*The desert planet of Tatooine
holds many secrets—
and a ghost from Leia's past. . . .*

Books by Troy Denning

WATERDEEP
DRAGONWALL
THE PARCHED SEA
THE VERDANT PASSAGE
THE CRIMSON LEGION
THE AMBER ENCHANTRESS
THE OBSIDIAN ORACLE
THE CERULEAN STORM
THE OGRE'S PACT
THE GIANT AMONG US
THE TITAN OF TWILIGHT
THE VEILED DRAGON
PAGES OF PAIN
CRUCIBLE: THE TRIAL OF CYRIC THE MAD
THE OATH OF STONEKEEP
FACES OF DECEPTION
BEYOND THE HIGH ROAD
DEATH OF THE DRAGON *(with Ed Greenwood)*
THE SUMMONING
STAR BY STAR
THE SIEGE
THE SORCERER

TATOOINE GHOST

TROY DENNING

BALLANTINE BOOKS · NEW YORK

Star Wars: Tatooine Ghost is a work of fiction. Names, places, and incidents either are a product of the author's imagination or are used fictitiously.

A Del Rey® Book
Published by The Random House Publishing Group
Copyright © 2003 by Lucasfilm Ltd. & ® or ™ where indicated.
All Rights Reserved. Used Under Authorization.
"Corphelion Interlude" by Troy Denning copyright © 2003 by Lucasfilm Ltd. & ® or ™ where indicated. All rights reserved. Used under authorization.
"A Forest Apart" by Troy Denning copyright " 2003 by Lucasfilm Ltd. & ® or ™ where indicated. All rights reserved. Used under authorization.

All rights reserved under International and Pan-American Copyright Conventions. Published in the United States by The Random House Publishing Group, a division of Random House, Inc., New York, and simultaneously in Canada by Random House of Canada Limited, Toronto.

Del Rey is a registered trademark and the Del Rey colophon is a trademark of Random House, Inc.

"Corphelion Interlude" was originally published by Del Rey in February 2003 as an e-book.

"A Forest Apart" was originally published by Del Rey in February 2003 as an e-book.

www.starwars.com
www.starwarskids.com
www.delreydigital.com

ISBN 0-345-45669-6

Manufactured in the United States of America

First Hardcover Edition: March 2003
First Mass Market Edition: January 2004

OPM 10 9 8 7 6 5 4 3 2 1

Dedication

For Hans
Wookiee at Heart

Acknowledgments

I would like to thank everyone who helped make this book possible. Thanks are due especially to: Andria Hayday, whose suggestions and valuable insight contributed to the story in a thousand ways large and small; to special *Star Wars* fans Ryan Holden and Elliot Courant, whose enthusiasm for the galaxy far, far away reminds me why this is important; to Dan Wallace and James Luceno for advice and answers; to all the people at Del Rey who make writing novels such a pleasure, particularly Shelly Shapiro, Kathleen O'Shea David, Colleen Lindsay, Colette Russen, and Laura Jorstad; to Sue Rostoni, Lucy Autrey Wilson, Chris Cerasi, Leland Chee and everyone at Lucasfilm for their *Star Wars* guidance and keen continuity eyes.

THE STAR WARS NOVELS TIMELINE

6.5-7.5 YEARS AFTER
STAR WARS: A New Hope

X-Wing:
  Rogue Squadron
  Wedge's Gamble
  The Krytos Trap
  The Bacta War
  Wraith Squadron
  Iron Fist
  Solo Command

8 YEARS AFTER STAR WARS: A New Hope
  The Courtship of Princess Leia
  A Forest Apart
  Tatooine Ghost

9 YEARS AFTER STAR WARS: A New Hope
The Thrawn Trilogy:
  Heir to the Empire
  Dark Force Rising
  The Last Command

  X-Wing: Isard's Revenge

11 YEARS AFTER STAR WARS: A New Hope
I, Jedi

The Jedi Academy Trilogy:
  Jedi Search
  Dark Apprentice
  Champions of the Force

12-13 YEARS AFTER STAR WARS: A New Hope
  Children of the Jedi
  Darksaber
  Planet of Twilight
  X-Wing: Starfighters of Adumar

14 YEARS AFTER STAR WARS: A New Hope
  The Crystal Star

16-17 YEARS AFTER STAR WARS: A New Hope
The Black Fleet Crisis Trilogy:
  Before the Storm
  Shield of Lies
  Tyrant's Test

18 YEARS AFTER STAR WARS: A New Hope
The Corellian Trilogy:
  Ambush at Corellia
  Assault at Selonia
  Showdown at Centerpoint

19 YEARS AFTER STAR WARS: A New Hope
The Hand of Thrawn Duology:
  Specter of the Past
  Vision of the Future

22 YEARS AFTER STAR WARS: A New Hope
Junior Jedi Knights series

23-24 YEARS AFTER STAR WARS: A New Hope
Young Jedi Knights series

 25-30 YEARS AFTER
STAR WARS: A New Hope

The New Jedi Order:
  Vector Prime
  Dark Tide I: Onslaught
  Dark Tide II: Ruin
  Agents of Chaos I: Hero's Trial
  Agents of Chaos II: Jedi Eclipse
  Balance Point
  Recovery
  Edge of Victory I: Conquest
  Edge of Victory II: Rebirth
  Star by Star
  Dark Journey
  Enemy Lines I: Rebel Dream
  Enemy Lines II: Rebel Stand
  Traitor
  Destiny's Way
  Ylesia
  Force Heretic I: Remnant
  Force Heretic II: Refugee
  Force Heretic III: Reunion
  The Final Prophecy
  The Unifying Force

CORPHELION INTERLUDE

A Short Story

A flight of comets hung just beyond the observation dome, their luminous heads arrayed in a ragged double arrow, their long tails striping the dark sky with silver splendor. The largest were visibly creeping across space, and one—blazing giant with a braided tail that seemed to stretch across half the system—rapidly swelling to the size of a hubba melon. The panorama was just as advertised, the perfect honeymoon view, and Han Solo could tell by the gabble of three-hundred beings packed onto the small viewing floor that everyone else thought so, too.

At Han's side stood Leia, dressed comfortably but fashionably in a sleeveless doublet and a pair of slinky zoosha pants that Han found especially alluring. Her brown eyes were fixed on the patio below, and on her face, she wore a cordial diplomat's expression that was more mask than smile.

Behind them, a swarm of droning Kubaz spilled out of the turbolift and brushed past, making pointed comments about blocking access to the viewing floor.

"Sorry about this," Han said to Leia. A stop to watch the Corphelion Comets had seemed a romantic way to start their honeymoon—least until they had discovered that it was the height of the season and every resort on the asteroid was badly overbooked. "I guess the private dome isn't so private, either."

"I don't care, as long as we're here together." Leia took Han's hand and started down a broad set of dark, hardwood stairs. "There's a pair of empty chaises out there in the middle. Once we settle in and order a drink, we won't even notice the noise."

"Sure. A Pink Nebula sounds good." Jostling for elbow space was hardly the romantic way Han had hoped to start their marriage, but things were bound to improve. Around Leia, they usually did. "Maybe the serving droid has earplugs or something."

They were halfway down the staircase when a brilliant starburst of radiance filled the sky. The Solos stopped to look and saw the giant comet splitting into a spectacular set of twins. The crowded patio fell silent.

"Now that's more like it," Han said.

The twins began to drift apart, their tails crossing as one comet angled toward the rest of the Corphelions. The other continued to swell in the darkness above the dome. Finally, when its head had grown to an apparent diameter of more than a meter, a nervous murmur began to build on the patio below.

Leia turned back up the stairs. "Maybe we should go back to the Falcon."

Han caught her arm. "Not so fast." He continued to study the approaching comet—rather, the darkness around its edges, watching to see how quickly and evenly its head was obscuring the distant stars. "I thought you wanted to see the Corphelions?" "Not this close, Han."

"Relax." As he had hoped, the stars on the comet's lower left were vanishing by the dozens; those on the upper right were disappearing only in twos and threes. "Everything's under control."

"You've said that before," Leia objected. "You're sure we don't need to go back to the Falcon?"

"I'm sure." Han slipped a hand down to the small of

her back. "And this time I mean it. Everything's under control, Sweetheart."

Leia glanced from Han to the approaching comet, then back to Han again. Her expression grew more trusting, and she smiled slyly.

"Okay, Flyboy." She took his arm. "My life in is in your hands."

They descended the rest of the stairs arm in arm. The comet had doubled in size during the last few seconds, its tail becoming a fan that curved across a quarter of the dome. A portly Bothan couple rose with their fur standing on end and turned toward the stairs, and that was all it took to send the rest of the crowd scurrying for the evacuation stations inside the asteroid.

Leia pulled Han into a quiet corner and reached up with both hands. As jabbering humans and growling aliens continued to shove up the stairs in a near-stampede, she laced her fingers together behind his neck and stared deep into his eyes.

Han's heart began to beat faster.

"How did you arrange this?" Leia asked.

"Arrange what?" Han was genuinely confused.

Leia gently pulled his head close to her mouth. "The comet." She flicked her tongue along the lobe of his ear, then continued in a sultry voice. "Come on, Flyboy, you can tell me. Did Wedge help you?"

"Wedge? You think Wedge is out there moving comets around?"

Leia gently nibbled his earlobe. It felt warm and . . . well, wonderful. "Lando, then. He has that big asteroid tug, and this is just his style. Grandiose, effective." She glanced over at the now-deserted patio. "And just a little bit devious."

"Lando's busy on Nkllon." Han was keeping one eye on the comet. "You know that."

"You won't tell me?" Leia slipped her hands under the hem of his tunic and playfully ran her fingers up his back. "You're sure?"

"Well, I'm—"

Leia dug her fingertips into the flesh behind his shoulders.

"Pretty sure," Han said. "I think."

The comet was the size of an Endorian moon now, and he was beginning to worry that his pilot's eye had gone weak. The different rates at which the head was obscuring the surrounding stars suggested it was approaching at an angle, but unless the stars on the right stopped disappearing—and soon—the comet would not actually miss the resort.

"Uh, Leia?"

"No—I've changed my mind, Han." Leia lowered her hands and, one arm still wrapped around his waist, turned to look at the sky. "I don't want to know how you arranged this."

"But—"

"Sshhh." Leia touched a finger to his lips. "I just want to look. It makes me wish we could forget everything back on Coruscant and stay here forever."

"You don't say?" The approaching comet was as large as a bantha now. Han glanced toward the empty stairs, trying to estimate how long he could keep his real secret—that he may have miscalculated the comet's trajectory—before they would have to make a mad scramble for the evacuation shelters. "I just might be able to arrange that."

Leia leaned her head against his shoulder. "If only you could."

"Oh, I could . . ." The comet grew so bright that its radiance lit the whole dome and there were no stars visible around it at all. Deciding that things were starting to get dangerous, Han pulled Leia out of the corner. "In fact—"

The white spike of an antitail finally appeared in front of the head, and the entire comet began to angle across the dome—away from the resort. Han exhaled in relief, then put on his best lopsided grin and turned to Leia.

Leia looked puzzled. "In fact what, Han?"

"In fact . . ." Han waited while the comet drifted over their heads to the other side of the dome, then said, "You're going to be really impressed with what I've arranged next."

Leia cocked her brow. "Pretty sure of yourself, aren't you?"

Han nodded. "I have a reason."

The asteroid entered the comet's tail, and billions of tiny dust grains exploded against the resort's particle shield. Space above erupted into a glittering veil of micro-flashes.

"Okay, I'm impressed," Leia said. "Really impressed."

"That was nothing," Han said. "This is what I was talking about."

He drew Leia close and lowered his lips to hers. She pressed herself tight against him and returned the kiss passionately, and that was how they remained until a loud cheer from atop the stairs interrupted them.

Han opened an eye and, finding an audience of two dozen comet watchers leering down at them, broke off the kiss. "Leia?"

"Yes, Han?"

"Maybe we should go back to the Falcon after all."

Leia took his hand and started for the stairs. "Han, I thought you'd never ask."

TATOOINE GHOST

Leia Organa, newly Leia Organa Solo, sat behind Han and Chewbacca on the flight deck of the Millennium Falcon. *The twin suns of the Tatoo system were hanging outside the forward viewport, a pair of white eyes blazing up from the black well of space. Like all twins, they were bound together by a tie as unpredictable as it was powerful. Sometimes, the bond boosted their luminosity far beyond that of two normal suns. At other times, it sent waves of ionic discharge pulsing across space to scramble circuits and reorient core-relative compasses. Today, the twins were assailing the* Falcon *with electromagnetic blasts, overloading her sensors and filling the cockpit speakers with static.*

As Chewbacca worked to raise the proper filters, the static faded from a roar to a crackle, then softened to a hiss, which rose and fell in a sharp rhythm. Puzzled by the odd snickering sound, Leia glanced over at the master comm console and found the reception indicator still scanning for signals. She leaned forward against her crash webbing.

"Han, do you hear . . ."

No sound came from her mouth. The snicker became a deep chuckle, and a nebula of black gas began to gather in front of the Falcon. *Han showed no reaction to* it. Neither did Chewbacca, even when it coalesced into the cowl of a Jedi cloak.

"Han! Don't you see . . ."

Again, her voice made no sound. Glaring out from beneath the cowl, the twin suns looked more than ever like eyes—heartless eyes, full of malice and power lust. Where the cloud was thin, crooked streaks of purple radiance created the impression of a twisted mouth and wrinkled face.

The mouth rose at the corners. "Mine."

The voice was cruel and distinct and rife with dark side power. Leia gasped—silently—and tried to raise an arm that had suddenly grown as heavy as the *Falcon*.

The smile became a sneer. "Mine."

Still, neither Han nor Chewbacca seemed to notice what was happening. Leia would have screamed, had her mouth been willing to obey.

The nebula began to thicken, and the purple wrinkles faded behind its inky veil. The twin suns dimmed to darkness, and the black cloud assumed the shape of a familiar mask—a mask of harsh angles and obsidian sheen, framed by the long, flaring neck apron of an equally black helmet.

Vader's helmet.

A chill wave of nausea washed over Leia. The curved eye lenses grew transparent, but instead of the blazing brightness of Tatooine's twin suns—or the angry redrimmed gaze of Darth Vader—she found herself looking into her brother's soft blue eyes.

"Luke! What are you . . ."

Her question remained as silent as the others she had asked. Luke's eyes grew hollow and hard and haunted, and the helmet moved slowly from side to side. Blue flickers of electricity snaked across the speech circuits behind the respiratory screen, but his words were rendered

*nearly inaudible by static crackling. Leia made out some-
thing about not following and staying out of darkness;
then Luke fell silent again. She tried to tell him that his
equipment was malfunctioning, that his voice had been
obscured, but before she could find a way to make herself heard, the helmet stopped moving.*

*Luke locked gazes and held her transfixed for what
might have been seconds . . . or minutes . . . his eyes now
the lifeless blue of ice. Leia grew cold, and frightened,
and the mask dissolved back into the black nothingness
of space, leaving her to stare out once again into the
mind-stabbing brilliance of the Tatoo system's twin suns.*

ONE

Instead of bed, where she usually awoke from her dreams, Leia found herself slumped forward in her crash webbing, ears hissing with static and eyes aching from the glare of two G-class suns. Han and Chewbacca were still busy at their stations, Han plotting approach vectors and Chewbacca setting sensor filters. The planet Tatooine was just drifting into view, its yellow sodium-rich sands glowing so brightly it resembled a small sibling star in orbit around the big twins.

A metallic hand tapped Leia's shoulder. She turned to see C-3PO's photoreceptors shining at her from the adjacent passenger seat.

"Pardon me for asking, Princess Leia, but are you well?"

"Don't I look well?"

"Oh dear," C-3PO replied, a diplomatic subroutine activating in response to her tone of voice. "Why yes, you do look as splendid as ever, but it seemed for a moment as though you might have overloaded your primary circuits."

"My circuits are fine."

"I'll need to confirm that later." Han twisted around and glanced over his seat with the same crooked smile that had alternately charmed and worried Leia since their first meeting on the Death Star. "Princess."

"Oh, really?" Leia straightened herself in her chair without fully realizing she was doing it. With his tough-guy good looks and eyes sparkling with trouble, Han still made her sit up and take notice. "And you think you can read my schematics?"

"Sweetheart, I know your schematics by heart." Han's smile faded, and his expression grew concerned. "Three-pio's right. You look like you've seen a ghost."

"Something like that. A bad dream."

Han looked doubtful. "I've sat in that chair. That chair isn't comfortable enough for dreams—good or bad."

"It's been a long trip," Leia said, perhaps a little too quickly. "I must have nodded off."

Han regarded her a moment longer, then shrugged. "Well, see if you can stay awake." He looked forward again, to where the twin suns were slowly being eclipsed by Tatooine's steadily swelling disk. "Until the sensors come up, we need to keep an eye out for other traffic."

Leia gazed out the canopy and began to search for the rapidly swelling silhouette of blocked starlight that would mean an approaching vessel. Her thoughts remained focused on the strange dream. It had a similar feel to the Force-vision she had experienced nearly five years earlier at Bakura, when her father had sent an apparition begging for the forgiveness she would never—*could* never—grant. But that had been his doing, not hers.

Han's hand rose into view between the pilot and copilot's seats, pointing toward a blocky silhouette floating some distance to one side of Tatooine's yellow disk. The twin suns were now completely hidden behind the planet, and Leia could see that the tiny silhouette was growing larger as they approached. It seemed to be staying in the same place relative to Tatooine, deliberately hanging in the shadow of the planet.

"That's too square to be a moon," Han said.

"And it's no asteroid, not hanging in one place like that," Leia added. "But at least it doesn't seem to be coming our way."

"Yet," Han replied. "How about those filters, Chewie?"

An impatient rumble suggested that the Wookiee was still struggling with the filters. Anyone else might have been frightened, but Leia found the groan reassuring, a touch of the familiar in a time of shifting alliances and random annihilation. When she had married Han six months ago, she had known Chewbacca would be an honorary member of their family, and that was fine with her. Over the years she had come to think of the Wookiee as something of a furry big brother, always loyal to Han and protective of her, and now she could not hear him growl without feeling that she lived in a safer place, that with Chewbacca and Luke and Han—when he was in the mood—and millions of others like them, the New Republic would beat back the Empire's latest onslaught and one day bring peace to the galaxy.

That, and she liked how Wookiee fur always smelled of trillium soap.

The comm hiss finally fell silent as Chewbacca found the right combination of filters. He brought the sensors up, fiddled a moment longer, then let out a startled *ruumph*.

"The mass calibration is off," Han said. "That reads like a Star Destroyer."

Chewbacca oowrralled indignantly, then sent the data readout to the auxiliary display beside Leia's seat and glanced back for her affirmation. She had to look only a second to see that he was correct.

"Sixteen hundred meters, six comm bands in use, and a TIE squadron circling on station," Leia said, feeling a little sick and worried. When the *Millennium Falcon* came across a Star Destroyer these days, it was usually because one was stalking the other. "I don't know, Han. The mass calibration looks fine to me."

As she spoke, the *Falcon*'s computer found a profile match in its military data banks and displayed the schematic of an *Imperial*-class Star Destroyer. Below the image appeared the vessel's name.

"The *Chimaera*," Han read. "Isn't she still in service to the Empire?"

"As of two months ago, she was one of their most efficient Destroyers." Leia did not need to look up the information. The death of Warlord Zsinj eight months earlier had emboldened the Imperial fleet, and the Provisional Council had been mired in war minutiae ever since. "Admiral Ackbar has been wondering what became of her."

"Deserters?" Han caught her eye in the canopy reflection. "Another captain wanting to set himself up as a warlord?"

"Please, no! The situation out here is already too confused." With the New Republic battling the Imperials over the scraps of Zsinj's empire and the surviving warlords exploiting the war to enlarge their own territories, *confused* was an understatement. Several times, the New Republic Navy had moved against one enemy to find itself engaging another, and sometimes two or three at once. "And the *Chimaera*'s commander isn't the type. By all accounts, Gilad Pellaeon is both loyal and competent."

"Then what's he doing at Tatooine?" Han asked. "There isn't a conflict zone within fifty systems of here."

Chewbacca groaned the opinion that it was someone else's job to analyze Imperial objectives, then began to plot hyperspace coordinates. Leia braced herself, more concerned with Han's reaction than Chewbacca's when she explained why they still had to risk a run planetside.

She was spared the necessity when Han scowled at the Wookiee's flying fingers.

"Chewie! I can handle this, no problem." Han looked vaguely insulted. "It's only one little Star Destroyer."

Chewbacca grunted doubtfully, then added a yawl about the folly of tempting fate for a piece of art.

"*Killik Twilight* means a lot to Leia," Han said. "It hung in the palace on Alderaan."

Chewbacca growled a long question that suggested they might be flying into a trap; the painting might not even be real.

"You can't forge moss-paintings," Leia answered. "Not anymore. They require strains that don't spread or reproduce, the cultivation of which was a closely guarded secret even in Aldera. That secret died with the rest of Alderaan."

"You see?" Han asked. "Besides, if the Imperials *were* trying to lure Leia to Tatooine, they wouldn't leave their Star Destroyer out in the open like that."

Han pointed at the tiny silhouette of the *Chimaera*, which had started an edgeward drift across the canopy as the *Falcon* eased past it toward the planet. Chewbacca stubbornly shook his head, reminding them of the syren plant on his native Kashyyyk, which drew victims to certain death with a scent so alluring it could not be resisted.

"Not a *certain* death," Han corrected. "Or there wouldn't be so many Wookiees in the galaxy."

Never one whose purpose could be deflected by humor, Chewbacca reiterated the questions that had been troubling them all since learning of the auction. Why was such a valuable painting being sold in a seedy spaceport like Mos Espa? Where had it been all these years? Why was it surfacing now?

The answers were a mystery—as much a mystery as the Star Destroyer's appearance here. At the time of Alderaan's destruction, *Killik Twilight* had been returning home from a museum loan on Coruscant. It had dropped out of sight, and Leia had believed the painting destroyed with her home—at least until Lando Calrissian reported that it would soon be offered at auction on Tatooine.

Chewbacca continued to press his case, maintaining that the *Chimaera*'s presence was no coincidence. With an Imperial Star Destroyer hanging off Tatooine, there would almost certainly be Imperials at the auction. The argument was all too sensible, and—though Chewbacca clearly did not realize this—one that made it all the more imperative that Leia attend the sale herself. She leaned forward and grasped the Wookiee's shoulder, and his tirade rumbled to an end.

"Chewie, everything you say makes sense. The Star Destroyer worries me, too. If this were just any piece of Alderaanian art, I wouldn't ask you to take the risk. But for *Killik Twilight*, I must."

Chewbacca studied her in the canopy reflection. He was a ferociously brave Wookiee—one who would never deny a friend's request for aid once he knew a matter to be important. Leia only hoped she could win his help without having to explain herself now. Han was still stinging from that whole Hapan incident eight months ago, and being asked to risk his beloved *Falcon* on behalf of the Provisional Council would not sit well with him at the moment. Maybe not ever.

Leia held Chewbacca's gaze with a sober expression that came to her face all too readily these days. Finally, he wrumpffed softly and nodded.

Han glanced over, his jaw dropped in disbelief. "That's it? She says *must*, and you don't even want to know why?"

Chewbacca shrugged.

"But you'll argue with me?" Han glanced at Leia's reflection in the canopy. "Those are some powers of persuasion you have there, Princess. You been studying with Luke when I'm not looking?"

"I'm no Jedi," Leia said. Then, slipping back into the flirty mood that had been the norm between them since their wedding—it had to be driving Chewbacca mad, judging by how he turned away to look out the viewport—she gave Han a sultry half smile. "Just your common everyday Princess."

"There's nothing common or everyday about you," Han replied in a tone so cloying that it made Chewbacca groan. "Or your hidden agendas."

"Hidden agendas?" Leia cringed inwardly as she vacillated between sounding innocent and playful and came off as neither. "We're just here to buy a moss-painting."

"Yeah?" Han's eyes assumed an amused twinkle. "Maybe Chewie's right."

"I didn't say he was wrong," Leia said, trying to sound cool—and failing. He had her, and he knew it. She *hated* that. "Han, I really want that painting."

Han shook his head. "Something here smells wrong." He began to ease the *Falcon*'s nose away from the planet. "In fact, I'm sure of it."

"Han!"

He glanced again at her reflection. "Yeah?"

"You'll draw attention to us."

Han shrugged. "What's it matter, if we're leaving?" He turned to Chewbacca. "You about done with those hyperspace calculations?"

Chewbacca snorted and, clearly not wanting any part of what was to follow, threw up his hands. Tatooine began to slide across the viewport, and Leia knew she had to call Han's bluff. He was too good a sabacc player to blank his cards without making her show her hand.

"Han, we need to be at that auction," she said. "If *Killik Twilight* is down there, we have to buy it. Thousands of New Republic lives depend on it."

"Really?" Han did not look at all surprised. "Imagine that."

Tatooine stopped drifting toward the edge of the viewport, but Han did not turn the *Falcon* back toward the planet.

Leia took a deep breath, then said, "There's a Shadowcast code key hidden in the painting. In the moisture-control circuitry."

Chewbacca's eyes grew as round as bubbles. Shadowcast was a secret communications network that had sent Rebel messages, encrypted within the commercial advertisements that paid for Imperial propaganda programming, via the HoloNet. The system remained undiscovered, and the New Republic still used it to send instructions deep behind Imperial lines to its most delicately placed spies.

Han's eyes only hardened at the corners. "Honey, I think we're about to have our first married fight. Why didn't you tell me the Provisional Council was behind this trip?"

"Because it's not," Leia said, sounding more defensive than she would have liked. Why did her political skills always desert her with Han? "I'm the one who said *Killik*

Twilight would be a good place to hide the code. I'm the one who thought the painting had been destroyed with Alderaan. This is on me, Han. The Provisional Council has authorized purchase funds, but only because Mon Mothma strong-armed them. She's the only one who knows why we're really here."

"Oh, *that* makes me feel better."

Eight months earlier, Mon Mothma had been among those urging Leia to cement an important strategic alliance by marrying the prince of a powerful consortium of planets known as the Hapes Cluster. Han still felt so betrayed by the Chief Councilor and the rest of the council that, despite several generous offers, he had so far refused to reactivate his military commission or assume any other formal role in the New Republic.

Han's reaction was only one aspect of the Hapan matter that Leia regretted. Had she made it clear to Queen Mother Ta'a Chume that marriage to her son, Isolder, was not really a possibility—and that, given her genetic heritage, she had no interest in bearing children—she might well have salvaged an alliance via some other arrangement, and she would not have hurt Han.

Chewbacca yawled a warning, and Leia looked over at the auxiliary display to find an assault shuttle and three TIEs departing the *Chimaera*.

"Nothing to worry about," Han said, studying his own display. "They just want to see if we get nervous."

Leia *was* nervous, and a little exasperated, but she didn't say so. Maybe Han had drawn the *Chimaera*'s attention, and maybe he hadn't. Appearing too relaxed was just as likely to raise suspicions as appearing too worried. *Anything* could raise Imperial suspicions.

"Han, I didn't mean to put the *Falcon* at risk," Leia said. "I only wanted to spend some time together, and I thought this trip would be a good chance."

"On a mission for the New Republic?"

"I didn't know it would be a mission," Leia said. "I'm sorry."

"So you thought we'd *enjoy* a little trip to scenic Tatooine, pick up the lost code key, maybe swing by Jabba's palace and relive old times?"

Chewbacca reported that the shuttle and TIEs were approaching on an intercept vector. Han adjusted the *Falcon*'s course enough to keep their line of escape open, then looked back at Leia.

"I don't see why this code key's so important anyway," Han continued. "They must have updated it by now. It's ten years old."

"Nine years old," Leia corrected. "And the code is updated every sixth broadcast. But even an old key would help the Imperials break the new codes. Worse, it would alert them to the existence of a network they haven't detected in nearly a decade. It would cost the lives of thousands of former agents still living on enemy worlds. And there's no telling how long it would take us to replace Shadowcast—or how many current agents we'd lose in the transition."

Han looked away, his gaze dropping to his instruments, and Leia knew she had him. He would play hard to get, pretending to think it over, but Han Solo always came through when it counted. That was his weakness, and she loved him for it.

"Han, I really do want *Killik Twilight* back," Leia said. "When you see it—"

"*When* I see it?" Han interrupted. "You're taking a lot for granted."

Chewbacca stopped monitoring the incoming assault shuttle long enough to turn and growl.

"I know she's my wife," Han said. "That doesn't mean

I'm responsible for dragging us out here. I can't control what she does."

Chewbacca dropped his eyes in exasperation, then awrooed at Han . . . twice.

"Me? *I'm* being Huttish?"

Chewbacca snorted an affirmative, turned back to the sensors, and reported that the TIEs were starting to accelerate ahead of the assault shuttle. Han spent a moment considering his copilot's charge, then glanced at Leia again.

"Me?" he asked. "Huttish?"

Leia held her thumb and forefinger a few millimeters apart. "Maybe," she said. "Just a little."

Han's expression turned from disbelieving to chagrined. He nudged the *Falcon*'s nose back toward Tatooine, angling for the planet horizon, where the twin suns were casting a crescent of white brilliance.

"I'm not doing this for the council," he said. "I'm doing it for you."

"I know you are." Leia's smile was perhaps a little too broad, and she could not resist adding, "And the council is grateful."

Han scowled, but his retort was cut short when the comm speakers crackled to life.

"CEC transport *Regina Galas*," a gruff Imperial voice said. "Maintain position and stand by for inspection."

Regina Galas was one of a dozen false transponder codes the *Falcon* used when traveling anonymously. Han turned to C-3PO.

"You're on, Goldenrod."

C-3PO tipped his head. "*On*, Master Solo?"

"Stall." Han pointed to the microphone above the auxiliary navicomputer interface. "Try Gand. They'll have to rig for ammonia, and that'll buy us some time."

"Of course," C-3PO said. "Perhaps I should suggest—"

"*Regina Galas,*" a smoother voice said. "This is the Star Destroyer *Chimaera*. Stand by for boarding, or we *will* open fire."

"Threepio!" Leia pointed at the comm unit.

C-3PO activated the transmitter and used his vocabulator to emit a staccato burst of drones and clicks. There was a long pause while the Imperials summoned a translator droid.

Han smiled, satisfied, and rose from the pilot's chair. "You know what to do, Chewie."

Chewbacca groaned and took the yoke, continuing to angle for the bright crescent at the planet horizon. Han reached past C-3PO's shoulder and linked the comm speakers to the *Falcon*'s intercom, then motioned for Leia to join him.

"I'll need you in back with me," he said.

Leia unbuckled her crash webbing, her heart rising into her throat. "Han, I don't know if shooting our way out of this—"

"Do I *look* like a gundark?" he asked. "If we shoot, we're dead."

Happy to know they agreed, Leia followed him down the access to the rear hold. By the time they opened the hatch, the Imperials were back on the channel with their translator droid, and it was conversing with C-3PO in a cacophony of buzzes and clacks. Han retrieved a small cargo pod, then took it into the main ring corridor and opened one of the smuggling compartments in the floor. He began to extract the cases of fine Chandrilan brandy that he kept to pay off spaceport masters, passing them to Leia to stow in the cargo pod.

"What are we going to do, bomb them with intoxicants?"

"You might say that," Han said. "It's called 'bribe-on-the-run.' This stuff is good currency, especially to a junior officer who probably hasn't seen a payment voucher in months."

"Han, didn't you hear what I said about Pellaeon?" Leia asked. "He won't go for that."

Han smiled. "He won't have to."

By the time he explained the details to Leia, the cargo pod was loaded and the *Chimaera*'s officer was back on the comm channel, sounding as irritated as only C-3PO could make a sentient.

"*Regina Galas* pilot, our droid assures me there is no reason a Gand can't speak Basic."

C-3PO replied with a long rattle of a question.

There was a momentary translation delay, then the officer replied, "My point is that I know you understand our instructions. Maintain position or you will be fired upon. Our targeting computers have you locked in."

Leia nearly fell as Chewbacca suddenly decelerated and started what felt like a turn back toward the *Chimaera*. She knew it was really a maneuver to put the assault shuttle between them and the Star Destroyer's powerful turbolasers. Han and Chewbacca had been running Imperial checkpoints since before there was a Rebellion. They knew every smuggler's trick in the data banks—and a few more.

"I said maintain position, not come about," the *Chimaera* officer barked. "And speak Basic!"

C-3PO replied with a stream of flustered clicking. Han and Leia chuckled with appreciation; they knew how frustrating the droid could be when he was agitated. They sealed the pod and ejected it through the air lock. When they returned to the engineering station in the main hold and brought the tactical array up on the display, Chewbacca had already brought the *Falcon* around and was accelerating away, with the assault shuttle now squarely between them and the *Chimaera*.

The officer began to yell. "Halt! Halt, or we'll open fire!"

"Open fire?" C-3PO said, still in the voice of a Gand but now speaking Basic. "Oh my!"

Chewbacca closed the channel and, laughing so hard his roars rumbled out the cockpit access tunnel, continued to accelerate. Unable to make good on the officer's threats without risking her own assault shuttle, the *Chimaera* held her fire. The *Falcon*'s new bearing ran roughly parallel to Tatooine's surface instead of toward it. But Leia knew that once they were beyond turbolaser range, or masked by the electromagnetic blast of the twin suns, Chewbacca would turn. Leia continued to watch the tactical display, expecting the Star Destroyer to maneuver for a clear shot or divert her shuttle, but she did neither.

"Good," Han said. "They think we're just spice runners. They'll stop to collect our jettisoned cargo, and then we're home free. The boarding officer won't want prisoners around to tell Pellaeon what was really in the pod."

"You're sure about that?"

Leia watched with growing alarm as the three TIEs passed the cargo pod, now angling to put themselves between Tatooine and their quarry. As long as Chewbacca continued on a straight course, they would be unable to catch the *Falcon*—but the instant she turned toward the planet, the TIEs would be in good position to cut her off.

"They don't look all that interested in a bribe."

Han studied the display, his jaw falling a little more

with each kilometer the TIEs put between themselves and the ejected cargo. For a moment, it looked as though the assault shuttle would also ignore the pod and stay behind the *Falcon*. Then a tractor beam activated in its stern, and it veered toward the bribe. Han sighed in relief, but grabbed Leia's hand and started for the laser cannon access tunnel.

"C'mon."

"Han, what happened to no shooting?" Despite her protest, Leia allowed herself to be dragged along. " 'If we shoot, we're dead.' You said that. I remember."

"I say a lot of things." They reached the access tunnel and Han jumped in, not climbing down so much as using the handholds to slow his descent. "But they're trying to grab the pod on the fly. The boarding officer needs us to make this look good, or his commander won't buy our escape."

Leia was already climbing into the upper turret. "How good?"

"Good. That Pellaeon must be a real stickler." The *Falcon* shuddered as Han test-fired his weapons. "Just don't hit anything. Hit something and we're—"

"Dead." Leia buckled herself into the firing seat. "I know."

She slipped on the headset and spun her turret toward Tatooine's lambent disk.

The canopy dimmed against the sapphire flash of an incoming turbolaser strike, and Leia's pulse stopped. She steeled herself to vanish in the crash of heat and light she had been half expecting to take her since the Rebellion began, then saw the tiny block of the assault shuttle silhouetted against the blossom of a distant eruption.

"What was that?" Leia gasped.

Chewbacca's rumbled answer made her stomach go hollow.

"They blasted it?" Han cried. "The brandy alone was two thousand credits!"

"It *does* eliminate our bribery plan." It was a bit of a struggle to keep her voice even. "What now?"

Han answered by laying a wall of laser bolts in front of the TIEs. "The shuttle, we can outrun," he said. "But we need to check those fighters. Just don't—"

"Hit anything." Leia activated her range finder. "I know."

At this range, the TIEs were little more than blue barbs of ion efflux. She brought her sensor-augmented sights on-line, and the claw-shaped images of three TIE interceptors appeared on her targeting display. She set her lead ahead of the TIEs an extra length, then another one. She added another half length to be certain, and squeezed the triggers.

The quad laser cannons fired in diametric sequence to minimize discharge shudder. Even so, the turret shook. Leia checked her sights, found the interceptors still trying to cut them off, and fired again. The *Falcon* was still at maximum range, and the bolts took an eternity to reach their destination. Most winked out well ahead of the TIEs, but some—Han's, she hoped—merged with the blue glow of the starfighters' ion drives. She fixed her gaze on her targeting display and continued to fire, praying that none of the images vanished. The Imperials were accustomed to smugglers running and generally did not work very hard to chase them down, but they would prove a lot more determined with any vessel that actually destroyed one of their own craft.

The distance between Han's bolts and the TIEs continued to diminish on Leia's display. She cut one of the lengths out of her own targeting lead, and their fire turned to an impenetrable storm. The Imperials lost their nerve and turned toward the *Falcon* so they could bring their own guns to bear.

"Barge drivers," Han sneered. "What kind of plasti-heads is the Empire recruiting for pilots these days?"

The TIEs opened fire, and tiny lances of green light stabbed out of Tatooine's yellow glow. The lines faded to nothingness kilometers shy of the *Falcon*, but distant blossoms of laser energy began to burgeon against the shields almost before Leia could disengage the lead adjustment on her sights.

Han's laser cannons began to stitch space alongside the TIEs. Leia followed his lead, and they forced the trio back toward the Star Destroyer. The image on her targeting display switched to true size, and the interceptors became thumb-sized blurs coming dead-on. Chewbacca continued ahead, keeping the assault shuttle between the *Falcon*'s tail and the *Chimaera*'s guns.

They were going to make it, Leia saw. No Star Destroyer in the galaxy was a match for Han and Chewbacca together. Once Leia and Han forced the TIEs into the *Falcon*'s rear quarter, Chewbacca would hide behind them and dive into Tatooine's atmosphere, and the *Chimaera*'s big guns would be useless—unless Pellaeon cared to attack a whole planet to stop one vessel.

And even the Imperials would not do that, not unless they knew the true identity of the *Regina Galas*.

The TIEs kept closing, swelling to the size of fists in Leia's display. She grew bolder, timing her shots to seize the area vacated by their dodges, forcing the interceptors to slip farther into the *Falcon*'s rear quarter with each swing. Han shaved his attacks even closer, nearly scorching their solar wing panels, daring them to try to cut off the *Falcon*.

Then the blast-tinting went black, though not quickly

enough to spare Leia a moment of flash blindness as another turbolaser strike—this one much closer than the first—erupted. Her shoulders hit crash webbing as the shock wave bucked the *Falcon*. Again her pulse stopped, and she hung suspended in that last infinitely long instant between life and atomization, and she did not realize she was still holding her triggers open until the synthetic rumble of the targeting computer announced the destruction of a TIE interceptor.

Leia cursed and released the triggers, struggling to blink the blast-dazzle from her eyes and not quite able to believe they had survived the strike.

"Sorry! I didn't mean—"

Chewbacca cut her off with an astonished yawl.

"The *Chimaera* hit it?" Leia gasped. "By mistake?"

"To make a point." Han's laser cannons opened up again. "She didn't like her TIEs being pushed around."

Leia checked her display and found the last two interceptors weaving wildly as they rushed for the *Falcon*'s forward quarter. She swung her turret around but was too distracted to open fire safely. Something here did not make sense.

"Pellaeon would never destroy his own interceptor," she said. "The Empire is too short of good fighters."

"A lesson the survivors'll never forget." Han's cannon bolts were dancing around the lead TIE in a tightening web of light. "If there are any." Finally, the interceptor had no place left to maneuver and flew into a dash of laser energy, exploding in a white cloud of fire and light. "He's using us as a training mission. I hate that."

"Han, you said *don't* hit—"

"Change of plans." Han began to fire at the last TIE. "Now we make it cost them."

Leia joined in, forcing the TIE into Han's stream of

fire. It bobbed and weaved in ever-smaller oscillations, but maintained discipline and continued on course—no doubt mindful of the lesson the *Chimaera* had delivered earlier.

Finally, it turned directly toward the *Falcon*, and the space beyond bloomed into brilliant smears of color as it opened fire. Leia kept her eyes fixed on the targeting display and held her triggers down, spraying bolts at the interceptor in tightening spirals, trying not to think about how large its image was growing, or how her display kept dimming, or why the turret's blast-tinting had gone black.

Finally, the TIE had no room left to maneuver. The pilot broke high, his wings and spherical cockpit rotating so smoothly that Leia did not realize he had changed attitude until the cannon bolts stopped coming.

"He's yours!" Han yelled over the intercom. "Roll me up, Chewie!"

Leia raised her cannons and thumbed the automatic lead active, but the TIE was already too far ahead. She managed only a few more shots before the computer designated it out of range.

"That's it, he's been recalled," Han said. "They aren't going to give us any more trouble."

Leia checked the tactical display and saw the assault shuttle still trailing them. No match for the *Falcon*'s speed, it was out of range and steadily falling farther behind, but it was coming.

"You're sure about that?" Leia asked.

"I'm sure. Experience isn't much good to dead pilots."

"What about assault troopers?"

As Leia spoke, the shuttle broke off pursuit and angled for the planet. Chewbacca was quick to parallel its course, keeping the shuttle between them and the Star

Destroyer, now traveling more or less in the direction they wanted to go. Leia kept waiting for the shuttle to turn toward the *Chimaera*, to weave or bob or try anything to give the turbolasers a clear shot, but it only continued its dive toward the planet, still angling in the *Falcon*'s direction.

Leia swung her turret around, unsure whether she should thank the shuttle pilot or open fire.

Han figured it out before she did. "Chewie, cut behind them! Go sandside, fast!"

Chewbacca didn't ask why. He brought the *Falcon* around so sharply that Leia had to close her eyes against the starspin, and then Han began yelling for her to bring her guns to bear.

Leia opened her eyes again and wished she hadn't. Space was flying past the canopy in a flashing whirl of stars and sand as Chewbacca spiraled toward Tatooine. She still had no idea what Han wanted her to be ready for, but she focused on the display and swung her cannons toward the assault shuttle.

Half a dozen blips appeared at the edge of the tactical screen, and her heart had barely finished falling before the interceptor symbols confirmed what Han had realized two moments before. Another flight of TIEs was coming fast from the blind side of the planet.

Leia forced her attention back to the firing display. With the *Falcon* gyrating so wildly, the turret broke into a nauseating whirring spin-dance as the servomotors struggled to keep the shuttle centered in the crosshairs.

"I have a lock." Noticing that Han had not yet opened fire, she asked, "Should I—"

"Not yet," Han said. "Chewie, see that sandstorm? The really big one?"

An affirming grunt came over the intercom. Leia

glanced out and saw only dizzying smears of yellow and stars whirling against a violet backdrop and felt instantly sick to her stomach. She fixed her gaze on the targeting display and hoped she was wrong about why Han had pointed out the sandstorm.

The *Falcon* shuddered and slowed abruptly. Leia wondered if they could have reached the outer edge of the atmosphere so soon, but there was still too much darkness outside, then Han was cursing and asking no one in particular if all the *Chimaera*'s pilots had a death wish. She saw the assault shuttle tumbling around the tactical display like a flitnat, connected to the *Falcon* by the invisible ribbon of a tractor beam that was pulling the two vessels slowly, steadily closer.

"*Now,* Han?"

"Not yet," Han said. "Chewie, launch the—"

A soft thud reverberated through the *Falcon* as two concussion missiles shot from their tubes, riding the tractor beam toward the shuttle.

"Now, sweetheart!"

Leia squeezed the triggers. The turret shook as the quad lasers loosed their fury. The center of the targeting display erupted into a dazzling glow, and her canopy darkened to black as the shuttle returned fire. All nonessential systems diverted power to the shields, and an ominous silence fell over the *Falcon*. She tried to aim down the tractor beam, but with the *Falcon* reeling half out of control, Leia was doing well just to hit the thing.

Then the missiles vanished into the glow. The tractor beam twinkled out of existence, and the brightness behind the crosshairs dissolved into a fading starburst.

Chewbacca wrenched the *Falcon* out of her tumble and dived straight for Tatooine. The tactical display showed the interceptors closing, but they remained well out of range. Leia brought her turret around and finally found the sandstorm Han had pointed out to Chewbacca—a raging swirl of amber that covered a tenth of the planet's visible surface. Even from space, she could see clouds of turbulence eddying up far above the primary plane of the storm.

Chewbacca sent the *Falcon* corkscrewing into a new helix of evasion. Leia checked her tactical display and found the TIEs still out of range and likely to stay that way. They could not cut off the *Falcon* without entering the atmosphere, a prospect even slower than taking the long route around the planet. Nor was the *Chimaera*, still sitting in a remote orbit, near enough to launch another boarding mission. There was only one thing the Star Destroyer could do to block the *Falcon*.

A bright line of turbolaser strikes erupted ahead, trying not to hit the *Falcon* but to force her toward the approaching TIEs. Chewbacca flew directly at the nearest blossom. The shields crackled with sapphire energy as they passed through the dissipation turbulence; then the *Falcon* was plunging into Tatooine's atmosphere, bucking wildly and engulfed in entry flame.

Han was instantly out of his seat, half tumbling and half climbing up the access corridor as Chewbacca struggled to control the ship at an air velocity approaching meteoric. The *Chimaera* did not fire into the atmosphere—no doubt because the captain believed the *Falcon* was about to crash anyway.

"Stay put." Han started toward the main hold. "Pellaeon's got to be as mad as a rancor. Those TIEs may follow us down."

"So where are you going?"

"Flight deck," he said. "When we slip into that sandstorm—"

TWO

A yellow cloud of windborne sand howled through the streets of Mos Espa, etching goggle lenses with microscopic scratch marks and transforming the city into a warren of dome-shaped silhouettes. The squall was the dying remnant of the same sandstorm that had concealed the *Falcon* from Pellaeon's TIEs, so Leia should not have been surprised to see two stormtroopers standing in the haze ahead . . . but she was.

After all, Han had spent half the night bumping the *Falcon* blindly through two thousand kilometers of storm-filled canyons so Pellaeon would not know whether the *"Regina Galas"* had survived its plunge into the sandstorm. They had hidden the ship in one of Han's former haunts, a huge but little-known smuggler's cave thirty kilometers out in the desert. They had strung an antenna and spent the morning eavesdropping on local comm channels, listening for anything that might suggest an Imperial search. Only then, after hearing no hint of unusual activity, had Han broken his speeder bike out of the *Falcon*'s hold and gone into Mos Espa to arrange ground transport for everyone else.

Leia should have known better. Pellaeon was an old-school officer, too careful and competent to make simple mistakes. Most Star Destroyer captains were, even in these days of strangled budgets and green crews.

Han took her arm and guided her forward. "It's okay to hesitate. They expect that." A small synthesizer hidden inside his mouth gave his speech a raspy Devaronian quality. It also altered his vocal profile so it would be unidentifiable by anyone using voiceprint technology to search for Han Solo. "But don't gawk."

She looped a hand through Han's elbow and did her best to fawn up at him as they approached the armored silhouettes. Though both she and Han were well hidden beneath the cowled cloaks and face coverings necessary to travel anywhere in even a mild sand squall, Leia felt as though she was parading past the Imperials in full Alderaanian Princess regalia. She and Han were two of the most famous faces in the New Republic, and she had no doubt that capturing—or killing—either of them would mean a hefty promotion for all those involved.

If Han was nervous, she did not sense it. He strode straight for the troopers, his goggled gaze rising to the flashing sign over the door behind them.

"Mawbo's Performance Hall," he said. "This is it."

"A dance house?" Leia gushed. "You take me to the nicest places."

Han looked at the stormtroopers pointedly. They returned his glare impassively from behind their dark lenses, then finally stepped aside. One even pulled the door open. Leia did not thank him.

They found themselves in a large sand-grimed foyer where a single Weequay guarded the entrance to a dingy cloakroom. His face was typical for his species, oval-eyed and so gnarled it resembled a mask of wrinkled leather. From the back of his head hung a long fan of two dozen seclusion braids, one for each year he had been away from his home planet. He was dressed—absurdly and obviously uncomfortably—in a new shimmersilk cape and undersized tunic purchased, no doubt, for today's event. Though he carried no visible weapons, Leia assumed by the way he kept his back to the wall that he had a large blaster pistol tucked beneath the cape—perhaps two. He was a Weequay, after all.

"Here for the art inspection?" he asked.

"That's right." Han pulled up his goggles, and Leia thought she saw a glimmer of alarm as he met the Weequay's eyes. *"Killik Twilight?"*

The Weequay shrugged. "Mawbo's got lots of stuff to auction in there." He extended a knobby-fingered hand for their cloaks. "Leave your covers here. She don't want sand in the back."

Leia and Han stuffed their goggles and face coverings into their pockets and passed their cloaks over. With her skin dyed pale blue and a pair of prosthetic lekku squirming down her back, Leia made a reasonably convincing Twi'lek consort to Han's bald, behorned, sinister-looking, and very red Devaronian. Both disguises were courtesy of New Republic Intelligence, complete with retina-concealing contact lenses and false prints affixed to the pads of their fingers. So when the Weequay sniffed the cloaks, then grinned and reached out to Han with his free hand, Leia was astounded.

"Thought I recognized that jet juice you call cologne, Solo," the Weequay said.

"Jaxal," Han quickly added. "Solo Jaxal, remember?"

A cold lump began to form in Leia's stomach. Weequays used scent to communicate with members of their own clan, so they were especially good at remembering smells. Obviously, the Solos' disguise designer had not anticipated that Han would meet a Weequay he knew in a Mos Espa "performance hall." Neither had Leia.

But the Weequay seemed to have no intention of betraying them. He merely nodded and tossed their cloaks on the pile behind him, then said, "Jaxal, that's right. Sorry I forgot."

"Not a problem," Han said. "Good to see you again, Grunts. I didn't think you'd still be working Tatooine dives."

Grunts shrugged. "Where am I going? Just 'cause Mawbo frees you don't mean she pays passage home. Got to earn that." He glanced in Leia's direction, clearly waiting for an introduction. When it did not come, he added, "I smell you're still with that furball partner of yours. Where is he?"

"He's around," Han said. Chewbacca and C-3PO were waiting at a local inn, in a rented room. "Funny place to hold an art auction."

Grunts nodded. "Mawbo's doing a favor for the guy who came up with the big painting. He's one of her old lovers."

"Isn't everybody?"

"Now that you mention it." Grunts waved a hand toward a weapons locker at the back of the cloakroom. "You're supposed to check your weapons."

"Already did," Han replied with a straight face. "They're working fine."

Grunts chuckled, then said, "Just keep them out of sight. Mawbo would whip me if she thought I'd missed them, and you know how she enjoys that."

He turned to open the door, but Leia asked, "What are those stormtroopers doing out there, Grunts?" She suspected she already knew the answer—*looking for the crew of the* Regina Galas—but Leia wanted to hear what cover story the Imperials were using. "Did Mawbo hire extra security?"

The Weequay looked vaguely insulted. "They're here with two officers. I made the stormtroopers wait outside."

Grunts glanced at Han with a look that seemed to suggest he teach his Twi'lek some manners.

Leia ignored the look and asked, "Officers? What are they doing here?"

"Same as everybody else, I guess." Grunts pulled the door open. "They want to be sure the stuff is real before the auction starts."

He waved them into a droning chamber that could be called a performance hall only in the sense that it had a stage—half a dozen stages, in fact. These platforms were scattered across the cavernous space, each one now supporting a small beverage or snack stand that did not seem to be drawing much attention from the rather sparse crowd. Here and there, the much-spilled-upon floor showed circles of cleanliness where the customary tables had been removed to make milling space. In the center of the chamber was a large main stage, and along the walls were dozens of private booths where the sellers were displaying the pieces they would offer at auction that afternoon. Judging by appearances, the few buyers were offworld art lovers attracted by the prospect of owning—or at least viewing—the famous *Killik Twilight*, while most sellers were local residents chasing a windfall by offering whatever they could find that might be worth something.

As Leia studied the crowd, she leaned close to Han. "Where do you know Grunts from?"

"Long story, but he can be trusted."

"With you, everything's a long story," Leia said. "How about the short version? I need to be persuaded."

Han sighed and started toward the nearest stage, where a statuesque Codru-Ji female with four arms, pointed ears, and a lissome build was serving drinks. Though she was discreetly dressed in a shimmersilk blouse and mood-color vest—currently scarlet—she

looked as uncomfortable in her new clothes as had
Grunts, and the smile she flashed as they approached
made Leia wonder how well *she* knew Han's smell. He
ordered a pair of cometdusters, then, as the clamorous
impassioning machine excited the molecules, leaned
close to Leia's ear.

"I know because I used to own him."

"What?" Leia was beginning to wonder whether eight
years fighting and working at Han's side had really been
enough before agreeing to marry him. "*You* owned a
slave? How could you?"

"I won him from Lady Valarian in a sabacc game,"
Han said, as though that excused it. "I set him free."

"After how long?" Leia demanded.

"As soon as we left the *Lucky Despot*," Han said defensively. "I wanted to hire him to help with cargo, but
he and Chewie took a big dislike to each other. Something about odors. He lost himself to Mawbo trying to
win passage home, and you heard the rest."

The drinks came, and the Codru-Ji accepted payment
with a slow wink. Han's answering grin was truly lecher-
ous, though in fairness that may have been due more to
his Devaronian disguise than what was going through
his mind.

Leia waited until the Codru-Ji was gone, then asked,
"So, when did you own *her*?"

"Her?" Han began making his way across the floor
toward the back wall, where a couple of dozen buyers
were lined up outside a well-guarded booth, waiting to
inspect *Killik Twilight*. "What makes you think I ever
owned Celia?"

Leia knew Han was baiting her. She was doing her best
not to ask how he knew Celia's name when she noticed
two Imperials near the end of the line. One was dressed
in the white utilities of an Imperial technician, but the

other wore the gray tunic and rank bar of a full bridge commander. The man was probably a direct subordinate to Pellaeon, and his presence told Leia all she needed to know about the Imperial mission on Tatooine. They would not have sent such a high-ranking officer to track down a group of smugglers. They had come for *Killik Twilight*.

Leia angled toward the front of the chamber, pulling Han toward a flamboyant display of Tatooine glitterglass. "You saw?"

"You don't overlook that insignia, not if you were at the Imperial Academy," Han whispered. "And those stormtroopers outside are just for show. No one sends a Star Destroyer watch commander into a place like this without plenty of protection."

They circled a satellite stage where an Elomin female was offering stems connected to a hookah reeking of stale water. Leia said, "They know. They must."

Han did not contradict her.

"I don't understand how they found out," Leia continued. "Only three of us knew, and the other two were on Alderaan when the Death Star destroyed the planet."

"Your boss knows. Maybe she—"

"No. If anyone understands the importance of keeping a secret, it's her." Leia paused, then said, "I'm sorry. If I had known this was going to get so complicated—"

"You'd have come anyway. And so would I. You know I wouldn't let you do something like this without me."

Leia squeezed his arm, silently thanking him for not belaboring her omission.

"Still, I wish you'd told me."

They reached the booth with the glitterglass and pretended to examine several garish panes in a flowing, organic style. A small signscreen claimed they had come from the palace of the famous Hutt crime lord, Jabba.

The panes were not even close to Jabba's taste, at least what Leia had observed of it before she had used her slave chains to choke him to death; he preferred representational art, the lewder the better.

A solitary Gran stepped toward the front of the booth, his three eyes gliding over Han's ostentatious robe, the mouth at the end of his long muzzle puckering into an eager grin. Leia pulled Han away, and they nearly tripped over the sellers running the next booth, a pair of furry waist-high bipeds with short muzzles and long tufted ears.

"Hey, Redhorns!" the first one said, taking Han's wrist. "You look like a being who knows quality. Come see the real prize at this junk sale."

The second grabbed Leia's hand. "This way." It pulled her toward their booth, where a third member of their group stood in front of a one-way mirrfield. "Just two credits. You miss out on this, and you'll be sorry."

The third member reached into the booth and adjusted the mirrfield opacity, allowing Leia to glimpse a disparate collection of local handicrafts, twisted columns of plasteel, and what looked like the insipid planetscapes usually found in the corridors of tourist-class nebula cruisers.

Han stopped. "Two credits, just to look?" He pulled loose, then reached over and freed Leia as well. "You've been spending too much time in the suns."

The little creatures blinked up at him with long-lashed eyes so brown and deep that Leia felt instantly drawn to them.

"If such a small amount concerns you, think of it as a deposit," the first one said. "It's fully refundable when you bid on one of our items."

"We won't be bidding on your stuff, okay?" Han pushed between the creatures and, drawing Leia after him, grumbled, "Squibs. They'll sell you a bucket of air if you let them, and keep the bucket."

They came to a booth filled with exquisitely colored bowls made of some material so delicate Leia could see the shelf through the bottoms. A signscreen posted by the Barabel seller claimed they were alasl bowls, recovered from deposits deep in the Jundland Wastes and hand-carved by Tusken Raiders. She would have liked to stay and study the vessels with an eye toward bidding, but the press of prospective buyers made it a poor observation post, and they needed to locate the watch commander's guards. When something went wrong, Han would want to know whom to blast.

They eased past the Barabel's booth and continued toward the back of the chamber, mentally tracing sight lines away from the Imperial officers and searching for someone attempting to keep them open.

"There's one." Han nodded toward a hulking, short-haired human feigning interest in a worthless lump of blaster-fused sandglass. "Not too subtle, are they?"

"For the Empire, that *is* subtle," Leia said.

They quickly found two more guards, a male–female team masquerading as a Kuati aristocrat and her telbun paramour.

Then they stopped at a booth containing several pieces of refined sculpture and half a dozen imagist gleaminks depicting Tatooine landscapes. Leia was particularly taken with a depiction of an approaching sand squall and an empty sandrock basin titled *The Last Lake*. Then she came to a single, oversized holocube.

The image was of a sandy-haired boy of perhaps nine or ten, standing in front of an old Podracer cockpit with a pair of goggles down around his neck and both arms raised high over his head. The joy in his grin was as contagious as it was innocent—he was clearly pretending he had just won a big race—but that was not what captured Leia's attention.

There was something about those eyes that compelled her to stand there and stare, to forget the presence of Han and the vendor and simply look. They were Luke's eyes, Leia realized. They were the same radiant blue, they had the same depth and softness as her brother's, and—most of all—they had a quiet intensity that burned as brightly as the twin suns themselves.

Leia saw again the white orbs that had taken the place of Luke's eyes in her dream aboard the *Falcon*, and she began to experience an eerie sense of connection to the boy. But this was not Luke; this boy's cheeks were too broad, his nose too small.

It was only a dream.

And dreams were not the future, Leia reminded herself. They were viewports into a person's private wisdom, hints of the truths kept trapped in the mind's forgotten recesses by the twin vornskrs of fear and desire. Those eyes aboard the *Falcon*, Tatooine's two suns, the Tatooine boy, they were trying to tell her something. But what?

For now, the explanation would have to remain a mystery, as would the reason the boy's image brought the dream so forcefully to mind. A slender, swarthy man of around fifty was approaching, his dark eyes fixed not on Leia's face, but on her hands. They were clasped just below her waist in a manner she often used when speaking in public. Her personal assistant, Winter, had gone so far as to call the gesture distinctive—and to caution her against using it when she wished to remain anonymous.

Cursing herself for falling into old habits, Leia quickly unclasped her hands and draped one over Han's shoulder. The man, apparently the owner of the holocube, raised his gaze and pretended not to notice. With black hair and dark skin, he had an air of reserve about him that suggested good breeding or—more likely on Tatooine—offworld training. He looked Leia directly in the eye and flashed an easy smile that seemed as sincere as it was bright.

"It doesn't surprise me that you find this holo so fascinating," the man said.

Leia felt Han bristle at the vendor's knowing tone. She squeezed his shoulder to caution restraint, then put on her best Twi'lek doxy attitude.

"Sure, I love little kids." She glanced around the booth for a signscreen identifying the holocube and found it on the floor, smashed and unreadable. "Especially human kids."

The vendor smiled shrewdly. "Of course. But the boy in this 'cube is no longer a child. It was taken when he won the Boonta Eve Classic, more than forty years ago."

"*Won* it?" Han scoffed. "Look, don't think you're talking to a pair of nerf herders here. Even when Podracing was legal, humans didn't have the reflexes to survive it—much less win, and especially not as kids."

The vendor ignored Han. "I don't want to part with it. He was my best friend, but times are hard. Still, if you'd care to strike a bargain before the auction, I'd be willing to offer it to you now."

"Yeah, I'll bet you would." Han pulled Leia away. "Come on, Tails."

As soon as they were out of the man's earshot, Han asked, "So who's the kid?"

"How should I know?"

"You were sure staring at him," Han said. "I didn't think you were such a fan of holography."

"I'm not. His eyes reminded me of someone—and we have other things to worry about. That vendor might have recognized me." Leia told him about the hands.

"Winter says I do that all the time in holocasts, and she's right. He might have been asking for a bribe."

"Or he might be an Imperial plant trying to draw you out," Han said. "I don't like this, and it's definitely not a good idea to draw attention to ourselves by starting a bidding war against the Empire."

He turned toward the Squibs' booth.

"Han, you can't be serious. What do a bunch of over-grown pack rats know about art?"

"Nothing." He pulled four credits from his robe. "But they know auctions."

The two Squibs in front of the mirrfield gave up on the Togorians they were harassing and watched with conde-scending smirks as Leia and Han approached. Han held out the hand with the credits.

"One word and we leave," he said. "Just show us the stuff."

The leader—at least Leia thought it was the leader—looked as though he was thinking of asking for more. Han put the credits back in his pocket, and the Squib sur-prised Leia by shrugging and turning to look for another customer.

Han sighed, and when he pulled his hand from his pocket, it was holding six credits. "We don't have all day."

The Squib's eyes brightened, and he held up ten fingers.

"Seven," Han said. "And it's not worth that much."

The Squib lowered one finger. Han pulled two more credits from his pocket, so now he was holding eight. Even then, they almost had to leave before the Squib fi-nally raised his palm and motioned for the money.

The Squib rubbed the credits against his furred cheek, then nodded and passed them to his fellow, who did the same thing and passed them through the mirrfield. Only after the third Squib had inspected and approved the coins did they allow the Solos into the booth.

It was filled with the same collection of used handicrafts, twisted plasteel—labeled by a signscreen FOUND SCULPTURE—and mawkish planetscapes Leia had glimpsed earlier. The Squibs immediately began to offer items for inspection, carefully rubbing each object against their furred cheeks before attempting to press it into Han and Leia's hands. And, mindful of the threat with which Han had opened negotiations, they did it all without speaking a word.

Han pushed a smashed cooling unit aside and said, "Stop! I told you before, we're not interested in your stuff. That's not why we're here."

The leader was so shocked he nearly dropped a chipped boneglass bowl. "You're not?"

This drew a pair of stern shushes from his fellows.

"Don't worry," Leia said. "We *want* to talk. We just needed to be someplace private first."

"Talk's not cheap," the second Squib warned.

"Time is money," the third chimed in.

Han turned to Leia and rolled his eyes. "You had to say it."

"Listen," Leia said. "We need you to do a job for us."

The booth fell silent, and the leader turned his head aside, glaring at her out of one eye.

"We don't do *jobs*. We're not *hirelings*."

"We want to strike a bargain," Han corrected.

"A bargain?" The leader clasped his small hands together. "What wares?"

"*Killik Twilight,*" Leia said. "We want you to buy it for us."

"We supply the funds," Han said quickly. "You have the fun."

The Squibs looked at each other, nodded, and the leader said, "Deal."

"But you have to buy *all* our stock," the second Squib added.

"We don't need your stock," Leia said. "We don't have anyplace to put it."

"Not our problem," the third said.

"We can get you a magnetic freight compartment."

"Won't even scratch your yacht."

It was growing difficult to keep track of which one was speaking.

"Only a thousand extra."

"How about we just pay you for your stock?" Leia asked. "And you can still sell it at the auction."

"Can't do that."

"*You're* buying it at auction. That's the deal."

"Look, we don't want your stuff," Han said.

"Then why are you taking the freight compartment?"

"We're *not*," Leia said.

"And we're not buying at auction," Han said. "We're not agreeing to that. We're not dumb enough to let you have someone run up the bidding."

"So how dumb are you?"

"Maybe just one—"

"*No!*" Han shouted. The Squibs fell silent and blinked up at him in shock. Finally he rolled his eyes and asked, "Okay, how much stock do you have?"

And they were off, the Squibs offering and Han and Leia counter-offering, pulling one element out of the deal and throwing two more in, the negotiation moving at the speed of sound and almost instantly growing as complex as anything Leia had seen as a New Republic diplomat. By the time they were finished, it was agreed that Han and Leia or their designated agent would bid on three items of their own choosing from each category, the maximum price to be determined by a complex formula based on bid increments, with each side being allowed one sleeper among the attendees.

"And *we* get the painting after you buy it," Leia said. "I just want to be sure of that."

All three nodded. "That's right," the leader said. "As long as you hold up your end of the bargain, a deal is a deal."

"Good. I'm Limba." Leia extended her hand. "It's been an education doing business with you. Jaxal is right—you guys are good."

The Squibs puffed out their chests visibly.

"You did all right," the leader said. He rubbed his cheek across Leia's palm, then across Han's, then jerked a thumb at his chest. "I'm Grees. That's Sligh."

Grees indicated the second Squib, who stepped forward and rubbed his cheek over the hands of both Han and Leia.

"And I'm Emala." The third Squib pressed her cheek to Leia's hand. "I've seen worse from a Twi'lek."

"Thank you," Leia said. "I think."

Han waited for Emala to nuzzle his hand, then asked, "Which one's coming to see the painting? I want to be sure you know what you're bidding on."

Emala and Grees turned to Sligh expectantly.

Sligh let out a heavy sigh. "*I'll* go." He shook his head in disgust. "But when I come back, I'm out front."

They emerged from behind the mirrfield to find the Imperial officers, having already completed their inspection, leaving the dance house. A tangible sense of relief filled the air, and the polite murmur intensified to an electric drone. More prospective purchasers appeared out of dark corners and the backs of the booths, and the beverage bars on the satellite stages began to do a brisk business. Leia, Han, and Sligh took their place at the back of the line and had to wait nearly an hour before their turn came to go through the mirrfield.

Instead of the painting, inside the trio found half a dozen of Mawbo's thugs in nylar tunics and shimmersilk capes, all holding blaster rifles trained on their prospective purchasers.

"Don't worry," a Rodian said. His cone-shaped snout twitched toward the dark corner to Leia's right, and someone came up from behind and blindfolded her. "Just a security precaution."

"How much security do you need?" Han grumbled. "You have a Weequay sniffer checking for blasters."

"You want to see the moss or not?"

Han fell silent. They were led through the back of the booth, down a long hallway, then up a liftglide into a quiet area reeking of acrid thaq smoke. Their blindfolds were removed. The trio found themselves standing in a dark chamber before a section of wall illuminated by an overhead glow panel and flanked by two Gamorrean guards. In the middle of the wall hung the velvety rectangle of a sublimely colored Alderaanian moss-painting, its moisture-control apparatus artfully concealed within an internal frame. It was smaller than Leia remembered, no more than fifty centimeters across, but even more beautiful and moving.

"Killik Twilight," a harsh female voice croaked behind her. "You got two minutes."

Leia wanted to protest that two minutes was not nearly enough, not after a decade of trying to keep its bold composition and subtle hues locked in her mind. She had thought it a treasure forever lost to her—and to future generations of Alderaanian descendants. And now here it was, hanging in front of her close enough to touch, with its stormy sky sweeping over of a city of Killik pinnacles and, in the foreground, its line of enigmatic

insectoid figures—the vanished species who had inhabited Alderaan before humans—turning to look back at
the approaching darkness. She could never look upon it
without marveling at the artist's prescience, wondering
how Ob Khaddor could have seen so clearly what Palpatine's rise meant for the galaxy . . . and how he could
have expressed his sorrow so beautifully and completely
in such a small space.

"You need to verify it, go ahead," the harsh voice said.
"But brush sampling only. No clipping."

Sligh instantly stepped forward, already turning his
furry cheek toward the painting.

Leia barely caught the Squib in time. "No!"

"Who's going to be buying this thing, you or us?"
Sligh demanded, the lip of his muzzle lifted in an irritated
snarl. "We have to check the merchandise."

"It's the real thing." Leia pulled the Squib away. "I
don't need a test kit to tell me that."

She glanced over to find Han staring at the painting,
his gaze fixed and his jaw slack with wonder.

After eight years together, it was good to know Han
could still surprise her.

THREE

Han had never been so moved by a piece of art. For the next two hours, as they sat at a local tapcaf waiting for the auction to begin, his thoughts kept returning to the painting, to how the Killiks were turning to face the storm. The image reminded Han that people—and bugs—were swept through life by forces they could not understand, that in the tempests life threw at them, they could control nothing but their own reactions. That was something Han tended to forget when the winds ran against him, and it was one of the things he loved most about Leia—the way she never flinched in a storm, the way she always stood firm while those around her were being blown off their feet.

Han wanted Leia to have that moss-painting. She had spent her youth looking at *Killik Twilight* every time she left her bedchamber, and it was the one physical connection to her family's palace that had survived the destruction of Alderaan. And, not that it mattered to potential bidders, it probably still belonged to her. Han would have hesitated to call the seller a thief—the moss-painting *had* been in transit, and galactic salvage laws applied to artwork like anything else—but there was a reason it was being sold on a lawless planet like Tatooine, and he was pretty sure it had nothing to do with the health benefits of dry desert air.

Like every tapcaf near Mawbo's Performance Hall, the one in which he and Leia sat was so packed that the air was almost humid with breath moisture. The customers—mostly bidders waiting for the auction to start—were chattering among themselves, decked out in their finest outfits and trying not to be too obvious as they appraised the competition. Slumped in a dim corner and doing their best to appear crassly involved with each other, Han and Leia drew few long glances. Chewbacca and C-3PO were in a tapcaf across the street, far enough away to avoid being associated with "Jaxal" and "Limba," yet close enough to come running in case of trouble.

Sellers from the auction began to arrive in ones and twos, among them the Barabel with the alasl bowls and the dark-haired man offering the holocube of the young Podracer. Han was not surprised to see Leia's eyes following the human toward a vacant counter stool. Though she seldom gave any work of holography more than a passing glance, there was clearly something different about this one—and Han felt sure he knew what it was.

He slipped an arm around the back of Leia's chair and began to stroke her prosthetic lekku. The head-tail responded with an appreciative squirm.

"You know," Han said, "you never did tell me who the kid in the holocube reminded you of."

"*He* didn't remind me of anyone. Only his eyes."

"Sure," Han said. "If you say so."

Leia was not taking the bait. "I do."

"Come on. You can say it. I thought the kid was cute, too."

"What makes you think I found him cute?"

"I saw the way you looked at him."

Leia shot him a glare that could have frozen a sun. "So?"

"So, maybe there's a reason."

Leia narrowed her eyes. "What kind of reason, Han?"

Han took a big gulp. He could see that Leia knew where this was going as well as he did, and he knew what kind of reaction to expect. But it was one of those risks a man had to take.

"Maybe it's because you like kids," Han said. "Maybe because you want one."

Leia's face went blank and emotionless, a sure sign that she was angry—really angry. Furious, even. She took a long sip of her drink and avoided looking at Han.

"We talked about children before we were married. I thought you understood."

"Yeah, I understood," Han said. "But I thought—"

"We *agreed*." Leia returned the glass to the table with a bang. "You can't just change your mind."

Han bit his tongue. How could he tell her he had not changed his mind—that his mind had changed him? That *marriage* had changed him?

"I know what we said," he allowed. "But has it ever occurred to you that you're being irrational?"

"*Irrational?*"

"Irrational." Han had to wet his throat. "How can a kid—"

"Please tell me you just discovered you had a child with Bria Tharen," Leia said. "Because I could live with that. Everyone has a past."

"Yeah, but I'm pretty sure mine doesn't include kids," Han said. Bria had been his first love, a willowy red-haired beauty who was one of the founders of the Rebellion—and who had died a martyr after double-crossing him to secure the plans to the first Death Star. "Bria *did* have her secrets."

"None of which has anything to do with this conversation, I take it."

"Afraid not." Han leaned closer and spoke in a near whisper. "I know we talked about this, but I can't believe the dark side really runs in your blood."

"That's not what I said," Leia corrected. "It's the power that runs in my blood. And power corrupts. I see that every day."

"Not always." Han took Leia's arm, then played his trump card. "Just look at your brother. No one is stronger in the Force than he is. If anyone was going to go be corrupted, it would be him."

Leia jerked away and, fixing her gaze on the tapcaf's much-blemished wall, gulped down half her drink. "Drop it."

"Look, I'm not saying we have to decide today—"

"You've known how I felt since Bakura." Leia still did not look at him. "I don't have the right to bring someone who could become another Darth Vader into the galaxy. If you can't live with that, why didn't you let me marry Prince Isolder?"

The mere mention of Isolder's name set Han's teeth on edge. The whole Hapan incident had shattered what little faith he'd ever had in politicians.

"What about—" Han heard his voice start to rise and caught himself. He checked for eavesdroppers and found none; with the auction approaching, the room was filled with an escalating drone that rendered conversations difficult to understand even at the same table. "What about Isolder?"

Leia finally turned and met his eye again. "What's that supposed to mean?"

"It's pretty clear," Han said. "Did you tell him you didn't want children?"

"It never came to that. *Someone* abducted me before negotiations went that far."

"Yeah?" Han saw the waitress approaching and

waved her off. "And what if negotiations had gone that far? Do you think Ta'a Chume would have allowed the wedding to take place knowing you didn't want children?"

Leia's composure broke, and she looked at him with tears welling in her eyes. "Why are you doing this?"

"Because you don't know what you want."

"And you do?" Leia asked.

"I see how your face lights up when someone lets you hold a baby," Han said. "And I saw the way you looked at that kid in the holocube."

"You're way off course—"

"You *know* I'm right," Han interrupted. "And you're afraid to admit it. The only reason you don't want kids is you're still afraid of your father—afraid of him and mad at him. And that's a lousy excuse for not having kids. Not when we both want them."

Leia waited until he had stopped speaking, then asked, "Are you finished?"

"Yeah. It's not that complicated."

"I agree," Leia said. "Because I'm sure I remember you telling me you could live without children. That's very clear in my mind."

Han shrugged. "I like being married. Maybe that's changed my thinking about kids." He lowered his gaze and stared into the dark ale in his mug. "I didn't realize how much I'd love this—being a family, I mean. I keep wondering what it would be like to shape a kid's life, to give him a safe place to grow up."

"Like the home you never had," Leia said.

"Yeah, like that," Han admitted. He had seen Leia take control of difficult negotiations often enough to know when she was trying to avoid the subject. "But you still haven't answered me about Ta'Chume and Isolder. When were you going to tell *them* you didn't want children?"

"I don't know."

"Maybe never." Han was not bitter about the suggestion; he was just trying to point out to Leia that there were *some* circumstances in which she might have had children. "Maybe you'd have risked it for the New Republic."

"I *would* have told them." Leia raised her chin. "With the power of the Hapes Consortium behind it, any child of mine would be *more* likely to become the thing I feared, not less."

Han's scowl was thwarted by the fang dentures of his Devaronian disguise. "Ta'a Chume would never have agreed to that."

Leia flashed him a typically sad Twi'lek smile. "Maybe that's why *I* wasn't so worried when the Hapans came to visit."

Half a standard hour later, Han and Leia sat behind the mirrfield wall of one of the performance hall's private booths, watching the main floor fill with spectators and bidders. Everything had the sound of money: the nervous laughter that rang like clinking credits, the electric babble that rose and fell with the familiar rhythm of market-day bartering all over the galaxy, the voices of bartenders and waitresses selling eyeblasters and pallies at prices ten times normal.

The Imperial watch commander stood in front of the primary stage, where the auction would take place. His science officer companion was gone, replaced by two burly bodyguards in full dress uniform. They were the only beings in the room with more elbow room than they really needed.

Han could see Grees, Sligh, and Emala pushing through the packed performance hall, approaching likely-looking

Twilight bidders on the pretext of offering them inside information on the auction merchandise. There were a few takers, and these the Squibs offered a thinly disguised sales pitch for their own wares. Sometimes the buyers paid for the advice and sometimes they didn't, but the trio never wasted more than a few moments quarreling before they moved to the next prospect.

They worked hardest trying to sell those who dismissed them most quickly, spending as much as three minutes arguing while they quietly assessed the competition. There were a few social climbers hoping to land a steal because the auction was being held on Tatooine, but most bidders were thuggish, hired more to protect the fund transfer chips they were carrying—a requirement of purchase—than for their expertise as auction agents. Once, Han caught a glimpse of Emala quietly slipping a vibroblade out of a hidden boot sheath while Grees and Slight kept the weapon's Aqualish owner occupied with a sales pitch.

"Those Squibs are good—maybe too good," Leia said. She was sitting beside Han at the booth's plastoid cocktail table, slumped down on an overstuffed wraparound lounger that would abide no other posture. "Are you sure we can afford that deal we struck?"

"It's under control."

Leia looked doubtful, the sensors in the base of her false lekku reacting to her mood and causing the tentacles to writhe in short, tightly spaced waves. "You know they have something planned."

"Yeah, but we have a Wookiee."

Han tipped his counterfeit horns toward Chewbacca, who was out in the theater enduring Sligh's sales pitch as they tried to size him up. He had dyed a red streak over his shoulder; a Wookiee could do little to disguise himself except change his markings. Chewbacca endured no more than five seconds of the Squibs' harangue, then bared his fangs and raised a foot, sending all three scrambling for cover.

"See? No problem."

C-3PO, whose disguise consisted of a false green patina, watched the exchange from several meters away. He started to push through the crowd, politely asking permission and excusing himself each time he eased past someone.

Leia activated her comlink and opened a channel to the droid. "What are you doing?"

C-3PO raised his own comlink. "They appear to need a translator. I was going to offer my—"

"No," Leia said. "Leave them alone."

C-3PO stopped, but did not lower his comlink. "Are you quite certain? The Squibs are trying to be helpful, and it sounds as though they have some interesting infor—"

"*No,*" Han said, speaking into Leia's comlink—and praying the Squibs were too frightened of Chewbacca to notice the droid approaching. "Just do your job."

C-3PO fell silent for precisely one second—the electronic equivalent of a sigh—then rotated his head toward Han and Leia's booth, practically shouting the location of his owners to any careful observer.

"As you wish."

Leia deactivated her comlink and rolled her eyes. "You're sure about this?"

Han shrugged. "What could go wrong?"

They spent the next few minutes trying to pick out the watch commander's backup. It was not difficult. Predictably, they had stationed themselves in pairs on opposite sides of the chamber, wearing nondescript tunics and dreary business tabards in a crowd that favored parvenu-flamboyant, thug-crass, or Tatooine-tattered. Seeming to sense the essential wrongness of these people, the spectators and bidders alike remained well apart, with the result that the Imperials stood out like rancors in a nerf pen. It was all much too obvious, and it took the next half hour to find the rest of the bodyguards, a dozen men and women scattered through the room in the garb of well-groomed ruffians or overmuscled natives.

Han also found the black-haired man who had tried to sell them the holocube of the boy Podracer, standing not too far from the Imperial commander at the front of the crowd. He was half turned, studying the room, not quite searching for someone in particular, but taking note of whom he did and didn't see. Han was still bothered by the way the man had focused on Leia during the pre-auction inspection, by how he had seemed so certain she would be drawn to the holocube, and—most especially—by how right he had been.

Precisely on the hour, a stout human woman with pale skin and almond eyes and a long tail of braided black hair stepped through the holographic cityscape at the back of the stage. She waited for the room to quiet, then glided forward in a slinky stride that had lost none of its poise or grace despite the forty kilograms she had added since her dancing days. In a voice roughened by hubba smoke, she welcomed the bidders to the auction and introduced herself as Mawbo Kem, drawing a laugh by commenting that of course the males in the audience knew that already.

When the theater grew quiet again, Mawbo announced that she would start the auction with a bang. Exactly on cue, the four-armed Codru-Ji who had served Han and Leia earlier stepped forward with the day's first offering cradled in her four hands. An instant later, a giant hologram of the featured item appeared beneath the ceiling.

To Han's surprise, it was the holocube of the young Podracer.

Several offworlders began to boo and hiss. The locals shouted them down and cheered even more loudly, and almost instantly the theater erupted into a tumult of cheering and jeering a little too heartfelt to be good-natured.

Ever the consummate show-woman, Mawbo remained silent, allowing the cacophony to build and add energy to the auction.

A single muffled click sounded from the comlink in Han's pocket: Sligh confirming that he should go ahead with their side deal. Han answered with a double click: *Go ahead.*

"Wonderful," Leia grumbled. "Wake me when they get to *Twilight*—sometime around midnight."

Despite her tone, her eyes were fixed on the hologram above the stage. Han had to turn away to hide his smile.

On the stage, Celia was using her two upper arms to hold the holocube above her head and parading along the perimeter of the stage in her haughty dancer's stride.

Mawbo said, "As you can see, this is the same 'cube displayed this morning in booth twelve. It's a one-of-a-kind original holograph of the only human Podracer ever to win the Boonta Eve Classic, taken four decades ago and now offered at auction by the pilot's best friend, Kitster Banai."

When the audience failed to erupt in skeptical jeers, Han said, "I can't believe they're buying this. There's an old racetrack just outside town. The locals ought to know humans can't pilot Podracers."

The dark-haired man who was offering the holocube— Kitster Banai—stepped to the edge of the stage and said something to Mawbo.

She nodded and, waving him back to his place with a thick-fingered hand, said, "For the offworlders out there who toured Kitster's booth after his signscreen malfunctioned, the boy in the holocube is Mos Espa's very own Anakin Skywalk—"

The theater again erupted into jeering and cheering, and the last syllable of the name was lost to cacophony. Mawbo asked for quiet, but it was slow in coming.

"What did she say?" Leia asked, again transfixed by the holocube. "Did she say Anakin *Skywalker*?"

"Maybe."

Feeling a little queasy, Han went to the mirrfield, as though moving that tiny distance closer to the holocube would make it easier to see any semblance between the boy and Leia. There wasn't much—high cheeks, the shape of the eyes and maybe the face—but enough that it seemed possible.

Han cursed under his breath, but kept his voice even as he said, "Definitely Anakin Skysomething. Luke did say he'd found something in a 'Net search that suggested your father might have lived on Tatooine as a boy."

"He didn't say it had been here." Leia stared at the table. "He didn't say it had been Mos Espa."

Han shrugged. "There aren't many cities on Tatooine." He slipped a hand into his pocket and clicked his comlink once—Sligh's no-bid signal. "It's not that surprising."

Leia took her time meeting his gaze. "You have no idea."

Sligh answered with a double click: bid.

Han repeated his no-bid one click and tried to pretend nothing was going on. "Well, at least the name explains it."

"Explains what?"

Han started to say the kid's identity explained why she seemed incapable of taking her eyes off the holocube for more than five minutes at a time, but he saw Leia narrow her eyes and decided another answer would be safer.

"How a nine-year-old human won the Boonta Eve Classic," Han said. "He had the Force."

Mawbo finally got the crowd quieted and wasted no time opening the auction. "Who will start the bidding?" She looked first to the Imperial commander in the front row. "How about you, sir? Young Anakin went on to make quite a career for himself."

Han was not surprised when the commander waved her off with a curt gesture. The officer was old enough to have served in the Imperial Navy during the height of Darth Vader's power, and the only people with more reason than the Rebels to fear Vader were the officers who served under him. Mawbo wasted no time looking for another bidder.

"One hundred credits!"

The bidder was hidden from Han's view by the crowd, but the reedy voice was all too familiar. Sligh was opening at a third the maximum Han had authorized, trying to scare off undecided buyers before they grew excited and drove up the price.

Mawbo's gaze dropped to belt high in the front row. "A hundred credits from the Squib in front."

"From a Squib?" Leia hissed. "Our Squibs are bidding on a 'cube of Darth Vader?"

Han shrugged, then single-clicked Sligh again.

"Do I hear—"

"A hundred twenty." The bid came from a straw-haired local woman in a tattered sand cloak.

"A hundred fifty," Sligh offered, still trying to scare off the others.

"What's he doing?" Leia sounded more alarmed than puzzled. "Do they *know* that's not what we want?"

"They know. Don't worry."

A Kurtzen in patched leathers bid 175, and Sligh countered with 180. Han single-clicked again.

Grees pushed through the mirrfield and thrust out a smooth-palmed hand. "Give me your comlink."

"What for?" Han said. "I'm just trying to make sure Sligh knows we're *not* interested in the holocube."

"Should have thought of that before the auction." Grees wagged his fingers for the comlink. "Pass it over. You're breaking Sligh's concentration."

"Thought of *what* before the auction?" Leia narrowed her eyes. "What's he talking about, Ha—er, Jaxal?"

There was no use denying it. Leia knew Han too well to be fooled, and he would only make matters worse by trying to play innocent. He pulled the comlink from his pocket and passed it over. "Call him off. We don't want the 'cube."

"Too late." Grees closed the channel and handed it back. "A deal is a deal."

Leia's jaw dropped. "*Deal?* You're trying to buy a holograph of my . . . of *Darth Vader*?"

"Anakin Skywalker," Han corrected. "And I didn't know who he was. I just thought you liked the picture. You could barely take your eyes off it."

Grees left the booth and disappeared back into the crowd. The bidding was already at 230, and now Sligh was trying to slow it down, taking it up in 2- and 3-credit intervals. The blond woman and the Kurtzen weren't cooperating.

"You thought I'd like a *holocube*." Leia studied him with a durasteel gaze, the counterfeit lekku thrashing on her back like snakes. "Of my *father*?"

Han spread his hands. "How could I know?"

By then, the bidding was at 260. Sligh jumped it

straight to three hundred credits and finally succeeded in scaring the other bidders. Mawbo tried to coax a higher offer by sweet-talking the Kurtzen and taunting the woman, then finally gave up and pointed into the crowd where Sligh was presumably standing.

"Three hundred credits to the Squib," she said. "Going once, twice—"

"Three hundred ten," the woman said.

"Three hundred eleven!" Sligh shot back.

"Hey! That's over the limit!"

Han opened the channel again and single-clicked the Squib, only to have him bid 320 a second later. He stepped out through the mirrfield, but Grees and Emala were nowhere to be seen. Asking Leia to wait for him, he pushed his way down the narrow aisle between the wall booths and the crowded main floor. Of course, Leia didn't wait. She was right behind him when he reached the front of the room, where the large VIP booths—the ones with the hidden doors that opened into the vicechambers in the rear of the theater—sat on elevated platforms mere meters from the stage.

"I thought I asked you to wait."

"You asked," Leia said. "What's going on?"

"I told him three hundred." The bidding was now at 420. "He's breaking the deal."

"And we're trusting them with *Twilight*?"

The hiss of a repulsor chair sounded from the adjacent booth, and Han looked over to see a pudgy human hand slipping through the mirrfield to beckon a service droid. On the smallest finger sparkled a big Corusca gem, set in a boxy ring too garish to be overlooked . . . or easily forgotten. Han started to ask Leia if she saw the hand, but she was already pulling him along behind the front row of bidders.

"Forget what's in the booth," she said. "The important thing is to rein in Sligh. If we end up with that holocube, I'll crack it over your head."

"But you saw the ring, right?" Han asked.

Leia pulled him close and lowered her voice. "There are a lot of ostentatious rings in the galaxy, my dear."

What Leia left unsaid was that one of those rings—the ring that Han had seen—belonged to Threkin Horm, the immensely corpulent president of the powerful Alderaanian Council. Seeing tremendous advantage—perhaps even a new homeworld for his people—in a union of the royal houses of Alderaan and Hapes, Horm had been the loudest of those urging Leia to wed Prince Isolder. That put him high on Han's list of bad guys.

They slipped behind the Imperials, drawing a wary glare and two well-placed elbows from the watch commander's bodyguards, and found Sligh standing alone in the buffer zone the other bidders had left around the Imperials. The bid was at 510, and Han had to pull the Squib out of the front row to keep him from making it 520.

"Put me down!" Sligh bared his teeth as though to bite, but did not dip his head toward Han's arm. "I'll have it in two bids!"

"Yeah? On whose credits?" Han asked. "The limit was three hundred."

"Three hundred?" Sligh asked, sneaking glances at the adjacent bidders. "What are you, broke?"

Han looked up to find the Imperial commander and several other inactive bidders looking in his direction. Too disciplined to smirk, the officer could not quite keep a patronizing light from his eyes.

"It's not too late to cancel the other deal, if that's what you think."

"Cancel?" Sligh's attitude changed from arrogant to alarmed. "You can't cancel. That's a separate deal."

"Try me."

Han dropped Sligh and led Leia back to the booth, all too aware of the eyes turned their way.

As they resumed their seats, Leia said, "I thought we hired the Squibs to *avoid* drawing attention."

"Yeah, but I didn't tell *them* that," he said. "They were setting up an angle."

"What kind of angle?"

Han shrugged. "With Squibs, who can tell?"

FOUR

The holocube of Anakin Skywalker went for an amazing thirteen hundred credits. The winner, a shaggy-chinned Gotal in a much-patched jumpsuit, looked as though he would have to indenture himself to the Hutts to come up with the money. But the smile on his flat face could not have been wider.

Han turned to Leia. "It must be a different Anakin Skywalker in that 'cube," he suggested, not entirely joking. "Because that just doesn't make sense."

"Power always attracts its worshipers," Leia replied.

With the holocube sold, Mawbo quickly moved on to other items, bringing them out by lots. She did not even wait for the highest bid before declaring some collections—usually the least valuable—sold. The exquisitely colored alasl bowls inspired the most spirited offworld bidding, earning enough to buy the Barabel seller a hunting range of a thousand square kilometers.

When the Squibs' lot came out, Han and Leia were relieved to discover that their Wookiee sleeper was more intimidating than the Aqualish the Squibs had recruited. The chipped bantha bone bowl opened for 2 credits, C-3PO bid 3, the Aqualish bid 100, Chewbacca bid 101. When the Aqualish made it two hundred, Chewbacca dropped out of the bidding and, growling softly, sidled up to the competition. The Aqualish never tried to inflate the price again. Within a few minutes, Chewbacca was the proud owner of a piece of twisted plasteel called *Dune Sea Cyclone*, a particularly drab holograph of Dantooine, and a tattered-but-guaranteed-genuine Tusken Raider utility belt.

Han spent the next hour of the auction pondering the pudgy hand he had seen. Humans heavy enough to require repulsor chairs for mobility were hardly rare in the galaxy, but people of such girth rarely braved Tatooine's sweltering climate without good reason. And, aside from Leia herself, who would have better reason to come to an auction of *Killik Twilight* than Threkin Horm? As president of the Alderaanian Council, it was Horm's duty to gather and safeguard what remained of the planet's lost treasures. Had anyone else held that post, Han would have found a safe way to let him know that another bidder had the same intention—a bidder with the resources of the entire New Republic at her disposal. But Han would not help Horm. Threkin Horm, Han would enjoy watching squirm.

A wealthy Bothan bought the last of the junk—a dozen glitterglass panes supposed to have come from Jabba's palace—just to get it off the stage. Then Mawbo announced they were ready to begin the bidding on the final item, the masterpiece *Killik Twilight*. A low murmur filled the theater as the bidders or their agents moved toward the front of the room. Most of the local sellers left to collect their credits, but not Kitster Banai, the swarthy vendor who had sold the holocube. Instead, Banai took a spot in the front row of spectators, securing a good place from which to see the moss-painting.

Han used his comlink to call C-3PO into the booth, but left Chewbacca in the crowd as a surprise reserve. If the Imperials knew about the code key hidden inside the painting, they would not take losing well.

When everyone was in the proper place, Mawbo flashed an alluring smile. "Are you ready?"

Without awaiting an answer, she waved a hand toward the back of the stage. Her Rodian security captain reappeared, stepping through the cityscape holograph with his crew: a dozen hulking, swine-faced Gamorreans carrying vibro-axes, supported by two burly humans armed with repeating blasters. Celia followed, holding onto *Killik Twilight*'s small frame with all four hands. She placed the painting in an easel erected by one of the Gamorreans.

A tense silence fell over the theater. At just fifty centimeters wide, the moss-painting was too small for most of the audience to see clearly. But all eyes were fixed on the giant holograph of it projected beneath the ceiling. Kitster Banai proved himself a man of taste and refinement by removing a small pair of electrobinoculars so he could look directly at the original.

Mawbo studied the row of buyers before her, then pointed at the Imperial commander. "How about you, General? Will you start the bidding?"

"Commander," he corrected. "Commander Quenton. My bid is a quarter million credits."

"A quarter million and one," Sligh said instantly.

This drew a titter from spectators and bidders alike, which, Han suspected, was exactly what the Squibs intended.

"Two seventy-five," Quenton said. He turned his head and stared first at the Squibs, then at the rest of the bidders, clearly trying to send a message of intimidation. When no one seemed willing to meet his eyes, he looked back to the stage. "That would be two hundred and seventy-five *thousand*."

Not one to be bullied while standing on her own stage, Mawbo fixed her almond-shaped eyes on him and said,

"I know what you mean, General. Would those be New Republic credits?"

From the booth, Han could see only the back of Quenton's head, but he guessed by the long silence following that the Imperial had not missed Mawbo's slight in questioning his ability to pay—and in continuing to address him by a rank she knew to be incorrect.

Finally, Quenton said, "The so-called New Republic has no right to issue credits. It is not a legitimate government. But for the purposes of this auction, the transfer will be made in gold peggats."

"Thank you." Mawbo graced him with a cloying smile, then betrayed her anxiety by looking away a little too quickly. "Who will make the next bid?"

Quenton and his bodyguards made a show of glancing down the bidding line, and no one seemed willing to break the silence.

"The Hutt spawn!" Leia leaned forward, her hands braced flat on the table. "He's trying to steal it."

"Steal it?" C-3PO cocked his head. "You seem to have misheard, Mistress. The commander bid almost three hundred thousand credits."

"Threepio, that *is* stealing it," Han said.

When no one bid against him, Quenton said, "The bid stands at two seventy-five, madam."

Mawbo shot him a fiery glare, then glanced down the line again. "*Killik Twilight* is Ob Khaddor at his finest and most subtle. Do I hear three?"

Again, there was silence.

Leia stood and went to the mirrfield. "Those Squibs were a mistake. They're letting him intimidate them."

"Give them time," Han said. "No one's bidding yet."

"And no one's going to." Leia smoothed her cloak, preparing to go out and do her own bidding. "This is a

bad idea. How I ever let you talk me into trusting a pack
of rodents—"

"Relax, will you?" Han slipped around the table and
caught her arm. "They made a deal. No Imperial is going
to scare them off."

Leia stopped short of leaving the booth, but neither
did she return to the couch.

On the stage, Mawbo glared openly at Commander
Quenton. "Very well," she said. "Two seventy-five
once—"

"Two seventy-five one." Sligh paused an instant, then
added proudly, "That's two hundred seventy-five thousand one *hundred* . . . in New Republic credits."

The clarification brought an involuntary snort from a
Kubaz on the other side of Quenton. Then Celia, still
standing beside the painting, covered her mouth with
two hands and tried not to snicker. Her failure seemed to
release all of the tension Quenton had so carefully in-
jected into the auction, and the rest of the theater burst
into laughter.

Mawbo smiled broadly. Seeming to find her own
courage again, she looked to the Imperial. "Two hundred seventy-five thousand one hundred to you, Commander Quenton."

"Three hundred," Quenton said quickly.

The Kubaz said, "Three fifty," and the auction was
off. The amount climbed to a million, then two, and
started toward three. The Squibs stood by silently, allowing the auction to seek its own level before they began to
bid in earnest. Though Han could not see them through
the dense crowd, he imagined they would be playing to
type, standing slack-jawed amid the other bidders.

Her faith renewed by how cleverly the Squibs had outflanked Commander Quenton, Leia watched in patient
silence as the amounts climbed toward the astronomical.

She seemed to take a secret delight in knowing others valued the piece as much as she did, but when the auction was over, Han knew she would regret every credit that had been diverted from the New Republic's hard-pressed defense budget.

The bid hit four million credits, and a small furry hand shot up in front of Kitster Banai's shoulder.

"Down here! I have a bid!" Emala jumped so high her pointed ears bobbed into view. "Five million credits!"

All heads turned toward the Squibs, and Mawbo stepped to the edge of the stage and peered down.

"Repeat that."

"You didn't hear us the first time?" Grees said from somewhere beside Emala. "Five million New Republic credits. That's a five with five zeros."

"*Six,*" Emala corrected. "A five with six zeros."

As all this was taking place, Sligh came slinking out of the spectator crowd with bulging cheeks. He slipped into Han and Leia's private booth and ducked under the table, then something began to clatter to the floor. Han looked down to see him spitting out fund transfer chips.

"You'll want to dump those down the waste chute," he said. "Real fast."

Sligh winked and departed again, leaving Han staring under the table as Leia's head appeared opposite his. Her jaw dropped when she saw the pile, then she simply began to scoop chips into her palm. Han joined her, and they dropped the chips down the booth's waste chute, where they would be drawn along a vacuum duct to a central disintegration unit.

By the time they returned their attention to the auction, the Rodian security guard was crossing the stage toward Mawbo, coming from the general direction of the VIP booths.

"What's going on now?" Leia asked.

Han could only shake his head. "Probably something to do with those chips we dumped." He reached under his cape and pulled his belt around where it would be easier to reach his holster. "Better check your blaster."

The Rodian whispered into Mawbo's ear. She looked toward the VIP booths and nodded, then turned to the bidders.

"In light of the sudden jump in price, the owner has requested funds verification."

Han barely noticed the approving grunts from the crowd, or the superior looks the other bidding agents threw in the direction of the Squibs. He was too shocked by what Mawbo had just said.

"*Owner?* Threkin Horm is the owner?"

"We don't know it's Threkin in the booth." Despite her words, Leia's voice was quavering with rage. "That hand could belong to anybody."

"I'm betting on Horm. Didn't his family control the spaceline that serviced Alderaan?"

"One of them."

"The one *Twilight* was on?"

Leia nodded.

Han rose. "I'd even give you odds."

She caught his arm. "Where are you going?"

"To see a thief." Even as he said it, Han realized that Tatooine was neither the time nor the place to seek justice. With the *Chimaera* in orbit, Mawbo's thugs controlling every door, and an Imperial infiltration squad just meters away on the other side of a mirrfield, the circumstances were hardly ideal for a citizen's arrest. He sat down and said glumly, "I just wanted to make sure it's him."

"I know." Leia's tone suggested she didn't believe a word. "We'll take care of Horm on Coruscant. We do know where he lives."

"Yeah." Han returned to his seat. "And how he's paying for that penthouse of his."

At the front of the theater, the Rodian had produced a comm-linked transfer pad and was descending a small lift-platform to the theater floor. Two Gamorreans were already waiting for him beside the stage.

"Please ready your transfer chips for a validation reading." Mawbo looked straight at Emala and Grees. "And if you can't cover a bid of five million credits, save us all time by retiring from the purchasing area now. I'll buy you a drink later."

A number of bidders left immediately, but the Squibs were not among them.

The Rodian security captain and his guards began to work their way down the line, sending bidder after bidder into the spectator area. An angry rumble built in the front of the room as a handful of agents realized someone had stolen their chips. Mawbo glanced quickly in the direction of the VIP booth, then nodded and reminded the bidders they were responsible for their own security. When a pair of Aqualish took offense and leapt onto the stage, the two humans loosed a flurry of stun bolts and sent them falling back to the floor.

The incident sped things along. The Rodian continued the verification as a Gamorrean dragged the Aqualish away. Several more bidders failed to find their transfer chips. They left without protest—especially after Mawbo moved the remainder of the Gamorreans down to the theater floor. The Squibs, of course, still had the chip Han and Leia had provided. When Quenton—a by-the-book Imperial officer all the way—discovered that his own funds chip was missing, he simply turned to a bodyguard for the backup. By the time the validation reading was completed, only the Squibs, the Imperials, and twenty minor plutocrats remained in the auction.

Leia cast a vaguely guilty look toward the disposal chute, but when she spoke, her tone was one of relief. "Our Squibs don't play fair."

"That's fair for Tatooine."

Once Mawbo recovered from the shock of seeing the Squibs still on the floor, she accepted their bid. The price steadily climbed, a quarter million at a time. By ten million, only the Squibs and the Imperials remained. At twelve million, Leia winced visibly, no doubt counting the number of blastboats or assault companies the New Republic would not be arming in order to recover the code key inside *Killik Twilight*.

At thirteen million, she bit her lip. "Sweetheart?" Leia removed her hold-out blaster from its thigh holster, then twisted one of her counterfeit lekku free of its collar. "How close would you need to be to hit my painting with that?"

She pulled a small silver sphere from inside the tentacle and placed it on the table.

"Oh dear," C-3PO said. "A thermal detonator."

"Relax, Goldenrod. It's a little one." Han picked up the detonator and tapped his Devaronian horns with it, then asked in a hurt voice, "How come all I got was vibroknives?"

"Smaller horns." Leia's tone was impatient. "How close?"

Han gazed through the mirrfield for a moment, pretending to study the situation, but really just thinking. In the unlikely event they survived an assault on the painting, he knew how terribly hurt Leia would be if it was destroyed—especially if she was the one who had directed it. Besides, he wanted her to have it back—if not in their home, then at least in a New Republic museum where she could go and visit it. He tossed the detonator in the air and caught it in his palm.

"How much time do we have?"

"The chip is only authorized to fifteen million," Leia said. "I'm sorry. I never imagined the bidding would go half that high, but with the Imperials here—"

"Yeah, we'll have to figure that part out later." Han tucked the detonator into his pocket, then motioned at the counterfeit lekku on the table. "Better put that back on."

Leaving C-3PO to wait behind, Han and Leia—still disguised as a sharp-toothed Devaronian and his Twi'lek companion—went to Horm's VIP booth. As soon as they turned toward the mirrfield, a pair of Horm's human bodyguards stepped out to block their way. Both were resting their hands on their holstered blaster pistols, and they seemed far more comfortable in their shimmersilk suits than Mawbo's staff.

The tallest pointed toward the back of the theater. "Refresher's that way, pal."

"The guy I'm looking for wouldn't fit, pal." The bid went to fourteen million credits, drawing a gasp from the audience. Han looked past the guards and addressed his own behorned reflection in the mirrfield. "You'd be smart to talk to us inside, Horm, unless you *want* everyone in the theater to hear who's selling the painting."

After a moment's hesitation, a pudgy hand emerged from the mirrfield. It waved them inside, where a pale Hutt of a human spilled over the safety rails of his high-capacity repulsor chair. With reddish brown hair cropped short and a nose so fleshy it was almost shapeless, the occupant of the chair was definitely Threkin Horm. He fixed a pair of beady brown eyes on Han and Leia, but showed no hint of recognition.

"What makes you think anyone here cares where the painting came from?" Horm did not offer them a seat;

there were none. The table and couches had been removed to make room for his repulsor chair. "Tatooine is
well known for its aversion to questions."

"I doubt anyone here does care," Leia said coolly.
"But a certain council on Coruscant would be very inter-
ested in knowing what their president is doing with
Alderaan's lost treasures."

Horm spread his hands. "The council has its expenses."

"Not many." The tips of Leia's counterfeit lekku were
twitching in anger. "The New Republic grants you office
space, and survivor donations far exceed salaries and
disbursements."

Horm smiled tolerantly, then waved his bodyguards
out of the booth and pointed to a switch on the wall.
"Activate the sound filter." Once Leia had done so, his
eyes narrowed to slits. "For a Twi'lek, you know a lot
about Alderaan's business."

"We do our research," Han said. With the offer at
fourteen and a half million, the auction was about to
end. "Now, you have a choice to make."

"How much do you want?" Horm asked. "And I
should warn you, if the figure is too high—"

"It won't be," Han said. "You keep everything."

"Really?" Horm lifted his brow folds. "Then why are
you here?"

"Because the painting shouldn't go to Imperials," Leia
said. "As an Alderaanian, you must understand that."

"You're appealing to my conscience?" Horm smirked.
"Blackmailers?"

"We're appealing to your sense of self-preservation,"
Leia said. "If the council finds out what you've been doing, you'll face fraud charges."

"And if they find out you sold *Killik Twilight* to Imperials," Han added, "someone will hire a bounty hunter.

So, either you spend the rest of a very short life hiding, or you walk away with"—he listened to the bid amount—"fourteen and three-quarter million. Decide now, because this auction's almost over."

Horm considered Han for a moment, then dipped his chins in a sort of nod. "Very well." His repulsor chair hissed as it tipped forward so he could extend a beckoning arm through the mirrfield. "I was appalled to see the Imperials here anyway."

A bodyguard stepped into the booth. By the time Horm had given him his instructions, the bidding stood at fourteen nine.

In an overly casual tone, Grees called, "Fifteen—"

The audience broke into an excited babble, drowning out the remainder of the bid and buying Horm's guard time to go to the stage. Mawbo raised her hands for quiet, but the crowd was not cooperating. Han thanked them silently.

The bodyguard went to the rear of the stage, where he was stopped by a Gamorrean who seemed to understand only that his orders were to keep people off the stage. Finally, the Rodian noticed and went over to talk with the bodyguard. By then, Mawbo had quieted the crowd. Ever the show-woman, she paused for dramatic effect, then looked back down to Grees.

"I think we all know what the bid was, but would you repeat it for the record?"

"Fifteen million credits." Grees managed to sound as though he was perfectly willing to go higher. "New Republic, of course."

The security captain started across the stage. All eyes shifted toward him, save for those of Kitster Banai, who had not moved his electrobinoculars from *Killik Twilight* since Celia had brought it out.

Quenton touched a finger to his ear, then glanced

toward Horm's booth. Someone on his team had figured out what Han and Leia were doing in there.

Quenton's hand shot up. "Fifteen million five!"

Mawbo started to acknowledge the bid, but the Rodian sprang the last few steps and caught her arm. He began whispering into her ear, and the theater broke into an inquisitive drone.

"Fifteen five," Quenton repeated.

When Mawbo did not acknowledge him, Quenton said something into his collar. A dozen fit-looking beings began to move in from the edges of the room, not running, but shouldering and pushing and heading straight for the stage. They were all about the size of large humans and of species with the same general body pattern, and they were all holding one hand beneath a cloak, cape, or jacket loose enough to hide the bulge of a weapon.

"Back to intimidation tactics," Han said. He commed Chewie and told him to stay out of sight behind the Imperials, then drew his blaster. "When will they learn?"

Horm's eyes went round with fear. "Where . . . how . . . You're not supposed to have weapons!"

"We're not?" Leia pulled her hold-out blaster from its hiding place on her thigh. "Remind me next time."

In front of the stage, Quenton repeated his bid yet again—this time with the smug air of a threat. "My bid stands at fifteen and a half million, madam."

Mawbo glanced down at him, then looked out at the infiltration team pushing its way toward the stage. Her dark eyes flashed in anger, but her expression remained otherwise unreadable as she weighed the costs of defying the Empire against the damage her reputation would sustain by allowing Quenton to push her around. Unable to counter the bid, the Squibs stood by silently, still appearing cocky and confident.

Mawbo's face fell, and Han knew which bad choice she had decided would cost her more. She met Quenton's gaze.

"I have been directed to accept the Squibs' last offer." A collective gasp filled the theater, and Mawbo looked toward Horm's booth. "The owner has decided it would be an outrage to sell the painting to the same Empire that destroyed Alderaan."

The Squibs whooped for joy and huddled in a tight little circle, snickering and chittering in their own language and casting smirks in Quenton's direction. He glared blaster bolts at them, then spoke into his collar.

The infiltration squad broke into a run, shoving spectators aside or just kicking them down and running over their backs. The crowd exploded in panic. Spectators began to push for the exits and brought the squad's progress to a crawl. Towering half a meter above the crowd, Chewbacca managed to look frightened and confused even as he eased forward behind the Imperials.

Mawbo ordered her Gamorreans to the front of the stage, then turned to Celia.

"Take the painting to—"

From somewhere deep behind the stage came a series of low booms, followed quickly by startled cries and the muffled scream of discharging blaster rifles.

"What's that?" Horm asked, his repulsor chair hissing as he leaned forward. "Were those explosions?"

"It wasn't applause," Han said. "Quenton has a squad coming the back way."

Horm activated a comlink and sent both bodyguards onto the stage to help guard the moss-painting.

Out on the stage, Mawbo's face grew stormy with rage. She motioned Celia to wait—needlessly—then turned back to Quenton.

The Squibs were already taking things into their own

hands, darting past the bodyguards, swarming the commander.

"Thief!"

"Our painting!"

Quenton went down screaming and flailing. His two bodyguards spun to help, their arms extending downward to activate spring-loaded sleeve holsters. Emala reached up and snatched a small silver weapon away as it appeared in the first guard's hand, then used it on the second one. There was no sound or flash, but the man cried out. He clawed at his throat and collapsed.

Mawbo watched in horror from the stage. "Stop! Not here!"

The surviving bodyguard plucked Grees and Sligh off Quenton, shaking them violently, trying to snap their necks. Emala shot him in the knee. He dropped the two Squibs, reached for his leg, pitched over forward, and did not move.

More fire sounded behind the stage, this time closer. Mawbo's human guards took their repeating blasters and vanished through the cityscape. A stray bolt came through the holograph and struck the valance above Celia's head. She screamed and abandoned the painting, rushing to a lift-platform concealed in the floor and descending into the stage.

Quenton scrambled to his feet, yelling for help and ordering his infiltration squad after the Squibs. Emala whistled, and the rodents scurried out of sight. Mawbo took her lead from Celia and raced for the back of the stage, leaving her Gamorreans to form a perimeter around the apron.

But a dozen Gamorrean security guards were no match for an Imperial infiltration squad, and Han knew it.

"Cover me!"

Han stepped out of the booth, and darts began zipping

past his head. He dropped to his knees, still looking for the source of the attack, then heard one thump into his false horn.

Leia's hold-out blaster began to spray dashes of color over his shoulder. A small hand grabbed his collar and pulled him back into the booth.

"What, did I marry a gundark?" Leia asked, crouching next to him.

More darts hissed over their heads, and Horm cried out several times. Judging by the anguished gasps that followed, the Imperials were using a fast-acting neurotoxin.

Chewbacca appeared at the edge of the panicked crowd, coming up behind a Kuati aristocrat and her telbun. He slammed their heads together, and they went down with sickening dents in their skulls.

Chewbacca growled in victory, then leapt away from a flurry of incoming darts. He came down next to an overmuscled man in an unstained farmer's tunic, then sent the Imperial flying in one direction and his weapon in another.

Darts started flying in Chewbacca's direction again. Han traced them back to a booth opposite Horm's and poured blaster bolts through the mirrfield. Finally, he hit the projector relay and revealed a glittergowned woman kneeling on the table with a dart shooter in her hands. She dived for the back of the booth, but Leia fired, and the woman hit the couch in a smoking heap.

Chewbacca roared his thanks. Grabbing an Imperial to use as a shield, he began to work his way toward Horm's booth.

The remainder of Quenton's infiltration squad emerged from the shrieking crowd and began to spray darts everywhere. The Gamorreans dropped without swinging an ax blade, and Han and Leia had to take refuge behind Horm's repulsor chair.

Han reached around the side and found he could just reach the controls. "Stick close. I have a plan."

"Han!"

Han stopped short of moving the chair. "Yeah?"

"What are you doing?"

"He's dead anyway." Han grabbed a thick wrist and tried to feel for a pulse. "I think."

"I did—I married a gundark." Leia pulled his hand down. "Use the detonator."

Han shook his head. "You don't want that. I know you."

"And how do you think I'll feel when the Imperials crack Shadowcast and start executing our agents?" Leia removed the detonator from Han's pocket, thumbed the fuse to twenty seconds, and activated it. "Do I have to throw this myself?"

"And you say *you* married a gundark!"

Han took the detonator, peered over the top of the chair, and saw the first stormtrooper emerging at the rear of the stage. *Killik Twilight* still rested on its easel.

"Fifteen seconds, fourteen . . ." Leia counted.

"I hope those troopers like art, because it's the last thing—"

"Han!"

Han stood and threw.

He did not see the Squibs until the detonator hit and began to roll toward *Killik Twilight*.

They were clambering over the *other* side of the stage. Han rushed out of the booth. "Emala, Sligh—detonator!"

He pointed, and the Squibs' eyes went to the silver orb rolling toward the painting. So did the stormtroopers'.

The Squibs dived over the front of the stage, and the troopers stumbled back through the cityscape holograph, firing wildly in Han's direction. Then a dark-haired man rose into view, riding the same lift-platform Celia had used to escape.

"No!" Han yelled. "Det—"

The man sprang onto the floor, kicked the detonator toward the front of the stage, snatched *Killik Twilight* off its easel, and raced for the far corner.

Han glanced at the holograph above the stage and instantly recognized the immaculately groomed hair. "Kitster Banai?"

Leia caught Han's collar again and jerked him into the booth backward; he did not see whether Banai made it out alive. All he saw was the white flash of the exploding detonator.

FIVE

The Weequay—Grunts—had been clever enough to bring Leia and the others into Espa Heights from the back side, so they were peeking down on the Banai household from a sand-choked alley directly above and behind the home. It was a typical house for this part of town, with one large dome and three smaller ones arranged in a diamond around a central courtyard. A tarnished maintenance droid was out using a shovelvac to clear the enclosure of the last of the storm deposits, so it was impossible to hear what sounds might be drifting out of the air vents in the roofs. But through the window bubbles in the dome walls, they could see flying dishes and overturned furniture.

Chewbacca glared at Grunts and growled.

C-3PO leaned over the shoulder of the crouching Weequay and translated this—rather diplomatically, Leia knew—as, "Master Chewbacca was under the impression that we would arrive *before* the Imperials."

"Who says we didn't?" Grunts retorted. "Even if they saw who took the painting, nobody is going to tell the Imperials where Kitster lives—not after Quenton crossed Mawbo like that."

Chewbacca rumbled an opinion that made Leia thankful Grunts did not understand Shyriiwook.

C-3PO said, "Master Chewbacca wonders how you

can be sure they aren't Imperials? Our vantage point is rather limited."

The Weequay spun on his heels and sent C-3PO stumbling back. "He saying I don't know what I'm talking about?"

Chewbacca snarled and started forward to explain himself in terms a Weequay could understand. Leia and Han rose and blocked his way. On the assumption that the Imperials would be watching for a Devaronian and a Twi'lek, they had both discarded their disguises and were now concealed only in heavy sand cloaks. Han turned to calm Grunts, and Leia stepped in front of the Wookiee, her neck craned way back so she could meet his gaze.

"Where do you think you're going, big guy?"

He informed her he was going to rearrange a Weequay.

Leia knitted her brow. "Chewbacca, we don't have time for this nonsense. We need to get down there and figure out what happened to Kitster and *Killik Twilight*." She pushed him gently back toward his place. "Besides, Grunts is taking a big risk by helping us. I want you to apologize."

Chewbacca grunted menacingly and glared at the Weequay over her head. Grunts glared back. Leia braced her hands on her hips and stood between them, silently demanding that the Wookiee do as she asked. Though she did not like to test him, she knew that he was almost as loyal to her as he was to Han. She gave Chewbacca her best stare, and finally he looked away, oowralling reluctantly.

"Master Chewbacca wishes to convey his awareness of Master Grunts's fidelity in keeping the secret of our identities," C-3PO said. "He also wishes to acknowledge that Master Grunts did not need to be asked twice when Captain Solo asked for help. He further explains that his temper is unusually difficult to control around Wee-quays, as their odor smells rather like a starved katarn coming up from the forest."

Grunts eyed the droid doubtfully. "He said all that in one groan?"

"Of course," Leia said. "Threepio doesn't embellish. He's a droid."

C-3PO leaned closer to Grunts. "I believe it is quite an apology, for a Wookiee."

Grunts murmured something that might have been ac-knowledgment or mockery, then looked back to the Ba-nai house and said, "It isn't Imperials. If it was Imperials, they'd have guards posted."

Chewbacca snorted quietly.

Grunts was instantly on his feet, fists clenched. "What'd he say?"

Han grabbed his sleeve. "Take it easy. Chewie said you're probably right." He unholstered his blaster. "But there's only one way to be sure. We need to go down and see."

Grunts pulled a light repeating blaster from beneath his sand cloak. The fur rose along Chewbacca's spine.

"Uh, Grunts, perhaps it would be better if you kept watch from here." Leia passed a comlink to the Wee-quay. "Whether anyone wants to cooperate with the Im-perials or not, it won't take Quenton long to find out where Kitster lives. We can expect a squad of storm-troopers anytime."

Grunts shot Chewbacca a baleful look, but clicked the comlink once to test it and nodded. He jumped up on a speeder-sized recycling bin and settled down on his haunches to keep watch.

C-3PO raised a hand. "Mistress Leia, perhaps keeping watch is a duty suitable for—"

"Forget it, Goldenrod." Han stepped over the side and

led the way down a short bank toward the Banai house. "We need someone to talk to that maintenance droid."

Leia followed, with Chewbacca herding C-3PO down the slope behind her. Once they reached the house, Han jumped off the embankment and landed lightly on the roof. Leia went next, and together they scrambled to the top of the rear dome.

Behind her, C-3PO said, "Oh, my. I'm afraid I'm not equipped for such maneuvers. Without repulsorlifts—"

Leia turned to find Chewbacca gathering the droid up in a Wookiee hug.

"Help!" C-3PO cried. "I'll be smashed to circuits!"

Chewbacca ignored him and took a running leap. He landed on the dome below the others, pinning C-3PO against the roof with his chest. He extended his climbing claws and pushed the droid up beside Leia.

Down in the courtyard, the maintenance droid's photoreceptors were shining up in their direction. C-3PO spat a burst of static at it, and the droid replied with a similar burst.

"How interesting," C-3PO said. "There are three Squibs inside. He says it's going to take a week to clean up."

"Squibs?" Leia looked at Han and shook her head, then grabbed his hand. "Cover us, Chewie."

They slid into the courtyard together, then covered Chewbacca while he descended into the courtyard with C-3PO. The pair landed with only a minor amount of clanging, soft enough so the maintenance droid's shovel-vac concealed the noise.

Leia led the way to the primary dome and peered through a transparisteel door. A blond woman in her midthirties was squatting in the corner, covering her head and biting her lip as the Squibs raced around, touching objects to their cheeks, then smashing them.

"Doesn't look like the Squibs found anything," Han whispered. "How should we handle this?"

"Well, it doesn't look like intimidation works," Leia said. "And we've got to do something about those Squibs anyway. If we can win the woman's gratitude, maybe I can get her to open up. She has to be worried about her . . . uh . . . father?"

Han pressed his brow to the transparisteel, then shook his head. "I don't think so. Pretty old to be a daughter."

Sligh sent a plate of blue alasl spinning into the wall above the woman's head, and she finally screamed.

Grees jumped onto her knees and yelled so loud his voice was barely muffled by the door. "Where is he?"

"I told you, at the auction!"

"Liar!" Grees hopped down in front of a carved bantha bone cabinet, then opened a drawer and sent an empty flatware tray flying across the room. "That's where *we* came from!"

Leia and Han checked each other to make sure their sand cloak hoods concealed their faces, then Leia opened the door.

Nobody inside seemed to notice.

"He m-m-must have left," the woman said. "How would I know?"

Sligh went to her side and snatched a comlink from her tunic pocket. "I'm sure a bright woman like you knows how to work one of these."

"You want me to call him?"

"Good idea!"

The woman extended a tentative hand, only to have Sligh slap it aside while he rubbed the comlink against his cheek.

"That's enough, you three," Han said, stepping into the room.

The three Squibs spun on their heels and, finding no

sign of head horns or tentacles, did not seem to recognize their business partners. They immediately spread out across the cluttered floor and began to ease forward.

"Leave while you still can," Grees said. He slipped a hand behind his back as though reaching for a blaster that Leia had already seen was not there. "This is no business of yours."

"Actually, it is." Leia waved Chewbacca and C-3PO through the door. "You might recognize our associates."

Grees's eyes narrowed. He barked something in Squibbian, and all three Squibs stopped advancing. "You." He glowered at Chewbacca. "You took us for a thousand credits."

Chewbacca showed his fangs and growled.

Grees was not intimidated. "There's always a next time, Wookiee. Don't think you've won this."

"He didn't do anything that wasn't in the deal," Han said. "You have a problem, you have it with all of us."

"Oh, *now* I'm scared." Sligh went over to Han and tipped his head back. The tip of his snout just reached Han's belt. "What happened to the horns, Ace?"

"Lost them in a firefight." Han tugged his hood forward, then pointed at the wide-eyed woman in the corner. "Why don't you apologize to the nice lady and leave? We'll take it from here."

"Leave?" Emala shook her head and stepped to Sligh's side. "That deal went sour. You tried to kill us. We're all very disappointed in you."

"If he had *tried*, you'd be dead." Leia put her blaster away. "And we kept our end of the bargain. Your credits are still waiting at Mawbo's, as soon as you want to go pick them up."

"Mawbo's?" Sligh scoffed. "Are you spacesick? Mawbo wouldn't let us through the door right now."

"Not our problem."

Han holstered his blaster, then looked to Chewbacca, nodded, and turned his palms up.

Chewbacca tossed his bowcaster over, then dropped to his knees and lashed out with both arms, sweeping Grees and Sligh into his grasp.

Emala leapt instantly onto the Wookiee's back, her sharp Squib teeth tearing out huge tufts of fur as she tried to rip her way down to his hide. He tucked the two males under one arm, then reached over his shoulder and plucked her off.

"Let go!" Emala ordered. "Don't make me rip your throat out."

Chewbacca rose, growling, and started for the front door.

"Stop!" Grees ordered. "You can't cut us out like this!"

Chewbacca left the Banai house and started up the street toward the alley, where, Leia hoped, he would be able to intimidate the Squibs into leaving. She went to the woman in the corner and, electing not to kneel in the jagged shards covering the floor, crouched beside her and took her hand.

"It's over," she said. "They're gone."

The woman turned a pair of shocked blue eyes on Leia. The lines at the corners were deep and long, the lashes dark and carefully curled.

"Those . . . those terrors were yours?" she asked.

"We had a business arrangement." Leia looked around the ransacked room, taking in the child-sized tunics, a speeder toy smashed under an overturned vidconsole, the four limbs of a stuffed bantha lying across the room from each other. "This was no part of it."

Han picked up an overturned chair and brought it over. "Things kind of got out of hand at the auction."

As Han said this, Leia watched the woman's eyes and saw no sign of surprise.

"The Imperials were there." Han brushed off the seat and offered the woman his hand, which she refused to take. "A fight started."

Still no sign of surprise, but the woman asked, "Are you here to tell me something happened to Kitster?"

The question was a ruse, Leia realized. The woman's composure so far suggested she already knew Banai was safe, which meant that she could probably lead Leia to him—and to *Killik Twilight.*

"We think Kitster escaped," Leia said. She had decided that Han was right about the woman's identity; a daughter probably would not call Banai by his first name. "Listen, we're very worried your husband—"

"Tamora," the woman put in. There was no hint of relief, only the quick information.

"I'm sorry," Leia said. "Aren't you married to Kitster?"

"More or less." Finally, the woman allowed Han to help her into the chair. "My name is Tamora."

"I see."

Leia continued to study the room. Ransacked though it was, the house was too clean for Tamora to be the type who left her children's clothes and toys lying around. Someone had warned her about the trouble at the auction, and that people would come looking for her husband. She had been rushing to leave when the Squibs arrived.

"Tamora, are your children safe?"

Finally, Tamora's eyes betrayed some hint of surprise. "My children?"

Leia picked up one of the small tunics lying on the floor. "The little boy who wears this." She pointed at the torso of the stuffed bantha. "And the girl who plays with that."

Tamora's manner went from evasive to angry. She stood and crunched across the room in her bare feet, stopping in the kitchen entrance to turn and face Leia.

"Ji and Elly are safe," she said. "They aren't here—and they don't concern you."

"If you're sure." Leia was careful to avoid looking toward the locked doors of the plasteel pantry in the kitchen. She needed to win Tamora's trust, and she was not going to do that by making the woman worry for her children. "You have nothing to fear from us, I promise."

"That promise would sound a lot more sincere on your way out the door," Tamora said. "Or at least coming from someone whose face I could see."

"I'm sure." Leia tipped her hooded head in acknowledgment. "But it's safer for all of us this way."

"If you say so," Tamora said. "You're the one with the Wookiee."

Seeing that she was making little progress, Leia took a moment to circle the room, searching for another angle into the woman's confidence. Had the reference to the Wookiee been a veiled suggestion that Tamora had guessed their identities? It was always possible, but Leia saw no advantage in pressing the point. Everything in the house hinted at the money troubles Banai had mentioned during the pre-auction inspection—an expensive durasilk-lined flatware tray lying on the floor among cheap plasteel utensils, the unfaded rectangles on the walls marking the pieces he had sold at auction, a corner left empty for an absent piece of sculpture.

Money was almost certainly the reason Banai had risked his life to steal the painting. In all likelihood, the promise of a big payoff was why Tamora had refused to be intimidated by the Squibs. To recover *Killik Twilight*, all Leia had to do was convince Tamora that she would pay more than the Imperials—more safely—and do so before Kitster sold the painting to Quenton.

Leia came to a transparisteel shelf hanging across from a pair of overturned reading chairs. There was only a little dust—probably just what had blown in through cracks during the storm—but enough to see that the empty place in the center had once been occupied by something square.

"This was where the holocube sat?"

"The Skywalker 'cube?" Tamora asked. "Yes. Kitster liked it there. I'd catch him staring at it sometimes, so lost in the past he wouldn't hear me come in."

"Really?" It was a hard thing for Leia to imagine, someone having memories of Anakin Skywalker that he actually wanted to revisit. "So they really were close? That wasn't a sales pitch?"

"Anakin was his best friend. I didn't want Kit to sell the holocube, but . . ." Tamora let the sentence trail and turned to wipe an eye. When she turned back, she was biting the inside of her lower lip to keep it from quivering. "After Anakin won the Boonta, the Jedi who took him sold his Podracer to a competitor. Anakin gave a few of those credits to Kit. It changed his life."

Behind Tamora, Han pointed to his chronometer, then made a circling motion with his finger. *Speed it up; the Imperials will be coming.*

She nodded to Han, then continued to draw the woman out.

"Changed his life?" More was required here than millions of credits. "How?"

Tamora crouched down and began to rummage through the knickknacks that had once occupied the empty shelf. Holocubes of Tamora and the children, Kitster at the gates of a bustling mansion somewhere out in the desert, a pair of bantha tusk figurines. Finally, she found an old flimsi-plast book and handed it to Leia.

"Kitster used the credits to buy this."

"Par Ontham's Guide to Etiquette?" Leia asked.

"A classic!" C-3PO crunched over, his heavy droid feet crushing the shards on the floor into an even finer grit. "I have a recent edition in my memory banks, of course, but I've never recorded an original monograph. May I?"

The grinding seemed to jar Tamora back to the present, and the trust that Leia had been working to build faded before her eyes. She pulled the book away from C-3PO's outstretched hand. "Thank you for sharing this." Leia passed the flimsiplast back to Tamora. "I take it Kitster put the information to good use?"

Tamora accepted the book, but when she spoke, the wariness had returned. "He became a steward at the Three Moons and earned enough to buy his freedom. Eventually, he became the majordomo on the Rendala Estate." She cast an uneasy look at the holocube of Kitster at the mansion gate, then seemed to recall Han and turned to face him. "But I doubt you came to talk about Kitster's past."

"Not really," Han said. "Look, we're not out to hurt him."

"In fact, we're even a little grateful to your husband for saving the painting," Leia said. It was more or less true; the confusion that followed *Killik Twilight*'s "res-cue" had helped her and the others avoid further Impe-rial entanglements. "And we're willing to compensate Kitster very handsomely for the risk he took. But now we need it back, Tamora."

"Back?" Tamora echoed. "Who are you?"

"That's not important," Leia said. "What is important is that we'll pay enough that you and Kitster will never have to worry about finances again. And we'll make sure you can enjoy it in safety."

"That's very generous of you," Tamora said. "I wish I knew what you were talking about."

"I think you do." Leia picked up a child's tunic. "You were rushing to leave when the Squibs arrived. You knew exactly what happened at the auction. Kitster commed you—or someone did."

Grunts's voice came over Han's comlink. "Stormtroopers at the base of the hill. A full squad."

Tamora's face paled, and she turned to look out the large window bubble in the front wall. The view did not extend beyond the homes across the street.

"Look, we're talking as much money as the Imperials." Han held out his hand and took a step toward her. "You owe it to your family to hear us out—and you don't want anyone here when the stormtroopers arrive anyway. Kids make pretty good bargaining chips."

"I told you, my children aren't here." Tamora retreated toward the kitchen. "But nice try."

"Nice try?" Leia motioned Han to stay back. "He's not kidding. They're going to tear this place apart. When they find your children, they'll take them hostage, and you'll be lucky to get anything at all for the painting."

"And, of course, *you* would never do the same thing," Tamora said.

"Have we tried to open those pantry doors?" Leia countered. "We're asking you to come with us, not telling."

Tamora's mask of resolve finally melted into indecision. "Kit said to trust no one." She was speaking more to herself than to anyone else. "He said the Imperials would try anything, and everyone else would be worse."

"And he was right." Leia felt sure that, with a little patience, Tamora would turn to them for help. She had no choice, really. "Kitster has gotten himself involved in some very serious business. I don't think he realizes *how* serious."

Tamora looked around the room, then shook her head. "I know he doesn't. He said to throw some clothes in a bag and go. I didn't even get to the bag."

"And then the Squibs were here," Leia said. "You never had a chance."

Han's comlink activated again. This time it was Chewbacca, telling them to come out the back way—and soon.

"Time's up." Han stepped toward Tamora.

Leia intercepted him and pulled him toward the courtyard door. "It's her decision."

They had barely taken a step before Tamora called, "Wait."

"Great." Han started toward the kitchen. "Let's get the kids."

Tamora continued to block the entrance. "Show me your faces."

"Look, you really don't want to know," Han said. "It will only put us all in more danger."

"You mean put *you* in more danger," Tamora countered. "If you want my help, you'll have to trust me this far."

Leia looked at Han, then nodded. "She's trusting *us*."

"Not yet," Tamora pointed out.

"Yeah—but it's not like we have a choice." Han pulled back his hood, revealing his handsome rogue's face. Traces of red dye still showed where he had not applied the removing cream thickly enough along the edges of his sideburns and hairline. "Maybe you've seen me hanging around. I used to spend a lot of time on Tatooine."

The way Tamora's jaw fell suggested that while she certainly recognized Han Solo, it was not from some seedy smuggler's cantina.

Leia also pulled back her hood. "I hope this will satisfy you." She glanced out the front window bubble—no stormtroopers yet, but they could not be far away. "Because we really do have to leave."

"Oh, I'm satisfied." Tamora started across the room, moving *away* from the kitchen. "We'll leave the back way. It's less noticeable."

"Uh—aren't you forgetting something?" Han was scowling and looking into the kitchen at the plasteel pantry. "Like your kids, maybe?"

"They're in the back." Tamora motioned Han into the adjacent dome area. "Do you really take me for the kind of mother who would lock her children in a pantry?"

SIX

With eight beings crammed into a four-person land-speeder, Leia had to sit on Han's lap while Chewbacca, who needed the room of the forward compartments, drove. Tamora sat on C-3PO's lap in the front passenger seat, guiding them through a maze of dust-choked alleys deep into what looked like Mos Espa's merchant quarter. Grunts rode in back opposite Leia and Han, grumbling to himself about Wookiee driving and holding the black-haired Banai children in his lap. Though neither one could have been more than six, they handled their fear with reserve, obeying their mother's commands without hesitation and generally remaining as quiet and unobtrusive as children could with streams of tears pouring out of their brown eyes.

Leia longed to comfort them, but limited her attempts to reassuring smiles and encouraging words. They did not strike her as the type of children who would react well to a stranger's embrace, and even if they were, she knew their mother would hardly welcome such familiarity from someone stalking their father.

"Turn there."

Tamora pointed down a side lane so narrow that Chewbacca had to stop and spin the landspeeder on its repulsorlifts before entering. Leia slipped a hand beneath her sand cloak where it would be able to reach her blaster more quickly. Though Tamora had already circumvented two stormtrooper checkpoints, Leia remained nervous. From what she had seen so far, Mos Espa was a bustling dome-warren where catastrophe lurked around each blind curve and trouble sat watching from beneath every shade awning. It was no wonder that Tamora had proven so wary; anyone who lacked vigilance in this city would soon perish.

That was something Leia would do well to keep in mind, even when dealing with Tamora. The woman had seemed duly impressed—even relieved—when she learned the Solos' identity, and she was hardly likely to cause trouble with her children in the landspeeder. But anytime a mission involved strangers and Imperials, betrayal was always a possibility.

And, so far, Tamora seemed unable to explain what Banai had in mind for *Killik Twilight*. She insisted he hated Imperials and—contrary to Leia's assumption—would never sell to them, but Tamora remained at a loss to provide another good reason for the theft. The only excuse she had suggested was that Banai had impulsively taken the painting to save it, and that he imagined he would eventually find a buyer from Alderaan.

It all sounded very noble, of course, and before the auction Leia had seen enough of Banai's collection to realize he was a fellow art lover. Yet this was also a man who had displayed a holocube of Anakin Skywalker in his *home*. It seemed to Leia that any decent man would have put the holocube away when he learned his friend had grown up to become Darth Vader.

Just as disturbing was the spirited bidding for the holocube. In any given group, there were always a few beings who glorified power even in its most brutal form.

But there had been *dozens* of local bidders. And hundreds of local spectators had seemed to think the holocube was a fine piece of memorabilia.

Maybe it was something in the Force around here, some sort of residual presence that blinded natives of Mos Espa to the monster Anakin Skywalker had become. That might even explain the waking nightmare Leia had suffered aboard the *Falcon*—some awful vestige of her father's childhood that had sensed her coming and reached out.

And if Anakin had left a trace in the Force, then perhaps Luke had left one as well. Both were powerful in the Force, and their residues becoming mixed might explain why she had seen Luke turning to the dark side.

Leia had no idea whether such a thing was possible, of course. But she liked that explanation a lot better than the others that kept running through her mind.

Tamora told Chewbacca to stop in front of a dingy mud-and-sand hut near the outskirts of the merchant district. Behind the hut stood a large enclosure of opaque fencing, topped every five meters by the electrodes of an antitheft field. Jutting up behind the barricade were the assorted canopies, turrets, and engine housings for vessels ranging from cargo skiffs to heavy space freighters. A band-cut metal sign above the door read WALD'S PARTS—GOOD AS NEW AT PRICES YOU CAN PAY.

If Tamora was telling the truth, Banai was waiting for her inside. Chewbacca opened the cowling, and they piled out into the poststorm doldrums. The dust seemed to hang here even thicker than in Espa Heights, trapping the heat and making Tatooine's already stifling atmosphere even more searing and unbreathable. But with the first sun hanging low on the horizon, the evening colors were worthy of Ob Khaddor. Above the roofs of the city hung a thick-banded sunset of scarlet, copper, and coral, topped by wispier ribbons of pink and yellow. And, growing swiftly larger, sinking down out of the brilliant curtain of color, were a dozen H-shaped silhouettes.

Leia pointed at the expanding shapes. "Han, are those? . . ." A familiar whine sounded from the direction she was pointing, growing louder and rising in pitch, and she knew the answer. "TIEs!"

Leia had barely spoken the word before the starfighters dropped in over Espa Heights and shrieked across the city, dust billowing off rooftops in their wakes. By the time Han and the others turned to look, the TIEs were on them, so low the air crackled with discharge from their ion engines. The squadron flashed past too fast for the eye to follow, trailing a series of sonic booms that blasted the dust-laden air into roiling gray haze, then screamed out over the desert and vanished.

"Now that's just impolite," Han said, trying to smooth his static-charged hair. "The spaceport ought to revoke Imperial landing rights."

Chewbacca, whom the ion static had rendered into a fair imitation of a two-and-a-half-meter bottle brush, groaned and pointed back over Mos Espa. A flight of five *Sentinel*-class landing craft was descending out of the lower sun, their noses already rising as they decelerated. At 54 stormtroopers per vessel, that would be 270 soldiers—a full assault company.

"Oh my . . ." Tamora gasped. "What has Kitster gotten us into?"

The look of panic on Tamora's face might have been counterfeit, but not the way her cheeks paled. No one could fake that. She turned to Leia.

"All that for a painting?"

"Imperial commanders are accustomed to getting their

way." Leia exchanged a worried glance with Han, then gently guided the Banai children toward their mother. "Why don't you take the children ahead."

"Of course . . . the children." Tamora held out her hands and cast a worried look back at the approaching troop shuttles. "We'll be inside."

Once they were gone, Han asked, "What do you think? Did somebody recognize us at the auction?"

"Maybe," Leia said. "We can't really know, but I think we should assume the worst." She cast a pointed glance in the direction of Grunts.

Han nodded and turned to the Weequay. "Uh, thanks for all your help, but—"

"This isn't my fight." The Weequay turned to go. "No way I'm sticking around."

Leia knew better than to offer a Weequay money for his help, but she wanted to repay him for the risks he was taking just by keeping their secret. "Grunts, if you want a lift offplanet—"

"Not bad enough to ride with the Wookiee." Grunts glanced in the direction of the landing craft, which were now fanning out across the city and raising their rear wings in preparation for touchdown. "Besides, when I do make it out of here, I want to get where I'm going."

Chewbacca rumbled something that sounded like "good idea" but might have been "good luck."

Leia and Han pulled up their sand hoods and followed Tamora into Wald's Parts. The interior was dim, relatively cool, and not all that dusty by Mos Espa standards. It was also a wreck, with repulsorlift elements, servodrives, and droid components scattered across the floor. Tamora and her children were in the rear of the hut, where the lower half of a vaporator lay diagonally across the door to the yard.

Han turned to Chewbacca. "I thought you handled the Squibs."

Chewbacca groaned indignantly.

"You left them locked inside a recycling bin?" Leia gasped. "Chewie, it must be an oven inside!"

Chewbacca shrugged and growled.

"I don't care how hard they are to kill," Leia said. "We can't leave them to bake."

"Kit?" Tamora was working her way through the disarray, peering under half-toppled shelves and into the dark corners. "Kitster, where are you?"

The children, hands firmly clasped in Tamora's, were adding their own voices to the search.

Han unholstered his blaster and turned to C-3PO. "Keep watch."

"Certainly." C-3PO trained his photoreceptors out the door. "At present, there is nothing out there but our landspeeder."

"Threepio, just tell us if someone comes this way," Leia said.

"Oh, I see," C-3PO said. "Certainly, Mistress Leia."

Han was already several steps inside, studying the room. Seeing that Chewbacca had already unslung his bowcaster and was quietly covering Tamora, Leia motioned Han to follow and went over to the service desk. The door to the rear office was closed. She leaned across the counter and found the floor littered with datachips, credit vouchers, and expensive compact power cells.

"Not a robbery. We aren't that lucky."

Leia started to go around the counter, but Han—ever the gallant, at least when it came to her—slid over the top and beat her to the office door. He hit the OPEN key on the control pad, and nothing happened.

"Locked." Han stepped back and pointed his blaster at the control pad. "Watch—"

The door opened a crack, and the muzzle of a blaster rifle appeared in front of Han's hood. Leia started to step behind the counter to position herself next to the door, but a droning Rodian voice brought her to a halt.

"Stay put, or his head is smoke." The Rodian shoved the blaster into Han's hood, forcing him back, but remained out of Leia's line of fire. "And you there, what were you going to do to my door?"

"Look fella, we're just trying to find a friend." Han was careful to keep his blaster pointed away from the Rodian, but he was also careful not to drop it. "We don't have anything to do with this mess."

"I don't believe you," the Rodian said, still speaking through the partially opened door. "You thought your friend might be hiding in my office?"

Chewbacca arrived at the opposite end of the counter and pointed his bowcaster through the door—apparently he could see the Rodian.

"Wald!" Tamora appeared from behind Chewbacca. "Put that thing down and let me see Kitster."

Wald did not lower the weapon. "What makes you think Kit is here?"

"Because he told me to meet him here." Tamora's concern sounded genuine and substantial. "He has business with these people."

"In my parts yard? What kind of business?"

"She can't tell you that," Han said.

"Then I guess I can't keep my finger off this trigger." Wald shoved Han's head back. "My strength isn't what it used to be."

"Wald!" Tamora scolded. "Will you stop that?"

"Sure, when I get some answers. You see what happened to my shop. I've got a right."

Han's knuckles were turning white, and Leia knew what that meant.

"Look, why don't we all put the blasters away?" She holstered her own weapon. "If we were really going to shoot each other, we'd have done it by now."

"I wouldn't be so sure." Han seemed to be glaring into the office. "I can be patient."

"Your kind of patience isn't what we need." Leia stepped over, took the blaster from Han's hand and laid it on the counter, then nodded at Chewbacca. "You, too. I think Wald here just needs Tamora to convince him that she's here voluntarily."

Chewbacca stared through the door for a moment, then growled ominously and set his bowcaster on the counter.

Wald kept his blaster pressed to Han's face. "Tamora, why don't you and the kids come into my office?"

Tamora rolled her eyes, then snatched the bowcaster off the counter and pointed it at Chewbacca. Leia began to fear she had misjudged the sincerity in the woman's voice, and the Wookiee growled softly.

Tamora ignored him. "Okay, Wald, we have the drop on them." She almost certainly lacked the strength to pull the bowcaster's trigger, but Leia was not going to tell her that. "*Now* will you believe me?"

Wald let out a sound that resembled a chemical cutting torch running out of fuel; then the blaster rifle disappeared into the office and a stocky little Rodian waddled into view. Leia always found it difficult to tell a Rodian's age—perhaps because so many of them pursued violent professions and died young—but the sagging of his sensory horns, the blotchy gray areas near the end of his thin snout, and the milky sheen of his bulbous eyes suggested that Wald was fairly old.

"Sorry about the blaster." He held a green hand out to Han. "No hard feelings, eh?"

"No." Han took the hand, teeth grinding so hard Leia could hear them. "Not many."

"Kit?" Tamora shoved the bowcaster into Chewbacca's arms, then grabbed her children again and led them behind the counter toward Wald's office. "Where are you?"

"He's not back there." Seeming to realize that a distraught wife would have to see for herself, Wald addressed himself to Han and Leia and allowed Tamora to look anyway. "He was here, though, with that moss-painting everyone's after."

Leia tried not to show her alarm at the word *everyone.* "And?"

"And Jergo—a Kubaz sellsecret—came in behind him and pulled a blaster. Jergo wanted the moss-painting. Kit wouldn't turn it over." Wald lowered his voice and pointed at a scorched hole in the ceiling. "He nearly got himself killed. I had to lay out Jergo with a hydrospanner."

"So where's the painting now?" Leia asked.

Wald made a point of turning toward the door of his office. "Let's wait for Tamora."

Han pulled a fistful of credit vouchers from his pocket. "Look, you've suffered a lot of damage here on our account. Maybe if we covered the cost of the cleanup for you."

The sensory horns atop Wald's head twisted outward in irritation. "The damage I suffered wasn't on your behalf. It was on Kitster and Tamora's. And you're *not* cutting the Banais out of this deal—whatever it is."

"Of course not." Leia took the vouchers from Han and pressed them into the Rodian's hands. "But we do feel responsible."

"Sure you do." Despite the cynicism in Wald's voice,

he took the credits. "I still think we should wait for Tamora."

A moment later, Tamora emerged alone, her eyes red from crying. Leaving her children in the office, she closed the door and went to Wald's side.

"Okay, Wald. What happened to Kit?"

"I wish I could tell you." Wald spread his hands and, glancing at Han and Leia, said, "But the truth is, I don't know."

"But you know something," Tamora pressed. "Tell me."

Wald repeated his account of knocking the Kubaz spy unconscious, then continued. "That happened a minute after Kitster commed you. For a while, we thought Jergo was just trying to take the painting and sell it, but then a squad of stormtroopers showed up."

"They didn't take him?" Tamora gasped.

"No." Wald glanced at Han and Leia. "Maybe I should tell you the rest alone."

Chewbacca started to growl, but Leia silenced him by raising a hand. They would get nowhere through intimidation. "It's Tamora's decision."

"It's okay, Wald," Tamora said. "I trust these people."

Wald regarded Leia and Han's hooded faces warily. "Kit said not to trust anybody."

"He told me the same thing," Tamora said. "And Kitster doesn't have the faintest idea what he's doing. These people do. They, uh, work for the owners."

"The owners?" Wald regarded Chewbacca and C-3PO, his snout twitching with interest. "They look a little rough for the artsy crowd."

"Looks can be deceiving," Han said.

"Will you please just tell us what happened to Kit?" Tamora pleaded. "Have you seen what's going on outside? The sky is filled with TIEs and assault shuttles. Kitster's about to get himself killed."

Wald reluctantly looked away from Han and Leia, then said, "He took my old swoop out into the desert."

Tamora's face fell. "*The* old swoop?"

Wald nodded. "It gets worse. He was going out through Arch Canyon."

"Arch Canyon?" Tamora gasped. "The one in the old Podracing course? *That* Arch Canyon?"

Again, Wald nodded. "He said it's his only hope of keeping the Imperials off his tail. He's right, but it doesn't make it any less crazy." Wald cast a disparaging look at Han and Leia, then added, "I told him he should just sell the painting to them and be done with it, but he wouldn't hear of it. He said *Killik Twilight* doesn't belong in Imperial hands."

Leia exhaled in silent relief; at least Tamora was right about that much. "So who *does* Kitster plan to sell it to?"

Wald looked back to Tamora. "You're sure you want me to tell them?"

"Yes, I'm sure," Tamora said. "Ji and Elly would like to see their father alive again someday."

"Okay." Wald stared at the floor and kicked a broken recording rod across the room, then said, "That's the thing. I don't think he means to sell it to anyone."

"What?" This from Leia, Han, and Tamora.

Wald looked to Tamora. "He wasn't thinking right. He just kept talking about some Devaronian and Twi'lek who tried to blow it up, saying he was going to take it someplace safe."

"Someplace safe." Leia could not believe what she was hearing. "On Tatooine."

"Of course, on Tatooine," Wald said. "He wouldn't be taking a swoop to Ohann, now would he?"

"I doubt it," Leia agreed. "Then what?"

"Well, I think he was hoping for a reward. He was going to send a message to Princess Leia." Wald waddled closer and squinted up beneath Leia's hood, obviously trying to make out her features. "Except I'm pretty sure he thought you were still on Coruscant."

Leia sighed. "Is there anyone in Mos Espa who doesn't know who we are?" She pulled back her hood. "I'm sure there's no use denying it."

Wald twisted his sensory horns back and forth and jerked a thumb toward Chewbacca and C-3PO. "A droid, a Wookiee, the painting—I'd have to be a lot blinder than I am not to figure that."

"Thank you for pointing that out." Leia and the others had realized all along that staying together would make them easier to identify, but things were happening so fast they didn't dare separate. She turned to Han. "At least we still have something going for us."

"For a little while." Wald pointed toward his security system, a small vidcam hidden in the ceiling corner. "I overheard the stormtroopers talking about their new admiral."

"Pellaeon?" Han asked.

"All I know is, he awes them," Wald said. "But you should know he thinks there's something in *Killik Twilight* the New Republic doesn't want the Empire to have. It's the only reason he can see for the Devaronian throwing a detonator at it."

Leia and Han exchanged looks of exasperation. They could hardly have stood by and watched the Imperials walk off with a code key that would mean the exposure of the entire Shadowcast network and the deaths of thousands of agents. But it was frustrating to realize that had they done nothing, the code key might well have spent the next decade hanging harmlessly in some admiral's stateroom.

"Thanks for telling us, Wald." Leia took a calming breath, then turned to Tamora. "Perhaps you'd care to comm Kitster? We could arrange a rendezvous."

Tamora nodded and activated her comlink. "Kit?"

A tiny echo of her voice sounded from the back of the room, beneath the toppled vaporator.

"Are you there?"

Again, the echo sounded from beneath the toppled vaporator. Chewbacca went to the back of the room and picked up a comlink identical to Tamora's.

"Chubba!" Wald cursed. "That's where Jergo grabbed him."

Leia sighed. "Would it be too much to hope that he told you where he was going?"

Wald spread his hands. "Someplace safe. That's all he said."

Leia turned to Tamora next but didn't even bother asking when she saw the look of despair on the woman's face.

"We'll never catch him in a landspeeder," Han said. "Especially not with a bunch of TIEs after him." He turned to Wald. "Do you have another swoop?"

Wald and Tamora exchanged looks. Then Wald said, "*I* don't—not one that can catch Kitster."

"It's the one Wald used to win his freedom," Tamora explained.

"Kitster and I built it from a design a friend's mother found in his room." There was more than a touch of pride in Wald's voice. "It was nearly as fast as a Podracer."

A strange feeling of déjà vu came over Leia, and she asked, "Who was this friend?"

"Anakin Skywalker," Wald said.

"You knew Anakin?"

"Of course I knew him." Wald sounded insulted. "He was my pal. We were slaves together."

Leia's jaw dropped. "My father was a *slave*?"

"Don't make it sound like something dirty," Wald said, growing defensive. "We were kids. It wasn't like we gambled our way into it."

"That's not what she meant." Han took Leia's hand and gave it a little squeeze to break her out of her shock. "It's just hard to believe that a slave grew up to be Darth Vader."

"Darth Vader?" Wald waved his palms dismissively. "That's a lie. Anakin Skywalker never became Darth Vader."

"Really?" Leia heard the ice in her tone, but found herself losing the battle to keep her temper under control. The Rodian's denial touched a deep and painful chord, for rejecting the truth of Darth Vader's identity was the same as claiming all his terrible deeds never happened. "And you know this *how*?"

"Because I knew *him*," Wald retorted. "You don't understand what it takes—what it took back then—for a slave to win his freedom."

"We do." Tamora tried to slip between Leia and Wald. "But what we really need now—"

Wald stepped around Tamora and continued to speak, his voice filled with admiration. "I thought it couldn't be done. But Anakin did it."

"So he got lucky and won a Podrace," Leia said. "That hardly makes him a hero."

"It does on Tatooine, dear." Han took Leia by the arm, then pulled her closer and said more gently, "Damp down your power core. We need this guy's help."

Han was right and Leia knew it. But this was a visceral issue, something so powerful there could be no compromise. Fortunately, it was also entirely unimportant—at least to the task at hand—and she knew she had to set her anger aside.

Leia took a deep breath, then said, "I'm sorry, Wald. Obviously, we have very different views of Anakin Skywalker."

"Obviously," Wald said. "And only one of us is right."

Leia clenched her teeth, swallowing a sharp reply. *Obviously,* she thought.

Tamora breathed a sigh of relief, then said, "About that swoop—"

"I'm afraid I must interrupt," C-3PO said, awkwardly picking his way through the debris strewn on the floor. "The Squibs are here."

"Squibs?" Tamora gasped.

She slipped behind Chewbacca, and Han and Leia pulled up the hoods of their sand cloaks.

"I'll get rid of them." Wald started toward the door. "I'm sure they're just here to sell me something I don't need."

He was too late. The trio came boiling into the hut, their fur ruffled and greasy, and their belt pouches loaded with all the broken comlinks, datapads, and glow rods they had retrieved from the recycling bins.

Wald met them three paces from the door. "Grees, Sligh, I'm not buying anything—"

"And we're not selling!" Sligh said.

The Squibs swept past the Rodian as though he wasn't there and came straight for Leia and Han, not quite able to keep their gazes from straying to all the interesting stuff scattered over the floor.

"I can't believe how you treated us," Emala said to Han. "We thought you were a player."

Grees waved the credit transfer chip at Han's belt. "Try to cut us out again, and we go straight to Mawbo with this. We'll pay her and take the painting ourselves."

"She doesn't have the painting." Han tried to snatch the chip away, but Grees was too quick for him. "And you can't pay Mawbo our money. She wouldn't activate that chip."

"You really want to try her?" Sligh asked. "After what happened to her performance hall?"

Wald came up behind the Squibs. "How are these three involved?"

"They're not." Leia pulled a two-thousand-credit voucher from her pocket and held it out to Grees. "We'll buy you out."

The Squibs shook their heads without bothering to look at the amount.

"There's no buyout option," Sligh said. "We were the successful bidders."

"So the painting belongs to us," Grees added, "until we receive the negotiated payment."

"And that isn't going to happen, not with two squads of stormtroopers keeping Mawbo's locked down tight," Emala said.

"I'm offering you twice what we paid for your, uh, wares in the auction," Leia said. "Take a look."

"Doesn't matter," Sligh said. "It's not the same fee."

"If that's the way you want to play it." Leia continued to hold the voucher out. "I'll cancel the transfer chip. You'll be out your fee *and* your proceeds."

The Squibs' eyes grew round, and Grees said, "We'll think about it."

All three began to back toward the door. Leia watched them go, then slipped the voucher into her pocket and turned back to Han.

"You were about to ask Wald something?"

Han's expression remained blank. "I was?"

"About a swoop?" Leia prompted. "Wald said *he*

didn't have another one that could catch the one Kitster took."

"Right. But what about the transfer chip? Shouldn't you be canceling it?"

"No need," Leia said. "Unless I'm there to authorize the transfer, the chip will self-destruct when they try to use it."

"It'll be nice to see someone getting the best of those three for a change," Wald said. The tiny mouth at the end of his snout actually formed a smile. "But I doubt I'll be much help with the swoop."

Tamora's face fell. "Wald, please. You know Kitster. He doesn't stand a chance out there—not with the Imperials chasing him."

Wald nodded gravely. "I know."

"Look, Wald," Han said. "If this is about the Darth Vader thing—"

"It's not." Wald's tone was sharp. "Do you think I'd let a friend die just because Leia Organa insulted her father?"

"Of course not," Leia said. "As I said, we have very different views of Anakin Skywalker."

Wald fixed his bulbous eyes on her a moment, then shrugged. "Why should a Princess believe an old Rodian junk dealer?" He turned to Tamora. "There's only one swoop that can catch the one Kitster took. You know where you need to go."

Tamora's face paled. "Ulda's?"

Wald nodded. "I know it won't be easy, but she has that old rocket swoop Rao used to fly. If you want, I'll take them over."

Tamora shook her head. "No, she'd see through that." She turned, and not seeming to notice whether anyone was following, said, "I have to go."

Leia lingered behind just long enough to be sure Tamora was out of earshot, then asked, "What's so terrible about this Ulda?"

"Nothing," Wald said. "Unless you happen to be Kitster's *second* wife."

SEVEN

As the landspeeder circled the outskirts of Mos Espa, Leia watched the terrain outside slip past. To one side of the vehicle rose the domed huts and walled docking bays of the spaceport city, a testament to the tenacious soul of galactic commerce—and to the resilient spirit of the profusion of species that called this bleak world home. To the other side of the speeder, a golden sweep of forlorn desert stretched across a measureless distance all the way to the purple wall of the departing sandstorm, a stark reminder of one's place in the Tatooine scale of things . . . and of the strength of will it took to survive such a planet.

Leia's thoughts kept drifting back to her father. Wald's revelation had caught her off guard. Learning that Anakin Skywalker had been a child slave painted him as a victim, an image so at odds with the monster in her mind that she actually found herself wanting to agree with Wald's outrageous assertion, to believe that her father had not been Darth Vader.

Perhaps more disturbing than Wald's revelation was the way Tatooine seemed to be working on her. She was starting to see Mos Espa not as the corrupt spaceport that it had appeared as they waited for the auction to start, but as the home of beings like Tamora and

Wald, who lived and grew old here and somehow found their measure of happiness. Even the desert was beginning to feel inviting. It still struck her as dangerous—more so than ever, in fact—but Leia was growing aware of its beauty, of its majesty of scale and subtleness of color, and of the promise of mystery waiting in its hidden heart.

Maybe she was simply growing accustomed to the place. Or maybe the Force was acting on her again, awakening some spiritual connection passed down from her father. Leia could not say which. She only knew that she was growing steadily more unsettled, that she felt like she was losing control of the mission. In everything she was learning about her father, in her dreams aboard the *Falcon* and during her previous visit, there was no denying the hand of the Force. It was not guiding her exactly, but it was certainly touching her, nudging her down dark alleys she did not want to explore.

The landspeeder entered a vast sunken arena at the edge of town. Though there was no barricade to control access, a metal sign arching over the outer edge of the lot read, MOS ESPA SWOOP ARENA. The SWOOP had been riveted over another word, with the PO still visible at the beginning and CING at the end.

Tamora directed Chewbacca around the far end and down to a row of dilapidated hangars designated OWNERS' ROW by a small sign display. The hangar doors had corrosion stains bleeding down the front and towers of sand piled high in the corners, and they looked as though they had not been opened in years. But most had Wookiee-sized portals in the center, with fans of hard-packed ground in front suggesting regular use.

Chewbacca opened the cowling, and they climbed out of the speeder's climate-controlled comfort into the dusty heat of a Tatooine late afternoon. Tamora—who'd had the foresight to leave her children with Wald—started toward a hangar in the center, where a small servo-droid greeter stood just inside an extra set of transparisteel doors. Leaving Chewbacca and C-3PO behind to make themselves a little less identifiable, Leia and Han raised the hoods of their sand cloaks and followed.

As they approached the doors, Han leaned close and asked, "How are you doing?"

"Fine." Leia knew what he was really asking, but she did not want to talk about it. "Why shouldn't I be?"

"I didn't say you weren't." Han was the one person who never seemed to notice her *don't press it* tone. "I just want to know what was going on back there with Wald. Why should you care if he thinks Anakin was some sort of hero?"

"Obviously, I don't." Leia regretted her sharp tone as soon as she spoke. She stopped and took Han's hand. "I'm sorry. I'm having a hard time with all this pro-Darth-Vader blather."

"Yeah, I keep wondering when somebody's going to tell us about the real kid," Han said. "The one who used to tie grenades on bantha tails."

Leia smiled, weakly. "It's a little worse than that."

Han lifted his brow and waited.

"Not here." Leia nodded toward the doors. "We've got a swoop to borrow."

"Later, then." Han smiled and kissed her, then tightened his sand hood and turned toward the doors. "If they have a holograph of your father mounted on a pedestal or something, try not to start an argument. It's going to be hard enough to convince this Ulda to help us save her ex-husband."

As it turned out, Ulda's was not the kind of place to display a holograph of anyone. A combination lounge and betting parlor that had been converted from an old Podracer owner's booth, it was clean but austere, with a bar and several betting windows in the rear. In front, three rows of plastoid tables were arrayed before a transparisteel wall that overlooked the track below. Though no race appeared imminent, a dozen beings sat together down in front, making notes on datapads and watching swoop mechanics take test runs.

Leia was surprised to feel her heart flutter as she began to see the magnitude of the dilapidated racing track. At least five hundred meters wide, it stretched a full two kilometers in each direction before vanishing from sight, curving away into a labyrinth of rocky pinnacles on one end and emerging from an immense plain of gray dust-pack on the other.

This was where her father had won his freedom. Looking out at the enormous banks of seats, Leia could almost hear the crowd roaring as Anakin Skywalker came tearing across the finish line. At that moment, he could not have known the path that lay before him. Life would have seemed so full of promise to him—to the only human ever to win the Boonta Eve Classic. Had he foreseen that day what winning would mean—what his victory would eventually cost him and the galaxy— would he have come in second? Would he have had the courage to remain a slave here on Tatooine?

A human woman of about fifty emerged from behind the bar and approached, her gaze locked on Tamora with a look that could only be described as astonished. Slender and tall, she had the high cheekbones and arced eyebrows of a Kuati aristocrat, an impression reinforced by her broad-shouldered gown and bejeweled belt.

"Well, well . . . Tamora Spice." She stopped and put her hands on her hips, looking Tamora up and down. "You've put on a few kilos—but bearing the children of another woman's man will do that to you."

Tamora's face reddened, but she resisted the temptation to make a sharp reply. "You look as lovely as ever, Ulda."

Ulda flipped a nonchalant hand. "Money." She smiled bitterly. "Speaking of which, I hear Kit put that awful holocube of his in Mawbo's auction."

Tamora nodded.

"Good riddance, I say." Ulda finally glanced at Tamora's companions, then—apparently seeing no sign beneath their sand hoods that they were beings of consequence—returned to tormenting Tamora. "Now that the Rendala Estate is closed, I suppose finances must be tight."

"We're managing."

Ulda pushed out her lip. "Pity. I thought you might be here for a loan."

"As a matter of fact," Han said. He stepped forward, his patience with the woman's harassment coming to a quick end—as Leia had known it would. "We do—"

Leia caught him by the wrist. "Let Tamora handle this."

"Yes, do." Ulda shot Han a laser-hot look. "Whoever you are."

Clearly, she was a woman who had been nursing a grudge for a long time, and Tamora was playing her just right. Leia pulled Han back to her side and whispered for him to stay there.

Tamora swallowed, then said, "My friend is right. We do need to borrow something."

Ulda's face brightened. "Really?" Still ignoring Tamora's companions, she took her to a nearby table and sat down. She did not invite Tamora to sit with her. "Continue. I'm going to enjoy this."

"Maybe not," Tamora said. "Kit's in trouble."

Ulda chuckled. "And why shouldn't I enjoy that? I think I deserve it."

"He's in *big* trouble," Tamora said. "The Imperials are looking for him."

"For Kit?" Ulda's expression hovered somewhere between shock and doubt. "Whatever for?"

Instead of answering, Tamora said, "He took Wald's swoop."

Ulda's face fell. "He did what?"

"He took Wald's swoop into Arch Canyon," Tamora said. "To get away from the Imperials."

"Kit can't ride swoops! And Arch Canyon . . ." Ulda let the sentence trail off and shook her head, then looked up at Tamora again. "You still haven't told me why the Imperials are looking for him."

Deciding now would be a good time to take control of the conversation, Leia stepped to Tamora's side. "He stole a painting they wanted."

Ulda stared up for a moment, obviously waiting for Leia to lower her sand hood. When Leia did not, Ulda shrugged and did not object. On Tatooine, it was wise not to press those who were reluctant to reveal their faces.

Instead, Ulda asked, *"Killik Twilight?"*

Leia nodded.

"Why?"

"We're still trying to figure that out," Leia said.

"To save it," Tamora insisted. "A Devaronian tried to destroy it at the auction, and Wald says now the Imperials think there's something hidden in it."

"Yeah, Kit was just trying to be helpful," Han said, ever the cynic. "And maybe he thought a few credits would be nice, too."

Ulda considered this, then shook her head sadly. "Either way, I'm going to miss him." She turned back to Tamora. "He used to come in here from time to time—at least when he still had something to bet."

"He did?" Tamora gasped. "In here?"

Ulda smiled sadly. "I knew he didn't tell you. Men—you can't trust them."

Tamora summoned her resolve. "Wald said you have Rao's swoop."

Ulda shrugged. "So?"

"So, I'm going after Kit," Han said.

Ulda's glare was directed at Leia. "Is that so?"

"My husband is an excellent swoop pilot." Leia motioned Han back. Kuati women rarely liked to be addressed by strange men. "And I'll be glad to pay for its use."

"That bike's not for rent," Ulda said. "Maybe I can let him take another."

"Another one can't catch Wald's," Tamora said. "If Kit sees someone coming up behind him, he'll hit the thrusters and be gone. You know that."

"We'll purchase Rao's swoop," Leia offered. "Is fifteen thousand enough?"

That caught Ulda's attention. She looked up into the darkness beneath Leia's hood, either trying to guess the identity of her visitor or calculating how much she could take her for.

"Thirty thousand," Leia said. "Kitster already has a twenty-minute lead."

"And you're not going to change that by getting your man killed." Ulda stood and turned to the group gathered down in the front of the parlor. "Ody, go fetch Rao. I need her to take her old swoop out—"

"You don't want to do that, ma'am." A blue-skinned Er'Kit with a large egg-shaped head and downturned ears turned to look back at her. "She couldn't pilot a landspeeder right now."

"Again?"

The Er'Kit nodded and went back to his datapad.

Leia exchanged a relieved glance with Han, then said, "I can't imagine that thirty thousand isn't enough, but—"

"It's not the credits," Ulda said. "I'd give it to you for twenty. But that thing's been the death of six riders. I bought it just to keep it off the track."

Han stepped forward. "Look, lady, if it has a seat and a thruster, I can fly it."

To Leia's surprise, Ulda did not lash out at Han for daring to speak to her. She merely studied him, then turned to Leia. "Let me see him ride a regular swoop first."

"We don't really have the time—"

"If he's good enough to handle Rao's swoop, you'll make up the time. It'll take ten minutes." Without awaiting a reply, Ulda turned to the front of the parlor again. "Ody, take this man down to the hangar. Let him take that old Novastar around the test track once."

The Er'Kit rose and, hobbling badly, started toward them. "The Novastar?"

"The Novastar. Do we need to have your ears flushed again?" Ulda turned to Leia. "Podracers. You have to wonder whether they have half a brain left because they used to race, or they used to race because they had half a brain."

It was a nice cover, but Leia was too careful a listener

to have missed the surprise in the Er'Kit's voice. There was something wrong with the Novastar. She turned to Han.

"Take the Wookiee along and give that swoop a close look. If you don't like it, ask for another." Leia felt bad enough about dragging Han into this mess without putting him at unnecessary risk. She turned back to Ulda and narrowed her eyes. "I'm sure Ulda wouldn't mind."

"What's not to like?" Han gave a quick head tip to show that he understood the warning, then turned to follow Ody. "They haven't made swoops like Novastars in twenty years."

Ulda smiled. "Your man *does* seem to know his swoops. Perhaps you'd care for a drink? It will be a few minutes before they're on the track."

"Eyeblaster." It was what Leia always ordered in her tough-girl persona. "Atomized, not fizzed."

"The only way." Ulda turned to Tamora. "Would you mind? I'm sure you remember where everything is."

Tamora glowered, then put on a false smile. "Of course not."

Whether Tamora intended it that way or not, it was the perfect play. Ulda watched her go behind the bar and smirked comfortably.

"Tamora was my best mixer." She gestured toward the front of the parlor. "A pity she had to steal my man."

Leia descended the stairs to the forwardmost row of tables, where the beings with the datapads sat watching the swoop tests. Most were simply old for their species, but one—a jagged-toothed Veknoid whose face was all mouth—was as hunched and battered as Ody, missing an arm and badly scarred from burns.

"Was that Veknoid a Podracer as well?" Leia asked.

"They aren't hard to identify," Ulda said. "Even swoop racers don't look that bad."

Motioning Leia to follow, Ulda led the way over to the Veknoid and leaned down close to his ear. It was a melted mess.

"Teemto!" Ulda was practically shouting. "Tell this lady about your Podracing days."

The Veknoid ignored her. Down on the test track, a swoop abruptly lost power and settled into the sand. He made an entry on the datapad in his lap, shielding it with his body so Leia and Ulda could not see.

"I'm talking into your good ear," Ulda said. "I know you can hear."

Finally, Teemto looked away from his datapad. "It was fast."

"That's all?" Leia asked. "Just fast?"

Tamora appeared with two drinks on a tray. Teemto grinned and took one of the drinks.

He winked his good eye. "Real fast."

Ulda's face reddened. She did not like being embarrassed in front of a guest—and especially not by a male. "And *you* would know," she said. "As I recall, that's how you lost your arm. Going too fast."

Teemto frowned and raised a finger to clean his ear.

"Um, Ulda, there's no need to press," Leia said. She had lived with Han long enough to know what the Kuati was doing; there was no faster way to make a pilot talk than to challenge his skills. "If Teemto doesn't feel like discussing it . . ."

Ulda ignored her and pointed at the stump of Teemto's missing arm. "You heard me. You lost that because you couldn't handle speed."

Teemto glared at Ulda a moment, then bared his jagged teeth and turned to Leia. "I was handling the speed just fine, until Hit Man Beedo threw a wrench in my starboard pod."

"That doesn't sound very fair," Leia said.

"Excuses," Ulda scoffed.

The reason Kitster had taken up with Tamora was growing clearer by the moment, though Leia was having trouble understanding why he had ever married Ulda in the first place. She glanced down at the track. There were a handful of mechanics and riders working in the pit area, but still no sign of Han.

"Tell the lady how your ears got melted off," Ulda said. When the Veknoid was not quick enough to answer, she added, "Or maybe you'd rather I call in my marker."

Teemto's expression changed from one of irritation to one of incredulity, but he grunted and squinted at Leia. "That happened in the Boonta. The Tuskens shot out one of my engines." He turned back to Ulda. "Got a vid to prove it. Now, want me to tell her how I lost my eye?"

Leia barely heard this last question. "The Boonta? The Boonta Eve Classic?"

"That's the one," he said. "The same year that human kid won."

"Anakin Skywalker?" Leia heard the shock in her voice and realized she was showing too much interest. The smart thing would have been to change the subject and hope no one noticed, but she wanted to know what kind of racer her father had been—how driven he had been to win his freedom. Besides, Han still wasn't out on the track. "Was the boy as good as they say?"

Teemto studied her for a moment, his big lips starting into a snarl, then he seemed to decide it was not worth the effort of defying Ulda and set the pilfered eyeblaster aside.

"Anakin was great. A human who beat Sebulba head-to-head?" He rubbed his burn scars, not seeming to realize he was doing it. "I'm just sorry so much of that race is a blank."

"But you raced him before that," Ulda prompted. "Tell her what kind of pilot he was."

Leia began to wonder if Ulda had guessed her identity; if so, she would only confirm it by changing the subject now. "It sounds like there was a lot of cheating."

"Not from Skywalker." Teemto stared through the transparisteel, his thoughts lost in another time, and chuckled. "That little human never cheated—still young enough to think you could win honest, I guess."

"Never?" Leia found this hard to believe. "Maybe you didn't notice."

Now Teemto did snarl. "Lady, you ever see a Podrace?"

Ulda took Leia by the arm. "Everyone says Anakin flew a clean race—apparently, he was one of the few." She pulled her toward the opposite end of the parlor. "Here's your man now. Perhaps we should watch from over here."

Tamora appeared with a fresh eyeblaster. Down on the track, Han and Chewbacca were following Ody out to the test loop, walking a battered swoop between them. The handicappers at the other end of the parlor sat forward murmuring, and Leia's stomach grew queasy. Han had bored her many times with tales of the races he had won as a boy, which—along with Dewlanna, the old Wookiee cook who had looked after him—seemed to be the only things he recalled fondly from his childhood. But there was something wrong about that bike. Really wrong.

"This has gone far enough," Leia said to Ulda.

"There's no need to worry." Ulda continued to watch them approach the test loop. "If your man is good enough to handle Rao's swoop, he'll be fine on this little Novastar."

Leia recognized a classic Bothan claim test when she saw one—put the subject in a situation where he either had to admit he was lying or prove that he wasn't—but this one had a hidden twist. And she didn't like hidden twists, not with Han's life at risk.

"I'm very fond of my man." Leia put as much ice into her voice as she could—and she had been told she could give a wampa the chills. "I would be very upset if an unnecessary accident befell him."

"Then I hope he's as good as you say." Ulda's carefully maintained poise slipped a little. "For both our sakes."

The trio reached the test loop, a thin ribbon of sand track circling the inner pit area, no more than a kilometer in length. Chewbacca held the swoop while Han climbed on. Ody spent a few moments trying to show Han the controls, then seemed to realize he already knew them and stepped away.

That was when Ulda pulled a comlink from her sleeve. "Ody, didn't he check the control vanes?"

Ody nodded and raised a comlink to his lips. "In the hangar."

Han activated the ion thrusters.

"So he fixed them?"

Ody shook his head, and Chewbacca stepped back.

"Then don't just stand there! Get him off that—"

Han twisted the throttle and was gone. Ulda's shoulders slumped, the handicappers stood and went gasping to the transparisteel wall, and Leia reached for the holdout blaster in her pocket.

Han was halfway down the first leg of the loop when

the swoop's nose suddenly came up, and he shot into the air like a missile.

Ulda was on her comlink instantly. "Ody! What's happening?"

Ody spread his hands, then Han reached the first turn, spun the swoop upside down, and began a sharp banking descent that carried him to the back side of the loop. He did not turn the swoop right-side up again until he was so close to the ground that a sand plume began to shoot out behind him.

Showing off, as usual.

Ulda let out a long sigh of relief, and the handicappers returned to their seats, jabbering to each other and making notes on the datapads. Leia left her hand in her pocket, still grasping the hold-out blaster.

Han climbed into the air again as he came to the second turn, then flipped the swoop over and repeated the maneuver. He was still rounding the corner when Ulda raised the comlink to her lips again.

"Ody, get Rao's swoop ready. And put a vidmap aboard."

The Er'Kit waved and started back toward the hangar— then hit the sand as a long line of white-armored figures on Imperial speeder bikes entered the track from the direction of Mos Espa. They rounded the curve, speeding toward the far end of the arena.

"Don't tell me," Leia said. "They're going into—"

"Arch Canyon." Ulda nodded toward the canyon mouth at the far end of the arena. "That's the fastest way in."

"Kit!" Tamora gasped.

Ulda surprised Leia again by laying a hand over Tamora's. "It's going to be okay. Your friend will find him first."

"He will?" This from Leia.

"Of course." Ulda continued to look at Tamora. "He'll know where Kit's going."

Tamora appeared dazed. "How?"

"Kit was mine for a lot of years." Ulda could not resist smirking. "And I guess I still know some things about him that you never will."

EIGHT

Rao's "swoop" was little more than a seat laser-welded onto the top of an old IPG Longtail Podracing engine, with a few jury-rigged control vanes, a big land-speeder repulsorlift to keep it off the ground, and a transparent plastoid pilot's cowling. A heavily dented engine housing and bloodstained seat suggested it was even more dangerous than Ulda claimed, and it was obviously a home design made to win races regardless of risk.

Han loved it, but the idea of riding the thing frightened him. It would be a little like life as a smuggler, he supposed. The trip was going to be fast, dangerous, and a whole lot of fun, but filled with wild detours and possibly subject to an unscheduled and violent end.

As Ody mounted a hands-off vidmap between the handlebars, Han slipped into the flight suit Ulda had insisted he would need, then spent a few moments walking around the machine, checking to see that all control surfaces moved freely. He had to admire the builder's insight into swoop racing. Because of the swoop's size, a factory engineer would have doubled or even tripled the size of the vanes, then relied on computer-assisted movement mechanisms to refine adjustments at high speeds. The builder of this machine had used *undersized* vanes, knowing they would be more forgiving at high speeds—

and less likely to malfunction in a sandy environment like Tatooine.

By the time Han finished his survey, the vidmap was mounted and programmed. Han's destination was an empty, isolated little house in the desert, about two-thirds of the way to Jabba's old palace.

"This is where Kitster goes to find peace of mind," Ulda explained. "I understand it has a splendid view of the Western Dune Sea."

"So you've never been there yourself?" Leia asked.

Ulda shook her head. "I had Kitster followed once, when I suspected him of seeing other women. It turned out he was gleaminking a desertscape." She cast a venomous glance in Tamora's direction. "Perhaps that's why I was so easily betrayed later."

Tamora's face reddened, and she bit her lip.

"Yeah, well, no use living in the past." Eager to change the subject, Han rubbed his hand along the swoop's engine housing. "I'll have to be careful about breaking the sound barrier with this baby."

"Yes, do." Ulda handed him a bulky helmet with a full-face mask, built-in comlink, and heads-up display linked to the vidmap. "It wobbles just before you punch through."

"Really?" Han forced a smile to cover his astonishment; he had been joking about breaking the sound barrier. "You can't be serious."

Ulda nodded that she was.

"Don't get so excited, Flyboy," Leia said. "You're not sixteen anymore."

"Good, because I couldn't have handled this thing at sixteen." Han closed his face mask and nodded to Chewbacca. "Give me a boost, will you?"

Chewbacca groaned and glanced over at Leia. Han

turned to find her jaw hanging slack with disbelief, her eyes brown and liquid with hurt.

"What are you worried about?" He opened the face mask and kissed her, making certain to linger until she let him go. "I *am* coming back, you know."

Leia was still thinking about Han's parting words half a standard hour later, as Tamora guided them through a warren of sand-and-mud huts in Mos Espa's poorest section of town. She was drawn to the scoundrel in him, to the aura of danger and promise that clung to him like a bad holo job. But it was the hero in her husband that she loved, his casual courage, the way he thought nothing of hopping onto a saddled rocket and racing out into a desert full of stormtroopers to recover a priceless painting with a secret code. The only thing Leia didn't like was the reason he was doing it. No man should feel compelled to put himself in peril to please the woman he loved.

But it was sweet that Han would.

They pulled up in front of a small shabby hut packed tight against dozens of other small shabby huts.

"This old slave hut came with the parts yard—I think it belonged to your father's master, Watto." Tamora waited until the cowling rose, then climbed out of the speeder and went to the door, opening it with a security code Wald had provided over a comlink. "Wald lets a lot of junk peddlers and stranded spacers stay here, so we won't attract much attention. It's a good place to lie low."

"Slave hut?" Leia followed Tamora through the door. "How many of these did Watto own?"

Tamora shrugged. "Wald has just the one."

Leia glanced around. Though dusty and disordered, the hut was more spacious inside than she had imagined, with a central vault and three bumpout rooms, one on the same level for cooking and two elevated sleeping chambers.

Despite the grime and a dismal shortage of windows, the place did not seem at all unappealing. In fact, it felt strangely . . . comfortable.

Though it had been Tamora who suggested staying there, Leia began to suspect something else had led them to the hut. As she looked around, she half expected to see a pair of white eyes shining out of a shadowed doorway, or to hear a wispy voice calling to her from the corner of an empty room.

Leia turned to Tamora. "Could this have been where Anakin Skywalker and his parents lived?"

Tamora shrugged. "Maybe—and there was just a mother, I think. Kit never mentioned Anakin's father." She ran a finger over the table and looked at the dust it picked up. "No cleaning droids here, I guess."

"It'll be fine. We won't be here that long." Leia saw a flash of impatience in Tamora's eyes and realized *she* might not have been the one Tamora was thinking about. "For us, I mean. If you think it's too dirty for Ji and Elly—"

"Hardly," Tamora said. "Those two would sleep in a sand dune, if I let them."

"Well, I'm sure we can find something around here better than that," Leia said. "Chewbacca will take you to fetch them from Wald's, as soon as I get something out of the landspeeder."

Chewbacca oowrralled a question.

"Our mobile holocomm," Leia said. "I need to send a message to Mon Mothma to let her know what happened at the auction."

Chewbacca nodded and fetched the holocomm from the landspeeder cargo bay, then left for Wald's with Tamora. After setting up the unit and calibrating the antenna dish, Leia sent C-3PO outside to watch for Imperial spy craft above the city. Though the New Republic used a synchronized ghost wave—a technological byproduct of the Shadowcast system—to camouflage its clandestine transmissions, Leia was taking extra precautions. So far, everything that could go wrong with such a simple mission had.

After computing the local time in the Coruscant government district, Leia decided Luke was the only safe person to contact. Her report could not be trusted to an attaché, and waking Mon Mothma at this hour would draw attention that Imperial spies might well notice—and the last thing Leia wanted to do now was provide the *Chimaera*'s new admiral any more hints as to *Killik Twilight*'s true importance.

And Leia had been wanting to talk to Luke since her dream aboard the *Falcon*, to see the smiling face she knew and loved and be sure all was well. Whether she should also tell him about what she had seen, Leia was uncertain. She did not want to be the one who put that fear into his mind—especially not when she remained so unclear about it. Besides, it had only been a dream.

She opened a channel to Luke's apartment. It took only a moment for a hazy, fist-sized image of his head to appear over the holocomm pad, his dimpled chin propped on his thumbs and his blue eyes fixed on the documents. Though the image was not distinct enough for Leia to be sure, she suspected the records were the ancient archives they had recovered from the *Chu'unthor*, the lost Jedi training vessel they had stumbled across on Dathomir earlier that year.

"Just a moment." Luke finished what he was reading, then looked up. "Thanks. Go ahead."

"Anything in there about Jedi Masters needing their sleep?" Leia asked.

Luke lowered his hands out of the image and stared at her across space. "Why would I sleep when I knew you would be calling?"

"*Knew?* Those training records must be . . ." Leia saw the corners of his mouth rise and, realizing she had fallen for the "Master act" again, let the sentence trail off. "I suppose you know what I want, too?"

"Of course." Luke's face remained straight. "To talk to me."

Leia rolled her eyes. "I'm beginning to wonder about that." She leaned toward the holocomm and spoke in a quieter voice. "Listen, we had some unexpected company at the auction."

Leia told Luke about the old code key hidden inside *Killik Twilight*, the Imperial attempt to purchase the painting, its subsequent theft, and how the situation had deteriorated since.

"I'm afraid we alerted the *Chimaera* to the painting's significance when we tried to destroy it," Leia said. "And matters just keep growing worse."

Luke nodded, but said, "You did the right thing. With the code key hanging in some admiral's stateroom, the New Republic would have had to scrap Shadowcast anyway. And if they found it later, there might still be a lot of dead spies."

"I know," Leia said. "But the way things stand now, if Han doesn't recover that painting first, we'll have our dead spies a lot sooner."

This time, Luke did not try to reassure her. "What can I do?"

"Not much, I'm afraid," Leia said. "Things are moving too fast for you to get here. But I need you to inform Mon Mothma—personally. Nobody else knows the real reason we want *Twilight*."

"I'll see her first thing in the morning."

"Thank you," Leia said. "And tell her that if she doesn't hear from us before Wraith Squadron leaves—"

"Leaves?" Luke interrupted.

Leia had a sinking feeling. "In two days," she said. "Don't tell me they're gone?"

"Wedge canceled a get-together we had planned for tomorrow night," he said. "He didn't say why, but I had the impression that something was happening sooner than expected."

"That's bad," Leia said.

The Wraiths had been scheduled to leave on a mission to Askaj to capture Grand Moff Wilkadon during his annual inspection of his tomuon holdings. The plan called for Wedge Antilles, who would be in command of the operation, to use Shadowcast to activate a cell of local resistance fighters who would provide most of the dirtside intelligence and firepower. If the network was compromised, either there would be no one to help the Wraiths when they arrived—or there would be an entire Imperial armada waiting to ambush them. Possibly both.

"Very bad," Leia added.

"Should I ask Mon Mothma to have a recall message sent?"

Leia shook her head. "We might do more harm than good. They're going deep, under total comm silence, and the only way to contact them is Shadowcast itself."

She did not need to explain that what Shadowcast offered in security, it suffered in speed. Every message had to be laboriously encoded, then inserted as a ghost wave into a predesignated commercial program and holocast on the regular schedule. What all this meant was that it would take at least a day to recall the Wraiths, by which time they could well be beyond the point of no return. And if Wedge had already activated the local resistance cell, there would be no way at all to stop them from beginning their part of the operation.

"We just have to get that code key," Leia said.

"And if you can't?"

"It'll take the Imperials at least a few days to crack the codes," Leia said. "That *might* be long enough."

"May the Force be with you, then."

"Thank you," Leia said, thinking of how ironic those words really were under the circumstances. "Tell Mon Mothma that we'll keep her informed. If she doesn't hear from us within two days, she should assume Shadowcast has been compromised."

"I'll tell her." Luke pursed his lips and, when Leia made no move to break the connection, said, "I sense there's more you'd like to talk about."

Leia smiled wryly and asked, "Is it the Force, or am I growing predictable?"

"A little of both. Had all you needed been someone to pass a message to Mon Mothma, you would have called Winter." He narrowed his eyes, and in the hazy hologram they grew dark and empty. "Something else is bothering you."

"This place, I guess," Leia sighed. "Luke, why didn't you tell me Anakin Skywalker grew up in Mos Espa?"

"How did you find that out?"

"I met his best friend," Leia said. "He still lives here. He's the one who stole *Killik Twilight*."

"Our father's best friend stole your painting?" Luke looked confused. "And you're sure he was a friend of our father?"

"His name is Kitster Banai," Leia said. "He put a holocube of Anakin Skywalker in the auction. And you still haven't answered my question."

Luke's head tipped forward. "Honestly, Leia, I just

didn't think you wanted to know. Every time I try to talk about our father, you get that look."

"That look? Thanks a lot." Leia looked away from the transceiver, silently cringing at the lecture she would receive when she told Luke about the other things that had been happening to her on Tatooine. She would start small and see how much she could stomach. "Did you know he was a Podracer?"

Luke's image nodded. "I did a name search over the HoloNet. He won his freedom in the Boonta Eve Classic. The only human ever, I believe."

"So they say," Leia said. "He's a local hero."

Luke smiled. "Really?"

"Really." Leia's voice dripped sarcasm. "They say he never cheated."

"That doesn't surprise me."

"It does me," Leia said. "I'm having a hard time believing a lot of what I'm hearing. Everybody who knew him loved him. They still do."

"Leia, he was just a boy. Do you think he came out of the womb wearing a breather and black helmet?"

Leia recalled her dream aboard the *Falcon*. "The thought *had* crossed my mind." She paused, wondering if she should—if she *dared*—tell him about that. It was a little like telling someone that you had seen how they were going to die . . . they might be better off not hearing it. "Luke, did you ever feel anything strange around Tatooine?"

"Define *strange*," Luke said. "You know what kind of place Tatooine is."

"I can't say. His presence, maybe—or yours." Leia told him about her conversations with Wald and Teemto and the odd feelings of familiarity she had been having around Mos Espa, leaving out mention only of her dream.

"I keep feeling like the Force is leading me down a Sky-walker path, and I'm not sure I like it."

Luke's head grew larger as he leaned closer to his holo-comm. "You don't have to like it. Just don't fight it."

Leia felt her ire rise. "You mean forgive him."

"I mean trust what you find." Luke's voice grew stern. "Leia, the Force isn't anyone's servant. The presence you're feeling has nothing to do with me or our father. If the Force is acting on you, it's responding to you."

"That's not possible," Leia said. "I'm no Jedi."

"You don't have to be a Jedi to be destroyed by your own fear and anger."

"Me?" Leia shook her head. "I may be worried about Han, but I'm not fearful in the way you mean—and I'm not angry at anyone at the moment."

Luke said nothing and waited. The image was too hazy to be certain, but he was probably staring patiently at Leia.

"Anyone *living*," she corrected. "Darth Vader doesn't count."

"Not really—Darth Vader isn't the one you need to make peace with. The Force is with you, and nothing you do can change that." Now Luke leaned so close to his holocomm that Leia could see little more than his eyes—blue, soft, and hazy. "Leia, you may be in danger here. If you're not careful, your fear and anger will only make you into what you despise."

NINE

At low velocities, the swoop handled like a falling rock, so Han went fast. Blaster-bolt fast. Pushing-the-sound-barrier fast, backed off just enough so the shock waves did not make the control vanes shudder. At that speed, Arch Canyon was a serpentine channel of speed-blurred rock, one impossibly tight turn following another, sandrock arch after sandrock arch, with the occasional stone pinnacle jutting up just to keep things interesting.

Han flew with one eye on the heads-up vidmap display on his face mask, watching the canyon's twists and bends snake down toward the blip that represented his location, toeing the control vanes long before the curves and leaning into each turn until it seemed his cheek would scrape ground. Side canyons flashed past at the rate of two or three a second. On the vidmap, they were inter-secting worms of display light; on the canyon walls, they were gaping instants of darkness.

Han loved the thunder of the big Podracing engine and the hiss of the canyon air sliding over the pilot's cowling, and even the way his stomach fluttered when a curve was too tight and he had to rock the swoop up on its side to bounce himself off a canyon wall with a quick blast from the repulsor engines. But Tatoo I was already sinking beneath the horizon, turning the crooked swatch of sky above the canyon into a crooked snake of crimson brilliance. As Tatoo II followed, evening shadows would begin to creep across the canyon floor, cramming the path ahead with phantom hazards, concealing the real ones beneath blankets of purple gloom. Han would be forced to crawl along at no more than a hundred kilometers an hour, and his superpowered swoop would become a lumbering rock compared to the nimble speeder bikes the stormtroopers were riding.

He had already blown past two groups of Imperials, startling the first squad so badly they had not even fired on him. The second squad had been less surprised, and when cannon bolts started to explode into the surrounding sandrock, he had been forced to flame them with the efflux from his swoop's overpowered engine. The less time he gave the next squad to prepare, the better. At this speed, all they would have to do was string a utility line across a narrow section of canyon, and he would never know he had died.

The message TUSKENS' ESCAPE appeared on the headups vidmap above the swoop's locator blip, and the crooked band of light denoting Arch Canyon split into three forks, each of which split again, and then again, forming a braided maze of deep-cut alleys that gave this section its name. A green line snaked its way through the labyrinth, denoting the fastest route to the desert retreat where Ulda said Banai was headed. Han rounded a bend and saw the three mouths of the Escape yawning ahead, the white blurs of a dozen stormtroopers vanishing down the center route.

Han checked his display and found the leftmost branch lit. "Suckers!"

He flipped a parting salute at the stormtroopers' back

and slid toward the left wall of the canyon—then glimpsed the blue dot of an ion engine bobbing along in front of the squad, perhaps a thousand meters ahead of the leader and slowly pulling away. Imperial speeder bikes did not have ion engines.

Racing swoops did.

"Blast!" Han muttered. "Kitster, what are you doing over *there*?"

Han toed the right-side control vane hard and barrel-rolled into the center branch. The vidmap error alarm beeped in his ear, and the alley into which he was heading started to flash red. He ignored the warning and opened the throttle wide.

The swoop seemed to hesitate, its controls shuddering so hard it felt like the machine was disintegrating. He leaned close to its body, trying to lower the center of gravity. The vibrations began to subside—then abruptly ceased altogether. The ride grew as smooth as that of a hovercar, and the roar of the big thrust engine faded to silence, leaving no sound in Han's helmet except the insistent beeping of the vidmap error alarm. He silenced it with a command, then came up behind the stormtroopers almost too fast. He barely had time to pull up the swoop's nose before he was gliding over the top of the rear echelon. His shock wave began to slam speeder bikes into the ground, but he was already past before any fireballs erupted.

The leader craned his neck to look over his shoulder, then he and two more riders broke formation, splitting toward the canyon walls where they would not be beneath Han's shock wave when he passed. The maneuver saved them—for a fraction of a second. Instead of being slammed into the ground, they were tossed out of control by Han's wake turbulence. The leader went into a wild spin and slammed into a canyon wall. Han did not see what happened to the other two, but no cannon bolts followed as he continued up the canyon.

The tiny dot of ion glow ahead rapidly began to swell as he closed on the fleeing swoop. He was just starting to make out the square shape of its back end when it came to another fork in Tuskens' Escape and dodged down the right branch—in the direction opposite the flashing green line on Han's vidmap display.

Why Kitster kept heading away from his desert retreat, Han could not say. Maybe Ulda had been wrong about his intentions, or maybe Kitster just did not see the odds in heading for his hiding place with a long line of pursuers on his tail. It hardly mattered. Once Han caught him, they would be heading for a quick rendezvous with the *Falcon*, where Banai would be paid for his "help" and offered transport to a safe sector for him and his family.

Han came to the fork and started down the right branch after his quarry. A fresh round of error alarms began to beep in his helmet. He silenced them with a voice command. Banai's borrowed swoop did not seem nearly as fast as Wald and Tamora had claimed. Within moments, a lumpy shape grew discernible on the seat, a rider hunching down behind the handlebars to cut wind resistance.

Not hunching. A rider sitting upright, twisting around to watch over his shoulder, somehow still weaving around sandrock pinnacles and hugging curves tight inside, somehow still seeing where he was going while he looked back at Han.

A short rider in a sand cloak and goggles, with a long snout.

A line of blaster bolts began to stitch back at Han,

coming over the shoulder opposite the one the rider was looking over. The guy was firing behind his head. Who did he think he was, Boba Fett?

The swoop vanished around a bend. Certain that the driver—he no longer thought it could be Banai—would expect him to come in tight, Han rounded the curve only half under control, sliding perpendicular to his direction of travel. The wind slipped around the cowling and threatened to blast him out of the seat, and he momentarily lost control as a swarm of blaster bolts flashed past and blew rock sprays off the canyon wall. He tipped the left control vane and hit the power.

The swoop shot upcanyon, and Han came up behind his quarry to find not one rider, but three—all short and dressed in identical sand cloaks. The Squibs, the one in front driving, the one in the middle sitting backward firing the blaster rifle, the one in the rear holding the one in the middle.

Han cursed into his helmet—first at them for drawing him off Banai's trail, then at himself for thinking they would let the matter drop after Leia tricked them at Wald's. Like all vermin, Squibs were persistent and resourceful.

Han wagged a finger at the one holding the blaster rifle, then followed them into the next curve. All three leaned into the turn together, the one in the middle still aiming at him, but no longer firing. He stayed close on their tail, taking the turn much wider, but keeping them in sight and continuing to gain on them the whole way. The one in the middle let her muzzle fall open—Han was close enough now to recognize her snout as Emala's—then holstered the blaster rifle.

Han drifted over to the opposite wall of the canyon so they would not be tossed around too badly by turbulence as he blew past. He waved as he went by, but did not bother trying to motion them off; nothing was harder to shake than a Squib who smelled credits. Besides, the more Imperials they drew off, the fewer there would be chasing Banai and *Killik Twilight*. With a little luck, Banai might even be getting away clean.

Sligh's voice came over the helmet's comlink on the same channel Han had used at the auction. "Solo, that you?"

Han chinned his microphone. "Don't know who you're talking about."

"Spare us the bantha bombs, Solo," Emala said. "I was listening at the door back at Wald's. We know who you are."

"We'd already figured it," Grees added, "soon as you showed up at Banai's without your horns and voice synthesizer."

"Then I'm surprised you're not in Mos Eisley by now, blowing your Imperial credits at Lady Valarian's."

"Us? Sell out a business partner?" Sligh's voice was indignant. "What do you take us for, Ugors?"

Han had to swerve to avoid a pinnacle and ended up ducking through a sandrock arch so small that when he came out the other side, his efflux rebounded off the exterior and came boiling back in a ring of orange heat.

"Uh, I'm busy here, guys." He was surprised to hear a quaver in his voice. "So if you're just comming to say thanks—"

"Say thanks?" Sligh interrupted. "What the poodoo for?"

"You just squared yourself by blowing those Imps off our tails," Grees added. "The deal's on again."

"Back on? Forget it—"

"You don't really want out, do you?" Emala asked.

" 'Cause then you wouldn't be our business partner, and we'd be free to talk to whoever we wanted about you."

Han grated his teeth together.

"What was that?" Sligh asked.

"Fine," Han said. "The deal's on. Just don't crash into any boulders or anything. I'm not coming back for you."

"No need," Grees said. "We'll find you."

Han closed the channel, then called up an overview on the vidmap and found two routes returning to the branch he needed. One was a long circuitous path that seemed to wind around the perimeter of Tuskens' Escape; the other was a diagonal slash that jogged and twisted through a maze of tiny channels, rejoining his route only a few kilometers ahead. This route was lined in yellow dashes.

"I'll take the short one," he told the vidmap.

"The yellow dashes indicate a hazardous route," the vidmap replied. "At the speed you're traveling—"

"The short one," Han repeated.

"Are you sure?" the vidmap asked. "Be advised that human reflexes will not be adequate to ensure your safety."

"Yeah?" Han took another look at the long route and saw that the time estimate had him rejoining his original route well after dusk. "They used to say that about my father-in-law."

Han half expected the vidmap to retort that his father-in-law had the Force. Instead, it simply shifted scales and indicated he should turn down the next side canyon. There was a big yellow CAUTION flashing under the display.

Han reduced his speed as much as was possible without turning the swoop into a flying rock, then began a long journey through a nerve-racking series of slot channels and serpentine passages that kept him too busy to worry about the deepening shadows in the canyon, or even about the growing number of dust devils he was flying through. All too often, he found himself bouncing along a boulder-choked chasm where a racing swoop's lack of ride stabilizers left him feeling like he was in a starfighter dogfight with the acceleration compensators turned off. At other times, he had to snake down a twisting gorge piloting by his vidmap alone, his own turbulence sending a billowing cloud of sand down the passage ahead of him.

Finally, Han came to the last cutover, a narrow crevice that ran absolutely straight with a smooth bedrock bottom, then intersected the branch he needed less than a kilometer away. The vidmap finally turned off the CAUTION warning. He tore down the channel in less than a dozen heartbeats.

Han did not see the speeder bike at the end until a white blur hurled itself out of the seat.

"Blast!" Han cursed.

More blurs hurled themselves from more seats.

"Stang!"

He shifted his weight toward the rear of his swoop, pulling the control handles up to lift the nose, and climbed a dozen meters in a breath. The Imperial speeder bikes flashed past beneath, along with the stormtroopers who had vacated them, and a sandrock wall loomed ahead.

Han rolled the swoop on its side and was a kilometer gone before the stormtroopers could send a cannon bolt after him. The swoop was shaking so hard he thought he had snapped a control vane—until he looked down to check the systems display and saw that his trembling hands were the cause.

"Come on, Solo," he said. "This is fun."

Running into the squad had to have been a coincidence—or so he told himself. The gorges of Tuskens' Escape were too deep and twisting for him to be tracked from the air. To maintain a surveillance lock, a craft would have to stay directly overhead, following him through every twist and turn of the canyon. And even if they had some hotshot pilot who could manage that, there was still no way they could have predicted his route and had a squad waiting to intercept him. Besides, had they been expecting him, they would have opened fire.

Unless they thought he was Kitster Banai and did not want to take a chance on destroying *Killik Twilight*.

Han was still trying to puzzle all this out when he came to a two-kilometer straight identified on his vidmap as Main Avenue. He risked a glance over his shoulder and searched the darkening sky for a TIE or some other craft that might be tracking him. Instead, he found the real reason the squad had been stopped—a kilometershigh wall of billowing sand and friction lightning, rolling back over the canyon from the direction of the Northern Dune Sea.

The sandstorm had reversed direction.

Han slowed to a crawl and hazarded a glance over his shoulder.

He was rewarded by the sight of a dozen speeder bikes rounding the corner into Main Avenue, blue stars flashing under their forward outriggers as they opened fire.

"If I'm not careful," Han said to himself, "this could get dangerous."

He hit the throttles and tore down the canyon, sprays of rock rising ever closer to him as the stormtrooper blaster cannons began to zero in. Han began to juke and jink like a fighter pilot; then another CAUTION message appeared on his vidmap. This one had an arrow pointing to the right and the words, DEAD MAN'S TURN—120 DEGREES.

Han decelerated hard and saw nothing but rock ahead. Trusting to the vidmap, he swung up on the wall and rode the repulsors into what looked like the side of the canyon—then a narrow slot opened ahead, and the rest was easy. With the shadows growing ever darker and longer, and the storm looming ever nearer, he followed the vidmap through Jag Crag Gorge. By the time he reached the other end, it had grown so dark and the dust squalls so frequent that he could not see the smoke rising at the outlet. In fact, Han would not have noticed it at all had his swoop not begun to chug and choke so badly that he had to stop to clean the silt from the clogged intakes.

But when he climbed off the swoop and raised his face mask to take a drink of water, the smell hit him like a Wookiee's fist, hard and familiar and acrid, the odor of burning power cells and efflux-blasted ground.

The smell of a crash.

Han followed his nose past a giant pinnacle of speckle-stone and out into a murky basin. The billowing black curtain of the approaching sandstorm was sweeping in across a vast expanse of level ground, but it was the half-circle scorch mark that caught his eye. Less than fifty meters away, it encompassed the twisted exhaust nacelle of a still-smoking Podracer engine. If there was anything else left of the swoop Kitster had been riding, Han could not see it. Feeling at once sorry for Tamora and her children and angry about what he felt sure would turn out to be the loss of Leia's painting, Han fetched a glow rod from his utility box and approached the crash site.

A few more pieces of Podracer engine and a twisted control vane lay scattered across the basin floor. But the rest of the wreckage was missing, and there was a deep tread mark on the straight side of the scorch mark. A few meters beyond that was another tread mark, running parallel to the first.

A Jawa sandcrawler.

Han spent a few more minutes searching the area for signs of Banai's blood or the moss-painting. When he found nothing, he activated his comlink and opened a channel to Leia. "It's me."

"Where are you?" Leia demanded. "It's after dark."

Han glanced at the approaching storm. "Yeah, it's beginning to look that way."

In the background, Chewbacca growled a question about Kitster and the moss-painting.

"Not exactly. I think they're both on a sandcrawler."

"A sandcrawler?" Tamora echoed in the background.

"Yeah." Han glanced down at the scorch mark. "My guess is he hitched a ride. I don't think he's hurt—"

"Hurt?" Tamora's voice grew louder. "Why would he be hurt?"

"Well, uh, he sort of ran into it."

A muffled thump sounded over the comlink.

"Tamora, there wasn't any blood—"

"Don't bother—she's out." This from Leia. "What about *Twilight*?"

"Same as Kit," he said. "No sign of moss. I think it survived the impact."

"Sounds convenient," Leia said. "Maybe he faked it?"

"That'd be the smart thing." Han ran his glow rod over the surrounding ground, but saw no footprints leading away from the crash site. "But I don't think so. He might have had time to arrange something with Wald, but I don't think he could have known there'd be a sandcrawler passing by out here. If he was going to fake a crash, he would have done it back in the canyon."

A sigh of exasperation came over the comlink. "So what now?"

"I guess I catch the sandcrawler." Han ran the beam of his glow rod down the tread trail and saw that it was traveling parallel to the approaching storm front. "Look, I attracted some attention on the way through the canyon. It probably wouldn't be a good idea for me to ride back to Mos Espa on this thing, and the sandcrawler seems to be heading more or less toward Anchorhead. Why don't we meet there?"

"When?" Leia asked.

Han glanced at the approaching curtain of sand. "Tomorrow morning," he said. "I doubt I'll make it before then."

Though it should have taken no more than ten minutes to overtake the slow-moving sandcrawler, four hours later Han was still struggling to catch sight of it. As the storm drew closer, the squalls—both sand and dust—grew constant, and the big swoop was as temperamental as it was fast. He could usually travel through a dust squall for three or four minutes before alarms started screeching and he had to stop to unclog the intakes. But sand stopped him after only a minute, and, as the storm drew closer, there was starting to be a lot more sand than dust. For every minute flying along the sandcrawler tracks, Han was spending three servicing the engine. He knew because he had timed it.

To make matters worse, the swoop had no lights, and the storm had turned the evening into one of those blacker-than-a-black-hole nights found only on stormy planets. He had to travel with the glow rod fixed on the vidmap, trusting to the heading arrow to keep on the same bearing as the sandcrawler. Whenever he stopped to clean the intakes, the first and last thing he did was find the sandcrawler's tracks and make sure the Jawas were still traveling in the same direction. So far, he had suffered only one close call, when he had drifted a hundred meters off course and been forced to spend another hour meandering back and forth across the basin floor with his glow rod trained on the ground.

It irked him to think that Banai was probably riding along in the relative comfort of a sandcrawler. As salvagers and traders, the little bright-eyed Jawas were all business, but unless you were a droid with salable parts, they were rarely hostile.

Han pulled the last of the sand out of the intakes, checked his bearing, and roared off through the darkness. The subtle shudder he had been noticing in the big engine was no longer subtle, no doubt because the sand was pitting the turbine blades and throwing the drive motor out of balance. There wasn't much he could do about it— at least not out here, in the face of an approaching sandstorm. Racing swoops, especially *this* racing swoop, were hardly meant for this kind of travel.

But Han *had* to catch that sandcrawler before the Imperials—and not only because he wanted Leia to have her painting. Politics on the Provisional Council were as cutthroat as an Ord Mantell sabacc game. If it became known that Leia had allowed a Shadowcast code key to fall into Imperial hands, there would be no shortage of Bothans and Kuatis claiming she was either incompetent or a traitor. Other councilors had been forced to resign in disgrace for less cause. And while Han was all too happy to have nothing more to do with the New Republic government, being forced out would devastate Leia—and that was not something Han would allow.

Besides, there were the spies to think of. They were just little guys trying to do their part, and they really didn't deserve to be tortured and executed. Half of the Provisional Council, sure, but not the spies.

A dozen small teardrops appeared in the storm ahead,

hazy, white, and so faint Han could barely make out the peculiarly steady glow of thermal exhaust vents. The lights were a good three or four meters off the ground, high enough that they almost looked like a squadron of low-flying fighters, and they were growing rapidly larger as he came up behind them.

A muffled thumping arose in the compressor area beneath the seat. Han shone the glow rod over the instrument panel, but reading status displays in this miasma was out of the question. He continued to accelerate, and the sandcrawler's anterior lights grew visible, creating a yellow-and-white halo that silhouetted the huge vessel's blocky shape against the storm ahead.

Han stayed directly behind the crawler as the dark form swelled to mammoth proportions. An alarm came on and the swoop began to lose power, but he continued to come up on the sandcrawler like an X-wing on an air balloon. He swung out to the leeward side—and a cacophony of alarms erupted inside his helmet.

The swoop started to sink, and Han cut thrust and deployed the emergency braking chute. The swoop decelerated hard, hurling him against his safety restraints so ferociously he thought he might end up with a broken pelvis. Then the swoop slammed down and bounced along the smooth desert floor, rocking from side to side against the safety skids, the emergency tail-drag keeping the nose up to prevent tumbling . . . and still Han almost caught the sandcrawler.

Almost.

He came to a rest close enough that the sandcrawler's stern was obscured by the dust rising behind its rear treads.

By the time Han realized he was still breathing—that the terrible pain in his body was only bruising—he was no longer in the dust cloud. He was back in the sandstorm, with the swoop rocking up on its leeward skids as the ferocious wind threatened to roll it. Han chinned his comlink and opened an emergency channel. The glow from the sandcrawler's exhaust vents was already starting to shrink.

"Hey, you in the sandcrawler!"

The speakers in Han's helmet remained dead and silent.

"You Jawas, stop! You've got salvage here!"

When the sandcrawler continued on its way, Han knew his helmet comlink was not broadcasting. He climbed out of the seat.

A storm gust sent him tumbling across the basin floor. By the time he stopped himself and got reoriented, the sandcrawler was fifty meters gone. Han opened his helmet face mask. Seventy meters. He ripped opened a utility pocket and pulled out his personal comlink. Eighty meters.

"Jawa sandcrawler! Wait. Stop."

Only static in response. Ninety meters.

Han rechecked the comlink and found it set properly on the emergency channel. How could they not be monitoring it? Jawas always monitored the emergency channels. That was how they knew where to find crashes.

More than a hundred meters now. The glow of the exhaust vents was growing hazy. Han tried the emergency channel again. This time the static spiked, and his heart jumped into his throat—until he noticed a white flash sheeting across the sky. Sand lightning.

The storm static was smothering the comm channels. With the comm equipment aboard the *Falcon*, maybe he could blast through. But not with the swoop's comm system—and certainly not with a personal comlink.

Han activated the channel search and staggered to his swoop through the buffeting wind, one eye fixed on the comlink signal light. It did not illuminate.

The sandcrawler had to be two hundred meters distant now, a line of exhaust vents fading into the stormy night. Han retrieved his helmet and crouched down on the sheltered side of the swoop, then opened a familiar channel.

"Leia? Can you hear me?" A crackle of static. "Are you there?"

TEN

A storm gust rocked the landspeeder up on edge, scouring the floater pads with sand and pushing it sideways across the desert floor. Leia leaned toward the high side, but the automatic equalizers activated, and the vehicle was level even before she realized what she was doing. Chewbacca grunted and brought them back to their original heading. If not for the heading arrow on the vidmap, it would have been impossible to tell the nose had drifted. The storm had closed in again, and two meters beyond the viewport the only thing visible was a yellow sand cloud roaring across the flat-as-a-table Great Chott salt flat. Even the twin suns made their presence felt only in a soft ambient glow that came from every direction at once.

Leia activated her comlink, tried to raise Han, and heard only white noise. Again. She had been trying to contact him since the night before, to tell him that they would be a little late to the rendezvous in Anchorhead. There were too many TIEs around to risk retrieving the *Falcon* from the smuggler's cave, so they would be coming via landspeeder. So far, she had been unable to reach him. She was starting to get worried. Very worried.

"I'm quite certain it's only the storm, Princess Leia," C-3PO said. "The static discharge has been playing havoc with my circuits all morning."

"But I've been trying to reach Han since last night."

"Oh my," C-3PO replied. "I was unaware of that. It might still be the storm."

Chewbacca growled a suggestion.

"Good idea," Leia said.

She tried to open a channel to Tamora, who had remained behind with her children in Mos Espa. The only reply was more white noise.

"You see?" C-3PO said cheerfully. "It *is* the storm."

Only the impossibility of twisting around in the tight confines to reach the seat behind her kept Leia from switching the droid off. "*We* weren't in the storm last night."

"Of course not," C-3PO said, missing the point. "We were in Mos Espa."

"And we couldn't raise Han."

C-3PO fell silent for a moment, then said, "Oh dear. Do you think Captain Solo could have been caught in the storm?"

Chewbacca growled darkly—not saying anything, just growling. They continued through the storm at a crawl, navigating by vidmap alone, eyes flicking between the instruments and the yellow blur outside, Leia trying to raise Han on the comlink every ten minutes. She timed the intervals carefully, not because she needed to conserve power, but because trying any more frequently would have meant she really believed Han was in trouble, and she didn't believe that. She *refused* to believe that. However Han Solo went, it would not be in a sandstorm. It would take more than that—a lot more.

Finally, a trio of small vaporator symbols appeared at the top of the vidmap, two in one corner and one in the other. They were still a long way from Anchorhead, but at least they were starting to pass the outlying moisture farms.

Pass might have been an overstatement. The storm gusts started to come more frequently and more power-fully, and visibility frequently fell to nothing. The land-speeder rocked and bucked, and there were times when the strain of keeping it level made the equalizers scream like an incoming TIE. An hour later, the same three vapo-rator symbols remained on the vidmap, still ahead of their position and accompanied by only one additional symbol. Leia felt fairly certain she could have walked faster—save that the instant she stepped outside, the storm would have swept her into the most unnamed of Tatooine's unnamed wastes.

Leia thought of Han out there struggling through the storm on an overpowered swoop. Immediately, she tried to replace the image with another: Han sitting in an An-chorhead tapcaf, drumming a single finger on the table-top while he waited for her to arrive. It was not a picture she could hold. Before she knew it, she was seeing the swoop lying on its side, half buried in a dune, the pilot's cowling packed with sand.

But this picture Leia was not imagining. She was actu-ally *seeing* it, there inside the landspeeder, hanging in front of her with the same apparent reality as Vader's mask in her dream aboard the *Falcon*. It looked like a hologram, but even more solid, more tangible. She reached out to touch it, expecting it to dispel as soon as she did. Instead, her hand sank into the image and van-ished from sight.

Leia would not let herself believe this was a vision. It was just another waking dream, or a hallucination caused by worry and fatigue. Anything but a vision. Anything but the future.

The image melted back into Leia's mind where it be-longed. She quickly chased it away completely by trying to raise Han on the comlink—and never mind that it had only been four minutes since her last attempt.

The reply was the same as always. White noise.

Leia sat, shaken, trying to remember what her brother had said Yoda told him about the future, but recalling instead only what Luke had told her last night, that the Force was with her, that her fear and anger would make her what she despised.

But not this way. Please, not by taking Han.

The storm lifted the landspeeder on edge and held it there. The equalizers began to wail again, the pitch rising toward the inaudible as they strained against the power of the wind. Chewbacca threw himself toward the high side, leaning across the center console to smash Leia against the compartment wall.

"We're going to roll!" C-3PO cried. "We'll be smashed to—"

"Threepio!" Leia gasped.

"Yes, Princess?"

"Lean!"

A dull clunk sounded against the compartment wall behind her, and the rising wail of the equalizers finally stabilized and began to drop. Chewbacca eased their nose ever so gently into the wind, and the landspeeder slammed down so hard the floor vibrated beneath Leia's feet as the floater pad struck ground. The Wookiee groaned in relief. He shunted extra power to the rear repulsors to keep the nose down, then continued forward into the teeth of the storm.

The vidmap error alarm began to beep, and Leia looked down to see they had been blown considerably off course. Now there were only two moisture farms on the display, one in the upper left corner, and one at the top of the screen. At the bottom—which meant directly

behind them—was a jagged line of mountains labeled
THE NEEDLES. The destination arrow was pointed toward
the upper right corner, flashing red to indicate they had
drifted. Chewbacca reached down, used the back of a
furry finger to thump the alarm override, and continued
toward the nearest moisture farm.

It was the smart thing to do. Even if the storm didn't
send them tumbling across the salt flat to smash into The
Needles, it would take another day to reach Anchorhead
at the rate they were traveling. They might as well sit it
out in safety and continue the journey when the weather
cleared.

Leia would have been happy to do just that, except for
one thing. "What about Han?"

Chewbacca urrharrrled that he was probably on his
second Gizer ale by now.

"You don't believe that any more than I do," Leia said.
"Han didn't make Anchorhead. I know it."

Chewbacca glanced over, his dark Wookiee nose
twitching in thoughtfulness. Finally, he asked *how* she
knew.

Leia shrugged. "I feel it—but not like it was with Luke
at Bespin," she said. "The sensation's not that strong."

Chewbacca nodded and remained silent, waiting for
Leia to continue in her own time. That was one of the
things she cherished most about the Wookiee, how he
never doubted or pressured a friend, how he simply
trusted. Leia focused her thoughts on Han again, trying
to imagine him in Anchorhead drinking a second Gizer
ale. Again, she could not hold the image, but this time it
was not replaced by anything. Even when she tried to see
a half-buried swoop, all that came to mind was blowing
sand. Who was she kidding? Even if she could be sure the
first image had been something other than her own worst

fear made manifest, there had been nothing in it to help her find Han.

Chewbacca let out an inquiring grunt.

Leia shook her head. "I have no idea which way to search. If we happen across any sand dunes, let's stop and take a look. That's the best I can do."

Chewbacca groaned that it was probably just as well. If they tried to go any direction but forward, they would just end up getting flipped anyway. Leia appreciated the kind words, but they weren't much comfort. She felt like she was letting Han down. Had she worked harder at developing her Force potential, she might at least be able to find him.

But developing her potential would have meant facing the dark side of her heritage, and even before her dream aboard the *Falcon* and Luke's warning, that thought had frightened her as much as having children.

Leia queried the vidmap for information about the moisture farms on the display. A line appeared beneath their destination, reading, NADON FARMS, FRESH PRODUCE ALWAYS AVAILABLE, WARNING: AUTOMATED SECURITY SYSTEMS. Beneath the other farm, the line read, RODOMON FAMILY FARM, CONTRACT SALES ONLY, WARNING: SECURITY SYSTEMS AUTOMATIC AND NONSENTIENT ANIMATE, NO VISITORS. This last statement was blinking in red.

The third farm returned to the corner of the display, and an information line automatically appeared beneath it: DARKLIGHTER FARM, FRESH PRODUCE AND GOOD CONVERSATION, STOP BY AND SEE US. Leia pointed at the symbol. "That one, Chewie. Let's wait out the storm there."

Chewbacca glanced down and grunted an objection.

"That's the farm where Luke grew up," Leia said. "Gavin Darklighter's parents own it now."

Chewbacca growled that the middle of a storm was no time for social calls. Knowing that his gruffness was no doubt out of concern for her safety, Leia smiled and nodded in agreement.

"It's a little farther, but the Darklighters' farm will be more secure." She was already resetting their destination. "Even if I wanted to, wearing a raised sand hood inside someone's home would raise suspicions. And with you and Threepio along, it wouldn't take our hosts long to figure out who I am anyway. I'd rather go someplace friendly from the start."

Chewbacca considered this, then nodded and turned the landspeeder onto the new course. The bearing was not as directly into the wind as the previous one, and Leia's corner kept trying to come up. The Wookiee adjusted the repulsors again, lowering the nose almost to the ground, then continued blindly into the storm.

None of the millions of scientific geniuses who lived in the galaxy had ever found a way to eliminate a human body's need for water. They could make suits that conserved every drop, they could build chem-reactors that synthesized it out of any breathable atmosphere, they had even discovered how to pressurize it to the point that a being could carry a week's supply on his belt in a massnulling clip.

But there was no pill or injection that negated the need for water. In a normal environment, a human being typically required two liters a day to stay efficient and alert. In a desert, a human needed ten to fifteen liters a day just resting in the shade, and double that if he was moving. If a man did not drink enough water, he would begin to feel weak and sick to his stomach; if he continued without drinking, he would develop a headache and grow dizzy, and his arms and legs might start to tingle. Next, his vision would dim, his tongue would swell, and his blood would thicken. It would grow hard to breathe, and his heart would stop.

Han was at the dizzy phase. With a pounding head and qualmish stomach, he felt as though he had spent a long night in the Mos Eisley cantina listening to Figrin D'an blasting off-key. Racing swoops were not designed to carry much cargo, and the four liters of water in the utility compartment had lasted only until midmorning. Now, tucked behind the pilot's cowling of the half-buried swoop, Han was doing everything he could to conserve body moisture: remaining still, breathing only through his nose, keeping his body and head covered, keeping his helmet face mask lowered. Though his limbs felt shaky, they were not tingling, and his vision remained as clear as could be expected when the only thing to see was a veil of blowing yellow. He guessed he would last another ten or twelve hours. If the storm had cleared by then, maybe Leia would be able to reach him. If not . . . well, Tatooine was an oven planet, and he was baking.

All for a painting—well, for Leia and the spies. And it was a heck of a painting. He had to keep that in mind.

Han continued to monitor his helmet comlink, but he did not broadcast. Even if he could have penetrated the storm static to reach Leia, he did not want her or Chewbacca coming after him. Not in this storm. All night long, the receiver had been crackling and snapping with storm static, but there had never been any voices. Now it had settled into a steady hiss of white noise like nothing Han had ever heard a sandstorm produce. To generate that much random static, this one had to be a monster, even by Tatooine's standards.

After another hour, a strange whine rose from the

comlink speaker. Han turned and began to dig sand out of the pilot's cowling, trying to find the comm system's squelch knob—then recognized the whine and realized it was not coming from inside his helmet at all. He rose to his knees and saw a blurry, H-shaped silhouette emerging from the storm ahead. In the yellow haze, it did not seem to be approaching so much as growing larger, but he had seen too many shapes just like it to doubt what he was seeing. A TIE fighter.

The starfighter screeched past overhead and became a shrinking ball of ion efflux, then vanished into the storm.

Han dropped back down behind the cowling, wondering what the chances were that it had missed his swoop. Not very good, he thought. Considering the size of the Tatooine desert and visibility in the storm, the starfighter had to be using some kind of advanced search sensor to locate him at all.

Han had just reached this conclusion when the whine began to build again, this time coming from the opposite direction. A dim H-shaped silhouette emerged from the storm, this time flying so low he was tempted to draw his blaster.

Before he had the chance, the TIE pulled up a dozen meters short and banked away into the storm. A meter-long capsule came flying out of the yellow haze behind it, arcing down toward the swoop. Heart thumping in his ears, Han sprang over the swoop and took off running, hunched forward against the wind with arms flailing, as though trying to swim through the blowing sand.

He was a dozen steps gone, sweating profusely and gasping for breath, before it occurred to him that if the capsule were a bomb, he would already be dead. Feeling foolish and lamenting the precious fluid he had wasted, he returned to the swoop and found the capsule buried to the control fins in the basin floor. A brilliant white strobe was blinking in the tail, and he knew a locator wave would be pulsing from a powerful transmitter somewhere deep inside.

"At least *someone's* going to find me."

Han sank back down behind the cowling and spent the next few minutes staring at the beacon. He had no idea whether the Imperials knew who they were chasing, but they clearly wanted *Killik Twilight* badly enough to risk much-needed starfighters searching for it. To survive, all he needed to do was wait until a squad of stormtroopers arrived to investigate the disabled swoop. Sure, there would be the humiliation of being captured, followed by a few days of torture, but Han had survived worse. He had *escaped* worse.

It was the interrogation that worried him. Leia had resisted Imperial interrogation more than once, but that was Leia. She had only to think of her duty to the New Republic, and she could endure anything. Han did not have the strength of her convictions. He doubted he could endure the needles and the hallucinogens and the sleep deprivation and still hold his silence. Eventually, he would start to admit things the Imperials had already figured out for themselves, such as the fact that he was on Tatooine to recover *Killik Twilight*. Then he would admit something they probably knew, perhaps that there was a code key hidden inside the moss-painting. Next, it would be something they might not know, like the existence of the Shadowcast message network, and then maybe he would be telling them everything they wanted to know.

Worst of all, they might even trick him into saying that Leia was here, on Tatooine, with no protection except C-3PO and Chewbacca.

Han drew his blaster to shoot the beacon, then realized that would only make his capture more likely. When the signal stopped, they would realize someone was still alive and rush to find the swoop again. The beacon would have to stay.

It was Han who would have to go. He removed the vidmap from its mounting, studied his options, then programmed his new destination, stood, and stumbled out into the storm.

At least the wind was at his back.

The vaporator symbol slid over the landspeeder's position blip. Leia looked up to find herself still completely lost, sand raking the forward viewports more ferociously than ever, the landspeeder rocking like a hawk bat caught in a hover racer's wake turbulence.

"Slow down, Chewie. We're there." Leia pressed her face closer to the transparisteel and could see no farther than the nose of their craft. "I think."

Chewbacca decelerated to a crawl and continued to ease forward. The words STOP BY AND SEE US appeared under the speeder's locator blip. The comm receiver crackled sharply, and a garbled noise that was probably a voice came over the speaker.

Leia glanced over to find Chewbacca looking at her with his furry brow raised, clearly hoping *she* had understood the voice. When Leia shook her head, his knuckle fur bulged so high she thought he would crush the steering yoke. This was one tense Wookiee.

Leia glanced over her shoulder at C-3PO. "Did you make that out?"

"I'm sorry, but the static interference is really quite terrible," C-3PO said. "All I could understand was 'come right sixty.' Sixty what, I don't know."

Chewbacca cursed with a growl that made even Leia blanch, then swung the nose right sixty degrees. The storm set the landspeeder up on edge so high that, had Chewbacca not been sitting on the raised side, Leia felt certain they would have flipped.

Another crackle came over the comm speaker.

"I detected no meaningful wave patterns," C-3PO reported almost before the noise had ended. "I suspect it was sand lightning."

A faint column of red light appeared a little farther to their right, shining up into the sandstorm. When Leia pointed it out, Chewbacca whoofed in relief—then nearly flipped the landspeeder when he tried to turn. Leia shifted to the high side of her seat and leaned across the console, practically climbing into the Wookiee's lap.

"See-Threepio, get on the high—"

"I am, Princess Leia," C-3PO said. "But I'm not heavy enough. We'll flip!"

Chewbacca groaned at the droid, then eased the nose a few degrees back into the wind and continued forward. Once the light was directly leeward of Leia's side window, he swung them full into the wind again, placing the red column directly behind them. The nose dropped, and he eased off the power, allowing the storm to push them back toward the glow.

"Well done, Chewie," Leia said.

The red light grew steadily larger and brighter in the rear viewport, shining up from behind a large sand berm. Chewbacca let the wind push them over the rim, and the wind calmed to a swirling gale. The landspeeder settled onto its repulsors in the heart of a sunken courtyard, not far from the red spotlight that had served as their beacon. Visibility improved enough to see a sturdy figure in a cloak waving for them to follow.

The figure led them through a barrier field into a

crowded and disorganized hangar, motioning them to park beside a modified S-swoop with three small seats where normally there was one. It took Leia a moment to realize the hangar was not just disorganized, it was torn apart, with a speeder bike lying on its side and hoversleds shoved hither and thither. Toppled tool cabinets lay along the walls with the contents spilled across the floor, while canisters of maintenance fluids lay heaped in the corner.

"This hangar was certainly much better organized when Master Luke inhabited this farm," C-3PO said. "I have seldom seen such a mess."

"I don't think this is its normal condition." Leia slipped her hold-out blaster into her pocket. "Don't shut down yet, Chewie."

Chewbacca groaned an affirmative, then the figure that had guided them into the hangar was beside the landspeeder, pulling back his hood. A moonfaced man with gray hair and long sideburns, he had the same brown eyes and warm smile as his son Gavin. Leia raised the cowling on her side of the speeder and saw the man's expression fade from welcoming to shock. After his eyes flicked to Chewbacca and C-3PO, the shock changed to fear.

"I was going to say you picked a devil of a time to come shopping for produce." He offered his hand to Leia. "But I know you didn't come from Coruscant looking for hubbas. What happened to Gavin?"

"Nothing!" Feeling a little foolish for not having anticipated this reaction, Leia took his hand and allowed him to help her out of the landspeeder. Upon seeing an official representative of the New Republic, any parent with a child in Rogue Squadron would react with alarm. "As far as I know, your son's in perfect health—assuming, of course, you *are* Jula Darklighter."

The man's easy smile returned. "Sorry—I guess you don't see many holos of me making speeches." He shook her hand, which he was still holding, and said, "Jula Darklighter. My son served on the *Mon Remonda* under your husband's command."

Leia returned Jula's smile. "I know. Lieutenant Darklighter is making quite a reputation for himself in Rogue Squadron."

This brought a proud flush to Jula's cheeks. He leaned down and looked into the landspeeder to address Chewbacca.

"You can shut her down, big fella. The Imperials have come and gone already." He stood up and smiled at Leia again, as though not quite able to believe what he was seeing. "At least now I know what they were looking for. I thought it was the Squibs."

"Squibs?" Leia's stomach twisted in a knot.

Jula gestured at the three-seated swoop. "Came in a couple of hours ago, the minute the stormtroopers left. They were in pretty sad shape."

"Good to see you again, Princess!"

A trio of familiar figures appeared from deeper in the hangar, coming from the direction of a lit doorway.

"No hard feelings about Espa Heights," Sligh said.

All three had sanisteam-ruffled fur and were stained head to toe with orange bacta lotion.

"You butted in," Grees added, "but no real harm."

Only their faces, which had been covered by masks and goggles, had no bare spots.

Leia narrowed her eyes. "What are you three doing here?"

"Is that any way to talk to your partners?" Emala asked, sounding hurt. "We're very happy to see *you*."

Chewbacca climbed out of the landspeeder and growled,

which C-3PO translated almost correctly as, "Master Chewbacca will thank you not to presume."

Jula frowned and looked to Leia. "You know these three?"

Leia sighed and nodded. "We're acquainted. But we're not partners."

"Wrong again, sweetheart." Grees stopped and propped his hands on his hips. "Han saved our lives, and now—"

Chewbacca snatched Grees and held him up in front of his face, asking the same question as Leia.

"You saw Han?"

"Isn't that what I just said?" Grees grabbed one of Chewbacca's thumbs in each hand and tried unsuccessfully to peel them back. "If you'd let me finish—"

"Where?" Leia grabbed the Squib by his utility bandolier. "When?"

"Not until that furwall puts him down." Emala stepped in front of Leia and shoved her in the thighs. "It'd do you good to remember the painting belongs to us right now."

"What? Are you—" Leia recognized the tactic as diversionary and caught herself. "Never mind." She waved her hands. "We'll deal with that later. Where's Han?"

Emala and Sligh exchanged smirks, then nodded together.

"He set things right in Tuskens' Escape," Emala said.

"We held the Imperials off so he could go after the painting." Grees flashed a plasteel smile. "We didn't want him going it alone, but no way we could keep up."

"Last we saw of him was a flaming dot streaking off into Mesa Flats," Sligh added. "That's some swoop he has."

"General Solo is here, too?" Jula asked.

"Captain Solo is no longer a general," C-3PO said. "He resigned his commission less than—"

"I'm sure Jula knows all about that, Threepio," Leia interrupted. The last thing she wanted right now was to rehash the events of the Hapan rift for Gavin Dark-lighter's father. "The whole galaxy knows about that."

Jula earned Leia's undying gratitude by nodding gruffly. "More than it needs to." He glanced at C-3PO. "And Han Solo will always be Gavin's general to me."

"He'll appreciate hearing that," Leia said. "Can you tell me how difficult it would have been for him to reach Anchorhead from Mesa Flats last night?"

Jula tried to hide his alarm by glancing toward the barrier field, but he was not quick enough to fool Leia—not when the answer mattered so much.

She grasped his forearm. "He couldn't."

"He didn't," Jula said. "No one did. The last thing we heard from Anchorhead was an alert advising travelers to seek shelter and ride the storm out. Nobody made it into town."

Leia didn't bother asking if he could be sure, or arguing that nobody was as lucky or resourceful as Han. She *knew* he had not made it to Anchorhead. She had known before they stopped.

Leia slipped back into the landspeeder and reached for the vidmap, only to find Chewbacca's long fingers already calling up an overview of the area. She turned to Jula.

"Could we have some water and a few power cells?"

"No." Jula leaned into the speeder and put his hand on her arm. "I can't let you do that."

Leia began to fish for credits. "I'll gladly reimburse—"

"Now you're insulting your host," Jula warned. "On Tatooine, that can get you thrown in a Sarlacc pit . . ."

Leia frowned. "I don't understand."

"I think you do." Jula took a remote from his cloak pocket and flicked it toward the barrier field, which instantly turned gold and opaque. "I can't let you go out there, not in this storm, not even for Han."

ELEVEN

On some level, Leia knew she should have been more interested in the farm. She should have been following Jula Darklighter and his family on a tour through the warren of whitewashed rooms that surrounded the central courtyard, trying to guess where her brother had slept, where he had played as a boy, trying to find the place where he had lain outside looking at stars and dreaming of becoming a starfighter pilot. Until she had actually come here to the moisture farm and seen the barren land that had been Luke's childhood home, she had not understood his upbringing, how much harder and simpler and lonelier his life had been than hers. Now that she was here, she could only stand in awe of the man he had made of himself . . . stand in awe and wonder if *she* could have risen so far from such modest circumstances.

But Leia had no interest in seeing the moisture farm. She only wanted to sit here in the aboveground entrance dome, staring out into the yellow haze, listening to dry thunder growl across the plain, watching the sand lightning sheet across the curtained sky, silently begging the Force to bring the storm to an end—or at least to let her hear over her comlink the faintest scratch of Han's voice.

Unfortunately, the Force did not answer prayers. An impersonal power that could be touched but never moved, it cared nothing for the individual and served only those who served it. The Force would not save Han. Only Leia could do that, and she had not prepared herself. She had been too frightened of what she might become.

A woman cleared her throat on the stairs leading up from the subterranean levels. Leia turned to see Silya Darklighter stepping into the small foyer, carrying a tray loaded with pungent hubba-rind tea and Tatooine flatbread.

"You be cross with Jula if you like, dear—I usually am myself." A thin woman no more than a third Jula's size, Silya had gray hair and a leathery face that made her look half again as old as the fifty years Leia estimated from Gavin's age. "But I won't have you sitting hungry. Not in my house."

"I'm not angry with Jula," Leia said.

Silya cocked a doubtful brow.

"Well, I *shouldn't* be." Leia offered a guilty smile. "He's right, and I know it. I'm just so worried about Han."

"We all are. Even the Squibs are plotting search coordinates."

"Of course. I'm sure they smell a tidy profit."

"One you'd do well to pay." Silya put the tray on a broad shelf built into the wall. "None of us knows the desert like those three, and with all these Imperials running around, we can't organize a big search party."

"Good advice. Thank you." Leia noticed there was only one cup on the tray. "You're not staying?"

Silya smiled. "I'm sure you want to be alone—I always do when I get like this about Gavin or Jula—and I need to fix something to take with us. Jula says we'll start the search as soon as the storm lifts. And since it's Han Solo we're looking for, it might be a little earlier than that."

Leia immediately began to feel more hopeful. "I can't tell you how much your help means to me."

"No need, dear." Silya filled the cup. "We've all been through the same thing out here."

"Thank you." Leia took the tea from Silya. "Any word about the sandcrawler? We mustn't forget that Kitster Banai is out there as well."

"Don't trouble yourself about Kitster," Silya said. "The Jawas will take care of him, and only the Sand People know this desert the way they do. They'll tuck their sandcrawler in someplace safe, then take him to Anchorhead as soon as the storm lifts."

"You're sure?"

"The sandcrawlers always stop in Anchorhead." Silya patted Leia's wrist. "He'll be fine—and so will your painting."

Leia winced at the faint note of reproach in Silya's voice, but resisted the urge to reveal the true reason for her concern, that *Killik Twilight* contained a secret that could cost the lives of thousands of New Republic operatives— among them Wedge Antilles, Wraith Squadron, and most of the Askajian resistance.

Instead, she asked, "How is Chewbacca doing?" When Jula had hardened the barrier field, the Wookiee had been even more furious than Leia. "I hope he hasn't started roaring again."

"Don't you worry about Chewbacca. Jula has him installing a magnetometer in our market skiff. As long as he's busy preparing for the search, he doesn't get too grouchy."

Leia rose. "I should be doing something, too. I'm not much good with sensor equipment, but I can help you."

"Another cook in my kitchen?" Silya's face turned stony. "I don't think so, dear."

"Oh." Leia felt as though she had ordered nerfburger at an Ithorian banquet. "Then I'll look after Threepio."

"No, dear. Your droid took himself for an oil bath."

Silya paused, looking a little puzzled, then confided, "It's eerie, how he knows his way around."

"He's been here before. Luke's uncle owned him for a short time."

"Of course—silly of me not to remember that." Silya's gaze grew uneasy. She took a step toward the stairs, then paused and removed a tiny datapad from her pocket. "Speaking of the Larses—this was left behind after they died. It has a few data skips, but you might find it interesting."

Leia flipped the instrument open and saw that it was actually a tiny vidrecorder and playback screen. "A journal?"

"Anya—my daughter—found it buried in the mushrooms under a vaporator last month. The next time Gavin comes home on leave, we were going to ask him to take it back for Luke. Maybe you could take it instead."

"Of course. So it belonged to one of the Larses?"

"I think so." Silya turned away a little too quickly and started down the stairs. "I only viewed it long enough to know it wasn't our affair. But I doubt Luke would mind if you looked. Maybe it will make the waiting a little easier."

Leia waited as Silya descended the stairs. The woman had obviously seen more of the journal than she cared to admit, but why she wanted Leia to look was puzzling. Probably, she was just trying to keep her guest's mind occupied. Leia resumed her seat and activated the journal.

The question ENTRY? appeared on the display. Leia asked for the first one, and a time stamp appeared in the lower corner. There was a place for a date stamp opposite, but a message read "Calendar file corrupted." A moment later, a dark-eyed woman appeared on the screen. She had a small upturned nose and brown hair pulled back, and she looked a little tired, her face lined by worry and weather. Despite her fatigue, she was still attractive in that hard Tatooine way, with a quiet dignity and serene composure that Leia perceived despite the small display.

No . . . not perceived, Leia realized. *Recognized.* It would be difficult to discern such traits in two seconds of viewing a tiny electronic image, yet Leia *did* know they were qualities possessed by this woman. She felt them much as she had felt Mos Espa growing more familiar, much as she had known when she entered the slave hut where her father might have lived.

The Force again, carrying her into the Skywalkers' past.

"All right. Who are you?" Leia leaned forward, studying the image more closely. "Luke's Aunt Beru?"

The mystery woman remained in the display, her brow furrowing as she concentrated on something. Her lips began to move, but no sound came. Leia adjusted the volume to maximum . . . then nearly dropped the journal when a warm female voice suddenly blared from the little speaker.

08:31:01

. . . *this thing still is not recording.*

A gravelly voice, not as loud, said, *"What are you doing, woman? I told you to clean my shop. Memory chips, you clean at home."*

The woman's image was replaced by a bald blue head with large selfish eyes, a hoselike proboscis of a nose, and a huge mouth containing a handful of chunky tusks. In the background fluttered a pair of wings, moving so fast they were a blur.

"Where did you get this?" the being demanded. *"Is it yours?"*

"I bought it with my memory-chip earnings," the woman said. *"I thought—"*

"Maybe I should sell it for disobeying me, eh?" The image in the display whirled as the being turned the journal over. *"But it's not worth much, I think. Back to work, or I will."*

The display went blank—the end of the first entry.

Leia took a sip of hubba tea and looked out at the roaring storm. Despite the diversion of the journal, Leia could not keep her thoughts off Han. She kept recalling the image of his swoop lying half buried in a sand drift, kept wondering whether what she had seen was accurate, what it meant, and—most of all—where Han was. The Force was acting on her; Luke had left no doubt of that. But what did it want?

The answer, of course, was nothing. The Force did not have desires or purposes. It simply *was*—or so Luke had told her.

And that knowledge was of little comfort to Leia. She could not deny that the image had come to her through the Force. But her inability to divine any clear meaning— any clear hint of what she was to *do*—made the waiting unbearable. Her mind was spinning with reasons Han *would* survive and reasons he would not, and she just kept feeling more guilty, more lonely, more tormented by her decision to let him go after the painting.

Leia looked down to find the journal flashing ENTRY TWO?

She told it to continue, and the woman's face appeared in the display, smiling.

19:47:02

You might enjoy something to remember Watto by, so I left that as entry one. He's not so bad, as masters go,

*and I do believe there are times when he truly misses
your mischief.*

*Annie, this diary is for you. I know you'll be gone a
long time, and that you'll be very lonely at times. So will
I. This diary is so that when you come home someday,
you'll know you were always in my heart. But your destiny lies in the stars. You will achieve great things in the
galaxy, Anakin. I have known that from the moment you
were born. So you must never believe you were mistaken
to leave Tatooine. Wherever you go, you carry my love
with you. Always remember that.*

The journal nearly slipped from Leia's hands. "Annie"
and "Anakin" had to be Anakin Skywalker, who had
once been Watto's slave. The woman was his mother . . .
and Leia's grandmother.

Leia paused, taking a breath, then asked for the next
entry. Her grandmother's face appeared in the display
and began to speak to her.

19:12:03

*Watto came back from a trip to Mos Eisley today with
bad news. He told me that Qui-Gon Jinn had been killed
in a battle on a world called Naboo. No one knows
whether he had a boy with him, but I'm terrified, Annie.
Do I still have a reason to keep this diary?*

*Watto keeps saying that I should never have let you
go, that you would have been better off staying his slave
on Tatooine. I can't allow myself to believe that . . . Qui-
Gon promised me he would take care of you, that he
would train you as a Jedi, so I must trust that you are still
all right. But who is watching after you? Who will train
you now?*

Annie, I'm so worried.

* * *

The entries for the next few months ran in much the same vein—though many had been destroyed by the data skips Silya had mentioned. Anakin's mother put up a brave front, recounting day-to-day events as a matter of faith that her son had survived and would one day hear them. But she also continued to search for news of his fate. One spacer reported hearing that there had been a boy at the battle, another a wild tale about the boy actually striking the critical blow.

Anakin's mother even spent what remained of her meager savings on a HoloNet news search, which yielded only the unsettling news that a boy had been seen shortly before the battle in the presence of the "slain Jedi Knight." Few other details were available, for the Jedi Council was remaining even more reticent than usual about the incident.

As Leia watched, she found herself reeling with emotion. She understood her grandmother's fear and frustration all the more keenly because of her own concerns over Han. Every rumble of dry thunder, every flash of sand lightning, made her worry more acute. Han would have run out of water at least twelve hours ago. No human could survive a full day without water in Tatooine's furnacelike atmosphere. Leia kept counting the minutes, the hours, wondering when this storm would let up—and she kept thinking of her grandmother, wondering how she had endured a wait that was so much longer.

Leia would not have wanted to be the one who told the gentle woman the awful truth about what had become of her son.

The wind had not blown Han into the snug little cave he had been hoping for, but the crevice was deep, sheltered, and a perfect mixture of sand and fleckrock. As long as he kept his back to the opening and his hood raised, he did not even feel the searing breeze worming its way in from the Great Mesa, and he thought he just might last out the storm, if he could only keep his tongue from swelling any more and closing off his throat.

Han scraped another handful of sand from the hole he had been digging and packed it on his cooking stone in a tight little mound. As powdery and gray as it looked, it was a wonder it contained any moisture at all. But it was cool to the touch, and on Tatooine, what was cool had water. Han held his helmet mask over the top of the pile, then used his blaster—set on stun—to heat the cooking stone.

The vapor that rose out of the sand wasn't even visible, but it collected on the inside of Han's face mask in three beads the size of his little fingernail. Before the moisture could dissipate into the arid atmosphere, he wiped the inside of the face mask with a scrap of tunic, then put the tiny rag behind his lips, and sucked the few drops of water into his mouth.

Han was past the point of thinking about his odds, or even wondering if he would ever see Leia again. His vision was dimming and his thoughts came slowly or not at all, and he had one goal in mind. He set the helmet mask aside and swept the warm sand away, then pulled another handful of cool sand from the hole and packed it in a tight heap. He held his helmet mask over the pile and pointed his blaster at the cooking stone.

Han squeezed the trigger, and the power pack depletion alarm chirped twice.

17:30:04

Today you're eleven years old, Anakin, and some of your friends have come over to say hello. They don't know what happened at Naboo, so don't be hurt if they . . . what am I saying? You're fine. Wouldn't I feel it if you weren't?

Here comes your friend Wald. I gave him some of your tools—but not the droid you were building. I'll keep him, just like I promised.

The green-scaled face of a Rodian child appeared in the display, his bulbous black eyes shining with delight and his tapered snout squirming in excitement.

"How are things at Jedi school? Study hard, so you can come back and free us. By the way, I'm building that rocket swoop you dreamed up. Kitster's helping me. I hope you don't mind."

Wald's face was replaced by that of a black-haired boy with a dark complexion and huge brown eyes. He smiled, then held up a flimsiplast pamphlet with a familiar title: *Par Ontham's Guide to Etiquette.*

"Look what I bought with the credits you gave me. Rarta Dal said she'll hire me to be her steward—but first I have to memorize the whole thing."

Banai's face was replaced by that of Anakin's mother, this time in profile as she told the pair to have a seat at the table—she just happened to have a fresh pallie tart in the oven. Once they had gone, she spoke into the journal again.

They are so proud of you, Annie—and so am I. You have given them the courage to dream of things they could not imagine. And honestly, I don't know what I will do when they stop coming around. I see your reflection every time they smile.

Perhaps that's why I bake so many pies.

Leia asked the journal to mark the current entry, then lowered it and stared out into the howling sands. She had finished Silya's flatbread and hubba tea more than two hours ago, and still the storm was in full blow. She clicked her comlink for the ten thousandth time and, when she heard nothing but white noise in reply, refused to despair. Until the storm ended, she could do nothing but assume the best and carry on.

She had learned that from her grandmother.

TWELVE

Even with a landspeeder and a swoop tied down in the rear cargo compartment and six chairs and a suite of emergency search sensors magnoclamped to the floor in the forward compartment, the Darklighters' market skiff was large enough to accommodate the search party in relative comfort. It was also heavy enough to avoid being tossed around by stray gusts, which meant that the minute the winds dropped beneath a hundred kilometers per hour, Jula had them loaded and under way.

Jula and Silya were in the driver's cabin, pretending to be exactly what they were: a pair of moisture farmers out searching for storm survivors. Leia and everyone else sat in the forward cargo area—which was refrigerated to retard produce spoilage—shivering and watching passive search sensors. After two frigid hours of breathing musky hubba gourd scent and looking at nothing but empty desert on her optical scanner, Leia was both overwrought and mind-numbingly bored. She recalled feeling like this on some of the military assaults in which she had participated during the Rebellion. There was something about a long ride into combat that brought out the silence in soldiers, turning even the most gregarious extrovert somber and reflective.

But they were not going into battle, and the question on everyone's mind had less to do with how they would react to the roar and the fury than with what they would find when they reached the primary search zone—a large fan of desert that Jula had calculated would be the most likely place to find Han. The Squibs had developed an insightful list of places where Han might have taken shelter during the storm and plotted a thorough grid pattern for doing a sensor sweep of the basin itself. But the truth was, they were not sure they would find anything. The search zone was based on everyone's best guess as to where Han had been when he commed to report Kitster's accident with the sandcrawler. For all they really knew, he could have been on the outskirts of Mos Eisley.

With the storm moving away, comm traffic was starting to return to normal. Still, Leia resisted the urge to try raising Han on her comlink. Several Imperial spy craft were already flying holding patterns high above the desert, no doubt monitoring all channels and analyzing every signal for clues as to the location of *Killik Twilight*'s thief. Han and Leia both used military-grade scramblers on their comlinks, so a transmission coming from a local market skiff was sure to bring a company of stormtroopers to investigate.

Instead, Leia tried again to picture Han waiting in Anchorhead, sipping a Gizer ale and drumming his fingers on the table. Again, the image simply vanished. This time, the picture in her mind didn't even fade to a half-buried swoop. She simply heard a muffled whine, so distinct and tangible that she scowled and looked at the ceiling.

Chewbacca garuumphed a question.

"Don't *you* hear them?" Leia asked.

"Hear what?" Sligh demanded, instantly suspicious.

Leia cocked her head. There was definitely a whine. "TIEs."

The Squibs looked from each other to Chewbacca.

The Wookiee spread his furry hands and shrugged, then Jula's voice came over the intercom.

"Stay off the sensors back there. We've got—"

A deafening shriek reverberated through the market skiff roof, a TIE flying by to take a look. There was also the rumble of something larger, muffled and in the distance ahead.

Leia glanced at the ceiling. "You heard that, right?"

The Squibs' fur was standing on end, and Chewbacca's nose was twitching in alarm.

"*I* certainly did," C-3PO said.

The market skiff began to decelerate, and Silya said, "We'd better go to Operation Bodybag, dears. It looks like an assault shuttle just dropped off a scouting patrol."

Chewbacca released a tarp that had been furled against the ceiling, and a matte painting of a dark wall dropped down to conceal their sensor equipment. The Squibs dragged a bodybag over near the door and piled in together. Leia climbed into her own, while Chewbacca had to use two, pulling one up over his legs and another down over his shoulders. They all took their weapons, but were careful to conceal them under their hips.

C-3PO was the last to take his position, deactivating the compartment's interior lights and plunging it into total darkness. He shut himself down and clunked up against the access door. A few minutes later, the market skiff came to a stop. Over the intercom—now muffled by the matte painting—Leia heard a stormtrooper speaking to Jula.

"Anchorhead Volunteers?"

That was the magnetic sign clamped to the side of the skiff.

"Search and rescue," Jula explained. The howl of the wind—and the patter of sand grains against plastoid armor—could be heard over his voice in the background. "You *have* noticed the storm, right?"

"Of course," the stormtrooper said. "State your business."

"Just did," Jula said, sounding sincerely angry. "Look at the side of the wagon. Search and rescue. We're looking for survivors."

"You won't find any here," the stormtrooper said.

"What about that big swoop?" Jula demanded. "Someone must've driven that thing out here."

"The swoop is not your concern," the stormtrooper said. "How many survivors have you found?"

"Same as usual," Jula answered nonchalantly. "None."

"None?"

"We do it for the salvage," Silya said, her voice sweet and brittle. "*Rescue*'s just a euphemism."

"A what?" the stormtrooper demanded. "Never mind. Open your skiff for inspection."

The intercom went silent. Leia cursed under her breath, then pushed her hand through the zipper and popped one of the odor capsules moisture farmers used to empty profogg warrens when the pesky creatures started to burrow near their hydroponics chambers. The reek didn't smell all that much like a human corpse, but it was awful enough to discourage a close inspection of the compartment. She closed the bodybag again and held her breath. She wished she could hold it forever.

The compartment door hissed open, and C-3PO fell into the stormtrooper. The man cursed through his voice filter, and the droid thunked down across the doorway—as planned. Leia's bodybag immediately began to warm as the hot desert air rolled into the compartment.

"Sorry," Jula said. "Load must have shifted. We're still getting some pretty good gusts."

"That smell." No helmet-mounted air scrubber was

powerful enough to completely eliminate the stench in the compartment, and the Imperial sounded like he was making a sour face. "What is it?"

"What do you think?" Jula countered. "We found a few folks . . . They were pretty far gone."

"I thought you were looking for salvage."

"We are—and we find a lot of bodies," Silya said. "Do you expect us to just leave them where they dropped?"

"Besides," Jula added. "Sometimes there's a reward."

The stormtrooper was silent for a moment. Leia had to take a breath and was grateful for the antigagging tonic Silya had spooned into their mouths before departing the moisture farm. It did not make the smell any less vile, but at least she was not fighting her own body to remain quiet.

"Any humans?" the stormtrooper asked.

"A few," Jula said. "If you're looking for someone in particular, feel free to climb in—"

"That won't be necessary," the stormtrooper said quickly. "We're looking for a man named Kitster Banai. Here's a holo—"

"Don't need it," Jula said. "I know Kitster. What makes you think you'll find him out here? He's not the type to—"

"I'll ask the questions," the stormtrooper said.

"Sure, if that's the way you want it." Jula launched into his next question without pause. "What about the fella who was flying that rocket swoop over there?"

Leia's pulse started to pound so ferociously she nearly missed the start of Jula's next question.

". . . take him off your hands? A body starts to stink awfully fast in this heat."

Body! Leia had to remind herself not to sit up. If the Imperials were still looking for Banai and there was a body, it could only be . . . she could not even bring herself to think it. But if it was, she was not leaving here without it. She would not leave her dead husband in the hands of a squad of—

"There isn't a body," the stormtrooper said. "Did you find any of these corpses around here?"

"Not close enough to be your swoop pilot," Jula said.

Leia started to breathe again. There was still hope. Han was on foot in the Tatooine desert with a wing of TIEs and company of stormtroopers looking for him, but those weren't bad odds. Not for Han Solo.

Outside the skiff, Jula continued, "These all came from up near the main speeder corridor. So . . . you have any plans for that swoop wreck?"

"The Empire's plans are not your concern, farmer. What about Squibs?"

Jula's voice turned resentful. "What about 'em?"

"Did you pick up any?"

"Squibs? Bloah, no—they never bring a reward."

The stormtrooper was silent for a moment, then asked, "You're sure you don't have Squibs?"

"I know what a Squib looks like," Jula said. "You don't believe me, climb in and have a look. Nobody back there's going to mind."

The stormtrooper's voice grew muffled as he turned and started to crunch across the ground toward the rear of the market skiff. "What's in the rear compartment?"

"Salvage." Leaving the skiff door open, Jula started after him. "How many Squibs did you say there were?"

"I didn't." The voices continued to fade. "Why?"

"Because I did find a swoop you might be interested in," Jula said. "It had three small seats that might have been . . ."

The voices grew too muted to understand, and Leia could no longer stand not being able to see outside. She lowered the bodybag seal just far enough to look. Outside the doorway, in the gauzy dust haze of a relatively mild forty-kilometer-per-hour wind, five stormtroopers were standing guard around the rocket swoop Han had been using. The vehicle lay on its side, half buried in a dune, the pilot's cowling packed with sand.

The swoop lay on the same side at the same angle as in the image that had appeared to her in the landspeeder. The dune covered the engine housing to the same height. Sand spilled out of the exhaust nacelle in the same fan-shaped pile and covered the pilot's cowling up to the same edge. The same worn corner was all she could see of the seat. Not close. Exact. There could no longer be any denying it—she had not imagined this, nor hallucinated it. Leia had experienced a Force-vision.

She was not really surprised. She had long ago come to understand—when Luke told her the truth about their father—that many of the diplomatic gifts she attributed to intuition were really the glimmerings of untrained Jedi potential. Leia thought back to her vision aboard the *Falcon*. She was touching the Force, just as Luke had said. But was he right about the rest? Was she in just as much danger as Han?

Jula Darklighter walked back into view, followed by the stormtrooper leader and two escorts, and joined the rest of the squad by the rocket swoop. He circled the derelict twice, then squatted on the windward side and stared at the ground. The leader came over and stood above him, his filtered voice asking some question Leia could not hear.

Jula shook his head. The stormtrooper demanded an answer. The farmer shrugged, then pointed at the ground and ran his finger out ahead of him, tracing a line into the wind out toward the horizon. The leader summoned five of his troopers and pointed at the ground, then pointed in the same direction. The stormtroopers nodded, then mounted their speeder bikes and fanned out across the desert, traveling for the windward horizon.

Jula turned and asked something about the swoop, to which the stormtrooper replied with a firm shake of the head. The farmer spread his hands and started back toward the market skiff, the squad leader following close behind.

". . . Empire thanks you for your help, citizen. And you will report any sightings of sandcrawlers or Jawas."

"Sure I will." Jula's tone was cynical. "But I'd look a lot harder if you let me salvage that swoop."

"I've said before that I have orders to hold it for inspection. You have my service number. Contact me after I've had a chance to speak with my superiors and tell them how helpful you've been. Perhaps they'll release it to you after they're done."

Jula stopped beside the market skiff and reached for the door pad. "If that's the only way."

"It is. The *only* way. And my superiors will certainly be inclined to look more favorably on your request if you have helped us locate that sandcrawler."

Jula hit the slap pad. "I'll bet they would."

The door hissed shut, and the market skiff resumed its journey. The compartment broke into a rustle as Leia and the others crawled free of the bodybags.

"What a smell!" Emala gasped. "I wish I *was* dead."

They reactivated the compartment light, and Leia went straight to the intercom.

"Jula, that was Han's swoop."

"So I figured," Jula said. "He was doing pretty well when he abandoned it, so don't you worry."

"Sure I won't," Leia said, using the same cynical tone Jula had with the stormtrooper. "How would you know?"

"I *know*," Jula said. "There was an Imperial locator beacon next to it, and he was smart enough to leave it in one piece when he left. He didn't want to be found."

"And that means he wasn't desperate," Silya answered. "When a man gets really thirsty, he *always* wants to be found."

"Okay," Leia said. "What did you find on the ground that sent the stormtroopers flying off?"

"Nothing."

Leia waited a moment for more explanation. When none came, she asked, "So where are they going?"

"Nowhere."

"I'm afraid Jula played them a bit," Silya offered. "He let them think he saw something he didn't. Then, they began to see it too, and off they went."

"They weren't very bright, even for Imperials," Emala said.

"Everyone knows thirsty men never go into the wind," Sligh added.

"Actually, I didn't know that," Leia said. "But it makes sense. What *did* you find, Jula?"

"It's what I didn't find," he reported. "You said Ulda put a vidmap on that swoop?"

"That's right."

"It's gone."

Chewbacca, who was helping the Squibs roll the concealment matte back up to the ceiling, growled a concern. C-3PO, still drawling a little as his systems came up, translated.

"Master Chewbacca doesn't see how that information is of any use. Unless we know where he intended to go—"

"My money's on the Jawa Raceway," Sligh said.

"How much?" Jula asked.

"Jula!" Silya scolded. "Don't you take advantage. We're north of there, Grees."

Both male Squibs flattened their ears, and Emala chuckled. Grees snarled at Emala, then asked, "Then you're thinking the Bantha Burrows?"

"That's where I'd go," Jula said. "What do you think?"

"We find more stuff in the Sarlacc Gardens," Sligh said.

"But Han's not from Mos Espa," Silya pointed out. "He wouldn't know about Monk's Well."

Leia looked to Chewbacca, who grunted negatively. Chewbacca had never heard of the place, so Han probably hadn't either.

"The Bantha Burrows," Leia said. "Well or no well, Han's not going near anything with *Sarlacc* in the name."

The skiff floor seemed to shift forward as they accelerated. "Go ahead and bring up the scanners," Jula said. "The Imperials know we're out here looking, so they're not going to get too curious even if they do detect us, and we might find something that tells us one way or another."

Chewbacca and the Squibs set to work. Leia grabbed a set of electrobinoculars, then opened the door far enough to have a clear view. Though the storm was over, the winds continued to stir up a thin dust haze, reducing visibility to a mere hundred meters close to the desert floor. But the sky was clear, so deeply blue it was almost purple. In the distance ahead, the first of the twin suns was already sinking behind a jagged spine of brown mountains, spraying the vista with a fan of golden rays. Leia adjusted her electrobinoculars to maximum view field and, trading Tatooine's stern splendor for any small chance of spying her husband, began to search the pearly gauze for any darkness or sharp-edged shadow that might be a man or a piece of equipment lying on the ground.

As Leia watched, she brought Han's face to mind, hoping the image would change into a Force-vision and provide some hint that would help them find her husband. The only change was that the image kept changing: the insolent but lovable scoundrel *trying* to rescue her on the Death Star, the smug lover about to be frozen in carbonite, the confused suitor on Endor, offering to step aside so she could be with . . . her brother.

Chewbacca came over to sit behind her, staring out over her head, and rested his paws on her shoulders. They were as heavy as a full field pack, but Leia tried not to let that show. As large as they were, they were also a comfort, and she knew the Wookiee had to be as worried as she.

He groaned a suggestion.

"I'm trying," Leia said. "But the Force and I aren't much use to each other right now."

Chewbacca squeezed her shoulders and groaned softly.

"It's *not* all right, Chewie," Leia said. "I got Han into this. I ought to be able to get him out. I owe him that."

Leia raised the electrobinoculars to her eyes again, and they continued across the flats. Finally, the skiff turned, bringing the door around so she was looking directly toward the mountains. The wind died and the dust haze lifted, leaving her to stare across several hundred meters of desert into a shimmering labyrinth of brown canyons and craggy cliffs, pocked with the dark circles of thousands of huge caves.

"The Bantha Burrows?" Leia asked.

"You guessed it." Emala appeared at her side and stood on her tiptoes to push Leia's electrobinoculars away from the canyon floors. "You look for urusais or skettos circling overhead."

"Okay. What are they?"

"Carrion eaters and bloodsuckers." Grees made no effort to be subtle. It was probably not a concept Squibs could comprehend. "If you see them in the air, that's good."

"And if I see them on the ground?"

"You don't want to," Sligh said. "That's why Emala's watching the ground."

They continued along the front of the mountain. Once, a trio of TIEs circled around to take a closer look at the market skiff. Leia mistook them for urusais for an instant, but the craft shrieked over and were gone before she could yell for Jula to stop. The search party spent the next minute wondering if the starfighters were carrying sensor equipment capable of spotting the partially opened door, but the craft never returned, and eventually everyone relaxed.

It took only five minutes longer for Leia to spy a cloud of leathery-winged creatures circling in front of a cleft in a canyon wall. With huge red eyes, snaggletoothed beaks half hidden beneath folds of greenish gold hide, and fan-shaped combs rising behind their heads, they were the ugliest things she had ever seen in the air. As soon as the creatures noticed the big skiff, they dropped lower and tightened their circle.

"Stop!" Leia lowered her arms and pointed into the canyon. Without electrobinoculars, the creatures looked like flitnats. "In the canyon."

"Urusais," Emala reported.

"Got 'em." Jula turned the skiff toward the canyon. "I'll swing around and bring the door as close to the cleft as I can."

A few moments later, a terrible banging erupted from the roof of the skiff.

"We're being bombed!" C-3PO cried. "We're doomed!"

"It's just rocks, chipbrain," Grees said. "The urusais are defending their claim."

The Squibs readied their blasters. Leia and Chewbacca exchanged nervous glances and prepared their own weapons. The banging grew to a constant din of thunder, and dents began to appear on the inside of the ceiling. Leia had C-3PO store a reminder to send the Darklighters the credits to purchase a new market skiff.

Finally, Jula swung the skiff around and pulled it up beside a hundred-meter fleckrock cliff. As vertical and smooth as any Coruscant wall, it was split down the center by the meter-wide cleft that Leia had spotted earlier. Even with the compartment door open only a crack, Leia could feel a breeze pouring out of the fissure—not exactly cool, but not as hot as the surrounding rock. It grew apparent that the cleft was actually a deep, twisting, sand-filled gorge that ran some distance back into the mountains. With the suns already dropping behind the horizon, it was also dark and foreboding.

The Squibs squeezed in front of Leia and Chewbacca.

"We'll take care of this," Grees said.

"You keep the urusais off us," Sligh added.

Chewbacca growled, and Leia shook her head.

"No way we're staying behind," Leia said. "That's my husband out there."

"We're thinking of you," Emala retorted. "The Wookiee will get stuck in three steps, and don't expect *us* to wait for you if Han was dragged back there by a baby krayt dragon."

"Let the Squibs do it, dear," Silya said over the intercom. "They'll be faster—and speed might be important."

Reluctantly, Chewbacca growled in agreement—and caught Leia by the arm to make sure she didn't do anything foolish.

Grees hit the slap pad, and the Squibs launched themselves into the fissure, scrambling along the sides of the gorge, leaping back and forth between the two walls, sometimes bounding off a boulder rising up from the floor.

A loud clatter arose as the urusais swooped over, dropping fist-sized stones into the crevice. Leia and Chewbacca opened fire from the door, blasting three of the creatures out of the air in as many seconds, and the bombardment ceased. After that, it was only a matter of firing the occasional bolt when one of the creatures swooped by to see what was happening.

A couple of minutes later, a strange croaking arose in the back of the gorge. Then the Squibs started to argue in angry voices.

"Han?" Leia started into the crevice, but Chewbacca held her back—and the firmness of his grasp made clear there was no arguing the point. "What's happening?"

Again, there was a strange croaking, and more Squib voices.

"Grees? Sligh?" Leia called. "Someone answer me!"

Chewbacca added a roar of his own, and Sligh finally came scampering back, bouncing from wall to wall, his ears flattened and his fur caked with wet sand. This time, not even a Wookiee could hold Leia back. She leapt out of the market skiff and began to slog into the sandy gorge.

"What is it?" she demanded. "What's wrong?"

"Wrong?" Sligh echoed. "Your mate's as bad as a Hutt, that's what's wrong! Are credits all he ever thinks about?"

"Credits?"

Leia stopped short, trying to puzzle out what Sligh was saying, then realized what he was telling her. If Han was arguing about money, he was alive—better than alive. He was awake; he was awake and determined not to be cheated.

Her fears of the last twenty-four hours left in a rush, leaving a void into which poured all the other emotions she had been struggling to contain—the confusion, the guilt, the anger. Like a runaway reactor core, she reached the flashpoint in a single instant of uncontrolled fusion and exploded with a speed and fury that surprised even her.

"Listen!" Leia snatched Sligh off the crevice wall and, paying no attention to the sharp fangs concealed in his cute little snout, lifted the Squib to her face. "I'll pay whatever you want! Just get my husband into that skiff! Now!"

But it was impossible to intimidate a Squib, even for Leia. Sligh simply stared back at her, then calmly reached over and began to pry her grasp open, finger by finger.

"You . . . humans . . . and . . . your . . . money!" He peeled her thumb back and dropped into the sand. "How can you think I'd take a credit? I'm insulted."

Leia scowled in confusion. "Then this isn't about—"

"Money? Only a Jawa would charge for saving a partner's life." Sligh took her hand and started into the cleft. "He's afraid we sold him out. He won't move until he sees you."

They clambered through fifty meters of sandy, boulder-choked gorge, then there Han lay, his head in Emala's lap, Grees slowly dribbling water onto his cracked lips. He looked absolutely terrible, with heat blisters all over his face and hollow cheeks and sunken, closed eyes. Leia dropped at his side.

"Han?" She took his hand and found it was as rough and hot as the cleft's stone walls. "Han, wake up."

Han opened his eyes. "Leia? Is that you?"

"Yes, Han. I'm here."

"You're sure?"

"I'm sure, Han."

"Good." He let his head drop back into Emala's lap and motioned Leia nearer. " 'Cause I gotta tell you something."

Leia leaned closer. "What?"

He pulled her down, bringing her ear close to his mouth, and whispered, *"Killik Twilight."*

"Han, don't worry about—"

"Listen! Don't tell the Squibs. It's going to . . ." His eyes closed, then opened a moment later. "It's . . ."

"Going to Anchorhead," Emala finished. She motioned the other two Squibs to take Han's feet. "Everyone knows that."

Han opened his eyes and flashed the Squib a look of horror. "They do?"

"Of course," Grees said, grabbing a foot.

Sligh grabbed the other. "Sandcrawlers always stop in Anchorhead."

THIRTEEN

The search party had rushed to Anchorhead not because it was close, though it was, and not because it had an emergency medcenter, though it did. They had come to Anchorhead because Jula Darklighter assured Leia that the Sidi Driss Inn would be as safe as anyplace on the Great Chott for Han to recover—and certainly the most comfortable. They had come, too, because the Squibs claimed that the only sure way to recover Kitster Banai and *Killik Twilight* was to intercept the Jawa sandcrawler in Anchorhead.

But the mission could wait. For the moment, Leia was enjoying a bath in one of the Sidi Driss's huge, sunken, Hutt-sized tubs. It had fixtures of burnished verdisteel and tiles hand-painted in stylized florals of cobalt blue and cinnabar red. It had blast scrubbers, pulse kneaders, and flab ticklers, and it had a rack full of snap-on nozzle attachments whose purposes Leia could only guess at. The water cost as much as Endorian port, but it came out of the nozzles steaming hot or refreshingly cool, straight or with bubbles, pure or suffused with any of a hundred different oils and unguents—plain or perfumed with the scent of any flower on Tatooine, which meant there were at least a dozen different choices.

And Leia was enjoying all this alone, while Han slept

in the next room with a hydration drip in his arm—
clean, cool, and out like a wreck. It hurt to think of all he
had gone through in his chase for Kitster and the painting, but he was safe now and recovering. Leia was thankful for that.

She was trying to sort out the rest. With the ordeal
over, she was starting to feel more grateful than frightened. Still, Han had been chasing the painting for her,
and Leia knew she had allowed her duty to interfere with
their relationship—again. Perhaps it had not been to the
same degree as during the Hapan crisis, and perhaps
Han had even been a willing participant, but she could
not have him risking his life for a government he no
longer respected. It was tantamount to using him.

The obvious solution was simply to avoid getting Han
involved in New Republic business, but Leia knew that
was about as likely as a Tatooine rainstorm. If there was
trouble within a dozen parsecs, Han Solo would find it.

Instead, Leia needed to do everything possible to protect him—just as she knew he would safeguard her in return. She was already an excellent shot with a blaster, as
well as a quick thinker and a fast talker in almost any cir-
cumstance. But, having accepted that she had experienced two visions since entering the Tatoo system, she
also realized she possessed more potential in the Force
than she had previously been willing to admit.

The trouble was, she could not shake the image of the
twin suns glaring up at her from the black well of space.
She could not forget those heartless eyes, glaring out
from beneath the black cowl, nor the face that lay behind
the dark mask.

The Force was a dangerous ally, and Leia knew she
was not ready to embrace it. Whenever she thought of
her father, she still saw Darth Vader overseeing her tor-

ture, or standing behind her as Alderaan exploded, or ordering Han frozen in carbonite. No, Leia was not yet good Jedi material, and perhaps she never would be. She was still too filled with anger . . . and also with fear, for whenever she thought of children, *their* faces belonged to Darth Vader, too.

The temperature-control jets activated and began to shoot cooling currents into the tub, a sign that Leia had been in the bath so long the water had grown as warm as the room. She turned up her hands and, seeing ten wrinkled Darwikian climbing pads where there should have been fingertips, decided she had been soaking long enough. She rose and walked up the Hutt ramp to the dryers, selected CRISP, and watched the goose pimples rise as the air blasted her dry.

Leia slipped into a robe and changed Han's hydration drip bag. She ached to lie down and curl up around him, but she was too unsettled to sleep and would only disturb him. And the deeper he rested now, the safer he and everyone else would be tomorrow. With so many Imperials around, the longer they remained in one place, the greater the chance they would be discovered and captured. She settled for kissing his unshaven cheek, then left the bedroom and closed the door behind her.

The sitting room had a complete entertainment center, but Leia was not interested. Her eyes went to the journal sitting on the table with her blaster, the portable holocomm, spare power packs, and some of the other essentials they did not dare risk leaving in the landspeeder. She had not looked at the journal since the search. There had been no time—but now, with the sitting room to herself, she could not resist.

Leia took a chair and asked the journal to play the next entry. Immediately, the image of her grandmother filled the display and began to speak—the dark, tan woman whose name Leia did not even know.

18:15:05

Still no word from the Jedi Council about what happened at the Battle of Naboo. Watto is beside himself with fury, complaining that if I can spend a hundred credits to send a message, then the Jedi can spend a hundred credits to answer. It worries me that it's taking them so long. Three days should be long enough to figure out whether you were at Naboo, and whether you're still alive.

As Leia asked for the next entry, the door buzzed for attention. She paused the journal and, leaving her grandmother's image frozen on the display, went to the entrance. The security screen showed a round-faced woman with dust-colored hair and a desert-scrubbed complexion. She was holding a tray of sliced fruit and iced friz.

Leia opened the door and stepped aside. "Dama, you're too kind. Thank you."

Dama was the proprietress of the Sidi Driss and younger sister to Luke's Aunt Beru. Jula Darklighter had assured Leia that Dama could be counted on to keep a secret—especially from Imperials, whom she hated for killing her sister and Owen Lars. From what Leia had gathered, the Sidi Driss had been just another farm on the outskirts of Anchorhead when Dama met her husband while accompanying Beru on a trip to meet Owen. They were married a few months later, and the slow transformation from a failing moisture farm to an elegant inn and watering stop had begun.

Dama slipped into the room and set the tray on the table next to the journal. "It's no trouble. I'm sure you're famished."

"Now that I'm clean, yes." Leia took a slice of pallie. "Any sign of the sandcrawler?"

"Not yet, but I'm sure it will come in tonight. There's a caravan waiting on a vaporator shipment, and it's not like Jawas to keep customers waiting."

"Did Jula and Silya leave safely?"

Dama nodded. "They disassembled the search sensors and removed the rescue signs. Even if the Imperials stop them, it'll be as if they never met you. And Jula said he'll send word to Tamora tomorrow, though I don't know how frank he'll be. If she starts running around Mos Espa looking to hire a party of rescue hunters, it won't take the Imperials long to figure out who she's looking for."

As Dama spoke, her gaze dropped to the journal and lingered there a moment, then she blushed and looked away. "I'm sorry," she said. "You must think I'm snooping."

"It's okay," Leia said. "It's hardly a council secret—just a journal Silya Darklighter asked me to give Luke."

Dama's brow rose. "Silya gave that to you?"

Leia nodded. "She said her daughter found it buried under a vaporator. I've certainly noticed enough data skips to support that."

Dama's expression grew more relaxed. "Of course. That makes sense."

Now it was Leia's turn to be confused. "How so?"

Dama studied the image a moment, then nodded.

"That's Shmi."

"Shmi?" Leia asked.

Dama looked up. "Shmi Skywalker."

Leia turned to face Dama. "You knew this woman?"

"Well, I wouldn't say *knew*. But I met her a few times, when I went with Beru to visit Owen before they were married." The memory caused Dama to blush for some reason, but she smiled and did not turn away. "I was supposed to be her chaperone, but the truth is I spent more time in Anchorhead with my own beau than at the farm."

Leia frowned. "I don't understand."

"Shmi was Owen's mother—his stepmother, really. Owen's real mother died when he was younger."

"Now I'm really confused. This woman is—was—a slave in Mos Espa." Leia paused, then asked, "She was Anakin Skywalker's mother, right?"

"That's what I was told, but I never met Anakin." Dama sat in a chair next to Leia, slipping smoothly from the role of innkeeper to new friend. "He was gone before Beru met Owen. From what I understand, it would have been better if he stayed with his mother."

"That has to be the biggest understatement I've ever heard." Leia studied the image of the slave woman. Of her grandmother, Shmi Skywalker. "Do you see a resemblance between us?"

Dama put her hand on Leia's and did not even look at the journal. "I saw it the minute Jula brought you into the lobby. Even if he hadn't told me that I needed to open the luxury wing and keep you out of sight, I think I would have seen it in your eyes."

"In my eyes? Really?" That was not the good news Dama seemed to believe. Leia poured herself a glass of friz and moistened her drying throat, then said, "I still don't understand how Shmi came to be Owen's stepmother."

"Owen's father bought Shmi from Watto."

"*Bought* her?" Leia's heart grew as heavy as fleckstone. "So Luke belonged to Owen and Beru?"

The thought occurred to her that she might have belonged to the Larses as well at one time. She began to have visions of being traded to some smuggler as an infant. It could explain how she and Luke became separated.

But Dama looked confused by her question. "Their property? Why would you think that?"

"Didn't the children of slaves belong to the masters, as well? My memory of Outer Rim law is pretty hazy, but I seem to recall that in most cases—"

"Shmi wasn't Cliegg's slave!" Dama chortled. "Where did you get that idea? He bought her freedom. He married her. This was after Anakin was freed and left to become a Jedi."

"I see." Leia thought of Shmi's struggles to find out what had happened to her son. "Did she ever see Anakin again?"

Dama shrugged and pointed at the journal. "You'll have to look in there." She placed her hands on the table and started to rise, then caught herself and stopped. "But I think my sister did meet Anakin once, after he became a Jedi and came back to rescue his mother from the Sand People."

Leia's blood went cold. "My grandmother was taken by Tusken Raiders?"

Dama's expression grew somber. "I'm afraid so."

"But Anakin—my father—came back and found her." Leia phrased this as a statement because it was what she wanted to believe. "He saved her."

Dama finished rising, then spoke in a gentle voice. "He brought her back." She laid a hand on Leia's shoulder. "I don't know whether she was still alive when Anakin found her—Beru would never say what he told them about that. But she was dead when he returned to the farm."

Leia found herself fighting to push down the lump in her throat. "What happened then?"

"They buried her, then Anakin left."

"On the moisture farm?" Leia asked. "Is that where she's buried?"

Dama nodded. "Out beyond the western edge of the sand berm. Cliegg's buried there, too. They used to stand there together and watch the twins set."

"I didn't see any headstones."

Dama shook her head. "After Luke arrived, I noticed their headstones were missing. All Beru would say about it is that Owen didn't see a need for anyone to know where Shmi was buried."

Leia was silent for a minute, trying to absorb everything she had just learned, then finally reached up and patted the hand on her shoulder.

"Thanks for taking the time to speak with me, Dama. It's late, and I know you have work."

"Not so much." Dama withdrew a datapad from her pocket and placed it on the table. The screen showed an image of the Sidi Driss's lobby. "It's linked to the security monitors—twenty different vidcams, all hidden. I gave a 'pad to Chewbacca, too. I thought you'd like to keep an eye on things."

"You're very thoughtful," Leia said. "It will take more than money to repay your kindness."

Dama waved her hands. "It's nothing. But I do need to ask one thing. It's about the Squibs."

Leia's pulse quickened. "They're not leaving, are they?" Without awaiting an answer, she stood and turned toward the door. "I thought Chewbacca was keeping an eye on them."

Dama cut Leia off at the door. "They're not going anywhere. That's actually the problem."

She looked away, obviously hesitant to bring something up.

"We'll pay for whatever they steal."

Dama shook her head. "Squibs don't steal, at least not the way you mean. It's just that they're using a lot of water. A *lot* of water—and I have a caravan watering up out on the edge of the property. I'll run dry."

"I'll have Chewbacca talk to them," Leia said. "He has a way of reasoning with Squibs."

"Thanks," Dama said. "I appreciate that—and so will the Askajians."

"Askajians?" Leia asked. "On Tatooine?"

"Refugees. They're the ones waiting for the sandcrawler—though I think their patience is at an end. They're packing up to leave tomorrow." Dama pointed at the datapad she had given Leia. "Keep that on. If the Imperials come, take the back way out. You remember what I showed you?"

Leia nodded. "The false room."

"Good." Dama opened the door and stepped into the hall. "I'll let you know if I hear they're coming, but you know how they can descend on a place. Worse than skettos."

The door closed, leaving Leia alone to reflect on what Dama had said about how Shmi had died. Well aware of the Sand People's reputation for cruelty, Leia found herself tormented by her own imagination, reacting viscerally to the very vagueness of what she had learned about the circumstances of her grandmother's death. How horrible it must have been, how frightening and lonely. Knowing that Shmi's one wish would have been to see her son again, Leia found herself hoping that Anakin had reached his mother before she died, that she had seen him just once as a Jedi. It was a strange feeling for Leia, for it forced her to see him for the first time not as Darth Vader, but as the son Shmi had loved so dearly. It sent a prickle down her spine.

Leia asked Chewbacca to deal with the Squibs, then checked on Han. Finding him sound asleep, she returned to the sitting room and replayed the previous entry. An administrator on Coruscant had finally replied to Shmi's 'Net message: Anakin was well, but the Jedi did not discuss the activities of their Padawans even with parents.

Even that was enough to elate Shmi. Leia asked for the next entry.

20:45:06

Kitster is coming over tomorrow with a vidrecording he has of the Boonta. I'm not sure I want to see it again, Annie. Watching it the first time was hard enough, and now I know that when you win . . . that I must give you to your destiny.

I remember when Watto bought his first Podracer and told you to fix it for him. You were barely nine, but you were so clever, getting it running all by yourself. Before I knew it, Watto had you test-driving it. I was so angry I threatened to plastiment his wings together and drop him in a solvent vat. And I would have, too, had anything happened to you.

12:18:07

Kitster is running late. Rarta Dal is keeping him very busy over at the Three Moons, so that holodisk he bought must be serving him well. He says he's earning enough to buy his freedom by the time he is grown. Wald is not so patient. When he finishes building his swoop, he says he's going to race his way to freedom. I hope he doesn't hurt himself—but it's wonderful to see them dreaming of such things. I think your example gives them courage.

Even your friend Amee has a plan, though she won't say what it is. I think she is still upset that I didn't keep her secret when she said she was going to marry you, so she would be part of the family when you won our free-

dom. But how could I have? That was the first I had heard of Watto's plans to have you race his Podracer.

Toydarians!

And you weren't much better. When I told you the Hutts were taking bets on which lap you would crash in, that no one believed you would finish, do you remember what you said?

"Then everybody's going to lose their money."

Leia checked the time. She knew she should arrange watches with Chewbacca and try to rest. But she also knew she was too agitated to sleep. With Han recuperating and stormtroopers scouring the desert, she was afraid the Imperials would find Banai and *Killik Twilight* first. Then there was the risk of being discovered themselves. Less populated than a single floor of their residence tower back on Coruscant, Anchorhead would make a pretty quick and easy search.

But most of all, Leia was frightened of how the journal entries were changing her perceptions, of how she was coming to view her father through Shmi's eyes as well as her own. He had been Darth Vader, cruel, brutal, and ruthless. He had stood for all Leia hated about the Empire, had *been* one of the things she hated about the Empire. And he had been Anakin Skywalker, the nine-year-old slave boy who was the center of his mother's world, who won a Podrace and inspired others to dream of freedom.

Leia was reminded of the old diplomat's paradox, that the facts often concealed the truth. She was entering into a new realm, driving out into that land of mirage and intuition where reality was never what it seemed, and the nature of an object depended on how one looked at it.

Sighing, she requested the next entry, and young Kitster Banai's smiling face appeared on the display and began to speak.

13:20:08

Hi Annie! I hope you get to see this someday. Wald and I tried to record your race off your mom's view-screen at the arena, but all we got were the voices of your mom and a few others. Then a couple of days ago, Rarta Dal gave me a vidrecording of the whole Boonta. I thought you might like it if I patched them together and saved it for you.

"*With my voice?*" Shmi asked. "*Oh, Kitster, I don't think that's a very good—*"

The display flickered, then shifted to a view of the Mos Espa Arena in its glory days, with a hundred thousand spectators sitting in the stands and a dozen and a half Podracers waiting on the track, engines roaring.

An odd voice said, "*Mesa no watch. Dissen gonna be messy!*"

The starting light flashed green, and all but two of the Podracers roared off down the track.

The reverberating voice of an announcer called, "*Wait, little Skywalker stalled!*" A moment later he added, "*Looks like Quadinaros is having engine trouble also.*"

Then Anakin's Podracer came to life and began to shoot orange flames from its engines.

"*Bloah!*" The curse was in Shmi's voice. "*It started.*"

Anakin shot after the others. After that, the image switched to a view of the front of the field, where the bru-tal nature of the sport became immediately apparent as the leader—identified by the announcer as Sebulba—pushed a competitor into a gorge wall. Another crash followed moments later, and by then Anakin was coming up fast.

By the end of the first lap, he was leading the rear pack and moving up on the leaders. He dodged through the flying debris of a wreck caused when a wrench flew out of Sebulba's Pod into the engines of a competitor. Another Podracer crashed at Dune Turn, after a band of Tusken Raiders shot out an engine.

Anakin came up behind Sebulba, and the third lap became a race only between them. Sebulba made his move in one of the canyons, repeatedly bumping Anakin's Podracer.

"Oh, that Dug!" Shmi sounded more worried than angry.

Anakin was forced onto a service ramp and launched what appeared to be hundreds of meters into the air, and it seemed certain he would crash. Instead, he did a quick control thrust and returned to the track—in the lead.

But the race was far from over. Sebulba came up hard on Anakin's tail. Then something fell off one of Anakin's engines. The engine started to smoke, Anakin lost power, and Sebulba took the lead.

"Skywalker's in trouble!" the announcer reported.

"Annie, be careful!" Shmi cried. *"Shut it down!"*

Anakin put out the fire and came up again. Sebulba resorted to old tactics and slammed into Anakin once . . . twice . . . three times . . .

"That little human being is out of his mind!" the announcer called.

The crowd gasped.

"They're side by side!"

The crowd groaned.

Anakin and Sebulba remained neck and neck, hooked together at the Pods.

The crowd returned to silence.

"They've pulled apart . . . they're coming apart . . . no, wait, Skywalker's regaining control . . . Sebulba's the one coming—"

Anakin crossed the finish line, leaving Sebulba spinning in the dust behind him, and the crowd broke into a tremendous, thundering cheer.

The image shifted scales and showed Anakin's Pod-racer coming to a skidding stop in the center of the track. He shut down his engines, climbed out of his cockpit, and was immediately greeted by Kitster and Wald. With the crowd converging around them, they took turns hugging him and slapping him on the back.

Leia paused the image and spent a long time looking at the young boy with the sparkling blue eyes, thinking how happy he looked . . . and how innocent. Had she known him then, had she never met Darth Vader, she might have agreed with Wald: She might have believed they could not be the same person.

Leia resumed viewing.

The crowd converged, and the three boys were lost in a swirling mass of humanity. The display flickered; then Shmi's face took the place of the arena, her eyes shimmering and wet.

I was so proud of you, Annie—I am so proud of you. And I am also happy that now you are safe at the Jedi Temple . . . where I hope you aren't doing such dangerous things!

Han's groggy voice sounded through the door, calling for Leia. She stopped the diary and rushed into the bedroom. He was propped up on his elbows, looking around the darkened room with an expression as pained as it was confused.

Leia went to the bed and took his hand. "How are you feeling?"

He squinted up at her for a moment, then finally flashed a cracked-lip smile. "Thirsty."

"I'll get you something to drink."

Han nodded eagerly. "Make it two. Gizers."

"I don't think so."

Leia fetched a glass and two canisters of bactade from the other room. She was glad to see Han awake, but she expected to see him more fully recovered after three bags of rehydration solution. He still looked weak. Dehydration could cause organ damage. If he wasn't better by morning, she would risk a visit to the medcenter. The Darklighters had warned her that most of the staff were city-beings who probably could not keep a secret while looking down the barrel of an Imperial blaster, but Leia would rather shoot a few stormtroopers than stand idly by while Han slipped away.

She returned to find him sleeping again. She changed the bag on his hydration drip, then checked his vital signs on the portable monitor and kissed his cracked lips. It was like kissing a Barabel.

She returned to the sitting room couch and picked up her grandmother's journal. For a moment, it refused to play again, but at last, after flipping through a few unintelligible data skips, it began.

15:36:09

I hope you will forgive some of the things I said on Kitster's recording. I truly wanted you to win—but even more, I wanted you to survive. You know how those races always frightened me.

I can't tell you how I struggled with the decision to let you race for Qui-Gon that day. When you noticed his lightsaber, you were so convinced he had come to free the slaves . . . it crushed me to hear him tell you the truth. But as Qui-Gon himself said, you give without thinking of yourself. How could I say no when you hatched your plan to win the parts they needed to repair their ship?

A slave boy helping a Jedi. To me, it seemed matters should have been the other way around. I would have said no, and I know you would have forgiven me. But you wouldn't have forgotten, either. For the rest of your life, you would have remembered the Boonta Eve and how your mother wouldn't let you help a Jedi. And that wouldn't have been fair to you. I couldn't deny you the chance to be the hero you dreamed of.

Leia continued to play the journal, listening to Shmi recount how well Kitster and Anakin's other friends were doing, and what kind of mood her master Watto was in that day. At times, she seemed genuinely concerned about the Toydarian, for he had begun to suffer bouts of melancholy. Shmi seemed to believe that Watto genuinely missed the boy. Leia had trouble accepting this, but was forced to at least allow for the possibility when Shmi reported that Watto had actually made a gift to her of the ten credits she had borrowed to help pay for her message to the Jedi Council.

Leia was finally starting to grow tired when Han's voice sounded from the bedchamber.

"Leia? Are you still up?"

"Yes, Han." Leia hit the STOP key and tucked the journal into her pocket. "Are you ready for those drinks now?"

"Are they Gizers?"

"Can you sit up?"

"Maybe you ought to come see."

Leia went into the room and found Han lying flat on his back. His hands were folded behind his head and he was smiling at her crookedly. And he seemed to know where he was.

"Come here," he said. "And take this drip out of my arm."

Leia went over to the side of the bed. "You're sure?"

Han grabbed her around the waist, then pulled her down on top of him and kissed her, very long and very deep.

"Yeah, I'm sure." He ran his hands under her robe, and the room suddenly grew warm. "It's gonna get in the way."

FOURTEEN

Han woke smothering in the perfumed silkiness of Leia's long hair, her soft skin warming his side and her breath tickling his ear. Sometime during the night, she had managed to reattach his hydration drip and return to bed without disturbing him, and now even his lips no longer felt dry. The room was comfortably cool, the sky window above the bed was blushing with the pink light of first sunrise, and everything was right with the world.

Except, perhaps, that muffled sound coming from the suite's sitting room. It had the familiar drone of an electronically filtered voice and the sharp rhythm of someone giving orders. Of a squad leader assigning tasks to his stormtroopers. Alarm bringing him instantly to full wakefulness, Han looked to the side table and found his blaster resting next to Leia's.

The electronic voice barked a command.

Han did not bother to detach himself from the hydration drip, or even to wake Leia. He simply tossed her blaster over the far side of the bed, then snatched his own weapon and rolled after it, grabbing her on the way. A burning line of pain shot up his arm as the hydration catheter tore free, then he landed on the floor, bringing Leia down on top of him.

Her eyelids rose half open, and their gazes met instantly. "Han?" She smiled dreamily. "My, you *are* feeling better."

"Sorry, not in front of company." He snatched her blaster off the floor and pressed it into her hand. "You know I'm not that kind of guy."

Leia's eyes opened wide. "Company?"

"Listen."

They fell quiet and listened to the muffled voices coming from the next room. It was too faint to understand words, but the stormtrooper drone was unmistakable. Leia pushed herself off him and started for the bedroom's oversized door.

Han sat up. "Hey! Don't go out—"

Leia stepped through the door.

Han sprang across the bed after her. "At least put on some clothes!"

When he peered into the sitting room, he found no stormtroopers anywhere. Leia was standing at the table, staring down at the datapad from which the electronic voices were coming.

"Dama lent this to me so we could keep an eye on the lobby," Leia said, picking up the borrowed datapad.

With a blaster in one hand and her brown eyes fixed on the datapad in the other, her long hair falling in a silky cascade over her shoulders, she seemed more breathtakingly beautiful than ever. Han knew he had to be the luckiest ex-smuggler in the galaxy; if they could just get past her fear of having children, he was pretty sure that when his time came, he would leave this universe with every wish he ever had fulfilled.

Leia looked up from the datapad and frowned. "Han, why are you just standing there?"

Han shrugged. "Too much sun, I guess."

"Well, you're bleeding all over Dama's floor." Leia

nodded at his arm, which was oozing blood from the rip where he had torn out the catheter. "Get a towel or something and come over here."

Han snatched a small towel off the bar and joined her at the table. The image on the datapad showed a squad of stormtroopers standing in the ornate lobby of the Sidi Driss, the leader's chest pressed against the counter as he addressed a Pa'lowick so frightened her thin limbs and long proboscis were quivering.

"I can't bring up those records," she was saying. "I'm only the night clerk. I don't have the password to check the day records."

The squad leader grabbed her proboscis and pulled her half over the counter, then pressed the nozzle of his blaster rifle against the lips at the end.

"But you can find someone who knows it."

"Yefffth," she said.

"Then do it." The leader released the Pa'lowick's trunk, freeing her to stumble back against the door behind the counter. He pointed to two of his troopers. "Accompany her."

"What do you think?" Leia asked. "Are we in for a fight?"

"I don't know." Han started toward the bedchamber. "But it wouldn't hurt to put our clothes on. If we have to leave in a hurry, the last thing I want is an all-over Tatooine tan."

"I think we're in for a fight." Leia followed, her gaze still fixed on the borrowed datapad. "It wouldn't hurt to make sure Chewie and the Squibs are awake."

"Better stay off the comlinks in case the Imps have a signal tracer in the air," Han said. "Which wall is Chewie's?"

Leia pointed, then dropped the datapad on the bed where they could both see it as they dressed. Han banged on the wall with his blaster, using a two-short, two-long sequence that had meant trouble nearly as long as he and Chewbacca had been flying together. Then, keeping his eye on the datapad, he reached for his trousers.

Once the night clerk and her escort were gone, a stormtrooper came over to the squad leader.

"You didn't have to be so brutal, Sergeant," the trooper said. "She was already going to cooperate."

"Sorry, sir." Even through the electronic filtering, the squad leader sounded anything but apologetic. "I thought brutal was the new style."

"*Efficient* is the new style, Sergeant." The officer's armor betrayed no outward sign of his rank. "And brutalizing citizens who don't need it is most definitely not efficient."

"Yes, sir," the sergeant said. "I didn't want to let them slip away."

"Yes, of course."

The officer brought his assault rifle up and calmly smashed the butt into the sergeant's helmet, knocking him to the floor. With the other stormtroopers looking on from behind their faceless helmets, the officer pointed his blaster rifle at his fallen subordinate.

"Tell me, Sergeant, do you feel like doing me any favors now?" the officer asked. "And be honest. That is an order."

There was a moment's silence, then the sergeant said, "No sir, I don't."

"Now tell me why you believe a brutalized citizen will do anything for us but the minimum required to survive?"

"I don't know, sir," the sergeant said. "She won't, I guess."

"Congratulations, Sergeant. You get to live." The officer pointed his weapon away from the squad leader.

"When the next citizen arrives, what interrogation style will you use?"

"Efficient, sir."

"Good." The officer motioned two subordinates to help the sergeant to his feet. "And you understand why it is so important for us to find these Rebels and their painting?"

"Because the admiral wishes to add it to his collection," the sergeant said.

Han, who had grown so absorbed with the lesson that he had nearly forgotten that the Imperials were in the same hotel, could almost see the officer's eyes rolling behind his helmet's lenses.

"What about the Rebels? Why is it important that we capture them?"

An eager recruit stepped forward. "Sir, because the admiral says it is. That is all we need to know, sir."

The officer did not turn toward the recruit. "Sergeant, you will control your squad."

"Yes, sir."

The sergeant leveled his blaster rifle at the offender, then thought better of shooting the man and glanced at the officer. When the officer shook his head, the sergeant settled for bringing the butt of his rifle up under the recruit's chin.

Han knew by the way the trooper's body went limp that he had been knocked unconscious.

"Whoever this new admiral is, he's teaching old rancors new tricks." Han's gaze remained glued to the datapad. "That officer isn't following Imperial doctrine."

"No, he isn't. But unless you want him teaching *us* new tricks, you'd better finish getting dressed." Leia motioned at the tunic hanging forgotten in Han's hands. "I have a feeling this squad isn't going to settle for a look at Dama's registration records."

Han slipped the tunic over his head, then rapped on Chewie's wall again. This time, he was answered by the acknowledging thuds of a Wookiee fist. The officer continued his exercise.

"Sergeant, do you need me to repeat the question?"

"No, sir. It's important to capture these Rebels because they are New Republic scum."

The officer remained expectantly silent.

"Because they were prepared to destroy the painting rather than let us have it," the sergeant continued. "Because they were wearing elaborate disguises at the auction, and the admiral wishes to know who they really are."

"Excellent, Sergeant." The officer stepped back to join the other troopers. "Handle this well, and I may promote you to platoon leader."

The sergeant's posture grew instantly more upright.

"I don't like that officer," Leia said. She was already dressed and strapping on her blaster holster. "He's good."

"Yeah," Han said. "And he's still using us for training exercises. I hate that."

The Pa'lowick and her escort of stormtroopers returned with a sleepy-looking woman whom Han remembered vaguely from when Chewbacca carried him into the Sidi Driss. She had a round face and dust-colored hair with eyes he could see glinting defiance even in the datapad's tiny screen.

The woman went to the counter and glared directly at the squad leader. "I'm Dama Brunk, owner of the Sidi Driss. If it's rooms you're looking for, you'll have to go down to the SandRest. We're booked solid."

The squad leader ignored Dama and turned his helmet lenses on the Pa'lowick. She quickly stepped behind Dama and began to quiver again.

"First," the squad leader said, "I apologize for the treatment your assistant received at the hands of my predecessor. Such brutality is not proper Imperial procedure."

The Pa'lowick's proboscis curled upward in surprise.

Dama narrowed her gaze and demanded, "Since when?"

"It's a recent directive." The squad leader continued to look at the Pa'lowick. "As you can see, he's been relieved of command and, I assure you, he will be punished when we return to our ship."

"Who do you think you're fooling?" the Pa'lowick demanded. "I know who pulled my nose."

"You're mistaken. The man who handled your nose has been punished and demoted," the stormtrooper lied in his electronic voice. He pulled the orange pauldron off his armor and snapped it onto the armor of the man next to him, then took it back. "I'm his replacement. We have codes of conduct and chains of command, and when they are not followed, action is swift."

"Sure it is," Dama said. "You wanted something?"

"A few answers. We're looking for some Rebels—"

"None here."

"I'm sure you believe that," the squad leader said. "But they wouldn't be wearing uniforms. We're looking for a man and woman, human, with a Wookiee and possibly a protocol droid—"

"I didn't register anyone like that." Dama turned to the Pa'lowick. "You, Keesa?"

Keesa shook her head.

Dama looked back to the Imperial. "Anything else?"

"How about Squibs?"

Dama shook her head. "None of them, either."

"You're certain?" the squad leader asked. "Because we heard three of them were seen in your lobby. They might have arrived on a three-seated swoop."

Dama's bearing grew tense. "Where'd you hear that?"

"Then it's true?" the squad leader asked.

Dama remained silent, obviously debating how to answer.

"We've got trouble," Han said.

The door buzzer sounded and Leia, who was already hanging water packs on her utility belt, went into the sitting room and admitted Chewbacca and C-3PO.

"What about the Squibs?" Han asked.

Chewbacca growled that they were at the end of the hall, finally asleep after a long night of water play.

"We'll collect them on the way out." Leia was furiously loading the portable holocomm and other equipment into a utility satchel.

On the datapad, Dama collected her wits and pretended to consult the inn's registry. "No Squibs," she said. "But we've got Ranats. Maybe someone was mistaken."

"Maybe," the squad leader said. "But you won't mind waking them, will you? We'll only disturb them for a minute—providing, of course, that *you're* not the one who was mistaken."

"Of course. We'll show you the way." As Dama turned to step out from behind the counter, she cast a quick glance into the hidden security cam and mouthed the word "go," then started down the corridor. "They're in the east wing."

"That's at the opposite end of the inn." Leia pulled her sand cloak over her head and threw Han's to him. "She's trying to buy us time."

"And not doing very well," Han said, now carrying the borrowed datapad along as he stuffed the last of his possessions into a utility satchel. "The Imps aren't buying it."

The display screen showed only two stormtroopers following Dama and Keesa toward the east wing.

Dama stopped and turned toward the squad leader. "Aren't you coming?"

"We want to disturb your inn as little as possible," he said. "Two of my troopers will be enough to determine whether your guests are Squibs or Ranats. The rest of us will wait here with Keesa."

Keesa's proboscis began to quiver again.

Dama glared at the stormtrooper, but could only nod. "As you wish." She squeezed Keesa's shoulder. "It'll be all right."

But, of course, it was not. No sooner was Dama gone than the squad leader turned to the Pa'lowick.

"You like your employer, I can see that."

Keesa nodded uncertainly.

"Then you don't want to see her hurt."

Keesa shook her head.

"And only you can prevent that," the squad leader said. "We know she's lying."

Keesa's eyes grew wide. "She is?"

The squad leader nodded. "Where are the Squibs?" he asked. "Where are the humans and their Wookiee?"

"I don't know."

"Don't lie!" the squad leader snapped. "Lie, and I'll—"

"Sergeant!"

The squad leader stopped and turned to face the trooper who had barked at him. "Yes?"

"Perhaps she really doesn't know," the trooper—the officer, Han assumed—suggested. "Does that prevent her from helping us?"

"I see your point, sir." The squad leader turned back to Keesa. "Very well, you are—"

"You *don't* see, Sergeant." The officer stepped forward and fixed his lenses on Keesa.

Han and Leia were already following Chewbacca and

C-3PO down a dimly lit corridor toward the Squibs' room.

"If you were trying to hide a party of several beings in this hotel, where would you put them?" the officer asked. "Answer honestly, and I promise no harm will come to you or your employer."

Keesa pointed down a corridor opposite the way Dama had gone. "The Hutts' luxury wing. There's hardly ever anybody in it, since Jabba and Gardulla stopped meeting here."

Han glanced over the darkened corridor down which they were walking. It was large and round, the way Hutts liked them, with glide ramps instead of steps where the hall changed elevations.

"Get ready," Han said. "We've got company coming."

But instead of sending the squad rushing off in the direction the Pa'lowick had pointed, the officer turned to the squad leader.

"Sergeant, summon B-squad back to reinforce us and send two men with Keesa to cover the secret exit. As long as she shows them to the proper exit, she is free to go once the Rebels reveal themselves."

"Yes, sir." The squad leader assigned two troopers to go with the quivering Pa'lowick and commed the other squad, then asked, "If I may, sir?"

"You have a question." The officer armed his weapon, and the rest of the squad followed his lead. "Proceed. Questions are good."

"Are you sure there's a secret exit?"

"With Hutts, there's *always* a secret exit." The officer waved the rest of the squad down the corridor, but held the leader back long enough to add, "And, Sergeant, *questions* are good. Doubts are not. If you expect to survive in my command, you *will* keep the difference in mind."

The squad leader snapped to attention. "Yes, sir."

The officer waved him forward and followed down the corridor at a run.

Han came up behind Leia at the door to the Squibs' room. "Sweetheart?"

Leia pressed her finger to the door buzzer and did not let it up. "Yes, dear?"

"You weren't planning on slipping out a secret exit, were you?"

Leia half turned and gave him a tight little smile. "Married less than a year, and you already know me so well."

Chewbacca groaned a warning about being sick.

"Then you'd better do it now," Han retorted, "because I don't think you're going to have a chance later."

He told them about the stormtroopers Keesa was leading around to cover their escape route, then activated a surveillance lock on the officer. The datapad would now show the Imperial wherever he went. If it came down to a fight—and that seemed likely—Han wanted to know where that officer was at all times.

Leia tapped the door buzzer, as though that would make the Squibs respond faster.

Han brought up a schematic of the building. The luxury wing was a four-room annex in the rear of the Sidi Driss, separated from the rest of the inn by a locked security door. The officer was already passing the first of two intersections before the main corridor dead-ended at the security door.

"What's taking those Squibs so long?" Leia complained.

"Whatever it is," Han said, "we either have to leave them or find another way to wake 'em."

"We can't leave them," Leia said. "They know too much."

Chewbacca extended his climbing claws and ripped the control panel off the wall, setting off an alarm buzzer in the room. He sorted through the tangle of wires, then quickly found the ones he needed, stripped all three by running them between his fangs, and crossed the bared lines.

The oversized door slid open to reveal Emala filling water bottles at the bar sink. Sligh and Grees were struggling to stuff more bottles into a trio of tattered backpacks larger than they were.

"Humans don't know the meaning of privacy?" Sligh asked.

"Sorry to interrupt your stealing," Leia shot back. "But we've got Imperials coming."

"Imperials?" Sligh hoisted his pack onto his back and—amazingly—managed to remain standing beneath the weight. "Why didn't you say so?"

Han checked the borrowed datapad and found the stormtroopers at the wing security door, the squad leader wiring a slicer box into the control panel.

Leia peered over his shoulder. "Trapped again," she observed. "How do you want to handle it?"

Han glanced around the ornate corridor. He found a repulsor couch hovering in front of a decorative panel that depicted a watery oasis he was sure existed nowhere on Tatooine.

"The secret exit behind there?"

Leia shook her head and pointed to the door across from the Squibs' room. "Through there. It's not a real room. Maybe we can pull a Smuggler's Fade?"

Han shook his head. "This officer's too good for that." He pointed back toward their door and the one opposite. "We'd better hit them with a crossfire ambush. Everyone into those rooms."

As the Squibs lumbered past, Han plucked a jug of water out of Sligh's pack.

"Hey! You're unbalancing—"

"It's not too late to bait our trap," Han warned.

When Sligh fell silent, Han tossed the water jug under the repulsor couch, then followed Leia and Sligh into the first suite. Chewbacca took C-3PO and the other two Squibs into the room opposite, and they were barely inside before the security doors opened. Han watched on the datapad as the officer and squad leader cross-stitched cautionary blasterfire through the doorway. The two subordinates charged down the corridor with their weapons at the ready, then stopped at the end, one turning around to cover up the corridor while the other peered through the still-open door of the Squibs' suite.

"Clear!" this one reported. He glanced around the corridor, then kneeled down in front of the repulsor couch and withdrew the water jug Han had thrown under there. "It looks like they've used the escape door."

"You're quite certain?" The officer was careful to remain hidden behind the security door bulkhead. "You're willing to wager your life on that?"

"Sir, yes I am."

"Then you are a waste of stormtrooper armor," the officer said. "Remove it so the Rebels won't damage valuable Imperial resources killing you."

"Sir?"

"That *is* an order, trooper." The officer looked across the doorway to his squad leader. "Summon the owner's escorts. We'll need them to flush the scum out."

"Hutt slime!" Han turned to his companions. "We have to take 'em now. Sligh, you hit the floor and fire down the corridor. Leia?"

"Yes?"

"You stay back and be the surprise reserve—"

"Han?"

"Yeah?"

"Not a chance."

Han sighed. "Okay, you and I fire across the corridor at the officer. Chewie takes the sergeant, and Grees and Emala help Sligh."

"Sounds good," Leia said.

"No way!" Sligh objected. "How come the Squibs have to drop on the floor?"

"Because you're closer," Leia said.

"And I've seen you shoot," Han said. "You couldn't hit the officer."

"Okay, no need to get nasty," Sligh said, slipping out of his heavy pack. "Just asking."

Han shook his head, then turned to Leia. "One more thing."

"I know." She rose on her toes and kissed him hard and long. It was almost enough to make him forget what they were doing, especially when she finally stopped. "You love me."

"Yeah, that, too." Han flashed her a scoundrel's grin. "But what I really wanted to ask is did you remember to recharge my blaster?"

Leia's eyes started to flash, then she caught Han's expression and got a pinched little smile.

"What do you think?" She propped a hand on her hip. "Can we get on with it?"

"Just trying to give that stormtrooper time to get out of his armor."

Han angled the datapad so that she and Sligh could see that the stormtrooper was obeying his officer's command— even if he was starting with his shin protection. Then, keeping one eye on the datapad, Han activated his comlink and gave the others across the hall their instructions.

"And what am I to do, Captain Solo?" C-3PO asked.

"Don't get left behind."

The officer cocked his head as though listening to a voice inside his helmet, then glanced toward the Solo suite. Though Han had expected the Imperials to be listening for comlink transmissions, he had not thought they would be so quick to pinpoint the source. The *Chimaera*'s crew was fast starting to look like one of the Empire's best.

Han dropped the datapad in the pocket of his sand cloak, then simultaneously commed Chewbacca and depressed the OPEN button. "Go!"

The door hissed, and Han and Leia began to pour blasterfire out through the widening gap. Several bolts ricocheted off the officer's helmet and breastplate, forcing him to roll into a corner behind the security door bulkhead.

Chewbacca's bowcaster chuffed once from the door opposite. A loud clatter sounded from the direction he had been firing. The acrid fumes of scorched plastoid began to fill the air, and the squad leader's kicking boots slid into view on the other side of the security door.

Suddenly, the corridor was quiet. Han looked down to find Sligh lying between his feet, no longer firing.

"I thought I told you—"

"Both dead," Sligh said, rising. "I guess our aim isn't that—"

"Han!"

Leia jerked him out of the doorway a few milliseconds ahead of a line of blaster bolts.

"Be careful, will you?"

Sligh dropped to his belly and wiggled back into the room, the fur on his back smoking from a near miss. Han tried to return fire and nearly lost his hand as the blaster bolts continued to pour through the door. He felt a hand on his hip, then glanced back to see Leia pulling the datapad from his cloak pocket.

"It's only the officer," Leia said. "He's out there alone."

Han peered at the display over her shoulder and saw the stormtrooper lying on the floor at the corner of the security door, arms crossed with a blaster rifle in one hand and blaster pistol in the other, keeping up a constant barrage of fire.

"So much for lower training standards and sagging morale," Leia said.

"Yeah, you'd think the Emperor had come back to life or something."

Leia winced. "Han, I wish you wouldn't say things like that." She slipped the datapad into her cloak pocket. "I wish you wouldn't even think them."

She grabbed Sligh's pack and dragged it over.

Sligh was instantly at her side. "You'd steal my water?"

"*My* water—I'm the one paying for it." Leia traded the straps with Han for his blaster. "You know what to do."

"Yeah." He lifted the pack and, surprised by how heavy it was, braced himself to throw. "Be ready."

"For what?" Sligh stepped toward the pack. "Wait!"

Han hit the Squib on the backswing and sent him tumbling across the suite, then whipped the pack around and launched it through the door.

Even one-handed, the officer was a good shot with a blaster rifle. No sooner had the black shape started flying toward him than he began to pour fire into it, melting the plastoid bottles and instantly superheating several dozen liters of water. Billowing vapor filled the corridor. Leia rushed past Han, pressing his blaster back into his hand, dancing into the steam and raising her pistol toward the officer's position. Han followed and saw a golden-brown blur launch itself from the opposite doorway, leaping toward a hazy white shape scrambling across the corridor, toward the control panel on the other side of the security door.

"Hold on!"

Han reached over Leia's shoulder, pushing her weapon arm down just as the brown blur flew past. A tremendous *thunk* sounded from the side of the corridor, followed by the clatter of plastoid armor sliding down the wall and the scrape of weapons being kicked away across the floor. Chewbacca roared in triumph, one hand holding what appeared to be the officer's head. Then he rowled in astonishment and fell backward, arms flying up to launch the head into Han's chest.

Han caught the thing in both hands and heard a tinny voice coming from the helmet speaker. "Sir? Sir, are you there?"

Leia filled the corridor with blasterfire again, and Han looked up to see a blurry black oval bouncing back and forth in the steam, growing rapidly smaller as the hazy white armor beneath it dodged down the corridor. Han dropped the helmet—the *empty* helmet—and added his own fire.

The officer dived for cover and vanished from sight, apparently around the corner of an intersection.

"Chewie, you okay?"

Chewbacca growled and started to clamber up.

A pair of indistinct red eyes appeared ahead, glowing through the dissipating steam from where the officer had escaped. Han locked gazes with the eyes and raised his blaster to fire, but Chewbacca rose and blocked his shot. By the time he could step around the Wookiee, the eyes were gone.

"Did you see that?" Han asked. "Red eyes?"

"Yes," Leia said. "The Empire using aliens? They must be getting desperate."

Or maybe just smart, Chewbacca suggested.

C-3PO came out of Chewbacca's suite, Grees and Emala close behind him. They were not quite staggering under the weight of their packs, but both were hunched far forward.

Han took one look and said, "You'll never keep up."

"Is that *your* problem?" Grees demanded.

"You'll be happy later that someone has water to sell," Emala added.

Sligh clattered up, loaded down with blaster rifles and utility belts stripped off dead Imperials.

Han shook his head and started down the corridor. "If they fall behind, Chewie, shoot 'em."

Sligh stopped to retrieve the squad leader's rifle and utility belt, and the weapons left by the officer.

Noisy as they were, the Squibs did keep up, and a minute later the group was sneaking out the side door of the Sidi Driss. Leia pointed toward the entrance of what had been a subterranean workshop when the Sidi Driss had still been a moisture farm.

"That's the garage."

"Doesn't look like they have anyone watching it yet." Han started across the dusty ground toward it. "If we hurry, we can be out of there—"

"You must be sunsick!" Grees huffed up, both hands hanging onto his pack straps. "The Imperials see a landspeeder or swoop leaving this town, there'll be an assault shuttle on it faster than a farm boy on a womp rat."

"You have a better idea?" Han asked.

"That would be hard?" Grees twitched his snout and pointed out toward the watering corral on the perimeter of Sidi Driss land, where the humped silhouettes of several dozen dewbacks were arranging themselves into a caravan line. "The idea is to *disappear* into the landscape."

Leia came to Han's side and took his hand. "Han?"

"Yeah?"

"That's a better idea."

FIFTEEN

The Askajians had paid a fortune for the right to water at the Sidi Driss, and they would not be hurried, not by Grees's threats or Sligh's pleas or Emala's promises, not even by the prospect of a battle erupting in the midst of their caravan, and Leia thought that was probably a good thing. For now, the surviving squad and a half of Imperials was too busy searching hangars and disabling landspeeders to worry about plodding dewbacks, but that would certainly change should the caravan show any sign of haste. For now, it was better to allow every beast its fill at the watering basin, to give each Askajian driver all the time he—or she—needed to gulp down that last liter or two from the spigot.

"P-P-Princess Leia!" C-3PO sputtered. He was strapped in a smuggler's sling beneath the dewback that would serve as Leia's mount, concealed from the side by low-hanging saddle blankets and lying far enough forward that his head dipped in the basin whenever the huge lizard lowered its scaly head to drink. "If this continues, my circuits will short!"

"Even without power?" Leia asked. She was standing beside the dewback, holding its reins.

"No, b-but corrosion is always—oh . . ."

Leia waited until the dewback raised its head, then

reached underneath its chest and flipped the primary circuit breaker on the back of C-3PO's neck. He emitted a wet pop and fell silent. As refugees from a desert world long under Imperial domination, the Askajians had been quick to strike a bargain with the Squibs to help the group track down the Jawa sandcrawler, which was now alarmingly overdue. But they had also made clear they would abide no disruptions to their business.

Leia only wished the Squibs were as easy to silence as C-3PO. All three were hanging beneath the adjacent dewback, strapped in a smuggler's sling and hidden from view like C-3PO. Despite this, they were chattering incessantly to the caravan leader, a round mountain of an Askajian who stood on the opposite side of the basin directing the final watering.

". . . give you a better price for tomuon wool than any Jawa," Grees was saying. The Squibs had been trying to strike a bargain ever since they had discovered what the caravan was carrying. Tomuon wool was prized across the galaxy for its sheen and comfort, and when this tribe of Askajians had fled their home, they had possessed the foresight to resettle on a desert world where their stock could thrive. "And *we'd* never tell the Imperials where to find your village."

"Neither would the Jawas," the leader, Borno, said. With his epidermal sacs gorged with water, Borno resembled an immensely corpulent human with a bluish pallor and heavy brow folds. "They don't know where it is. No one does. We like it that way."

"Very wise," Sligh said. "We can see you're a shrewd being who appreciates the value of a credit—which *we* can get you. Imperial or New Republic."

"We don't need credits." As Borno spoke, he was careful not to look toward the dewback. Even with only a dozen stormtroopers to search all of Anchorhead, there always seemed to be one set of electrobinoculars turned their way. "We need our vaporators. They're on the Jawa sandcrawler."

"Our credits are better than Jawa vaporators," Emala said. "With our credits, you can buy vaporators—vaporators that won't break down."

"*All* vaporators break down," Borno said. "If you knew anything about vaporators, you'd know that."

"You've never owned a Tusede Thirteen," Sligh said quickly. "Someone like you would really appreciate the quality. Self-cleaning condenser filters, redundant sensors, magno-shielded intake vents, everything a shrewd buyer like you would want."

"That so?" Despite the query, Borno looked unconvinced. "Then I guess there wouldn't be any need to find out why the Jawas are so late in their sandcrawler. That would be a real bonus."

The Squibs fell abruptly silent. Valuable as tomuon wool was, it was worth only a fraction of what they stood to earn by recovering *Killik Twilight*.

Finally, Sligh said, "You're too smart for us, Borno. We'd better stick to the plan."

"As long as you can really locate the sandcrawler," Grees added. "If the Imperials find it first, you can forget about your vaporators."

"Yes, so you have told me," Borno said. "Besides, we already have a Tusede Thirteen. Those extra features are just more things to go wrong."

The Squibs' dewback stopped drinking, and Borno motioned it away. The driver led it over to the caravan column, being careful to keep himself between the beast and the Imperials watching from Anchorhead. Hanging in their smuggler's harness behind the long saddle blanket, the Squibs were well concealed, but it always paid to be careful when there were stormtroopers about.

Han was the next to lead his beast forward. Like Leia, he carried a long Askajian herding spear and wore a huge sand cloak over thick pads of musky-smelling tomuon wool tied to his stomach, back, and shoulders. He still seemed skinny for an Askajian herder, but too large and round to be one of the humans the Imperials were seeking. The disguise would probably work, as long as the stormtroopers remained at a distance and the morning light did not grow too revealing.

Leia was less confident of Han's ability to wear it. The battle at the inn had left his face pale and drawn, and she could tell by the weight of her own disguise that the extra padding would take a toll on his strength. Were it not for the Imperial threat—and the fact that the Squibs would pursue *Killik Twilight* alone—she would have insisted on taking shelter at the Darklighters' farm for another day or two.

Chewbacca was strapped beneath Han's mount, his big shoulders squeezed tight between the dewback's front legs. Though his head also sank into the water as the beast lowered its mouth to drink, he accepted the dunking with remarkably good grace—perhaps because he could sense how uncomfortable Han and Leia were in their disguises.

"I'm sure that alien officer called the rest of his company," Han said to Leia. "If we're still here when they come, it'll take more than a hundred Askajians to keep them from searching the caravan. You're *sure* this is a better idea?"

"Honestly, I don't know." Leia watched as their landspeeder emerged from the vehicle storage room of the Sidi Driss, its finish flushing pink in the morning light. Behind it came a pair of stormtroopers walking the Squibs' swoop. "But had we left town in our landspeeder, how long do you think it would have taken the officer to call in a flight of TIEs?"

"Not long." Han glanced at his mount's long tongue lapping water out of the basin, then whispered, "They've figured us out, Leia. They must have."

Leia nodded. "I think so." Her stomach knotted with worry—not for herself, but for Han and Chewbacca. "I never imagined recovering the painting would lead to so much trouble. I feel terrible about the way I dragged you and Chewie into this."

"Yeah, like I'd rather be home wondering what's happened to you." Han looked at her from beneath his sand hood. His eyes were sunken and hollow. "Besides, you *know* I'm the only one who can get you out of this mess."

"Really?" Leia folded her arms across her wool-padded chest. "And you're certain I need someone to rescue me right now?"

Han waved a hand toward the Sidi Driss. "Yeah."

"You seem to have forgotten why we were there in the first place." Leia spoke in a deliberately even voice. "*I'm* not the last one who needed rescuing."

Leia's mount finished drinking, and Borno signaled her to leave. She led the beast away from the basin, freeing the spot for the last dewback in line, and went over to join the caravan column. Several Askajians were careful to remain between her and the town, filling water jugs at the clean-water spigot or walking a few steps alongside, chattering merrily in their own language. She was grateful for their caution. C-3PO's metallic finish had been smeared with a mixture of dewback saliva and dung ash as a safeguard against a saddle blanket being inadvertently drawn aside, but it never hurt to be cautious.

The caravan was forming a tight defensive column, three animals abreast with the rider in the middle leading one cargo beast to each side. Leia walked her mount into the center position at the end of the line. Two Askajians helped her into the saddle, then taught her to stop her mount by hauling upward on the reins and to turn it by tapping its head with her herding spear. Once she confirmed her understanding, they brought two cargo beasts to flank her and secured the fibrasteel reins to a pair of saddle rings behind her legs.

"Your mount should stay ahead of the pack beasts," one of the Askajians advised. "But if you feel a rein pressing the back of a leg, strike the pack animal across the nose. That will slow it."

"What if I want it to go faster?"

This drew a deep Askajian laugh. "You won't."

A few minutes later, with Han and the last Askajian in line behind Leia, Borno opened the flush valve to send the unused water back to the recyclers, then lowered the basin's sand cover and joined the rest of the caravan.

A light hoverscout emerged from Anchorhead, one stormtrooper standing in back at the speeder's blaster cannon. Two more Imperials were visible through the front windows. The one in the passenger's seat wore the blaster-scorched shoulder pauldron of a squad leader.

Borno stopped near Leia and Han and pretended to check the cargo straps on the dewbacks they would be leading. "Do the same as everyone else," he said quietly. "I'm sorry, but if they realize we're hiding you, the deal is off. This caravan is too important to my people to risk it in a firefight."

"We understand, Borno," Leia said. "And we're sorry for putting you in any danger at all."

"A caravan is always in danger," Borno replied. "And you have nothing to be sorry about. On Askaj, we had a saying: those who wish to rid themselves of fleegs must clean the hair of their neighbors."

"A wise saying." Leia's scalp began to itch beneath the sand hood.

"And one that applies double to Imperial fleegs," Borno replied. "We will do what we can to keep our part of the bargain."

Borno departed.

Behind Leia, Han asked softly, "What's *our* part of the bargain?"

"Who knows?" Leia glanced over her shoulder, more to make certain he was holding up than to make herself heard. "All I could get out of Emala was that Sligh made an excellent deal, and not to worry. They always have our interests at heart."

Han winced. "I hate it when they say that."

As the hoverscout angled toward the caravan, Borno barked a command and pulled a repeating blaster from beneath his sand cloak. The rest of the Askajians followed his lead, exchanging their herding spears for an astonishing array of weaponry ranging from sniper rifles to power blasters more than capable of piercing an infantry vehicle's armor. Leia removed her blaster from its holster and propped her elbow on her hip, so that the weapon would be in plain sight. Though Askajians were a peace-loving people, the Imperials had obviously taught them the value of intimidation.

The stormtrooper gunner started to swing the blaster cannon around, but the squad leader quickly waved him off. The hoverscout pilot closed to within twenty meters of the caravan and flew slowly alongside. The gunner kept his helmet lenses fixed on the cargo line, while the squad leader studied the riders in the center. They passed Borno without incident and rounded the front of the column, then came slowly down the other side.

When the hoverscout reached the end of the column, it stopped. The squad leader leaned out of his window.

"Very well. You are free to leave."

The Askajians responded with a chorus of belly laughs so deep it sounded like sand thunder. Borno took his time walking to the head of the caravan, stopping to check cargo straps and chat with drivers. Though Leia knew he was only putting on a show of contempt for the Imperials, she could not help wishing he did not have such a flair for the dramatic. Every minute they tarried brought the rest of the stormtrooper company a minute closer to Anchorhead.

Finally, Borno reached the front of the caravan and hoisted himself into his saddle. Without looking back toward the Imperials, he boomed a command in Askajian that caused his followers to hide their blasters again and take up their herding spears. Then, at last, he urged his mount forward, and the caravan left Anchorhead behind.

The dewbacks were sluggish and slow at first, plodding along barely faster than Leia could walk. But as the suns warmed the morning air, the creatures grew steadily more energetic, and it was only a few minutes before the caravan was ambling at a swift pace. By the time the last blush of Second Dawn had faded from the air half an hour later, the purple crags of the Jundland Wastes could be seen rippling in the distance ahead.

They rode for only a quarter hour more before the Squibs began to complain about chafing. Though most Askajians could speak Basic, they paid no attention and kept up a merry prattle in their own language. Leia glanced back to check on Han and Chewbacca.

The Wookiee, barely visible in the shadows beneath the dewback's chest, was using the skirts of Han's saddle to pull his weight off the straps. He caught Leia looking and flashed a friendly snarl to show he was doing fine. Han was sitting too upright, staring straight ahead with an artificial smirk across his lips, obviously aware that Leia was checking on him and just as obviously trying to appear stronger than he was.

"Drink something," she mouthed.

Han raised a water bottle to his lips, then made a sour face and said, "You owe me some Gizer."

Then a familiar whine sounded in the sky. Leia looked toward the noise and found herself staring into the blazing white eyes of the two suns, Tatoo II quivering and flickering like something alive as it chased its twin higher into the sky. She turned away, trying to blink the blindness from her eyes.

The whine grew more distinct.

"Han—"

"TIEs," he confirmed. "Coming out of the suns, subsonic. They're just taking a look."

As the whine grew louder, the dewbacks broke into a nervous trot, and the Askajians were suddenly too busy slapping their herding spears across the pack beasts' noses to continue talking. Leia felt a rein against the back of her leg and turned, bringing her spear down across the nose of the offending beast. By then, the whine had grown to a shrill howl. She glimpsed an H-shaped silhouette dropping into the sky beneath Tatoo I. It swelled almost instantly into a TIE fighter—a fighter that came screaming up on the caravan from behind, flying so low that Leia and everyone else ducked instinctively.

The dewbacks bellowed and would have scattered had the fibrasteel reins not snapped the pack beasts back toward the lead mounts. As it was, the entire caravan burst into a panicked gallop and bolted across the salt flats in a column. Then the TIE's ion drives appeared in the sky ahead, and Borno's mount broke to the right, leading the rest of the caravan after it in a long curving arc. Leia nearly bounced out of the saddle before she managed to get her weight into the stirrups, and even then she came close to flying off each time the seat slammed into her from below.

The TIE went into a steep climb and did a wingover, then fell ominously silent as it began to dive back toward the caravan. The dewbacks dropped out of their gallop and began to rumble to each other in low, barely audible tones.

Then the whine started again, and the TIE swelled in the sky, now coming at the caravan from the flank.

This was too much for the dewbacks. They turned as one and fled in rank. Leia glimpsed Han beside her, a Wookiee hand hanging on to the saddle alongside his leg.

The TIE shrieked past overhead, trailing panic and the harsh smell of ozone. Leia's dewback broke right, dragging the pack beasts along and slamming hard into Han's trio. All six creatures nearly went down, but the lead mounts pushed off each other at the last minute and dragged their followers back to their feet. Leia spied a pebbled flank ahead and frantically slapped her spear into her dewback's head, barely turning it in time to avoid another collision.

The caravan dispersed, galloping across the plain in a hundred different directions, and Leia thought for a minute it would scatter to the far corners of the mesa. But once the whine of the TIE had faded, a low thrumming almost too deep to hear began to roll across the plain behind her. Her mount and the pack beasts turned toward the sound immediately and continued at a dead run.

Leia hauled back on the reins, trying to slow down until she could see what was causing the sound, but the effort was useless. When her mount slowed, the pack beasts charged forward, their fibrasteel leads pinning her legs against the saddle skirts. When she slapped the herding spear across their snouts, her mount charged ahead.

She finally began to feel vibrations in her stomach and realized her dewbacks were thrumming in reply, and she gave up trying to slow them. A few moments later, she began to see other riders charging toward the same spot she was, converging on Borno and his mount.

As Leia arrived at the edge of the throng, Sligh was complaining, "How can you leave us under here? We won't have a hair left on our bodies!"

Borno ignored the Squib and his fellows, issuing a series of commands in his own language. His drivers quickly arranged the dewbacks into a giant outward-facing circle and linked each creature to the two adjacent, connecting the whole caravan together via the sturdy fibrasteel reins.

Leia was impressed with Borno's foresight. After making his initial pass, a good reconnaissance pilot would return a few minutes later to record a second set of pictures and data that would show how the subject had reacted to his first pass. Often, the differences between the two were more telling than the data itself.

As they waited for the TIE to return, Leia glanced over and found Han waiting with his herding spear leaning against his leg and both hands braced on his saddle pommel. The muscles on the backs of his hands were trembling visibly.

"Drink some water," Leia said.

"Just did." Han straightened his back and patted the water bottle hanging beneath his cloak, then seemed to wobble in the saddle. "Why do you keep saying that?"

"Because you're looking a little shaky," Leia said. "You shouldn't be out in this heat, not so soon after yesterday."

"I don't think the Imperials are giving us a choice," Han said. "Except maybe a nice climate-controlled berth on the *Chimaera*."

Chewbacca groaned an opinion about that possibility.

"I don't care for how it would end, either." Leia reached into her satchel and removed the vidmap Han had taken off his borrowed swoop before abandoning it, then called up a schematic of the area. "But the Dark-lighter Farm isn't far."

"Not far at all," Emala agreed from beneath her dew-back. "You could be there in half a day at most, even by dewback."

"So?" Han demanded.

"So you shouldn't be out in this heat," Leia said. "You haven't recovered. I'm sure the Darklighters will hide you for a day or two."

"*Us,*" Han corrected. "I'm not going anywhere without you."

"Han, you know I can't," Leia said.

"Sure you can," Emala said. "Your partners will recover *Killik Twilight.*"

"You?" Leia glanced in the Squibs' direction. Her view of them was completely blocked by the adjacent dewbacks, but she shook her head anyway. "*You're* the biggest reason I need to go."

"You don't trust us?" Sligh gasped. "When have we ever given you reason to be so rude?"

"Trust is earned," Leia said. "You have a little work to do."

"And you'd rather let your mate die than take a chance on us?" Grees demanded. "Some heartless jillie you are."

"That's enough out of you three," Han said. "I'm not going anywhere without Leia, understand?"

Leia shook her head in frustration. "You're impossible."

"Yeah? I'm not the only one."

An uneasy silence fell over the area as nearby Aska-jians politely averted their gazes and tried to pretend they had not overheard the argument.

Leia sighed, then turned to Han and ordered, "Drink some water."

Han glanced over, not quite scowling, and said, "You, too."

They pulled their water bottles from beneath their cloaks, then tipped the necks toward each other in a silent toast. They drank together, the mystified Askajians watching and murmuring as they puzzled over erratic human behavior.

After Han finished drinking, his gaze remained fixed on the blazing sky. "That didn't take long."

A familiar whine rose from the direction of the sun. Leia barely had time to put away the vidmap and her water bottle before the TIE was on them, screaming over the caravan so low that she was sure a lucky Askajian could have planted a spear into one of its solar panels. The dewbacks bellowed wildly and tried to scatter, but found themselves pulling against their fellows and went nowhere. The circle simply undulated until the starfighter was past, then settled back into stillness as the craft climbed into the sky.

Borno shouted a command, and the Askajians began to draw their blasters from beneath their sand cloaks. The TIE did a wingover and approached on a vector perpendicular to its first pass. Again, the alarmed dewbacks attempted to flee and found themselves restrained by their neighbors. The Askajians added to the panic by shooting into the air, clearly trying to send a message by firing directly at the starfighter. Leia doubted they really meant to bring it down; Borno struck her as a competent enough warrior to know that the best way to bring down a low-flying craft was to put a wall of fire up in front of it.

Leia glimpsed a pair of pods—sensor and imaging—hanging beneath the cockpit where the blaster cannons would normally be, then the TIE was gone, climbing into the sky, wagging its wing panels and shrinking into an H-shaped dot. The Askajians cheered in triumph and, not waiting to see if it would return, began to free the dewbacks from the circle.

Borno rode over and waved a puffy hand at Chewbacca and C-3PO. "We can unstrap your friends now." He turned his narrow eyes toward the Squibs, then added, "And those three, as well—so long as they don't try to sell me any more vaporators."

"*Sell* a shrewd tomuon herder like yourself?" Sligh said. "That's impossible."

"We assumed someone of your intellect would want the best," Emala added. "Our mistake."

Borno chuckled. "The wise ones say you must never ask galoomps to stand still. I see this is so." He motioned to the driver of their dewback. "Free them. We would not want even a Squib down where they will get smashed when we reach rough terrain."

Han dismounted and set to work unstrapping Chewbacca, but Leia remained in her saddle.

"Borno, forgive me for questioning your wisdom," she said. "But these Imperials seem more thorough than most, and they have a very clever commanding officer. I think they'll be back with an assault shuttle."

Borno smiled broadly. "Of course they will, but they will look out there." He pointed in the direction the caravan had been traveling so far, then swung his massive arm in a ninety-degree arc, pointing toward a shimmering blue-brown curtain that might or might not have been the foothills of the distant Needles Mountains. "And we will be there."

Han stopped working on Chewbacca's straps long enough to peer in the direction the Askajian was pointing. "Why there?"

"Because that is where my vaporators are," Borno

said. "There is a hiding place about three hours from here where the Jawas go when the winds are too strong. If the sandcrawler isn't there, it will be a good place to start searching."

"Then what are we waiting for?"

Leia slipped out of her saddle and, trying not to gag on the musky stench of the dewback's belly, quickly unstrapped C-3PO.

Chewbacca and the Squibs had a few bald spots where the slings had rubbed off their fur, and C-3PO complained bitterly about the sand in his servomotors. Otherwise they all seemed to have survived the ride relatively intact.

Borno pointed at C-3PO, then asked, "Can the droid ride?"

C-3PO answered in Askajian, drawing an incredulous guffaw from Borno and several other caravan drivers within earshot. Oblivious to their reaction, C-3PO turned to Leia and translated.

"I explained to Chief Borno that I'm an excellent rider. If he wishes, I can supply a complete listing of the eight hundred ninety-seven different vehicles in which I have been a passenger."

Han said, "Threepio can't handle a dewback."

"I thought as much." Borno told his drivers to arrange mounts for Chewbacca and the Squibs, then waved C-3PO toward his own huge dewback. "You, I take."

"Take?" C-3PO turned to Leia. "Pardon me for saying so, Mistress Leia, but I fail to see what use a protocol droid of my sophistication could possibly be to a tribe of . . . herders. Especially in a sandy climate like this."

"He means you're to ride on his dewback." Leia pointed him toward the animal. "Ownership isn't being transferred."

"Thank the maker!" C-3PO went to Borno's mount, where a pair of Askajians were waiting to heft him into the saddle. "I am sure to make your ride a pleasant one. Perhaps you would enjoy a recitation of the *Song of the Dongtha Slayer* in ancient Askajian? My memory banks contain all seven hundred twenty-two known verses."

Borno paled. "I am very glad you are not giving me this droid," he said to Leia. "But perhaps now *would* be a good time to make payment."

Leia's stomach knotted. "Of course." She glanced at the Squibs. She was not happy to see them busy inspecting the dewback they would soon be riding. "I'm unaware of the final price, but I'm sure we have more than enough to cover it."

"It isn't much." Borno extended his hand. "Who carries the vidmap?"

"The vidmap?" Han exploded. "They're giving that away?"

"They cannot?" Borno's expression quickly went from perplexed to angry. "But they did."

"What my husband means is we still have need of it," Leia said.

"So do I," Borno said. "That's why I agreed to take it."

"*Agreed* to take it?" Han glared across the circle at the Squibs. "They offered it to you?"

"Of course they did," Leia said. "How else would Borno have known about it?"

Borno glanced from Han to Leia. "They should not have done this?"

"No," Leia said quickly—too quickly.

Borno's face turned the color of a volcanic eruption, and he barked something at his drivers. They immediately stopped what they were doing and began to unstrap the Squibs' saddle.

"My apologies," Borno said. "I should have checked with you before taking the word of rodents." He cast a dark look in the Squibs' direction, then asked, "So, what *are* you willing to pay for our help in escaping the Imperials?"

Under any other circumstances, after-the-fact would have been an awkward time for a negotiation. But on Tatooine, in the middle of the desert with the possibility of an Imperial assault company dropping in any moment, the timing could not have been more perfect for Borno.

"I know you're not interested in credits." Leia was thinking of the Askajian's reaction to the Squibs' attempts to buy his tomuon wool. "So what would interest you?"

Borno glanced briefly at C-3PO, then shuddered visibly and spoke in a matter-of-fact tone. "The vidmap."

Chewbacca groaned, and Han said, "I told you. We need that."

"Then why did the Squibs offer it?" Borno demanded.

No sooner had the Askajian asked than Leia saw the answer. The Squibs knew this terrain. She and her companions did not.

Leia turned to find Grees leading the other two over.

"You've got a death wish?" Grees demanded. "Turn over the vidmap."

"And place ourselves in your hands?" she asked. "I think not."

"It's either that or watch your husband die of thirst out here—right before you," Grees said. "We struck a bargain with Borno."

"A bargain that leaves us dependent on you." Leia phrased this as a conclusion, not a question. "How convenient."

Sligh shrugged. "You said make a deal with the caravan to save us. We made the deal."

"Give him the vidmap," Han said.

Leia turned. *"What?"*

"Sligh's right. A deal's a deal." Han shrugged. "Besides, what choice do we have? Let Borno leave them here to die?"

"*Them?*" Emala gasped. "After all we've been through together, you talk like we're not even partners?"

Leia stepped over to her dewback's flank and opened the utility satchel hanging from her saddle. After digging her way past the holocomm, the first thing she found was the journal. She was tempted to see if she could convince Borno to take one or the other instead of the vidmap, but she would need the holocomm later, and she was not ready to give up her grandmother—not after finding her so recently. Besides, a deal was a deal. She put the journal back and fished around until she found the vidmap, then went over to Borno's mount and passed it up.

"Now take us to our sandcrawler."

SIXTEEN

It was only midmorning, and already Leia felt as though she had a crystalplas skull—as though the twin suns were blazing through her sand hood and baking her brain in hot bright light. Even through her darkened goggles, the plain ahead was a shimmering white haze, with the cruel blue hoax of a mirage sea always rippling just on the horizon. The air was still and stifling, every breath a suffocating blast.

The caravan was moving fast, trotting toward the hideaway that Borno had assured them would have been the Jawas' first choice of shelter during the storm. The search would continue from there, depending on what they found . . . and whether they found anything at all. Again, Leia had the feeling she was being influenced by the Force, drawn out into the wilds of Tatooine—though she could not imagine to what purpose. The Great Chott was as empty as it was vast; as far as she could tell, there was no place to conceal another surprise about her family—or anything else.

The Askajians were scattered across the plain, being careful to form no rows or columns that would make the caravan easier for a high-flying surveillance droid to identify. Their globular bodies neither swayed nor rocked on their mounts, despite the dewbacks' spine-hammering gait.

Han rode ahead and off to one side. His pack beasts had become mounts for Chewbacca and the Squibs, so he did not have any extra dewbacks to lead. Still, the heat was taking its toll. He was wobbling and bouncing, and occasionally he struggled to stay in the saddle.

Leia urged her dewback forward and drew alongside him. With his eyes and face hidden by his goggles and scarf, it was impossible to read his expression. But Leia could tell by the way his shoulders slumped and his chin drooped that he was not doing well.

"Hey—" It hurt to talk, Leia's throat was so dry.

Han's dark goggles swung in her direction. The slump vanished from his shoulders—a brave front for her benefit—but his chin continued to droop. Not a good sign.

Leia held up a finger while she slipped her water bottle beneath her face coverings and drank. The contents were as hot as caf. "You remembering your water?"

Han displayed the bottle in his hand and nodded listlessly. "If you're trying to send me off to the Dark-lighters' farm again, forget it." His voice was too muffled to reveal anything more about his condition. "I'm not the one who sounds like a profogg . . . much."

Leia smiled behind her scarf and felt her lips crack. "I've given up." That was a small exaggeration. "I want to talk about something else."

Han's goggles remained fixed in her direction. "Yeah?"

"I, uh . . ."

Leia's throat went dry again, and this time it had nothing to do with the heat. There had been few opportunities to really talk since the auction, and Leia had kept much to herself. She had not told Han about the two visions she had experienced. Nor shared Luke's warning about how the Force was moving her, or even mentioned her grandmother's diary. And she needed to tell him, to make him understand there was good reason for her fear of having children, that as much as she wanted to, it was not a choice she felt free to make . . . not until she had put to rest the dark face she had seen aboard the *Falcon*.

"You were saying?" Han asked.

The distant hiss of a craft in flight sounded behind the caravan, and they both turned to see a wavering sliver of ion efflux creeping across the sky. The vessel itself was not visible, not even as a faint glint, but the length of its ion tail suggested it to be a sizable craft—probably one of the *Chimaera*'s intelligence launches, eavesdropping on local comm traffic.

The sight reminded Leia of another problem: sometime soon, she needed to find a safe place to set up the portable holocomm and make a progress report. Otherwise, Mon Mothma would be forced to assume that *Killik Twilight* was lost and Shadowcast compromised, and she might well decide to recall the Wraiths—regardless of what that would mean for the local resistance fighters.

After watching the efflux for a moment, Leia asked, "What do you think? Signal interceptor?"

Han shook his head. "The Imperials must have finished searching Anchorhead by now. That's got to be an assault shuttle." He did not add that when the shuttle pilots failed to locate the Askajians where they expected to, the *Chimaera*'s admiral would launch an all-out search to find them. The entire caravan had known that since slipping away from their original route two hours ago. "That what you wanted to talk about?"

Leia shook her head. "Han, I . . ."

The Squibs appeared on the other side of Han, all three riding in the same saddle and bouncing half out of control.

"Gartal!" Leia swore. "Perfect timing, as usual."

"You're looking a little shaky, Cap," Grees said. He

was sitting in front, gripping the pommel with both hands, the reins threaded under his palms and wrapped back around his knuckles. "Listen to your mate, or you'll make a widow of her."

"I'm doing fine." Han turned to face the Squib. "Not that it's any business of yours."

"That's just like you." Sligh rode in the middle, both arms wrapped around Grees's waist, his far elbow wrapped around the middle shaft of the herding spear. "You never think of anyone but yourself. How do you think *we'll* feel having to leave *you* behind when the heat knocks you out?"

"I'm sure it'll just tear you up," Han said. "Don't do me any favors."

Leia remained silent. She and Han could hardly hold a serious conversation in front of the Squibs.

"We *are* trying to do you a favor," Emala said. She was in back, holding on to the butt of the herding spear with one hand and Sligh with the other and bouncing higher than both of her companions. "We're as close as we're going to get to the Darklighter Farm—"

"No."

Chewbacca rode up on Leia's other side, sitting astride the dewback as though he had been born to it, his feet hanging down past its belly. Bracing himself on one of the cargo beasts Leia was leading, he leaned across and oowrralled at Han.

"I said *no*." Han glanced over at Leia. "I suppose you're a part of this?"

"This is the first I've heard of it, but—"

"Yeah, sure." Han shook his head. "You never give up, sweetheart. That's one of the things I love about you."

"Han, if I said I wasn't a part of this, then I wasn't."

"Okay, so you weren't part of it."

"But that doesn't mean it's a bad idea."

"It doesn't mean it's a good one," Han said. "I know how this works, Leia. First I agree to go, then you work me over until I think going without you is the best idea I've ever had. I've seen you do that to planetary governments a hundred times. I don't have a chance."

"You're not a planetary government," Leia said. "And I'm not trying to talk you into something you don't want to do."

"No?" Han's voice cracked with dryness. "Then what did you want to talk about?"

"Orbital surveillance." It wasn't a lie—not really. She had been wondering about orbital surveillance since the overflight by the TIE reconnaissance craft. "You know the *Chimaera* has to have spy satellites in place, and we're not exactly under cover."

"More than you think." Han took a long drink from his water bottle, then continued, "No sensor in the galaxy is delicate enough to find us right now. The reflection blast is hiding us."

"Reflection blast?"

"The Great Chott is a giant mirror." Han waved a hand at the pale surface of the surrounding salt plain. "With two suns shining down, this time of day all a spy satellite sees is heat and light—same for a high-flying surveillance drone. If the Imps want to find us again, they have to come down low—and that takes time."

"That's why Borno waited until the suns were up to change directions."

Han nodded. "He knows his evasion strategy." He turned and looked into the shimmering whiteness ahead. "I just hope we find some cover soon. Once that shuttle reports we aren't where we're supposed to be, it won't take them long to send a flight of TIEs out on a search grid."

An Askajian rode up behind them, arriving with such silence and suddenness that when he spoke, Leia nearly jumped out of her saddle.

"Why are you bunched together like this?" He gestured at the sky with his spear. "You make it easier for the sky eyes to see us. Spread out, or Borno will take your mounts and leave you for the white shells."

The Squibs drifted away immediately. Chewbacca, who never responded well to threats, flashed fangs and glared until the Askajian finally looked away.

"If you please," he said more politely, "we shouldn't take chances."

Chewbacca grunted an apology that, judging by the way the Askajian's eyes widened, Leia was sure the rotund being did not understand. Chewbacca snickered and angled off a bit. Still hoping to have a private word with Han, Leia lingered a moment to see if the Askajian would allow them to remain together.

"Please," he said. "It is even more important for *you* to separate. You are leading pack beasts."

"Of course." Leia wished she had a set of fangs to flash, but she knew the Askajian was only trying to protect them all. She glanced in Han's direction and, slowing her mount, asked, "Can we talk later?"

"You know we can." Han's goggled eyes lingered on hers. "I'm not going anywhere."

Leia fell in twenty meters behind him. Even at that short distance, the heat distortion reduced his shimmering figure to an unrecognizable silhouette, but she would at least be able to tell if he fell out of the saddle or let his mount wander. She felt her tongue sticking to the roof of her mouth and reminded herself to drink. The water was hotter than ever. She forced herself to swallow three long gulps, then put it away. In this heat, she would have thought any water would taste good. But the stuff in her plastoid bottle was beginning to have all the flavor of rancor drool. She set a chime on her chronometer to remind her to drink again in a quarter hour.

The plain became rocky and broken, with pockets of soft sand lying between boulders the size of droids. The caravan's progress slowed to a crawl, the gait of the dewbacks growing slow, rhythmic, and swaying.

Han's rippling figure seemed to twist in the saddle and look back in the direction from which they had come, and Leia knew he was thinking the same thing she was. Those TIEs had to be starting their search grid by now, and when they found the caravan this time, the equipment hanging beneath their cockpits would not be sensors and cameras. They would take action to stop the caravan, and quickly.

It soon grew apparent that the dewbacks were better off picking their way without guidance from their riders. With another hour to their destination and nothing to occupy her thoughts except worries over Han and the Imperials, Leia needed something to keep her mind occupied. She slipped her herding spear into its carrying sleeve and tied her reins to a tethering loop on the saddle, then took her grandmother's journal out of her pocket and began to view entries.

It wasn't long before Shmi reported an interesting surprise.

19:17:10

Today I came home to find a Falleen waiting on our steps. She was a very rough-looking lady, Annie, and not only because of those narrow eyes and sharp teeth. She was even taller and more beautiful than most females of her species, but her hair had been singed off, and she had a fresh burn across her nose. And there were holes in her jumpsuit that showed scarred scales and swollen bulges along her spinal ridge.

She had a plasteel box sitting beside her, so I thought she had brought some memory chips for me to clean. I told her she would have to pay in advance—I've been cheated by spacers before, even if they're usually Corellians—but she told me the box was from Coruscant. She apologized for taking so long to get it here and explained that it had been a gift from Qui-Gon Jinn.

Annie, I was so excited I forgot all about the box. Here was someone from Coruscant, who knew Qui-Gon. That meant she had to know you. But she claimed to be only an errand girl from the Jedi hangars and said she didn't know anything about Temple business. I didn't believe her. I told her I wanted to know who was taking care of my son. Finally, she said you were in good hands, and I shouldn't worry.

I don't think she was really an errand girl, though. I didn't see a lightsaber, but she could have been a Jedi— she seemed so certain of things. I so hope she told you about her visit, because then you will know how happy I am that you are following your dreams.

As the entry ended, Shmi's eyes grew glassy with tears, and Leia was surprised to find her own eyes tearing. It seemed wrong to condemn Anakin for following his dreams—yet those dreams had become a nightmare for the rest of the galaxy. If only Shmi had known what his destiny would be . . . would she have had the strength to deny her son's help to the Jedi, to make Anakin live out the rest of his life in bondage?

It was not a decision Leia felt certain she could have made.

19:19:11

Oh, yes—the box! Inside there was a message from Qui-Gon explaining that while he and his Padawan waited for the Jedi Council to test you, he had asked someone to start a galaxywide HoloNet search to . . .

The display clouded with static, and Shmi's voice faded to an inaudible scratch. Leia replayed the entry several times, and managed to make out a few more lines:

"Imagine, a Jedi like Qui-Gon taking . . . when there must have been so many . . . his attention. The galaxy is going to . . . fortunate he came into our lives."

Leia gave up trying to make sense of the entry and looked up to find Han slumped over, hanging half out of his saddle. She grabbed the herding spear and urged her mount to catch up, but the beast groaned in irritation and refused to move any faster over the broken ground.

Han's head rose alongside his knee and seemed to peer back at her, though it was difficult to tell in the rippling air, and he remained slumped over for several moments more. Finally his body rose upright, and a crescent of white desert light appeared between his seat and saddle as he stood to check the stirrup he had been adjusting.

Leia let out a groan of her own and returned the spear to its carrying sleeve. She forced herself to gulp some water. It was hotter and more foul tasting than ever.

18:20:12

Watto behaved very strangely today. When he sent me out to buy his nectarot, he gave me five extra truguts to buy some pallie wine for us to share—and he insisted I get it from Naduarr because "I should taste the good stuff." I hardly knew what to make of it!

It turns out he had heard about the Falleen's visit, and

that she had come on a ship from Coruscant. All he wanted was to hear how you're doing—well, what he asked was "how many Podraces has the boy won." I told him the Jedi don't allow their students to enter Podraces, but that you're doing well with your training.

I'm sure I wasn't stretching the truth, Annie, and the news seemed to calm Watto. Sometimes, I think he really misses you . . . though of course he won't admit it. He just grumbles that if he hadn't let "that Jedi" cheat him out of you, he'd be richer than a Hutt by now.

The entry ended, leaving Leia a little perplexed about Shmi's patience with her Toydarian owner. But many relationships were complicated, and she had learned in her work that few beings could be painted without shades of gray.

As Leia continued to view entries, it quickly grew apparent that losing Anakin had indeed affected Watto profoundly. The Toydarian continued to blame others for his "bad luck." But, according to Shmi, he no longer cursed at her, and he trusted her to run the shop while he went to bid on wrecks. He even continued to give her a few truguts every week to buy Naduarr's pallie wine, though he did not always insist on having their drinks together. And while Shmi never acknowledged Watto's right to own her, she seemed to feel for the Toydarian as well, sometimes defending him to customers who insulted him behind his back.

Then, after four years of routine entries, Shmi appeared in the display smiling as she had not smiled since the box had arrived from Qui-Gon.

17:06:13

A settler came into Watto's today, a great brattle of a man. Very gruff and to the point. Shmi lowered her voice and did a fair imitation of a human male. *"I need a set of booster coils for a SoroSuub V-Twenty-Four,"* he said to Watto, *"and don't try to rob me. I know your reputation."*

She slid into a flawless imitation of Watto's gravelly whine. *"Then you know I am only an honest business-being trying to keep his doors open in this miserable dustbin of a city. And the V-Twenty-Four is a classic. Those coils will cost you, if I have any."*

I've heard Watto use that line a hundred times, but there was something about this settler that made me want to help him, a sense of desperation maybe . . . or maybe his proud blue eyes and the way he carried himself. I told Watto we had plenty of booster coils, that I had dusted off a whole stack that morning.

"Good," the settler said. He looked directly at me, and my knees went weak, the way Amee says hers do whenever she sees Roc or Jerm or nearly any boy. *"I'll take two of 'em."*

Shmi began to laugh. *Watto was so angry he knocked a carton of power cells off the counter turning to yell at me.*

Leia forced down some stale water and checked to see that Han was still upright in his saddle, then continued to view the journal. The next few entries were short, consisting mostly of Shmi's ritual of telling Anakin how proud she was of him and how much she loved him. There were also a few mentions of the settler, noting with obvious disappointment that Shmi had not seen him again and probably never would—but she was glad to have helped him.

Watto proved surprising philosophical about the sale, telling Shmi he had only lost a few truguts anyway, and that she could make it up to him by cleaning the memory chips of a used navicomputer. A few days later, he even seemed to grow concerned about her happiness, giving her an afternoon off and buying a bolt of cloth so she could make herself a new robe.

About two weeks later, Shmi's mood was noticeably brighter.

23:29:15

The settler came back today! He was looking for fifty vaporator condensers. Watto was still so angry about the booster coils that he wouldn't offer a reasonable price, so the settler left.

But when Watto sent me for his nectarot, I found the settler waiting outside. He walked with me to Naduarr's. I was a little nervous, but he has a jolly manner that makes him easy to talk to. He asked if I had been punished for helping him, then apologized when I told him about the extra work I had to do cleaning the navicomputer's memory chip—even though it was really nothing.

Then he asked me why I had helped him. I laughed and started to say I just wanted to get even with Watto for yelling at me, but there is something about this man that wouldn't let me make light. There is something about his eyes that makes you want to speak your heart—they're blue, Annie, not quite as blue as yours, and so sincere and kind and warm.

Before I knew it, I had admitted the truth: that I had done it because I found him so handsome.

He actually blushed! Then he smiled and held his hand out to me. He is a good man, Annie, and it's wonderful to have a new friend. His name is Cliegg . . . Cliegg Lars.

SEVENTEEN

The droning sound came so faintly that Leia thought the sand had finally fouled the heat vents on the palm diary. Terrified the memory circuits would melt, she thumbed the POWER key and continued to hear the whine, then finally looked up to see Han's wavy figure twisted around in his saddle, his dark goggles studying the sky behind her. Leia turned as well and found Chewbacca and the Squibs and the shimmering blobs of several nearby Askajians also squinting into the sky.

The diary's heat vents were fine. It was a TIE making the noise.

Leia raised her arm, cocking it at a steep angle so she could block both suns, and still found herself staring into a rippling blue-white inferno. She searched until puddles of darkness began to swim across her vision, then closed her eyes against the pain and looked away. Wherever that TIE was, she only hoped the pilot and his instruments would be just as blinded as she was by the blistering heat of the Great Chott.

The droning faded a few moments later, and when it wasn't followed by a sonic boom, Leia knew they had escaped detection. Had the TIE spotted them, either the sound would have continued, constantly changing directions as the pilot circled to keep them under surveillance, or it would have grown steadily louder and more shrill as he descended for a strafing run.

Once her vision cleared, Leia activated the timing function on her chronometer. Assuming the TIE was flying a search grid, knowing the interval between passes would prove critical if they were to have any chance at all of evading detection. She returned the journal to its pocket and took up her herding spear and reins. There was nothing *she* could do to make the dewback move faster over this treacherous terrain, but she suspected the creature might find the scream and roar of a TIE blaster cannon more convincing.

Han was wobbling more noticeably in his saddle, but remained alert enough to keep drinking. Over the next ten minutes, Leia saw him tip his water bottle up twice and realized he, too, was using his chronometer alarm to remind himself to drink.

The brown wall of the distant mountains continued to hang on the horizon, and the blue sweep of a mirage still hovered at their base like a floating lake. Below the mirage, there lay a new desert apparition, a writhing stripe of darkness that appeared to have no worldly source. This was the first Leia had seen of it. The last time she had looked up to check on Han, the line had not been there. Noticing that it was a little thicker and blacker at one end than the other, she wondered if it might be the *Chimaera*'s shadow, cast from orbit above the Great Chott. It was not ordinarily Imperial procedure to bring a Star Destroyer so close to a planet unless they intended to bombard it—the Empire had lost capital ships to turbolaser ambushes before—but so far this new admiral had proven anything but ordinary.

The droning sound returned, this time loudly enough that Leia had no doubt about its nature. She checked her chronometer and discovered the last pass had come fourteen minutes ago, *then* shielded her eyes and turned to look. It took a few moments of searching, but she finally found a blue flicker of ion discharge bouncing along low on the horizon, blinking in and out of sight as it was obscured by curtains of rising air. The caravan had one more pass, if they were lucky, before the TIE was close enough to see them.

Leia glanced around, trying to distinguish Borno from all the other wavering blobs ahead. He had warned her that if it came to a fight, he would have no choice except to surrender them to the Imperials, and Leia failed to see how they could escape being caught in the open. And leaving the caravan had its advantages. Without the dewbacks, she and her companions could burrow under the boulders and hide from even a close-range sensor sweep. Besides, if the Askajians continued without them, perhaps the Imperials could be persuaded there had been nothing unusual in the caravan's sudden change of direction.

But Borno, wherever he was, did not seem interested in leaving them behind. Perhaps he saw the same weakness in Leia's plan that she did: without the Askajians, she and her companions would survive no more than a day in this desert. He probably thought they had a better chance of survival in Imperial hands. The scattered caravan continued at its same rolling pace, the TIE droning across the sky behind it, Han swaying in his saddle as he stared back toward the horizon.

Leia tried to urge her dewback close enough to see how he was holding up. Her mount broke into a trot for all of two paces, then nearly dumped her when one of the cargo beasts it was leading misplaced a foot and stumbled. After that, the creatures refused to move any faster, no matter how often she struck them with the herding spear.

The distant whine of the TIE faded to silence, and Leia reset the timer on her chronometer. Fourteen minutes if they were lucky. It wasn't much time. Unless she and the other non-Askajians left the caravan now, they would have no time to dig in and hide. But how could she explain her plan to the others without risking the use of a comlink? The caravan continued to amble onward at the same slow pace for another two minutes, then she heard—almost felt—a low thrumming similar to the sound that had recalled the stampeding dewbacks earlier.

Han's dewback, and the ones carrying Chewbacca and the Squibs, broke into a clumsy gallop and rushed forward, staggering and stumbling. Leia's mount started after the others, but stopped when it discovered it was still tethered to the pack beasts. It began to groan angrily and toss its head. The Askajians began to free their cargo animals, and more dewbacks lurched after Han and the others. Puzzled—and hoping Borno had some plan other than headlong flight—Leia twisted around to release the pack beasts tethered to her own saddle. She had barely undone the second knot before all three creatures broke into a clumsy trot.

The herding spear caught behind a rock and flew out of her grasp, and Leia spent the next few moments bent over backward, struggling to keep her feet in the stirrups and grabbing for a tethering loop. The heat made a difficult task nearly impossible, and by the time she finally caught the knot, her goggles were so steamy she couldn't see.

Leia barely had the strength to drag herself upright, and when she did, her head was spinning with heat fatigue. She lifted her goggles and allowed the steam to dissipate into Tatooine's arid air, then lowered them and saw that the shadowy line ahead had widened into an immense wedge of darkness. She turned and looked over her shoulder, convinced she would find the *Chimaera* eclipsing the suns.

Nothing above her but two blazing orbs.

Leia looked forward again to find the caravan converging ahead, the pack beasts outpacing the mounts. The Askajians weren't far behind, with Chewbacca close on their tails. But Han and the Squibs were rapidly losing ground, the Squibs remaining on their mount only through acrobatic grace. Han was slumped forward with both arms wrapped around his dewback's neck. Leia kicked her heels into her mount's flanks and slapped the side of its neck, trying to urge it toward Han. The creature didn't even seem to feel the blows.

Then the other dewbacks started to disappear.

At first, Leia thought they were just pulling far enough ahead to vanish behind a shimmering curtain of heat. But as she continued forward, she noticed that they were becoming larger and less wavy when she lost sight of them. The shadow beneath the mirage was rapidly growing wider and steadier, and the dewbacks all seemed to be disappearing about the same distance from it.

Not disappearing, but descending. The dewbacks' legs would vanish first, then their bodies, and finally their heads and—as the first Askajians reached the brink—their riders. Then the shadow slid out from beneath the mirage and resolved itself into a broad deep canyon. Chewbacca reached the rim and followed the Askajians out of sight.

A moment later, Han finally slipped out of his saddle.

Leia was instantly standing in her stirrups, pulling her scarf down and yelling, "Chewie! Wait!"

Her parched throat managed a loud croak, not much more. Still, one of the bouncing Squibs turned and glanced back. Leia pointed at the spot where Han had fallen—she could no longer tell his body from the rippling stones.

"Han's down!" Her voice cracked and fell short of a yell. "Get Chewie!"

The Squib shouted something back that she could not understand, then one of them began to bounce up and down even higher on their saddle and wave a pair of arms, and the other two began whacking their mount's neck, trying to force it back toward Han.

The dewback continued after its fellows.

As long as the beasts were thrumming, Leia knew she could neither steer nor slow her dewback. She pulled her foot free of the stirrups and brought her leg around so that she was riding entirely on Han's side of the beast. The imbalance caused it to veer in his direction, and—unable to see him lying among the rocks—she began to worry about trampling him.

Then the Squibs leapt out of their saddle, spreading their sand cloaks to catch the air as they dropped. It was no help. One after the other, they hit the ground, were overcome by their momentum, and started bouncing.

Leia could have kissed them.

Learning from their mistake, she watched for a sandy stretch, then kicked her remaining foot out of the stirrup, pushed off, and covered her head.

Her feet sank to the ankle, and she slammed down on her side, the wind leaving her lungs in a single gasp.

Normally, she might have lain there in pain trying to get her breath back, but she had jumped from the oven onto the broiler—literally. The sand was so hot it began to burn her skin through the heavy sand cloak, and she found herself rising to her feet almost before the pain registered in her shoulder.

Leia looked down and found her arm hanging at her side. She tried to lift it and nearly sank to her knees.

"Stang! When it rains it . . ." She glanced up at the sky and shook her head. "We should be so lucky."

Emala came scrambling over, leaping from boulder to boulder. Ten meters behind her, Grees and Sligh were pulling Han to a seated position.

"Are you crazy, jumping off a moving dewback?" Emala demanded.

"At least I didn't try to fly." Leia flopped her limp arm toward the Squib. "Hold that. Brace yourself."

Emala grabbed the offered arm with both hands . . . then pulled up her feet and let her whole weight drop on Leia's wrist.

There was a loud pop, and this time Leia did sink to her knees.

Emala stuck her furry little face in front of Leia and batted her long lashes. "Better?"

Leia spoke through clenched teeth. "I'm going to . . . kill . . . you."

"Then who will help with your mate?" Emala asked, looking distinctly unimpressed. "Besides, I was only thinking—"

"Don't say it. Don't even think it." Leia stood and tried her arm. An electric bolt of pain shot through her body, but the hand rose. "But thanks."

She followed Emala over to the others, where Sligh and Grees each had one of Han's arms draped across their shoulders.

"How is he?" she asked.

"Heavy," Grees said. "Grab a leg and let's go."

"In a minute." Leia went around and slipped her hand under Han's scarf and felt his pulse. It was shallow and slow. His skin was as dry as a stone, and nearly as hot. "He's stopped sweating. That's bad."

"So, you want to leave him?" Sligh asked.

"No!" Leia checked her chronometer. "But we don't have time to keep going. That TIE's due back in two minutes."

The Squibs peered toward the canyon. Down this close to the ground, the mirage waters seemed closer. They could no longer see the canyon's rim, only the dark shadow that had been their first hint of its presence.

"So what?" Grees started to pull Han forward. "It hasn't seen us before."

"It'll be closer this time." Leia looked around for something resembling shelter, then finally pointed at the thin sliver of shade behind a large boulder. "Help me lay him over there, then find the shady side of a rock for yourselves."

The Squibs looked doubtful, but did as she instructed, placing him in close to the boulder. Though hardly cool, the sand wasn't quite so searing without the suns beating down on it, and Leia told herself it wouldn't hurt Han to lie there for a few minutes.

The drone of the TIE stalker arose thirty seconds later and quickly built to shrill whine. This time, it was close. Had Leia dared to raise her head above the rock, she felt certain she would have seen the solar panels streaking across the near horizon.

Still listening to the sound, she raised Han's goggles and opened his cloak—the closures were difficult to work with one hand—then emptied her water bottle onto his face and clothes. Hot as it was, the moisture would still have a cooling effect as it evaporated.

Han's eyes opened, glassy and unfocused, and he rasped, "Another bath already?"

"Just a shower." Unsure whether he was joking or hallucinating, Leia cradled his head in her lap and pulled the water bottle off his belt. "Can you drink?"

"Got a Gizer?"

"A little warm water."

"That'll do." Han grabbed her shoulder to pull himself up, then scowled when she winced. "What happened?"

"Fast stop," Leia said. "I separated my shoulder—not bad. I can still lift my arm."

Han nodded, then finally seemed to hear the whining TIE and glanced skyward. "Tell me it's not your shooting arm."

"It's not."

"Good. No worries." He took the water bottle and swallowed a few gulps, then made a sour face. "You call that a *little* warm?"

The whine of the TIE faded. Leia put the water bottles away and called the Squibs from their hiding places, but Han didn't want them banging his head on rocks and insisted he could walk on his own. Leia found herself regretting every excuse she had ever used for not learning to use the Force to levitate stubborn husbands.

Han lasted almost a dozen steps before his eyes rolled up and he collapsed again. Leia reached out to catch him, instinctively using both arms, and now she *really* regretted not learning how to levitate things. Once she had recovered from the pain, they carried him, Grees and Sligh taking the front, Leia and Emala the rear.

Following the caravan trail across the broken terrain proved more difficult than expected. That close to the ground, the air was so superheated, and the reflection of the suns so brilliant, that when Leia tried to look for tracks all she saw was a painful shimmering radiance. She settled for traveling in the general direction of the shadow and quickly discovered that moving at even a brisk scramble was too fast. Within a minute, all four were staggering from the heat and exertion. Within three minutes, they had to stop to rest and drink.

"How far . . . can it be?" Grees cupped his hands around his goggles and peered into the rippling air. "It didn't look that far."

"This close to the ground, the mirage effect is more pronounced." Leia did not add what she had learned during her Rebel military training: that in a desert, distances were usually three times what they appeared. "We'll reach the canyon soon."

The Squibs looked at her as though she had just told them it was going to rain, then put away their water bottles and picked up Han again. This time, they moved at a deliberate walk, and five minutes later, the darkness finally slid out from beneath the mirage and resolved itself into the canyon again.

Sligh stopped and, nearly letting Han slip, pointed away at an angle. "Where's that Wookiee going?"

Leia looked in the indicated direction and saw a wavering tower of fur loping across the desert past them. She dropped Han's leg and waved.

"Chewbacca!" When he stopped and turned in their direction, she added less loudly, "Hurry!"

He arrived a few moments later, glassy-eyed, roaring with joy, and staggering from the heat.

Leia checked her chronometer. "Chewie, we have four minutes before—"

Chewbacca was already throwing Han over his shoulder and turning back toward the canyon. The Squibs bounced away after him, and Leia started after them at a slow jog she hoped she could maintain in this heat. Within two minutes, she was staggering and gushing sweat. But the curtain of heat shimmer had lifted to reveal the golden walls of a sandrock canyon, descending through the desert floor in a series of stony terraces and shadowy overhangs. And across the canyon, the mirage had contracted to a thin band of blue running along the furrowed slopes at the base of the brown mountains.

Leia's pulse began to pound in her ears. She slowed to a

walk. The canyon's rim lay twenty meters ahead. She had plenty of time to reach it—as long as she didn't collapse.

Her vision began to darken at the edges. She pulled her water bottle off her belt and, finding it ominously light, recalled what she had done with the last few swallows.

Her shoulder started to throb, then her head was spinning. Ears ringing. No, not her ears—her wrist. That chiming was the alarm on her chronometer. One minute.

Leia's vision narrowed, and she felt like she was suffocating. She ripped the scarf off her face and raced to catch Chewbacca and the Squibs, no longer sweating, just growing steadily warmer beneath the bright Tatooine suns.

"Chew . . ." She couldn't hear her own voice. "Chew . . ."

No good. Chewbacca reached the rim of the canyon and began to grow shorter as he descended a steep slope; then the Squibs disappeared over the edge. The strength left Leia's legs.

She continued to run anyway, teasing out three more steps as her knees buckled. Her vision went to black. She dived, blindly, for the canyon rim.

The ground fell out beneath her. For a moment, Leia feared she was sinking into unconsciousness, that she was really lying out in the open on the edge of the plain where it would be easy for the TIE's sensors to pick her out.

Then her tender shoulder erupted into pain. She felt herself tumble twice, bowling over a pair of small soft bodies before finally coming to rest against a furry tree trunk of a leg. A faint shrieking filled her ears, and she thought for a moment she had hurt one of the Squibs. Then she recognized the sound's steadily rising pitch. The TIE had arrived.

Leia lay for what seemed an eternity, wondering if she had made it into the canyon far enough, if the rim would shield her.

The TIE's approach seemed to take forever. Her vision went from a gray blur to a golden brilliance, and the sound of its engines began to echo off the canyon's far wall. It occurred to Leia that the starfighter's search vector might bring it directly over the gorge this time. A Rebel pilot might even take it upon himself to make a pass up the chasm, but Imperial pilots did not deviate from orders. They followed procedure. Almost always.

Leia waited, listening to the engine shriek bouncing off the golden walls. Her vision cleared, and she found herself staring down the canyon. She half expected to see the black panels and cockpit sandwich of a TIE fighter screaming around the bend.

But this pilot continued to fly the assigned pattern. The pitch of his shrieking engines went from rising to falling, the echoes drifted away up the canyon, and finally the whine vanished altogether.

The next sound Leia heard was Sligh's angry voice.

"Is that the way you repay our help?" he demanded. "Trying to kill us?"

"The deal's off!" Grees declared. "You can't be trusted."

Leia pushed herself into a sitting position, then had to lie back down when her head began to spin.

Chewbacca's face appeared over her, grumphing.

"I'm fine." Leia pushed herself to her elbows. "I just need water."

Chewbacca snatched a water bottle out of Emala's hands and passed it to Leia. She drank greedily. Then, once her head stopped spinning, she sat up and saw the reason the Squibs were trying to cancel the deal again. In the bottom of the canyon, hidden in the cool shadows beneath a sandrock overhang and barely visible, was the rear tread of a Jawa sandcrawler.

EIGHTEEN

Fifty meters from the overhang, Leia knew something was terribly wrong. The Askajians had stopped just inside the shadows and were milling about on foot, holding their dewback reins in one hand and their weapons in the other, clearly ready to fight or flee, and possibly both, on short notice. From deeper in the recess—it was really a huge disk-shaped erosion cave—came the raucous squawling of a flock of urusais; as more of the sandcrawler grew visible, the ground around it seemed to be squirming with their wings and serpentine necks.

But it was the smell that told the story. Though it was easily ten degrees cooler in the bottom of the canyon than it had been up on the plain—and another ten degrees cooler in the cave's shadows—Tatooine's temperature always remained formidable. And no smell in the galaxy was more unforgettable than that of battle casualties decaying in the heat.

Chewbacca groaned at the stench.

"Me, too," Leia said. "But I can stand a little retching if it gets Han some shade."

As sapped by the heat as Leia and Chewbacca, the Squibs did their best to trot ahead and get the first look at the sandcrawler. Leia still could not understand what—aside from profit—truly motivated this trio. Hutts—and

Threkin Horm—aside, they had to be the most selfish beings she had ever met, yet twice now they had not hesitated to risk their own lives to save Han's. Perhaps they saw some advantage in keeping him alive. Leia thought it more likely they simply operated by a code of conduct no one else understood. They clearly placed great significance on partnerships and adhering to bargains, yet their interpretations of the terms were so fluid that any agreement was rendered useless. They were the ultimate spokesbeings for the Lando Calrissian philosophy: anything to help a friend—as long as your interests converged. After that, it was everyone for himself.

The Squibs reached the cave a dozen paces ahead of Leia and Chewbacca. They shouldered their way through a tangle of plump thighs to the Askajians' front rank—then promptly stopped and yielded their lead. Leia saw why a minute later, when she and Chewbacca joined the group.

The floor of the huge cavern was carpeted with snarling urusais. They were crouching over the bodies of murdered Jawas or—in a handful of cases—slain stormtroopers, hissing and beating their scaly wings at the encroaching Askajians. Scattered among the scavengers was all manner of smashed equipment: speeder parts, dismembered droids, broken vaporators—most still in the crate—and a pair of Imperial hoverscouts, one lying on its side near the front of the sandcrawler, the other on its top near the back.

"So now we know why the Jawas did not keep their appointment," Borno said, joining Leia and the others. "The Imperials found them."

"Not really," Leia replied. "A *patrol* found them."

"I fail to see the difference."

Chewbacca groaned an explanation.

"That's right," Leia said. "The Imperials didn't find the sandcrawler—they lost a patrol. If the *Chimaera* knew about this, there would already be an intelligence squad down here tearing the sandcrawler apart."

Chewbacca growled another possibility.

Leia shook her head. "If the Imperials were going to ambush us, we'd be under attack already." She checked her chronometer. Less than ten minutes until the next pass. "And if they knew where we were going, why would they be flying a search grid?"

Chewbacca grunted.

"Let me guess," Borno said. "That means, 'Good point'?"

Chewbacca nodded, and C-3PO emerged from between two dewbacks.

"What a crime!" the droid cried. "Jawas are certainly no friends of mine, but what those stormtroopers did to them violates war accords as old as the Old Republic itself. And what they did to the droids . . . why they find it necessary to kill prisoners is beyond me!"

"Because they don't understand droids," Borno said. "Or technology in general."

C-3PO turned to face the Askajian. "I beg your pardon, sir, but in my experience the Empire has proven quite fond of technology."

"He's not talking about the Imperials, Threepio." Leia looked over the droid's shoulder to Borno. "Are you thinking Sand People?"

"I believe so. They must have attacked while the stormtroopers were searching the sandcrawler." He pointed a thick hand toward the sandcrawler's boarding ramp, which was surrounded by a random spray of metal dimples. "Those holes were made by slugthrowers."

Leia nodded. "Borno, I don't want to be disrespectful

to your trading partners, but we have only nine minutes before the next pass. There's a good chance he'll be directly over the canyon, and I could see—"

"The tread, of course. I saw it too." Borno issued a rapid series of orders in Askajian. Then, as the dewback drivers leapt into action, he translated for Leia and Chewbacca. "We will bring rocks to hide the tread. I doubt the dead will mind if they must wait a few minutes longer before we see to them."

"I'm afraid they have to wait longer than that." Leia waved her good arm at the urusais. "If they take wing and start circling—"

"Yes, it will alert the Imperials," Borno said. "I think the Jawas would understand."

"Actually," C-3PO began, "Jawa tradition is quite—"

"Threepio," Leia interrupted.

"Yes, Mistress Leia?"

"Not now."

"Of course. I was only trying to explain—"

Chewbacca snapped in Shyriiwook, and C-3PO retreated behind Borno. "No, I would not care to join the Jawa droids at all."

Leia checked her chronometer. "Eight minutes."

She motioned the others to follow and led the way to the back of the erosion cave, where the ceiling sloped down to meet the sand and the area was clear of battle casualties. The air was refreshingly cool—or at least not hot—and almost damp. She used one hand to smooth a place and had Chewbacca put Han there, then began to hand empty water bottles to C-3PO.

"Find our dewbacks and refill those from the water bladder," she ordered. "And be quick about it. Chewie, see if you can find a suit of stormtrooper armor with a functional cooling unit. Grees, I'd appreciate it if . . ."

Leia turned to address the Squib and discovered that neither he nor his two companions were anywhere to be seen. "What happened to the Squibs?"

The others glanced around, then C-3PO pointed across the squirming, scaly mass of urusai flesh toward the boarding ramp of the sandcrawler.

"I believe they are over there, Mistress Leia."

Chewbacca growled and turned to pursue the Squibs.

"No, Chewie," Leia said. "Armor first."

Chewbacca glanced at Han, then back to the Squibs, and groaned that Han would be furious to awaken and discover that he was the reason the little thieves had sneaked off with *Killik Twilight*.

Leia shrugged. "Han's been angry with me before." In the coolness of the cave, she knew Han would probably recover even without the stormtrooper suit. Right now, however, she was not taking chances. "I'm sure this won't be the last time."

Chewbacca looked at the sandcrawler and oomphrayed another protest. Despite what Han claimed, he really *did* care about the Shadowcast code key.

"Please, Chewie," Leia said. "We'll deal with the Squibs later."

"Mistress Leia," C-3PO interrupted, "I should point out that bargaining with the Squibs later will prove quite difficult. They feel that you cheated them by not revealing that the credit voucher you gave them was identity-coded, and they don't believe you have the funds currently available to match what they can negotiate from the Imperials. I'm quite certain that if they recover the painting, they intend to contact the Imperials and leave us to our fates."

"Really." This was pretty much what Leia had guessed, but it still angered her to hear. She glanced at her chronometer. Seven minutes. In the front of the cave, the Aska-jians were busy sweeping away sandcrawler tracks and stacking rocks in front of the tread she had seen earlier. "And you know this how, Threepio?"

"I heard the Squibs talking about it," the droid said. "Apparently, they are of the opinion that no one but a Squib can understand their secret trading language, but as I happen to be fluent in more than six million—"

"I *know*, Threepio." Leia turned to find Chewbacca waiting expectantly, glancing back toward the sand-crawler. "Chewie, will you just get the armor?"

Leaving Leia with the one bottle that still contained anything, Chewbacca and C-3PO scurried off to do as she had asked. Leia took two gulps of hot water, then raised Han's goggles and used the rest to wet his face and clothes. She watched carefully for any sign of stirring, hoping the moisture would have the same effect as last time, but a small cough was the only sign at all that he felt it.

Leia glanced back across the cave floor, dreading what the Squibs might find. If Kitster Banai had still been aboard the sandcrawler when the Tuskens sprang their ambush, Leia would be making a very difficult comm call to Tamora—the kind *she* hoped never to receive.

Leia returned her attention to Han. The color was al-ready coming back to his face, but she needed him to wake up. Drinking was the only way to get fluids into his body short of reattaching the hydration drip—which they no longer had.

Leia leaned close to his face. "Listen up, nerf herder. I'm tired of doing all the heavy work around here." She kissed him on the lips and began to feel dizzy—and not in the usual way. Han wasn't the only one who needed to drink. "Come on, Flyboy. Time to wake—"

Her vision narrowed, then Han's eyelids fluttered open, and she willed herself to stay conscious.

Leia smiled. "That's better . . ."

But his eyes weren't looking at her. They were glassy and vacant, the pupils fixed and dilated.

"Han!" She grabbed his shoulder and began to shake him. "Where do you think you're going? Come back here!"

As if obeying, a pair of white pinpricks appeared in the depths of his pupils. They rose toward the surface, swelling into tiny balls of pale flame and spilling out over the irises until they completely covered the eyes, two tiny suns crackling and hissing in a pair of dead empty sockets.

"Han?"

Leia's tongue had swollen to twice its size, and the word died rasping in her mouth. She turned to wave Chewbacca over and found the shadows beneath the overhang suddenly as thick as a nebula, the Wookiee's form indistinguishable from dozens of other ghostly silhouettes gliding through the murk.

Finally, Leia understood what was happening. *Not another Force-vision—please not this one.*

A soft crackling arose beneath her, and she forced herself to look down. The white suns were still burning in Han's eye sockets.

"*Mine.*" Though the voice was Han's, the tone was not. The tone was hard and sibilant and uncaring. "*Mine.*"

"No," Leia rasped. "Please."

The white spheres in Han's eyes flared. "*Mine.*"

Leia's first instinct was to repudiate the voice, to slap the apparition across the face and order it to go away. But it would only be Han she was hitting. Visions could not be vanquished by striking them. They were much more difficult to be rid of than that. They had to be understood.

A sleepy snarl—*Han's* sleepy snarl—sounded at Leia's side. Thinking the vision had taken some strange new turn, she glanced over and was baffled to see him lying next to her, encased in a suit of white stormtrooper armor. His head was propped on a rolled sand cloak, and a wall of fur was kneeling beside him. She looked forward—*up*—again. Han's face continued to hang above her, the white spheres in his eyes now golden and shining more faintly.

"How wonderful!" The voice was familiar, but it was not Han's—it was far too chirpy and obeisant to be Han's. "Princess Leia seems to be recovering!"

A deep voice rumbled something in Shyriiwook that Leia could not quite catch.

"I really don't think it's my place to make the Princess do any—"

The deep voice growled again. The face above her—no longer Han's, and not all that close to human—recoiled, banging the low stone ceiling with a distinctly metallic tone. A fleshless hand slid under Leia's neck and lifted her head.

"Mistress Leia, may I offer you some bactade?"

"Threepio?" Leia gasped. "What happened?"

"I'm certainly no medical droid." C-3PO's face changed from the visage of Leia's vision—or had it only been a dream?—to its normal golden self. "But it appears you collapsed."

Chewbacca growled ominously.

"Would you please drink some of this?" C-3PO held a bottle filled with brown liquid to her lips.

Beside Leia, Han sprayed a mouthful of bactade over Chewbacca's chest. "That's not Gizer! It's not even ale!"

Chewbacca snarled a threat, then returned the bottle to his patient's lips. This time, Han drank.

Leia pushed herself up and was surprised to find her own torso encased in white armor. Her injured shoulder was sore, but it held.

"What's . . ." She let the question trail off, noticing how cool her body felt, and took the bottle. "How long have I been unconscious?"

"We found you one standard hour and twenty-three minutes ago," C-3PO replied. "Master Chewbacca had to fight three urusais—"

"An *hour*?"

Obviously, the Askajians had succeeded in camouflaging the sandcrawler's presence. Leia glanced out into the cave and found the floor still swarming with urusais, three lying nearby with broken necks. The Askajians had dragged the smashed vaporators over to one side of the cavern and, hoping to salvage what they could, were exchanging their tomuon wool for the new cargo. Ever the opportunists, the Squibs were busy ferrying the wool onto the sandcrawler.

Leia ignored them and, still shaken from her vision—or was this one only a dream?—she turned to Han. "How are you feeling?"

"Awful. Head like a bantha stepped on it." He jerked a thumb at Chewbacca. "And this furbag keeps trying to get me to drink stale mudwater."

Chewbacca groaned defensively.

"I don't care when you mixed it," Han said. "It still tastes like mudwater."

"Mudwater or not, you need to drink it." Leia was determined to keep Han healthy. She forced a smile and raised her bottle. "I will if you will."

Han looked as though he had just walked into a performance hall to find a Gamorrean dancer on stage.

"Afraid?" Leia asked.

"Yeah, right."

Han snatched the bactade from Chewbacca, but continued to eye Leia. At first, she thought he was just waiting for her to drink first, but when she raised her bottle, he made no move to follow.

"What's wrong?" she asked.

"Nothing." Han lifted the bottle to his lips and, still looking at her, spoke around the opening. "Just thinking you look hot in white."

Leia ran a hand through her hair and found it caked with sand and sweat. "Yeah—hot is right."

She managed to down the entire bottle of bactade, though the chalky taste was so terrible she wondered if she would ever be able to enjoy a mud-colored drink again. Han, she was happy to see, had also finished his.

"Another?" he challenged.

Just the thought of bactade made Leia want to retch, but anything to keep Han healthy. She smiled and said, "Why not?"

"Set 'em up, Chewie," Han said.

Chewbacca grumbled that this was no time for a drinking contest, then gestured across the cave floor toward Borno, who was ambling in their direction with a Jawa cradled in the crook of one huge arm.

"It appears the Tuskens neglected to kill someone," C-3PO observed. "Isn't that marvelous?"

Leia and Han glanced at each other, then Han said, "I wouldn't put it that way to the Jawa, Threepio."

Borno stopped at the edge of the group, and Leia saw that the Jawa was holding one leg out straight and trying to keep it from moving.

When she and Han started to rise, the Askajian waved them off. "Save your strength. You'll need it when we leave."

"Leave?" Leia thought of her vision and cast a nervous eye toward the bustling Askajians. "How soon will that be?"

Borno shrugged. "A quarter hour. As soon as we are loaded."

Chewbacca snarled a question.

"Master Chewbacca wishes to inquire about the Imperials," C-3PO translated. "They may still be in the area."

Borno relaxed and gave a dismissive wave. "We have not heard any TIEs in an hour. And no Imperial in the galaxy can find me in these canyons."

Leia exchanged glances with Han; they had both heard similar boasts before. Chewbacca growled another question.

After C-3PO translated, Borno shook his head. "We did not come across the moss-painting you asked about, or any humans except the dead Imperials." He cast a pointed glance at the sandcrawler. "But the Squibs would not let us into the upper portions of the sandcrawler."

Han turned to Leia. "You let them have *Twilight*?"

Leia shrugged. "We had other things to worry about."

"Other things?" Han demanded. "After all I've been through to get it? After all *we've* been through? What could be more important than that?"

"*You*, Han," Leia said. "I told Chewie to take care of you and forget about the Squibs."

Han scowled, looking more disappointed than angry. "That wasn't very smart, was it? Chewie's the big one."

"Han—"

"You should have sent *him* after the Squibs and stayed here to take care of me yourself." Han did not seem to notice that Borno and Chewbacca had stopped talking and were now listening to him and Leia. "Maybe then you wouldn't have collapsed—"

"Han!"

"Yeah?"

"I *did* stay," Leia said.

"Stay where?"

"Here, with you."

"You did?" Han's scowl changed to one of confusion. "Then who was watching the Squibs?"

Leia shook her head. "No one."

That seemed to take the efflux out of his nacelles. His jaw dropped and he stared off toward the sandcrawler for several moments, then finally asked, "So you just let the Squibs go after *Twilight* alone?"

Leia nodded.

"Because you were worried about me."

Leia nodded again.

"Well . . ." For once in his life, Han seemed at a loss for words.

Chewbacca groaned a suggestion.

"Huh?" Han asked.

Chewbacca added an explanation.

"I suppose that *is* what you say." Han turned to Leia. "Thanks."

"Don't mention it." Leia pasted on her most diplomatic smile, then gathered herself to rise, adding under her breath, "Nerf herder."

Borno reached down with his free hand and spared Leia the exertion of lifting herself to her feet. "We will drop you in Motesta. There is an Imperial deserter there who can be trusted."

Leia's mind flashed on the image of Han's eyes just before the suns had appeared, when the pupils were fixed and dilated. Perhaps the dream had been a vision and perhaps not, but suddenly she could not bear the thought of continuing to travel with the Askajians.

"Do not be troubled because Gwend was once an Imperial." Borno grew thoughtful for a moment, then added, "He is the one who helped us come here. And he is helping another tribe come soon. That is why we need the vaporators."

Leia began to have a sinking feeling. Askajians were not known for their wanderlust—quite the opposite. If another tribe was coming to Tatooine, there was good reason.

"How soon?" Leia was thinking of Wedge's secret mission to Askaj—and of the possibility that Mon Mothma would recall Wraith Squadron if she did not hear from Leia before long. "After Grand Moff Wilkadon's tour?"

Borno's jaw dropped. "How did you guess?"

"The timing seemed close," Leia said. "Do you know if they have left Askaj yet?"

"Not Askaj. But they have left their village. We will not hear from them again until they reach Tatooine." Borno studied her carefully, then asked, "They have already committed themselves to payment. Will their ship be waiting?"

"I hope so." Leia didn't know how else to answer. She didn't know the details of the mission, but after such a bold operation, it wouldn't be unusual for New Republic Intelligence to relocate a group of resistance fighters— leaving them behind would be a virtual death sentence. She laid her hand on Borno's arm. "I think I know the transport line they'll be using. I have to contact them anyway, and I'll certainly urge them to be on time. But Borno, we can't continue with your caravan."

"You want us to leave you?" Borno glanced around the cave. "Here?"

"Uh, yeah," Han said, also rising. "We've got to find that painting." He glanced at Leia. "Right?"

"Right," Leia agreed.

Borno looked doubtful. "Forgive me for saying so, but you are a hundred kilometers from the nearest hut, the Squibs have already claimed salvage rights on the sandcrawler—" He ignored the angry outburst this drew from the Jawa. "—and they have no intention of giving you a ride—even if they do get it started. I am sorry, but I do not think you humans will do very well walking."

"We won't need to," Leia said. Maybe she was just shaken and maybe not, but—for the first time since coming to Tatooine—she felt in her stomach that she was making the right decision. "There are two hoverscouts and plenty of spare parts from the sandcrawler lying around. I'm sure we can cobble something together." She glanced at Chewbacca. "Can't we, Chewie?"

Chewbacca spread his arms and grunted.

"You see?" Han said, stepping to Leia's side. "We'll be fine. Have ourselves a look around, make a couple of repairs, and we'll be on our way home."

Borno studied them carefully for a moment, then asked, "You doubt my judgment? You do not think the stormtroopers are really gone?"

"I think it would be dangerous to underestimate these Imperials." Part of Leia's mind wondered if she wasn't condemning them to a slow and thirsty death—or a fast one, if the Tuskens returned—but it was a very small part, one she felt more comfortable ignoring than her instincts. "But I am *certain* we have pushed our luck as far as we dare. Should you run into Imperials later, it will be better for everyone if we aren't there."

Borno spread his hands in imitation of Chewbacca and grunted. "If that is your choice."

"It is." Leia was about to tell Borno not to deny seeing them if the Imperials *did* find his caravan—then a better idea occurred to her. "Borno, how you would like a portable holocomm?"

Borno's already narrow eyes diminished to slits. "What would I have to do for it?"

"Not much," Leia said. "Just call the Imperials and tell them you left us back in the Great Chott, after their TIE frightened you and you changed your mind about helping us."

"Lie to Imperials?" Borno grinned hugely. "Nobody is better at that than Askajians."

"Good." Leia explained her plan.

Borno nodded. "I can do that." He extended the arm holding the Jawa, drawing a hiss of pain from the little being. "We found this survivor hiding in a vaporator crate. I was hoping you could help him. He seems to have broken a leg."

"Of course." Leia looked into the glowing eyes beneath the Jawa's hood. "I'm no doctor, but I have field-dressed my share of wounds. I'll do what I can, if you like."

"*Go mob un loo?*" the Jawa jabbered.

"He wants to know how much it will cost," C-3PO translated.

"*Tomo!*"

"My apologies," C-3PO said to the Jawa. "*She.*"

Leia smiled. "It won't cost—"

"I don't know," Han said, cutting her off. He made a show of examining the Jawa's leg, then turned to Leia and gave her his *play-along-with-me* look. "That's a pretty serious break."

"Han!" Leia said. "How can you even think—"

She was interrupted when Chewbacca peered over her shoulder and agreed with Han that it was the worst break he had ever seen.

C-3PO duly translated this into Jawa.

The Jawa made a lengthy reply.

C-3PO translated, "She says the break is not as serious

as it looks. She will give you three ion blasters and not a power cell more."

Han and Chewbacca glanced at each other and shook their heads, and then Leia understood.

She peered at the leg and asked, "What's that lump? It looks awfully big."

"I can see my presence is no longer required here," Borno said. He laid the Jawa on the ground, then tipped his many-jowled chin to Leia and the others. "I will be ready when you are."

"I'll be along as soon as I'm finished here," Leia replied. The Jawa made another offer.

"She can add a fine T-eleven repeating blaster," C-3PO said.

"A T-eleven?" Han scoffed. "That was old when Tatooine had lakes."

"Any vidmaps?" Leia asked. Borno still had theirs, and he was not offering to return it. "We could use a vidmap."

"A *working* vidmap," Han clarified.

The Jawa hissed in pain and jabbered, *"Yanna kuzu peekay, jo."*

"She has no vidmaps," C-3PO said. "But she can tell you how to find anyplace you're looking for."

Han scowled at this. "Isn't this the sandcrawler that picked up that crashed swoop a couple of nights ago?"

The Jawa nodded, then, through C-3PO, asked how he knew.

"Because I was following it," Han said. "And you left *me* out in the storm."

The Jawa chortled something that sounded like "uh-oh."

"She apologizes—"

"Yeah, I got it," Han said. "And she's sure there was no vidmap on that swoop?"

The Jawa went into an elaborate explanation that, when

C-3PO translated it, amounted to "no one in the clan understood the swoop either. Who flies a rocket-powered swoop around in the middle of a sandstorm? Kitster Banai had to have a death wish, or be crazy, or possibly be on the run from a Hutt. In any case, he was on a racing swoop, and racing swoops don't have vidmaps."

Leia recalled that Ulda had made that old Podracer pilot install one on Han's before selling it to them. "But did Kitster survive? Did he have—"

The Jawa jabbered an interruption, which C-3PO repeated as, "Herat would like to remind you that you are currently in negotiations over the price of repairing her broken leg. If you wish to discuss the price of the information you are seeking, she would be glad to open those negotiations *after* you have completed the repair."

"Why don't we trade straight across?" Leia suggested. "The information for the repair?"

"*Oog,*" Herat snarled.

"No," C-3PO translated.

"You're holding back?" Leia could hardly believe it. A broken leg, her crew massacred, surrounded by strangers, and Herat was still maneuvering for advantage. The New Republic should have negotiators like her. Leia met the Jawa's yellow gaze with new respect, then began to roll up her sleeves. "Well, if a T-eleven and three ion blasters are the best you have to offer, so be it. You get what you pay for in this galaxy."

Herat turned to C-3PO and chattered a long sentence.

"She says you have the hearts of a Hutt," C-3PO translated. "But she is in pain and doesn't wish to walk with a limp for the rest of her life. She will tell you what happened to Kitster Banai and his painting."

A short chortle.

"*Or* his painting," C-3PO corrected.

"She drives a hard bargain." Leia sighed. "Now let's talk about painkillers."

Herat broke into a rapid twaddle.

"The Tusken Raiders took them both," C-3PO translated. "She can show you where to catch them."

"She can?" Han sounded truly excited. "For that, we'll throw in an airsplint."

"We will?" Leia turned to Han. "You want to chase down a tribe of *Sand People*?"

Han shrugged. "It's a great painting."

"Sure it is." In her mind's eye, Leia recalled the white suns that had taken the place of Han's eyes. She began to worry that the dream had not been warning her about the caravan after all; that this had been the path she must not choose—or that the nightmare would come true no matter which she chose. Perhaps that was what the voice meant when it kept saying "mine," that no matter what she did, the future—at least this part of it—would end the same. To Han, she said, "It's a great painting—as long as the Sand People keep it watered."

Han scowled, clearly confused by her sudden reticence to go after the painting. "It has a moisture-control device. A really *great* moisture-control device."

"I'm aware of that," Leia said. "But these are Tusken Raiders. Things will get dangerous."

"*Get* dangerous? What do you think . . ."

Han let the sentence trail off, then shook his head, his brow rising in guilt or anger—even Leia could not tell which.

The Jawa chittered a question.

"Herat asks why the Imperials are so interested in a moisture-control device," C-3PO said. "And if you can please finish your negotiations with her before opening any more between yourselves. She is in a certain amount of pain."

"None of her business and in a minute." Han kept his eyes fixed on Leia. "I thought you wanted to recover the painting. *I* want to recover it."

Leia stared at him. "Why, Han?"

"Like I said, it's a great painting." Han glanced at the Jawa, clearly trying to decide how much he could reveal. "One I wouldn't want the Imperials to have."

"Why, Han?" Leia repeated. "And I'm not talking about how useful the moisture-control device would be to them. I want to know why *you* wouldn't want them to have it."

Comprehension dawned in Han's eyes. "Because I don't want it hanging in some Imperial admiral's stateroom." His tone was growing defensive, a sure sign that they were treading ground close to something he did not want to admit—perhaps something he did not even understand himself. "Didn't I say that already?"

"Not good enough," Leia said. "You're no longer a member of the New Republic government *or* military. What do you care if it falls into enemy hands?"

"I care, okay?" Not even waiting for Leia to shake her head, Han continued, "I've been a nerfhead lately."

"*Now* we're getting somewhere."

"*Mambay,*" the Jawa chittered.

"Herat hopes so," C-3PO reported.

Leia ignored them both and waited for Han to continue. Han shot her a *don't-push-it* look, but said, "I don't know what I've been thinking, acting like the Provisional Council is the whole government. Don't expect me to sit down with Mon Mothma or Borsk Fey'lya anytime soon, but I've got too much on the table to turn my back on the New Republic now." He thought for a moment, then frowned. "And you're the biggest part of it, Leia. Nothing's going to change that."

Leia grew almost dizzy—in the good way. "And I wouldn't want it to."

Chewbacca groaned.

Leia took Han's hand and would have kissed him, except the Jawa was watching.

"We have to try," Han said.

Leia nodded and said, "In that case, we had better accept Herat's offer." She motioned for the medical kit and turned back to the Jawa. "Where can we catch the Sand People?"

Herat replied with a long burgle.

"After you have set the leg," C-3PO said. "She wants to be sure you don't try to change the terms again."

"Okay," Leia said. "That's fair."

Chewbacca groaned and slapped his brow.

"Now you've done it." Han shook his head in frustration. "We'll never get paid."

Herat tittered an angry reply.

"She says she is not that kind of Jawa," C-3PO reported.

"Sure she isn't." Han rolled his eyes and winked at Chewbacca. "You ever heard that one before?"

Herat exploded into a flurry of invective.

"My goodness!" C-3PO gasped. "I don't think I should repeat *that*!"

Herat was still cursing when Leia, taking advantage of the distraction, grabbed the Jawa at the ankle and pulled. There was a soft pop, and the depths beneath Herat's hood fell dark as her yellow eyes blinked shut.

"Uh, Leia, dear?" Han asked. "Maybe you missed that part about not getting paid. No matter what they say, with Jawas it's strictly payment up front."

"Han, are you saying you were willing to let that poor creature suffer until she told us what we want to know?"

"Well, when you put it like that . . ."

"Besides, she has a broken leg," Leia added. "She's going to need a ride."

Han raised his brow. "That's what I love about you."

"Quick learner?"

"Tough negotiator."

Two hours later, Leia and Han were ten kilometers down the canyon, kneeling in the shadows of a small tributary gorge with the proper orientation to obtain a signal, watching the seconds pass on their chronometers and waiting for Mon Mothma to come to the comm station in her private apartment. While still sore, Leia's shoulder had benefited enough from the bactade that she could use her arm almost normally—as long as she didn't mind the pain.

Most of the Askajian caravan had long ago vanished into the labyrinth of desert canyons, but Borno was ten meters up the gorge, sitting astride his dewback and ready to take the holocomm. Chewbacca and C-3PO were waiting with Herat at the mouth of the little ravine, the repulsorlift engine of their captured Imperial hoverscout still running. The Squibs were—presumably—still back in the erosion cave, trying to bring the reactor core of their "salvaged" sandcrawler on-line without the initializer core that Han had found lying among a heap of debris strewn through the cavern by the Tusken Raiders.

"What part of *hurry* doesn't the chief councilor understand?" Han asked. Like Leia, he still wore pieces of stormtrooper armor with the cooling unit turned to high. "It's been two minutes."

By now, Leia knew, the duty officers aboard the *Chimaera*'s intelligence launch would be reporting a suspicious HoloNet transmission to their watch commander—possibly even Commander Quenton from the auction. About five minutes after the commander was notified, the first flight of TIEs would arrive and find Borno standing atop the rim of the canyon beside the holocomm, waving them down. It would take perhaps another fifteen minutes—thirty, if the Solos were lucky—for an assault shuttle to arrive.

If all went well, the company captain would believe the tale of contrition he found on the datapad Borno left behind and rush off into the middle of the Great Chott without even bothering to track down the caravan leader. If matters went horribly, Borno had promised he would not be taken alive—and Leia believed him, if for no other reason than his determination to keep secret the location of his village.

Mon Mothma's image finally flickered into existence over the holocomm, her hair disheveled and her eyes still heavy with sleep. "Leia? I'm sorry—"

"It's okay," Leia interrupted. "But I'm transmitting hot. We have only sixty seconds before I have to shut down."

Mon Mothma's expression grew suddenly more alert. "I understand. Have you recovered the painting?"

"Not yet, but neither have the Imperials," Leia said. "And I have news about Wraith's mission. Local intelligence suggests that indigenous forces are already moving into position and can't be contacted. Repeat, they cannot be contacted."

"*Local* intelligence? On Tatooine?"

"It's a long story, and we don't have the time," Leia said. "But I believe it to be reliable."

The worry lines around Mon Mothma's mouth deepened. "Leia, after Luke passed along your report, I made the decision to recall the Wraiths. The order has already been coded. It goes out in thirty hours."

"Can you cancel?"

Mon Mothma bit her lip, her gaze dropping in thought,

then finally shook her head. "Not without the painting. We don't know how long it would take the Imperials to start cracking the codes with an old key—"

"But they would know about the network," Leia finished. "And that might be enough."

"You know what we would be risking."

Leia did—a Star Destroyer battle group, complete with Wedge Antilles, the Wraiths, and probably the Rogues and several other crack squadrons as well.

"I understand," she said. "But give us the thirty hours."

"Us?" Mon Mothma asked.

Leia nodded. "Han's on board with this."

Mon Mothma smiled. "Tell him welcome back. The New Republic has missed him."

Leia glanced over and found Han sneering at the hologram. "He'll be very happy to hear that. And please tell your aides to monitor all channels of communication. I don't know how we'll be contacting you again, but it won't be with this unit."

"I will," Mon Mothma said. "And Leia—may the Force be with you."

"Thanks—we're going to need it."

Leia ended the transmission, then immediately shut the unit down and opened the outer case.

"That's what I don't like about that woman." Han knelt beside Leia and removed the ghost-wave encoder, then rerouted the signal feeds so the unit would operate as a normal holocomm. "She always makes the safe play."

"It's the right play, Han."

"You see—that's another thing I don't like."

Han zipped the transmitter into a pocket, then closed the case and carried the unit over to Borno.

"Thanks, pal." Han passed the case up. "You be careful."   •

"And you, my friends. May the sand never melt your boot soles."

"May you always find shade from the suns," Leia replied. "If there is ever anything else the New Republic government can do for you, please—"

"Do for us?" Borno laughed. "I do not think so, Princess. Governments are what we are hiding from."

The Askajian turned and, waving a pudgy hand, urged his dewback into a gallop.

NINETEEN

For a change Han felt pretty good about being on Tatooine. No price on his head, no hibernation sickness, no Jabba the Hutt—that alone made the place a sun-planet paradise. He was at the wheel of an agile hover-scout flying all-out through the heart of the Jundland Wastes, the afternoon shadows just beginning to camouflage the boulders in the canyon bottom and the prettiest woman in the galaxy clutching the crash bar beside him.

Maybe Leia had been thinking about the same things—and about how she'd almost lost Han again—as well. She was constantly fussing over him, offering him water, checking to be certain he was cool enough, generally telling him she loved him in a thousand small ways. Not that he was complaining, but Han failed to understand why. He had been acting like a Hutt since their return from Dathomir, treating the Provisional Council as though it was a rival and all but demanding that Leia choose between them.

Then, when she had chosen him over duty back in the cave, he had finally seen that this was one bluff he could not afford to win. Withdrawing from the council would give Leia a huge marker to call in, and sooner or later, Han would have to sacrifice something in return—maybe high-stakes sabacc, his wanderlust, or possibly even the *Falcon*. Whatever it was, he knew he could not surrender such a big part of himself and remain who he was, just as he knew that Leia could not give up her work on the council and remain the woman he loved.

Mostly, though, Han really did not want the Imperials to get their hands on that code key. Whatever his feelings toward the Provisional Council—and they remained ambivalent, at least toward Mon Mothma and the others who had been so ready to condemn Leia to a loveless marriage—Han loved the New Republic, and he would have hated himself for allowing his hurt feelings to cost it one of its most effective and best-kept secrets.

But Han was not about to admit any of this. He was enjoying the attention too much—though he *was* tiring of hearing Leia say, "Careful, nerf herder."

Almost as good as all the attention from Leia, Han had finally outsmarted the Squibs. With the sandcrawler's initializer core hidden in the speeder's cargo bay, Grees and his compatriots would still be in the cave, struggling to bring the reactor core on-line when Herat returned with her clanmates to bury their dead and reclaim their property.

Even the Imperials were behaving as expected. Ten minutes after Han and the others parted ways with Borno, a trio of TIEs had begun to circle the Askajians' position. Twenty minutes later—by which time the Solo party was seventy kilometers away—the expected assault shuttle had arrived on the scene. Han would probably never know whether the Imperials had sent a squad to capture Borno—and if so, whether they had succeeded—but the shuttle had spent only a few minutes on the ground before streaking back into the heart of the Great Chott.

Now Herat was guiding Han and the others through a labyrinth of deep canyons and narrow gorges, where it would prove difficult—practically impossible—for any spy satellite to find them. Their goal, the Jawa had explained, was an oasis deep in Tusken territory, a sacred ghost village on the far side of the mountains. An entire tribe of Sand People had once been found dead there, hacked to pieces by an angry ghost—or so the Sand People believed. Now all Tuskens stopped there to present gifts and make sacrifices before leaving the area. Herat assured them that the Sand People intended to offer Kitster and his painting to this "ghost." All Han and Leia need do to recover *Killik Twilight* was wait until the Tuskens departed, then walk down and get it.

But if they wanted to save their friend, they would have to elude the Tusken sentries and sneak into the village without being killed. If that was their intention, Herat hoped they would understand if she waited in the hoverscout with the engines running and the blaster cannon armed.

Assuming things went smoothly, Han thought they might be back aboard the *Falcon* by dawn—in plenty of time to report their success to Mon Mothma. They continued through the canyons for another hour before Herat finally guided them into a narrow, rising gulch, then climbed to a vast sandrock plateau painted in crimson and rust by the setting suns.

Han stopped the hoverscout just within the gulch.

"I don't know about this," he said. "It'd be pretty easy for an Imperial eye to spot us out there."

Herat babbled a ten-second reply.

"She says it's the only way," C-3PO replied. "But we are a long way from the Great Chott, and there is no shortage of speeder traffic out here."

"*Hubaduja,*" Herat added.

"At least two or three vehicles per week."

Han glanced over at Leia, who continued to clench the crash bar with one white-knuckled hand. "What do you think?" he asked.

"Yes, let's go out where you can drive *really* fast." She shook her head. "Why are you asking me? I don't know where this 'ghost oasis' is."

She finally released the crash bar and activated the hoverscout's on-board holomap, which instantly displayed the designator SSC17 at the center. An instant later, a three-dimensional holograph of the immediate area appeared around the symbol, showing SSC17 at the edge of a small crab-shaped plateau, the maze of canyons through which they had just come delineated behind it in great detail. There were only three other designators on the map, one at the front of the display showing six buildings labeled SETTLEMENT, one on Leia's side of the plateau reading HERMITAGE—ABANDONED, and a third, on Han's side near the rolling sands of the Great Dune Sea, marked MONASTERY/PALACE—OCCUPANTS UNKNOWN.

Han pushed a finger into the holograph and stopped at the settlement. "That the place, Herat?"

The Jawa answered, and C-3PO translated, "You are certain you can guarantee that her clan's sandcrawler will still be at the cave when she returns, Captain Solo? She is most nervous about the Squibs."

Chewbacca asked if there was a spare initializer on board.

"No," came the answer.

"Then it'll be there. What would the Imperials want with a rolling recycling factory?" Han wiggled his finger in the holograph. "Is this the place or not? We can't leave this holomap on all evening. We didn't have time to deactivate the transponder."

"You didn't?" Leia gasped. "You might have mentioned that before you let me turn it on."

"Relax," Han said. "It's an *Imperial* transponder. Even if the operator notices the signal, he's not going to get too worked up about it."

Herat chiddled doubtfully, then continued.

"She says the oasis is beyond Wayfar, and more toward the old Kenobi place. Your bearing should be about a third—"

"Kenobi?" Leia repeated. "Obi-Wan Kenobi's?" She hadn't realized they were so close.

The Jawa shook her head and explained that it belonged to old Ben Kenobi.

"She says he has been gone for quite some time," C-3PO added. "But I'm sure it's the same place. Master Luke made the same mistake when—"

"We get it, Goldenrod." Han moved his finger to the indicated place. "That about right?"

Herat chiddled that it was. Han set a waypoint on the compass, then shut off the holomap and started across the plateau, Leia muttering something to herself about Luke, Obi-Wan, and thinking things through.

A stop at Obi-Wan's was out of the question. Leia knew that. With the Imperials searching for them, Kitster bound for sacrifice at the ghost village, and Wraith Squadron on the verge of being recalled from the Askaj mission, they had no time for side trips. But she could not stop thinking about the hermitage. Luke's journey as a Jedi had begun there, and he had told her once that he found it a good place to go to think matters through.

The few times Leia had been there, she'd felt the same—and thinking matters through was something she was feeling an increasing need to do. The encounters with her father's old friends, her grandmother's diary, the visions—or hallucinations, or whatever they were—it was all too much to ignore. The Force was touching her in a way it never had before. Perhaps it was only her father, reaching out to her as he had at Bakura, seeking the forgiveness she had refused to grant him then. Perhaps it was a response to all the transitions she had been going through during the last few years—from hero of the Rebellion to public servant, from Princess to ambassador of a lost world, from single woman to wife. Or perhaps it was the Tatoo system itself—the twin suns exerting some peculiar influence on her Skywalker bloodline, just as they sometimes grew impossibly luminous or played electromagnetic sabacc with starship sensor systems. She was not fool enough to pretend she knew.

What Leia did know was that she could not ask Han to take her to Obi-Wan's. Every hour of delay in reaching the oasis increased the likelihood that Kitster Banai would be sacrificed to the ghost-spirit and that the Imperials would find them again, and she would not endanger others while she tried to sort out her own jumbled feelings. No matter how powerfully she was beginning to feel she should.

Besides, Leia had another way to explore her connection to this place and to her past. With Han finally steering a straight course and three more hours before they reached the oasis, now seemed a good time to resume viewing her grandmother's journal. It might even keep her mind off Han's piloting.

21:18:16
Today, I came home to find Cliegg Lars waiting on my stairs with a huge carton of produce from his farm— pallies, a hubba gourd, bloddles, podpoppers, even a bristlemelon. He said prices were down in Mos Eisley so he decided to try his luck up here, but I think he had another reason for coming ... at least I hope so. He

*showed me how to burn the spines off the bristlemelon,
and we shared it for dinner. I don't know if I have ever
tasted anything so sweet before.*

"What are you listening to?" Han asked. Leia was
glad to see that he kept his eyes focused through the
windscreen, for night was falling and they were flying
along at a speed that only Han Solo could think was safe.
"That voice sounds vaguely familiar."

"It should," Leia answered. "It belongs to Shmi
Skywalker—my grandmother."

Han peered over into Leia's lap. "Your *what*?"

The Jawa erupted into panicked jabbering.

"Dear oh dear!" C-3PO yelled. "We'll be smashed—"

Chewbacca let out a scolding growl, and Leia looked
up to see a plume of dust ahead rapidly swelling into a
cloud.

"All right, don't get your fur all matted," Han said.

He casually steered into the thickest part of the dust
plume, and, through Han's window, Leia glimpsed the
flailing club-tails of a dozen wild galoomps. The hoverscout emerged on the other side of the cloud and continued on its way.

"Your grandmother?" Han asked, this time keeping
his eyes forward.

Leia explained the journal's significance and how she
had come by it.

Han shook his head in amazement. "That must be
something, knowing who your grandmother is."

"Only if I don't end up plastered to the backside of a
bantha." Leia turned the journal so he would not be able
to see the display. "Keep your eyes on the . . . well, whatever's out there."

"Just keep the volume up. I'm interested, too."

Leia did not miss the envy in Han's voice. He had no idea who either of his own grandmothers might be; he had been raised aboard a tramp freighter with no knowledge of his real parents, and the closest thing he had ever known to a grandmother was Dewlanna. That was another thing they had in common, she supposed—and it was probably part of the motivation behind his desire to have a family.

20:08:17

Cliegg brought his son, Owen, up to help load some vaporators he was buying—though I suspect the vaporators were an excuse to introduce us. He could have bought them in Mos Eisley more easily. Owen's about your age, Annie, with his father's square face and blue eyes. He doesn't resemble the way I picture you, but it was impossible to look at him without thinking of you, and how you must be changing from the little boy I knew.

After that day, all hint of resentment seemed to vanish from Shmi's attitude toward her master. She cheerfully did everything Watto asked, sometimes even anticipating his requests or tending to tasks he had not thought of himself. This only served to make the Toydarian more clinging and possessive, often to the point at which he found excuses to keep Shmi at the junkyard until well after dark. Shmi never complained, even when Watto kept her so busy she had no time to do more than point the diary camera at the stars and whisper to herself that she knew Annie was happy and doing well. And this entry she never failed to make, for Anakin remained at the center of her thoughts—even when it became obvious that Cliegg had fallen as much in love with her as she had with him.

At least once a week, Shmi would return home to find Cliegg waiting on her steps with a box of produce from his moisture farm, occasionally even with a bouquet of hubba blossoms. It wasn't long before she gave him the security codes.

20:51:18

While I was having my weekly drink with Watto today, he told me that my "suitor" had tried to buy me for a landspeeder. Watto seemed to think I would be insulted that Cliegg had not offered more, but I'm not. Watto doesn't understand how much a landspeeder is worth to a moisture farmer.

The next months went by quickly. Cliegg tried several more times to buy Shmi, eventually offering much more than a slave of her age could be expected to bring. Instead of being angry with Watto for taking advantage of Cliegg's feelings to drive up the price, Shmi seemed to accept the Toydarian's refusals with amused patience, as though she knew he would eventually yield.

It seemed to Leia that Watto's behavior was closer to that of a jealous beau than an owner. He began to keep Shmi closer to him than ever, occasionally closing shop so he could take her on journeys to bid on wrecks. Twice, he even made a side trip to show her the sights, once taking her to Mos Eisley and another time to see the magnificent alabaster pinnacles of the Rock Palace. The whole time, according to Shmi's diary, he talked about nothing but how hard the life on a moisture farm was, and he even stopped at a couple to show her.

Shmi told Watto that she wanted him to sell her to Cliegg for a fair price. Watto told Shmi not to see Cliegg anymore.

Shmi reported that she laughed in his face.

Soon after, she came home late to discover Cliegg waiting in her hut for the second time in a week.

06:22:19

I poured us some pallie wine and made a light dinner, then Cliegg announced he had talked "it" over with Owen. They had decided to sell the moisture farm so they could buy me from Watto. And if Watto refused, they were going to swat him and use the money to buy us all passage offplanet.

I had to explain about the transmitter bomb—again. Besides, it would take a lot more than the price of a moisture farm to make a miser like Watto sell his only friend. Cliegg snorted when I called myself Watto's friend, but I am. I've grown fond of him over the years ... and he misses you, Annie. That gives him a warm place in my heart.

But I think Cliegg is the one, Anakin. I've waited five years for someone I can trust, and now I know I've found him.

I'm going to show him what Qui-Gon sent.

Leia sat slumped in the seat beside Han, faintly aware of her tender shoulder and feeling distinctly inadequate in the presence of her grandmother's memory. Watto had been Shmi's master—and her son's—for *years*, and still she had somehow found it inside herself to forgive him. Leia had been Jabba's slave for one *night*, and she had strangled him with the chain that bound her.

Of course, there was a world of difference between Watto and Jabba.

Over the next few weeks, Shmi was consumed with mysterious "preparations," though never so much so that she forgot her nightly affirmation of faith in Anakin's well-being. She seemed at once contrite and elated, as though she felt guilty about how much she was going to enjoy what she was planning. As excited as she was, she never explained what she was preparing for—deliberately, Leia thought.

Leia asked for the next entry, and her grandmother's face appeared in the display looking as radiant as a moon. Shmi began by whispering into the journal.

09:58:20

Annie, we have completed our preparations, Owen is ready to play his part, and something special is about to happen. I know you will want to see it. And I'm so excited, I want a record of this, too.

Shmi's face was replaced by the cluttered counter area in Watto's shop. The image was small and blurry, for the palm diary appeared to be sitting on a shelf some distance away. Several minutes passed, then a sandy-haired youth of about fifteen came striding into Watto's shop. If this was Owen Lars, he could not have been dressed less like a moisture farmer's son. He wore a fine tomuon wool cloak over an immaculately tailored shimmersilk tunic, with a new belt and boots of krayt hide—a disguise that the greedy Watto seemed unable to look past.

The Toydarian was on the youth like a sketto on a dewback. *"You are looking for something I can help you with."* It was not a question. *"I have the finest merchandise in Mos Espa. Ask anyone."*

"I have." The youth—undoubtedly Owen Lars—glanced around the shop, then picked up a set of infrared sensor goggles and examined them thoughtfully. *"I may have been misled."*

Both voices sounded tinny and faint, for the journal recording device had not been designed to pick up such distant speech. Owen tossed the goggles aside, drawing a stifled chuckle from Shmi and—as the lenses broke—a strangled gasp from Watto.

Owen reached for an expensive recording rod.

Watto bit his tongue and allowed the young man to pick it up. *"You are looking for personal recorders?"*

Owen turned and, casually flipping the rod back and forth by its base, said, *"No."*

Watto hovered in front of him and tried to snatch the instrument, missed, tried again, then gave up.

"A droid? I have the finest reconditioned droids in the city."

"No." Owen turned and started toward the back door, walking out of the display. *"I was told on Nal Hutta that you actually have one of Renatta Racing's old needle ships on your lot."*

"I do!" Watto vanished out of the display after Owen, calling back, *"Bring me a glass of nectarot, slave, and whatever my young friend here would like."*

"A glass of yardle, if you please."

"Yardle?" Shmi's voice was clearer—and clearly disapproving. *"That is a little strong for someone your age. How about a nice glass of ruby bliel."*

"Bliel!" Watto stormed. *"Get the boy his—"*

"Ruby bliel will be fine," Owen chuckled. *"I shouldn't forget that I'll be flying for Pavo Prime this afternoon."*

"Oh, Pavo Prime. I've always wanted to visit there."

Their voices vanished through the door. The display showed Shmi rushing past to fetch the drinks; then the image shifted wildly as she carried the journal into the exterior lot. The next image showed Owen and Watto descending the boarding ramp of a sleek silver-finished racer. Then the display went dark as Shmi slipped the journal into a pocket.

"... *her get a bit ragged,*" Owen's voice said. "*But I could always turn Father's maintenance crew loose on it.*"

"*Indeed, you could.*" Watto's voice grew louder as he fluttered closer to Shmi. "*Who is your father?*"

Owen ignored the question. "*Very well, we can take it for a test flight.*"

Watto's voice dropped. "*I'm afraid we can't do that. It doesn't have the Tobal lens.*"

"*It doesn't have the Tobal lens?*" Owen's astonishment sounded very convincing. "*Then why are you trying to sell it to me?*"

"*I thought maybe you could get one yourself. They are not very expensive, but they are hard to come by out here.*"

"*They're hard to come by everywhere,*" Owen said. "*That's why Renatta Racing Systems went broke.*"

The sound of Watto's wings slowed to barely a flutter. "*I could let you have it cheap—a hundred thousand.*"

"*Without the lens, it isn't worth a credit.*" Owen's voice faded as he walked away.

Shmi let him move out of earshot, then asked Watto, "*A Tobal lens . . . would that be an oval crystal about the size of my head, full of sparkling colors?*"

"*It might be.*"

"*Would it leave you blind for a time after you look at it?*" Shmi asked. "*And perhaps even scatter optical data, if you bring it too close?*"

"*You've seen one!*" Watto cried. "*Where? Tell me before he gets away!*"

"*Cliegg,*" Shmi said.

"*Cliegg? Your boyfriend Cliegg?*" Watto's voice grew disappointed again. "*What would a moisture farmer be doing with a Tobal lens? He never owned a Renatta needle ship, I think.*"

"And where else would I have seen it?" Shmi asked.

Watto was silent for a moment, then droned off yelling, *"You, boy, wait!"*

Shmi laughed, then said quietly, *"Thank you, Qui-Gon."*

The entry ended, and Chewbacca groaned a query.

"It doesn't matter if Watto figures out where the lens came from," Han said. "He's already bitten on the kid. There's no way he's gonna let that deal slip through his fingers. Do you know what a Renatta needle ship is worth—if you can find someone who wants it?"

Leia looked up to see that Second Twilight had come and gone. Two of Tatooine's moons were already rising on the opposite horizon, throwing soft stripes of silver and amber over the dark desert, and the ground ahead was nothing but shadows and shapes.

Han continued across the plateau at top speed, clearly enjoying piloting an Imperial hoverscout.

"Han, can you see all right?" Leia asked. "I'm having a little trouble."

"Who needs to see?"

This brought an alarmed jabber from Herat in the back.

Chewbacca chuffed in amusement. Han tapped the window in front of him, upon which, Leia now saw, glowed the faint color lines of a heads-up display.

"Terrain scanners," Han said. "This baby's got every—"

A static crackle sounded from the speaker in the equipment console, then a cloud of light began to take shape over the holographic pad between the seats.

Han frowned over at Leia. "Did you activate—"

"It's not my fault," Leia said.

"The communicator!" Han pulled the throttle back and released the steering wheel, sending the hoverscout into a deceleration skid. "Smear the holocams!"

Han spat onto his fingers and smeared the saliva over a pair of small lenses on his side of the vehicle. Leia did the same for hers, and Chewbacca growled an alarmed question from the back.

"I don't know where they are," Han said. "I'm not the one sitting—"

"Maybe there aren't any in back," Leia said.

The cloud of light began to take the shape of a head, and Han's voice dropped to a whisper. "I guess we're about to find out." He glanced over his shoulder and motioned C-3PO closer. "You're on."

"Me?" C-3PO complained. "I didn't do very well the last—"

"You!" Leia ordered. Han could not answer without risking a voiceprint identification, and the rest of them were out of the question. There weren't many woman, Wookiee, or Jawa stormtroopers.

The holographic head resolved itself into the squinting face of an Imperial officer. "SSC-Seventeen, is that you? Report."

C-3PO stared blankly at the holograph.

"Seventeen? Your transponder is off and you're completely out of the operations area. Explain," the voice demanded. "What's wrong with your projector? All I'm getting is glowcloud."

Leia held her fists in the air. To C-3PO, she mouthed a single word.

"Oh dear," C-3PO began. Chewbacca groaned and Han shook his head, then the droid's vocabulator assumed the raspy, weak voice of an injured man. "Blood . . . it's everywhere."

It was not the word Leia had mouthed—that had been *Tusken*—but it would work.

"We're doomed!" C-3PO continued in his dying-man voice.

"Doomed?" the officer demanded. "Give me a sitrep, trooper."

Han motioned Chewie toward the blaster turret, then drew his own blaster and began firing out the driver's-side weapons port.

"What's that?" the officer demanded. "Who's attacking you?"

"Reb—"

Leia waved furiously, then angled her fingers in front of her lips.

The droid slipped into his own voice. "Tusks?"

Leia made a circling motion with her fingers, trying to get him to say the second syllable.

"Oh, *Tuskens*!" C-3PO's voice resumed the raspy quality. "They're everywhere! We'll be destroyed!"

"Negative, trooper." The holographic head turned to talk to someone out of cam view. "We'd better get some help over there right away."

The officer remained silent for a moment. Han and Chewbacca continued to fire, the Wookiee occasionally letting go with what sounded very much like an anguished human death scream.

Then a series of plinks began to sound against the exterior armor on Leia's side of the speeder. She looked over and, as a slugthrower projectile splatted itself against her transparisteel window, let out an involuntary scream.

"They're being massacred," the holographic head said. "Just listen to that trooper!"

Bringing her voice under control—and cringing every time a new slug struck her side of the vehicle—Leia leaned back and peered around the web of frosted transparisteel where the projectile had struck. In the distance, two lanky, rag-swaddled Tusken Raiders were standing silhouetted in the moons' silver light, taking turns firing at the hoverscout and shaking their weapons in the air.

"Oh my!" C-3PO's voice slipped again. "There *are* Tuskens!" Then, catching himself, he added, "*More* Tuskens!"

Another slug struck the window, completely frosting the transparisteel. Leia reached for Han's arm, but Chewbacca was already bringing the heavy blaster around to drive off the warriors.

The officer began to speak to them again. "Seventeen, we need to know your exact position. Activate your holomap."

Leia looked back and found Han shaking his head.

"I'm sorry," C-3PO said in the wounded-man voice. "But the holomap seems to be malfunctioning."

"Malfunctioning?" There was a pause while the officer absorbed this, then he continued, "Just hold yourselves together, Seventeen. There's a TIE following a sandcrawler not too far from the plateau where your transmissions are originating. Keep firing your blaster. He'll find you."

"Find us?" C-3PO screeched. "That won't be necessary."

More projectiles began to plink the armor behind Leia. She ignored them and joined Han in frantically nodding to C-3PO and mouthing that it *was* necessary.

"Oh dear me! What am I saying?" the droid cried. "We need help. All we can get. Come as quickly as you can!"

Han sighed in relief, and Leia motioned for the droid to continue.

"We're in terrible trouble!"

Leia pulled her blaster and turned to shoot the comm unit, and found Han already preparing to do the same thing.

"Oh my . . . we're doomed!"

They pulled the triggers together.

"Okay, Flyboy," Leia said. "Get us—"

A loud pop sounded from the window behind Leia's head, then something hot buzzed past her ear to splat against the interior of Han's window. A circle of transparisteel frosted into the web pattern of a slugthrower hit.

"Out of here?" Han finished.

He opened the throttles, and they shot into the night.

TWENTY

Eyes glued to the blue lines of the terrain scanner's heads-up display, Han angled the hoverscout across the desert floor on a new vector, automatically memorizing bearing, speed, and time so he could calculate a new route to the oasis without activating the holomap. With the Imperials mounting a rescue operation and the Tuskens watching them already, this could be harder than he had thought.

And he had come close to losing Leia back there. A little farther back, and the slug would never have reached his side of the compartment. He glanced over and found Leia watching him, her face pale and her lips still trembling from the close call.

"Careful, Han," she said.

Han returned his gaze to the schematic on the windscreen. "Close, huh?"

"Too close." Leia's tone was brittle. "They almost got you."

"Me? I'm not the one they were shooting at."

"No, I suppose not." Strangely, this seemed to strengthen Leia's voice. "But we need to find some cover. That TIE will be coming soon, and I'm beginning to have a bad feeling about our conversation with the *Chimaera* back there."

"*Beginning* to?" Han said. "It gave me the chills."

Chewbacca growled a comment from the backseat.

"You're right," Leia said. She reached over and touched one of the environmental controls on the abdomen of Han's stormtrooper armor. "He hasn't turned down his cooling unit."

Han finally found a deep ravine and slowed to a crawl, then ran back and forth along the rim several times to scare out any lurking creatures—and to draw the fire of any Tusken sentries camped nearby. When neither happened, he dropped into the ravine, parked them on the dark side of a huge boulder, and, after a last glance around the moonlit crags, powered down all systems except the blaster turret.

"Oh, this looks safe," Leia said. "The Tuskens will never think to look down here."

"Safe as our own bed back in Coruscant," Han replied. "Why don't you play your grandmother's journal? I'm dying to know whether Watto fell for it."

"Sure you are," Leia said. "You're just trying to keep my mind off the Sand People."

"No, really." Han waited until she bent over to retrieve the dropped journal off the floor, then glanced over his shoulder at Chewbacca, pointing two fingers at his eyes and motioning him into the blaster turret. "I see where you get your nerve."

"You do?" Leia came up beaming, journal in hand, just as Han turned forward again. She glanced back at Chewbacca, who was trying hard to look innocent as he rose into the blaster turret. "I saw that—and thanks."

Leia activated the journal and held the display out. Han saw the desert-hardened—though still attractive—face of a chestnut-eyed woman who looked every bit as beautiful and dignified as he imagined Leia in twenty years. She spoke in a whisper.

* * *

16:04:21

*Now the bite, Annie. I feel . . . well, I don't really
know how I feel. My heart is pounding so hard, and my
hands are trembling. I shouldn't feel guilty about cheating Watto—but I do. Or maybe I just feel sorry for him.*

Shmi's face was replaced by the hazy image of a cluttered counter area. A few minutes later, a burly human
farmer entered the frame carrying an energy-shielded
cargo box. Shmi appeared in the display again and kissed
him on the cheek, then he set the box on the counter. A
potbellied Toydarian fluttered out of the office behind
the counter and went to the box.

"*This is it?*" Watto's voice was barely audible. "*Let me
see.*"

He reached for the clasps, but the farmer—it had to be
Cliegg Lars—put his hand on the box.

"*Price first.*" His voice was deep and easier to hear.
"*Then the lens.*"

"*I only want to see the merchandise. You think I'm going to pay you a fortune for a closed box?*"

"*Terms first.*"

"*Terms? That lens was mine anyway. I know it was.*"
Watto turned to face Shmi. "*That Jedi sent it to you. Do
you think I'm stupid?*"

"*It belongs to Cliegg now,*" Shmi said. "*If you want it,
you must deal with him.*"

Watto turned back to Cliegg. "*All right, then. If the
lens is real—and it fits my ship—I'll give you a quarter of
what I sell it for.*"

Cliegg remained silent, his hand on the box.

"*Say something! My buyer is leaving in an hour. If I
don't have the lens installed by then, it's worth nothing
to me.*"

"*You know what I want. It's not money.*"

"Shmi? You'd be better off taking the money. With that much, you could buy a dozen like her."

"I want Shmi."

Watto considered this a minute, then said, *"I'll tell you what. I'll give you a quarter interest in the ship and Shmi both. You can take her one week a month."*

Cliegg picked up the box and turned to leave.

"Done! She hasn't been such a good slave since she met you anyway." Watto turned to Shmi. *"You've wanted to go with him all along, haven't you?"*

"Yes. I've told you that."

"So you have." Watto seemed to sag in the air, then he glanced at his chronometer. *"Let me see the lens. I need to hurry if I'm going to catch the buyer before he goes to Pavo Prime."*

"First you give me the deactivator wand," Cliegg said, *"and tell me where the transmitter bomb is hidden."*

"It's behind her jaw, on the left." Watto touched his own chin to illustrate, then reached into his vest and produced a small electronic wand. All of the status lights were dark. *"Here's the wand, but you won't need it. I deactivated her transmitter a long time ago."*

"What?" Shmi gasped. *"When?"*

"A few months after I lost the boy." Watto turned away and looked as though he was wiping his eye. *"The way you were moping around, I was afraid you would get yourself blown up."*

"You mean I could have left? Anytime?"

Watto shrugged. *"But you didn't."*

Watto passed the wand over to Cliegg, then fluttered down to the box and reached for the lid clasps.

"Watto!" Shmi called. *"Wait a—"*

But Watto was already opening the box. A spray of iridescent light spilled out beneath the lid, and the journal display erupted into brilliant flashes of color.

Watto's voice could barely be heard. *"You've blinded me!"*

The entry dissolved into a white blur.

"The lens," Han surmised. "I've heard about those. They were used to power the old Renatta photon drives. They say a good Tobal lens could convert heat to light at close to a hundred percent efficiency."

"My data banks indicate that it could be fully one hundred percent," C-3PO reported. "Depending, of course, on the skill of the gemologist who shaped it."

Herat started to ask something, but was drowned out by an urgent growl from Chewbacca. Han turned to find the Wookiee pointing into the sky behind them, where the twin efflux needles of a nearby TIE were making a slow curve across the night. After their little show depicting the Tusken assault, it was probably attempting a "rescue."

They watched in breathless silence as the needles vanished behind the wall of the ravine, then waited another two minutes for the TIE to return. When the sky remained dark—or at least free of TIE efflux—Han cautiously moved the hoverscout up to the gully rim.

"Anybody see anything?" He and Leia had to lower their projectile-webbed windows to get a clear view of their own quarter of the sky. "Take all the time you need."

After ten minutes of looking, they were finally convinced the TIE was gone. They emerged from the ravine, and Han started for the oasis again.

They had traveled only a few minutes before Leia said, "Han, maybe we should duck over to Obi-Wan's and give things a few hours to settle down."

Han took a moment before answering, not trying to decide whether Leia was right, but wondering what had come over her. She was not the type to get her circuits shorted by a close call.

Finally, he said, "Kitster may not have a few hours. And your boss will be recalling the Wraiths in twenty-two hours."

Leia sighed, then nodded. "I know that. But there's something I really need to tell you."

Alarm whistles started to go off in Han's head. *"Again?"* He glanced over at Leia, who was biting her lip and staring at the floor. *"Now?* It's a little late to be telling me the Provisional Council wants you to swing by Obi-Wan's and pick up an old lightsaber."

Leia shook her head. "I wouldn't do that to you."

"There's always a second time."

"Han, there just hasn't been a chance to tell you." Leia gestured at the windscreen, reminding Han that he was piloting. "Since we came to Tatooine, I've been having, well, some Force-experiences."

"Force-experiences?" Han asked, once again paying attention to the terrain display. "Like what? Waking up in midair? Talking to dewbacks? Accidentally moving sandcrawlers around with your mind?"

Leia took a deep breath, then said, "Visions. Sensations."

"My wife has been seeing things?" Han asked. "Is that what you're telling me?"

"It's more complicated than that," Leia said. "That dream I had on the way insystem? It was Luke wearing Darth Vader's mask. At least, I think it was Luke."

Han began to worry. "But it was only a dream, right?"

"That's what I thought," Leia said. "Until I saw your swoop abandoned in the desert."

"What do you mean, 'saw'?"

"In front of my face, Han, like a hologram. It looked exactly the same as when we found it with the Dark-lighters." Leia paused, as though she was going to add another example, then said simply, "I've been having Force-visions."

Chewbacca groaned a question.

"I'm not as sure of the sensations," Leia said. "I just keep finding certain things here on Tatooine familiar . . . and I'm fairly sure the Force has been guiding—make that *pushing*—me much of the way. My father has popped up too many places in this journey for it to be coincidence."

"Let's talk about the oasis again," Han said. "You've seen something bad there?"

"This is more of a sensation," Leia said. "Like going there now is a bad idea."

"I could've told you *that* without the Force," Han said. "But I don't see that we have any choice—or that things will settle down if we wait. When that TIE doesn't find us, the Imperials will get suspicious. And those Tuskens didn't just happen to be camped nearby when we stopped. They were watching their back trail."

Chewbacca groaned his agreement, adding that the sooner they hit the oasis, the better Kitster's chances—and theirs. Chances of what, he did not say.

But Herat had a completely different idea, which C-3PO explained after the Jawa's long jabber.

"Herat thinks it is incumbent upon you to turn around and help her reclaim her clan's sandcrawler from the Squibs, as your assurances that they would never activate the reactor core are obviously without merit."

"Not a chance," Han said.

"How can she know it was her sandcrawler the TIE was following?" Leia asked.

Herat chittled a reply.

"How many sandcrawlers do you think such a small area can support?" C-3PO translated. "One."

"Then we won't have any trouble finding it later, will we?" Han retorted.

He continued toward the oasis, troubled by what Leia had told them, but uncertain as to what else they could do. The Squibs knew this country. There was a good chance they had figured out what had happened to the painting and were on their way to the ghost oasis. And that meant the Imperials soon would be as well, given that they were tracking the sandcrawler from the air. Han and Leia's best chance—probably their *only* chance—was to beat everybody else there. But they were still an hour away.

After a few minutes of travel, Leia seemed to decide that Han was right about the detour and resumed viewing her grandmother's journal. Focusing on the terrain scanner, Han listened with half an ear as Shmi described her hurried move to the Lars moisture farm. She took only her clothes, her journal, and a droid Anakin had started building years before.

The next six months of entries were more sporadic and filled with data skips. But Han caught enough of the story to know that while Shmi loved both Cliegg and Owen deeply, she missed Anakin more every day. Her nightly entries grew longer and more filled with reminiscences about his childhood, and she sometimes lapsed into speculation about what he might be doing at the Jedi Temple, or where he might be traveling in the galaxy.

Finally, Leia came to an entry that was completely intact.

20:07:22

Annie, today your mother is a married woman. Cliegg waited until last month to ask me—I guess he wanted to be certain it was him I loved and not just freedom. It was a simple ceremony in Anchorhead. Owen came, of

course, and a few of Cliegg and Owen's friends. Kitster,
Wald, and Amee were there, and they asked about you. I
wish you could have been there, but I know the Jedi
wouldn't have allowed it, even if the message we sent
had been accepted. And I understand, I truly do.

I just wish you could have been there.

Watto surprised us all by showing up uninvited. I
thought he would make a scene when he saw Owen, but
he just squinted and said, "You!" Then he offered Cliegg
a discount on used parts and told me that if times grew
hard on the moisture farm, Wald wasn't doing such a
good job as his assistant. He still hasn't found a buyer for
the Renatta needle ship—but he's asking a million cred-
its! Who does he think is going to buy it?

Shmi fell silent a moment, then continued.

Owen makes me miss you so much, Anakin. I can't
look at him without thinking of you—not that I see you
when I look at him. That's not what I mean. Owen is
strong like his father: pragmatic and certain of his ways,
grateful for simple joys and for his life on the moisture
farm. Your eyes were always on the stars. Even as a
young boy, you had to prove yourself to everyone you
met, be the best at everything you did. To you, this won-
derful place would have been a prison.

But I love you both so very much, and I'm sure that
if—no, when—you and Owen finally meet someday, you
will be great friends.

Leia asked for the next entry, then cursed.

Han glanced over to see datelines blinking past with
no entries, or entries so filled with electronic snow that it
was impossible to see a face.

"More data skips?"

Leia nodded, then asked, "Han, do the heads-up displays in Imperial hoverscouts have retinal trackers?"

"Uh, no."

"Then I suggest you keep your eyes on the terrain scanner," Leia snapped, "because I can't see a thing in the dark!"

Han looked forward and casually steered them around a bantha-sized boulder he really hoped no one else could see.

Leia continued to struggle with the journal. Finally, a year later, she began to reach intact entries again. Mostly, they were typical farm stuff—talk about crop plantings, the low moisture content in the air, worries over market prices.

20:32:23

Today started a disaster, Annie. I opened the number three growing vault to discover I hadn't set off enough stink capsules the night before, and profoggs had ruined a whole crop of tangaroots. It was too much for me. After the dry winds and the pallie blight, I began to feel like I had brought a curse to the farm. I just sat down in despair.

And that's how Owen found me. He is so kind, Annie. He told me it wasn't my fault, that he had checked the vault the night before, too. I don't believe him, but it was a nice thing to say. We started to clean up, and I asked how we were going to stop the problems we have been having.

Do you know what Owen did then? He caught a pair of profoggs, then held up the scaly little beasts and offered to show me how to make profogg stew.

It wasn't until evening that I began to see what he was really trying to say, Annie. The three of us were eating the profogg stew—and it tastes even worse than it sounds—and Cliegg and Owen were talking about the low price of water, and about how we wouldn't make much recapturing the moisture from the ruined crop. Cliegg shrugged and said, "We don't own the farm, it owns us."

Then Owen slurped down a big spoonful of stew, made a satisfied sound, and said we were looking at this the wrong way. What we really needed to do was start a profogg ranch! You had to be there, eating that awful stew to understand, but we all broke out laughing, and we didn't stop until tears came.

That's when I finally understood the secret of being a moisture farmer, Annie. You can't fight life out here. You just take what Tatooine gives you and find a way to use it.

Leia shut off the journal and fell silent. Han started to ask if something was wrong, then noticed that the terrain was starting to break up into ravines ahead—a sign that they were moving closer to the edge of the Dune Sea.

"*Mine,*" Leia whispered. "Mine."

"What?" Han asked.

"Nothing." Leia shook her head. "Sorry. Just something I've been trying to understand."

"Yeah?"

"I'll tell you when I do."

When Han glanced over, her eyes were closed, her head tipped back as though her mind had retreated to some other world.

"*Mine,*" she whispered.

"Yours?"

Leia's eyes snapped open, and she pointed into the darkness on her side of the hoverscout. "Turn here."

"Turn?" Han looked over. When Leia did not immediately remind him to watch the terrain scanners, he knew it was important. "Here?"

Leia nodded and continued to look out over the dark desert. "We have to stop at Obi-Wan's."

"We talked about that." Han continued on his current course. "The sooner we get there, the—"

"Han, trust me." It was not a request. "We *have* to stop at Obi-Wan's. We're not going to save Kitster or anyone else unless we do. There's something there we need."

"What?" Han demanded. "A spare lightsaber? Wookiee armor? Assault artillery?"

"I don't know," Leia said. "I have this feeling. I have to trust it."

Chewbacca howled disapprovingly.

"Indeed," C-3PO agreed. "I have always had the utmost faith in Mistress Leia's feelings. Especially when it means *not* rushing into combat."

"Oh, a *feeling*." Han shook his head in surrender, then started the long swing toward Obi-Wan's. "Why didn't you say so?"

TWENTY-ONE

Even deep into the starlit desert night, it was clear that Obi-Wan had chosen the site of his hermitage as much for its safety as for its beauty. More house than hut, the dwelling had been built on a promontory at the edge of the Western Dune Sea, high enough above the rolling sands to afford a good view of approaching vehicles and far enough back to avoid being assailed by a constant curtain of blowing grit. The only other approach, the narrow and winding gully up which Herat had guided them, was visible along its entire length from a window bubble near the back of the abode. And with curving lines and a buff exterior the same color as the surrounding terrain, the structure blended into its environment so well—at least at night—that Leia hadn't recognized the building until the hoverscout passed within three meters of it.

"I don't see any spare turbolasers lying around." Han turned the vehicle around so they could leave quickly in an emergency, then raised the access panels. "Where do we start?"

"I don't know." This wasn't something Leia wanted to admit. She had hoped that as they drew nearer to the hermitage, her feelings would grow clearer. Instead, her sense of needing to be here—her sense of security—remained strong, but her idea of why had grown more ambiguous. "I guess we just see what we find."

"Great." Han drew his blaster and motioned Chewbacca into the blaster turret. "It'll probably be a krayt dragon."

"*Bbberddle awdoway tchters,*" Herat chiddled.

"Kenobi's house is too small for krayt dragons, but watch out for anoobas," C-3PO translated. "If you don't mind, I'll wait here to help keep watch."

After a quick moonlight reconnaissance of the area—there was little to examine but an old vaporator pad behind the house—Leia and Han returned to find C-3PO keeping watch in the blaster turret. Chewbacca was kneeling in the back, reaching into the cargo area behind the seat, where Herat lay tucked into a corner clutching something to her chest. They were snarling and squawking furiously, producing a noise that sounded like fighting womp rats.

Han opened the rear cargo hatch and plucked Herat out by the scruff of her hood.

"Are you two trying to wake the whole neighborhood?"

Herat jabbered something and tucked a military datapad under her cloak. Chewbacca roared at her.

"Threepio?" Leia called.

C-3PO continued to study the sky. "How very interesting. Mistress Leia—"

"Threepio, will you stop stargazing and do your job?" Han nearly had to shout to make himself heard.

"Of course, Captain Solo, but this—"

"Threepio!" Han lifted Herat higher. "What's Herat saying?"

"That she found the datapad and it belongs to her." C-3PO looked back into the sky. "You really should—"

"Later, Threepio," Leia said. "We'll tell you when we want to know."

Chewbacca rumbled that he only wanted to see the pad because he saw a picture of Han on it. Of course, the Jawa understood none of this—which, Leia knew, was the problem.

"Herat," she said, "we'll make you a deal."

This instantly calmed the Jawa. *"M'kwat kenza?"*

"Let me see the datapad for a few minutes, and you can keep it."

Herat chittered a long question.

"She would like to know how much rent you will pay."

"How much will you pay me not to drop you?" Han asked.

Herat pulled the datapad from beneath her cloak and passed it over. Leia quickly found a message titled, "Commander's Directive TS3519 Re: Suspected Rebels." In quick succession, the display showed file images of Han, Leia, and Chewbacca.

A communications officer's voice identified them by name.

"*Chimaera* Intelligence has reason to believe said Rebels are the ones seeking *Killik Twilight*. Command directs they be captured alive. Any trooper slaying one will cost his platoon a week's liberty and one month's wages. Fines are cumulative, should more than one be killed."

"They certainly know who we are," Leia said. "That's bad."

"Yeah, but they're not supposed to kill us," Han said. "That's good."

The directive continued, "Command further directs that if they cannot be captured alive, they be slain regardless of the aforementioned consequences. Any trooper or troopers allowing said Rebels to escape will be tried and executed for crimes against the Empire. His platoon will be denied liberty for a year and forfeit their pay for the duration of their service."

Han's jaw fell, but he managed to collect himself after a moment and say, "That's not so bad. They'll hesitate. That's all the advantage we need."

Chewbacca groaned and nodded.

A new image appeared on the datapad, this one of a stock YT-1300 freighter similar to the *Falcon*. "*Chimaera* Intelligence believes they are traveling on the *Millennium Falcon*, a Corellian Engineering Corporation stock light freighter similar to this, possibly traveling under *Regina Galas*, *Sweet Surprise*, *Longshot*, *Sunlight Franchise*, or another false transponder code. Said ship is believed to be somewhere in the area of Mos Espa. Any trooper reporting the location of this ship to *Chimaera* Intelligence will be promoted two ranks and have all previous fines and punishments canceled."

"*That's* bad," Han said. "If someone tells them about that smuggler's cave, we're in big trouble."

Chewbacca rowled a question.

Leia checked the date stamp on the directive. "Two days ago."

"We're in big trouble," Han said.

After the message ended, Leia scanned the directory, looking for more directives that might prove informative. She found a message from the previous day, referencing *Killik Twilight*.

The display showed an image of the painting. A different communications officer's voice explained what Wald had already told them in Mos Espa, namely that their effort to destroy *Killik Twilight* had alerted the Imperials to its importance.

"Under no circumstances is this painting to be destroyed," the voice instructed. "Any trooper responsible for the painting's destruction will be tried and executed as a traitor. Any unit allowing the Rebels to escape with or destroy the painting will forfeit pay and liberty for the remainder of their service."

"Now we know what the Imperials are doing to cut labor costs," Leia observed.

She started to shut off the message, but Han reached over to freeze the image. Leia thought he had seen something she had not, but found him lost in thought, just staring at the image and trying to recall what it looked like in person. *Killik Twilight* had that effect on people.

"Mistress Leia, would you like to know now?"

"Know?" Leia had almost forgotten the droid had something to tell them. "Yes, now would be good."

C-3PO pointed along the edge of the Dune Sea, his finger indicating a group of stars just above the horizon. "I believe there may be a flight of TIEs over there."

"TIEs?" Han dropped Herat roughly in the speeder and grabbed the electrobinoculars. "Where?"

With the electrobinoculars' reduced field of vision, it took Han longer to find the circle of moving stars than it did Leia. There were six of them, winking in and out in a steady pattern as they wheeled out over the dunes and then back over the rugged crags of the Jundland Wastes.

"Got 'em. Twin drives. Definitely TIEs, about fifteen kilometers away." Without lowering the electrobinoculars, Han asked, "Herat, would that ghost oasis be over there?"

"Bzabzabert, uqiqu! Chichichi!"

"She wants to know why she should tell you anything, you cheater," C-3PO said. "That is strictly a translation, of course. She says her leg is throbbing."

Chewbacca snatched Herat out of the hoverscout and

held her over his head. Leia thought he was probably only trying to help her see the TIEs. Really.

"*Yuyu.*"

"That's what I thought." Han turned to Leia. "We'd have come in right under them. Good thing I trusted that feeling you had."

"Good thing," Leia said.

She hoped her feeling would not cost Kitster Banai his life—or the New Republic the Shadowcast code key. But they would not have saved either by riding into an Imperial trap. Better to think of some way to defang the ambush, *then* go in.

That was why she had felt so uneasy about going straight to the ghost oasis, Leia was sure. After her vision in the cave, she had followed the Force and declined Borno's offer to take them to safety. Then, as they had traveled across the plateau, the Force had acted on her again, guiding her away from danger.

Now all Leia had to do was figure out why the Force had been drawing her toward Obi-Wan's—why simply thinking of his home had filled her with such a powerful sensation of security and comfort. And she had to do it quickly.

"Let's have a look around," she said.

Han passed the electrobinoculars to Chewbacca and motioned him back into the blaster turret, then entered the house with his weapon drawn. When no fire broke out, Leia grabbed the glow rod out of their utility satchel and followed.

A small dwelling with whitewashed walls and clean curving lines, it was basically a single large room divided into sections by square pillars. Since Leia's last visit, the place had clearly been ransacked many times and played host to dozens of creatures both sentient and otherwise. The footing for a primitive stove, some plumbing cavities in the walls, and a ventilation hole in the ceiling indicated where someone had stripped the kitchen of its appliances. In a niche at the back, next to the window overlooking the rear approach, stood a dusty workbench with no tools. Across from the bench lay a shredded mattress that looked as though it had most recently served as the bed of a womp rat sow. None of this did anything to diminish the aura of stark comfort and spiritual serenity in the home's simple design.

Leia walked through the different areas, allowing the glow rod to roam at random over the walls and debris, doing her best to let the Force guide her hand where it wished. The last entry in Shmi's journal had finally convinced her that it was the Force drawing her to Obi-Wan's, and that she would be wise to trust it. *We don't own the farm,* Cliegg had said, *it owns us.* She believed that to be the message of the voice in her vision. *Mine.* Luke and Han and everything that Leia counted as hers, they all belonged to the Force. *She* belonged to the Force. *Mine.* Like life on Tatooine, one could not fight the Force. One could only surrender to it and find a way to use what it offered. *Mine.*

"Anything?" Han asked.

"Not yet."

"Maybe there isn't anything," Han said. "Maybe you were only feeling the danger at the oasis."

"Maybe." Leia shrugged and tried not to think about the little spiny thing that her glow rod had just sent scurrying through a window. "But I still feel the need to be here."

"What do you mean, *feel*? Like Luke feels?"

"How do I know what Luke feels?" Leia retorted. "I'm no Jedi. But I do think it's the Force. It's too strong to be anything else."

Han took the glow rod and began to run the beam

around the house. "I'm just saying it would help if we knew what we were looking for."

"Maybe," Leia said. "And maybe not."

Leia and Han spent the next few minutes searching the house, peering into dusty crannies and rearranging the debris that mysteriously accumulates in any abandoned dwelling. They found little of interest and nothing to justify the sensation Leia had been experiencing. Finally, Han took the glow rod and swept the light over the kitchen a few times, lingering on the power outlets and the empty areas in the corners and under the cabinets.

"What's missing?" he asked.

"His recipe box?"

Han shined the glow rod on her shoulder. "Funny." He turned and started for the back of the house. "The cistern. The power generator."

Leia took him to a trapdoor hidden beneath the workbench and descended into a large cellar. A dozen of the black spiny things she had noticed earlier scurried into the corner together to make a single big spiny thing, and a few ten-legged arachnids began to hiss and vibrate in webs on the ceiling.

Anything of any value had long ago been taken by Jawas or broken by Tuskens. The generator was among the former, the cistern the latter, its lid lying in the bottom in three pieces.

"Nothing," Leia said. "Let's get out of here."

"Not so fast."

Han dropped into the cistern and stooped out of sight, leaving Leia in the dark with arachnid webs rustling above her head.

"Han, I mean it. Let's get—"

"You'd think a Jedi would be more original."

The broken lid pieces landed beside Leia and sent half a dozen spiny things chittering back into the dark.

"Han, give me that blasted—"

"Hold this."

Han passed Leia the glow rod, which she promptly swept across the floor and ceiling.

"I mean on the plug, Leia."

"Plug?" Leia shined the glow rod into the cistern and found Han squatting again, probing at something between his feet. A pair of clicks sounded, then he pulled a thick plastoid lid off the bottom and set it aside. "What did you find?"

"The oldest smuggling trick in the book." Han peered into the dark hole beneath the cistern. "A submerged compartment." He withdrew a bag about as large as his torso and passed it up to Leia. "That what you're looking for?"

Leia opened it, found an ancient datapad and a star chart inside, and felt no change in her experience of the Force. Not that she would have. Just because she had decided to trust the Force did not mean she could expect to tell a premonition from a shiver. She would have to talk to Luke about giving her some guidance.

"I have no idea," she said.

When Han found nothing else, they took the datapad and retreated back outside. Chewbacca had noticed some TIEs flying what looked like a reconnaissance grid and moved the hoverscout down among some boulders where it would prove difficult to detect. Otherwise the Imperials seemed no closer to discovering their presence.

Leia activated the datapad and found herself looking at Obi-Wan Kenobi's gray-bearded face.

"I am waiting, my friend."

"Waiting for what?" Leia asked.

"The watchword."

"This has to be it!" Han whispered.

"*This has to be it* is not the watchword," Obi-Wan's image said.

"May the Force be with you," Leia said.

Obi-Wan smiled patiently. "And with you, too, my friend." The image returned to its previous state. "*May the Force be with you* is not the watchword."

Leia placed her thumb over the microphone slot and turned to C-3PO. "You talk to it."

"Me? But I don't know the password. Just because we share a common chip—"

"See if you can reason with it," Leia said. "If I try again, I'm liable to trigger a security wipe."

"I see. I will certainly do my best."

Leia removed her thumb. C-3PO and the datapad exchanged electronic garble for less than a second before the display went dark. Chewbacca let out a derisive groan.

C-3PO turned and cocked his body to look up at the Wookiee. "I see no need for name calling, Chewbacca. It was quite cooperative, for a datapad."

"If that's cooperative, I'd hate to see rude," Han said.

"Let's hear what it said." Leia turned to C-3PO. "Is there anything helpful in there?"

"Not at the current time, I'm afraid," C-3PO said. "The datapad was kind enough to tell me it was being used to store research on hyperspace lanes entering the Unknown Regions. Master Kenobi may have been thinking of leading a mission to search for something called the Outbound Flight Project."

"What's that?" Leia asked.

"I'm afraid that's all the datapad would tell me," C-3PO said. "When I asked for an explanation, it suggested that Obi-Wan's real friends would know what it was and shut itself down."

Leia turned to Han and Chewbacca. "Does *Outbound Flight* mean anything to you?"

"Nothing." Han looked toward the oasis. "And especially nothing that will help us get past those Imperials."

Chewbacca shook his head as well.

"Oh, and the datapad needs a charge," C-3PO added. "It hasn't had fresh power in years."

Leia plugged the datapad into the hoverscout's recharger—warning Herat that it was spoken for—then turned back to Han and Chewbacca.

"I'm sorry." Leia was running out of ideas. "I just don't know why I made you come up here."

"I must say, I'm very glad you did," C-3PO said. "Otherwise, I'm quite sure we would be racing down some narrow, winding canyon exchanging blasterfire with a whole squadron of TIEs by now."

"For once, the droid has a point." Han put his arm around Leia's shoulder. "Let's give ourselves half an hour to think. Maybe we can come up with a good way out of this mess."

"And maybe we can't." Leia put her hand on Han's. "But what can we do? This is Tatooine."

Toward morning, they were still thinking—thinking that the situation just kept growing more hopeless. Five minutes after Leia and the others had sat down to think the night before, a pair of assault shuttles had landed near the oasis and debarked two companies of stormtroopers, one into the Jundland Wastes and one into the Dune Sea. An hour later, there had been a few blaster flashes, not enough for a real battle, and the TIEs and the shuttles had departed together. Han was betting that stormtroopers were taking hidden positions around the ghost oasis, surrounding the Tuskens and waiting for the Solos to arrive.

Leia was betting that he was right.

She was sitting at the edge of the bluff with Han, her shoulder throbbing dully, but feeling good enough that she insisted on taking her turn with the electrobinoculars. If there were any TIEs above the oasis now, they were too high to see even at a magnification of several hundred times. Behind them, Chewbacca was cursing repeatedly and loudly as he struggled to remove the transponder from the hoverscout's holomap without triggering a tamper signal. They still had no idea how they were going to sneak past two companies of stormtroopers, rescue Kitster Banai, recover *Killik Twilight*, and survive long enough to inform Mon Mothma of their success. But they did know they would need a working holomap, and that meant the transponder had to be removed before they went anywhere.

"How many moss-paintings did Ob Khaddor grow?" Han had "borrowed" the Imperial datapad from Herat's salvage heap and was again transfixed by *Killik Twilight*. "How did he do it?"

"If you're going to become a Khaddor devotee, you should probably know that the proper term is *design*, not *grow*," Leia said. "And I'll never tell how it's done. No good Alderaanian would."

"Not even to your husband?"

Leia softened her voice. "To my husband, maybe." She glanced over from behind the electrobinoculars. "But to one of the fastest smugglers in the galaxy? I don't think so."

"That's *the* fastest," Han said. "And it's criminal to let a whole art form die off like that. I can't believe that's what Alderaanians want."

"Careful, Han. Your sensitive side is showing." Leia would never have guessed Han Solo to be the moss-art type . . . but then again, Khaddor's work was not just any moss-art. "And letting it die is the whole point. It underscores the plight of Alderaanian culture. It's also one of the favorite themes of one of the planet's best-known painters."

"Khaddor said that?"

"Not in so many words," Leia replied. "But he never passed on the refinements that allowed him to design such deep colors. And it's inherent in the work. You only have to look at it."

Han was silent a long time, and Leia looked over to see him studying the image in the datapad. Finally, he shook his head.

"I am looking at it," he said. "And I don't see that."

"It's a warning about the cost of surrendering to darkness."

"It's not."

"Han, everybody agrees. The finest critics in the galaxy—"

"I don't care," Han said. "Everybody's wrong."

Leia sighed in exasperation, then gave the electrobinoculars to Han and took the datapad. "It's probably the colors in the display. You can't expect an electronic version—"

"It's not the colors." Han raised the electrobinoculars and began to watch the oasis. "I thought the same thing when I saw it at Mawbo's."

Leia studied the image. The colors were hardly as rich as the real thing, but the tones were true. And with its stormy sky sweeping in over the Killik city and the insectoid figures peering over their shoulders at the approaching darkness, it was still beautiful, and it still had the same profound effect.

"You don't see the Killiks fleeing the storm?" Leia asked. "You don't see how they're going to vanish because they've turned their backs to the darkness?"

"Nope."

Han's voice had assumed that stony tone it did when he had not only made up his mind, but also concluded that anyone who disagreed with him had the brains of a rock worrt.

Nothing bothered Leia more.

"Then what *do* you see?" Usually, she had to consciously inject the impatience into her voice; this time it came naturally. "Perhaps you'd care to enlighten me?"

"I would." Han lowered the electrobinoculars and tapped the datapad down near the bottom of the display. "What are the Killiks doing there?"

"They're glancing back at what they're about to lose," Leia said. "Also, Khaddor didn't want to show their faces. Nobody knows what the Killiks really looked like, so it was his way of not presuming."

"He said that?"

"Not in so many words," Leia replied, trying to remember what critic had made the point. "But it's obvious."

"Not to me," Han said. "They aren't looking. They're turning. Look at the way their bodies are twisting at the waist."

"This is a datapad. You can't be sure—"

"I can't, but *you* can. You saw that painting every morning for how many years? And you're telling me you can't close your eyes and remember whether their bodies were twisting?"

Leia did not need to close her eyes. The twist was there, subtly and only in the leaders, but it was there. Most critics considered it an uncharacteristic awkwardness of form and attributed it to a design problem in the growth medium.

"Even if you're right, it doesn't mean they're turning," Leia said. "They're insectoid. You can't presume to know their anatomy."

"And neither could Khaddor. He could have painted—designed—them any way he wanted. And he designed them twisting at the waist. He designed them turning toward the storm."

"Your point being?"

"They know it's coming, and they're turning to face it," Han said. "Khaddor isn't trying to warn anyone about the cost of surrendering to darkness. He's talking about how you meet it. You turn and look into it."

Leia fell silent, at first trying to think of an argument against Han's point, and then realizing how futile such an attempt was. They were arguing interpretations, and Khaddor would have been the first to agree that the interpretation belonged only to the eye of the beholder.

"I bet Ob Khaddor didn't like critics much," Han said. He had that cocky *I-won* smile Leia always loved—except when it was directed at her. "Did he?"

"Not much." Leia would not deny a fact. "But everybody else doesn't have to be wrong for you to be right. A painting can mean more than one thing, you know."

"No kidding?" Han's smile grew cockier than ever. "So you admit it . . . I'm right?"

"Of all the arrogant . . ." Leia finally caught the playful tone in Han's voice and realized he was not trying to humble her, only trying to insist on the validity of his own unique vision. And that was one of the things she loved about him. Most of the time. "I guess that's what I said, isn't it?"

"So what you see depends on how you look at it?" Han slipped an arm around her waist and pulled her close. "Like a lot of things."

Leia let him, but she knew when she was being outflanked. Han was not talking about *Killik Twilight* anymore. He was certainly not talking about the situation with TIEs over the oasis, either. He was talking about the future. Again.

"Han?"

"Yeah?"

"Shouldn't one of us be watching for Imperials?"

The arm retreated, and Han's voice grew serious. "We have to talk about this, Leia. You're not the only one who gets to make the choice."

"No? Then I hope you're ready to consider adoption." Leia regretted the retort as soon as she uttered it. She felt sure she would love adopted children as dearly as her own, and without any of the attendant fears. But by the time she turned to apologize, Han was already rising. "Han, I'm not closing the discussion. But please not here, not now. Not with tomorrow hanging over us."

"Why?" Han's eyes caught a moon's reflection and burned down on her in silver. "What's going to happen tomorrow?"

"Nothing." Leia had to look away. "I won't let it."

"Yeah? Well, it might happen anyway—but you can't be afraid to look. That's what Khaddor's saying, Leia." Han passed the electrobinoculars to her. "Keep an eye on the oasis. Time for me to make a circuit."

Leia returned to watching the oasis, so upset she barely registered what she was seeing. She would call what they were having frustrations more than troubles, but Han was certainly right about the need to talk. Unfortunately, her feelings about Anakin Skywalker remained too confused for any intelligent discussion about children—and now was no time to let the matter consume her attention. It was dangerous, even.

She lowered the electrobinoculars long enough to activate the journal, then returned to her vigil and asked for the next entry. Leia and Han had spent much of the night listening to her grandmother ponder Anakin's destiny and recount her hard-but-happy life on the moisture farm, and Leia knew the narrative would occupy just enough of her attention to keep the rest of her mind focused on the oasis.

21:45:24

Owen caught me celebrating your birthday out on the sand berm. Twenty years old—you and Owen, both! Owen has a lovely girlfriend now, Beru Whitesun. Neither has said so, but I'm sure they're thinking of marriage. Watching Owen grow, I always find myself wondering about you. Are you happy? Have you become a Jedi Knight yet? Would I recognize you if I saw you?

With you, I have nothing but questions—questions and love. And I do love you, Annie. I hope you know that—and also how proud I am of you. Always and forever.

The next day, Shmi reported that they were hearing banthas out on the plain. Leia's heart grew increasingly heavy as the following entries grew more concerned with the presence of Tusken Raiders, reporting tracks and probes of the security perimeter. Cliegg's moods turned dark, and Owen actually began to seem apprehensive. Shmi confessed to being worried for the safety of young Beru, who was staying with them for a few days.

22:45:25

Today, there are more Tuskens out on the plain. We can't see them, but the lowing of their banthas carries for kilometers. Owen and Cliegg keep saying we'll be all right, as long as we don't go out at night. I'd feel better if they didn't make such a point of keeping their blasters within reach, even inside. But there isn't much food out here for banthas; the Tuskens will have to move on soon.

And Cliegg is going to the Dorr Farm tomorrow, to start organizing local farmers. We'll be fine, Anakin, I'm sure.

Leia continued to watch the stars gleam above the oasis, searching for efflux trails or anything else that might indicate an Imperial movement, and asked for the next entry.

No sound came from the journal.

Suspecting another data skip, Leia said, "Advance to next entry."

When the journal continued to remain silent, Leia glanced down to find a message on the display: END DATA.

Leia shut off the journal and forced herself to return to her duties—though she had to keep blinking tears away so she could see through the electrobinoculars. How the journal had come to be where Anya Darklighter found it, she could not even guess; there were a thousand possibilities. The one she favored was that Shmi had been carrying it in a pocket when the Tuskens came, and had tossed it there hoping Cliegg or Owen would find it and one day give it to her son.

What Leia *did* know was that the journal had never made it into Anakin's hands, or it would not have been found beneath a vaporator. She wondered whether it would have made a difference in her father's life, had it been given to him—and whether it had remained there all those years to make a difference in hers.

Leia began to experience a profound sense of regret and self-doubt as she thought of Anakin Skywalker. Did she regret not knowing him? Hardly. She had come to hate and fear him as Darth Vader, and the last thing she had ever wanted was to know him better. But self-doubt? Leia had plenty of that. She could hardly think of Anakin

Skywalker without questioning half the life decisions she had made in the last five years.

But the feelings went deeper than that. The regret—a regret she *knew* she did not feel—weighed on her like a shielding cloak. It was physical and wearying, an emotion so enervating it rooted her to the ground. And the doubt was deeper than any she had ever experienced, a questioning so profound she felt raw and bottomless inside.

Leia found herself staring out across the desert without realizing she had turned away from the ghost oasis. Though the rolling sands were still swathed in night shadow, the moons were already dropping behind the horizon, and Tatoo I was kindling a golden gleam along the crest of the highest dunes. The sight filled Leia with a sense of loneliness and grief that was almost more than she could bear, and she finally understood the source of her powerful feelings.

Obi-Wan Kenobi.

Leia could almost feel him behind her, brooding over his failure as the first sun's light crept across the sands. How terrible the burden must have been, how deep his sorrow, that she could still feel it nine years after his departure. Had he stood here each morning, reciting the names of Jedi and friends lost to Darth Vader's saber? Had he reviewed his every conversation with Anakin Skywalker, reexamined every lesson he had taught, rebuked himself each dawn for his inadequacies as a Master?

Leia thought that perhaps he had.

Sitting there where Obi-Wan had stood every morning, she could feel how he had allowed his doubts to rule his life. For years, Obi-Wan had thought of little else but his fallen student, had allowed his concerns to cloud his thoughts—just as Leia had been allowing her own anger and hatred to dominate her view of her father.

Could that be what Leia's vision was telling her—that she needed to forgive her father for her own sake? That if she allowed her anger at him to rule her life, she would be harming no one but herself and Han?

So absorbed was Leia that she did not hear Han's hurried steps crunching the gravel behind her until he was within a dozen steps. Knowing what a stickler he was about keeping proper watches, she brought the electrobinoculars up and swung her gaze back toward the oasis.

"Who do you think you're fooling?" Han demanded.

"Sorry." Leia was so excited that her voice sounded anything but apologetic. "Han, I think I have it. What we came here for."

"Can you tell me about it later?" Han motioned Leia to her feet. " 'Cause we gotta leave, and quick."

Leia was up instantly, though her stomach was sinking. "Imperials?"

"Worse." Han displayed a small transistor with a long wire antenna, the kind used in tracking devices. "Squibs."

"Those vermin have been following us?"

Han nodded. "The sandcrawler is coming up the canyon."

"You're sure it's them?"

"Herat seems to think so," Han said. "We may have to leave her behind, if Chewie can't catch a Jawa with a broken leg."

Leia stopped so abruptly that Han ran into her and knocked the electrobinoculars out of her hand. "That's it!"

"What?" Han grabbed the electrobinoculars off the ground, then took Leia by the arm. "The hoverscout's in the rocks, remember?"

"We don't need it." Leia pulled free of his arm and started down the gully at a run. "Not yet."

"Hey!" Han called, racing after her. "Where are you going?"

"To strike a bargain!" Leia called over her shoulder. "I think Tatooine just gave us profoggs."

TWENTY-TWO

By the time the sandcrawler's blocky shape could no longer be seen rocking over the crests of the rolling sands, Tatoo I was spreading its golden light across the entire vastness of the Western Dune Sea. Leia glanced back at Han, who lay atop the hoverscout's forward cargo compartment scanning the sky with the electrobinoculars.

"It's gone," she reported. Along with Chewbacca, C-3PO, and the Squibs, she was about ten kilometers from Obi-Wan's, waiting in the mouth of a shadowy canyon at the edge of the Dune Sea. "Anything?"

"Still just the one TIE trailing it." Han lowered the electrobinoculars and slipped off the hoverscout. "Looks like your plan's a go."

"*If* Herat keeps her word," C-3PO pointed out. He was in the front passenger's seat. "Personally, I never find it advisable to trust a Jawa."

Chewbacca, sitting behind the steering yoke, gave a testy grunt. "That has nothing to do with it," C-3PO said. "I didn't believe for a moment Mistress Leia would include me in the deal."

"Pretty cocky for a droid," Han said. He turned to Leia. "But Threepio has a point. Herat's taking a big risk. Maybe she'll decide it's too big."

"That depends," Sligh said. He and Grees were in the back, working on the built-in comm units of a pair of stormtrooper helmets they had salvaged back in the cave. "Have you double-crossed *her* yet?"

"We haven't double-crossed anyone," Leia said. "You were the ones who called the deal off in the canyon. We were under no obligation to return the initiator to you."

"Speaking of that, how *did* you restart the reactor core?" Han asked.

"The baradium charge from a thermal—"

"Sligh!" Grees barked. "Did they *pay* for that?"

"Then she'll do her part," Sligh said, immediately switching back to the question about Herat. "That's why we told you to promise her a diagnostics kit from the *Falcon* instead of your protocol droid. A Quaxcon Mark Fifteen is too valuable for a Jawa to pass up. She'll take the risk, as long as she thinks you'll come through in the end and drop the kit."

Tinny static emerged from the speaker of the helmet in Grees's lap. He flipped a switch under the chin padding, then nodded and turned to Sligh.

"The droid was right." Grees passed the helmet forward to Chewbacca. "They switched modulation. It's Secure Blue."

"Of course," C-3PO said. "The Imperial datapad assured me that changing modes is standard procedure when communications equipment is captured."

Sligh made the frequency change in the helmet he was working on and passed it forward as well.

To Han, he said, "We're placing a lot of trust in you."

"Then why risk her life?" Han gestured at Emala, who stood beside Leia in a buff-colored sand cloak. She held a stormtrooper blaster rifle much too large for her and was loaded down with a water pack that weighed half what she did. "We don't need company that bad."

"I'm coming to help you find the ghost oasis," Emala said. "We're only thinking of the objective."

Though Leia knew the Squibs were more interested in protecting their own interests than assuring the outcome of the mission, she didn't even try to argue. Aside from Herat's insistence that simply recovering her sandcrawler wasn't enough compensation for the risk she was taking, this had been the largest sticking point in the hurried negotiations. The Squibs simply refused to go along with the plan unless one of them accompanied Leia and Han to the ghost oasis—and no matter that it might compromise the pair's disguises.

Leia took her helmet, then glanced down at Emala. "I just hope you can hold up," she said. "Without temperature-controlled armor, it's going to be a long hot walk."

"That's why she's going," Grees said. "She's the tough one."

Emala's ears perked with pride.

Han rolled his eyes, then took his helmet and clasped Chewbacca on the forearm. "Don't hit anything. And when you get the *Falcon*, don't scratch—"

Chewbacca cast his eyes at the sky and rowled in mock annoyance.

"Han, that ship still has scorch marks from fighting the first Death Star." Leia turned to Chewbacca and said, "Scratch all you want. Maybe he'll finally paint the blasted thing."

Chewbacca nodded enthusiastically and activated the repulsor engines, then started up the canyon with C-3PO and the two male Squibs, casually waving over his shoulder. It was, Leia knew, the Wookiee way of parting under such circumstances; to make a fuss would be to suggest he didn't think they'd be seeing each other again.

Han put his arm around Leia's shoulder, and together they watched as the hoverscout disappeared around the corner.

"So," he asked. "You really think this will work?"

"I don't know." Leia turned to face him. "Have a better idea?"

Han smiled. "Yeah." He slipped both hands around her waist and pulled her toward him until they bumped chest plates, then leaned down close. "This."

Emala groaned.

Leia ignored her and kissed Han until her stomach began to flutter, then kissed him a little longer. Not because it might be the last time, she told herself, but because they were in this together. At last, she pulled away and smiled up at Han.

"Time to march, trooper."

Leia and Han put on their helmets and started toward the oasis, Emala trailing half a kilometer back to serve as a rear guard—and to stay out of sight, in the event they ran into an unexpected reconnaissance team. They were careful to remain in the shade along the base of the cliffs, both to stay out of the sun and to reduce their chances of being seen by far-flung sentries—Imperial or Tusken.

Despite the cooling units in their captured armor, the going was slow and uncomfortable. On the sandcrawler, Han had pieced together a suit of salvaged pieces that almost fit, but Leia had been forced to pad hers out with tomuon wool. Even then, the shin and forearm guards were simply too long for her, and every step was a struggle to bend her ankles, knees, and elbows. It took them four hours of wading through sand and scrambling over rocks to cover the next four kilometers, and by the time they finally ducked into a cranny in a small side canyon to wait, Leia was both exhausted and sore.

Still, she counted her blessings. Kitster Banai was certainly worse off by far—if he was alive at all. And if they failed to recover *Killik Twilight* in time to contact Mon Mothma, hundreds of Askajian resistance fighters were certain to endure torments far more painful at the probe tips of Imperial interrogator droids.

Emala crept up a few minutes later, her movements so stealthy and her sand cloak such perfect camouflage that she was almost past before Leia noticed and stepped out of hiding to wave her over. The Squib looked even more tired than Leia, and she sank into the shaded cranny with a weary sigh. Her water pack was three-quarters empty.

"How are you feeling, Emala?" Leia asked.

"I've made it this far, haven't I? Don't think you'll leave me passed out in this—"

"Easy there," Han said. "We only have your interests at heart."

Emala shot him a doe-eyed glower that only managed to look endearing. "Don't expect me to fall for that. I know you humans."

"Do you need to rest?" Leia asked. "Chewie and the others should be at the edge of the salt flats by now. They can't leave the canyons until we give the signal."

Emala took a long draw from the water tube hanging over her shoulder, then stood and brought her blaster rifle to port arms. "I've got your backs."

Leia put her helmet back on, then removed a captured comlink from her equipment belt and glanced at Han. Fearful that any signal over their own comlinks would lead enemy eavesdroppers down on them, they had decided to confuse the issue by communicating over the *Chimaera*'s own comm net. With any luck, the Imperials wouldn't even notice the extra traffic.

"Chubba!" Emala reached up and briefly depressed the transmit switch. "Will you just click it and see what happens?"

Chewbacca's double click answered almost instantly.

Leia and Han crept down the gulch until they had a clear view of the sky over the Dune Sea, then Han raised the electrobinoculars and knelt down to watch. A minute passed . . . two . . . Leia began to wonder if Herat had decided not to take the risk after all.

Then Han finally said, "They're buying it."

He passed the electrobinoculars over, and Leia saw a dozen TIEs—a full squadron—dropping down over the Dune Sea. She activated the range finder but saw only a 1 followed by two blurs of changing numbers.

"A hundred kilometers? That can't be right!"

"Closer to a hundred fifty, I think," Han said. "Herat must have the sandcrawler's power core running close to critical. She wants that Mark Fifteen."

"She deserves it."

Leia passed the electrobinoculars back, then clicked the captured comlink again. This time, Chewbacca did not answer, for they were trying to communicate as little as possible to avoid drawing attention. But Leia knew he would be piloting the hoverscout down the last few hundred meters of canyon and out onto the Great Mesa, racing for the *Falcon*'s hiding place. Assuming the diversion kept the Imperial eyes focused on the Dune Sea long enough for him to melt into the general traffic patterns running between Mos Espa and Mos Eisley, they had guessed this part of the trip would take about an hour. The entire return journey—assuming the *Falcon* was still in the smuggler's cave when he reached it—would take about three minutes.

A series of blue hyphens flashed in the distant sky.

"They're firing," Han reported.

"At Herat?" Emala asked.

"Can't tell," Han said.

"They're warning shots." Leia was recalling the command directive they had seen. "*Chimaera* command wants us alive. Even more than that, they want to know where we are. They won't take the chance of hitting the reactor core and vaping the whole crawler."

They watched in silence for two minutes more, Leia's ears aching to hear a voice coming over the built-in comm receiver in her helmet, an officer issuing orders or a trooper asking a question, anything to indicate how the *Chimaera* was reacting to the diversion. Normally they would have. But, exhibiting a discipline lacking in Imperial troops since the days of the Emperor, the two companies of ambushers maintained comm silence, and she heard nothing over the channels to suggest one way or the other how well her plan was working.

"Blast!" Han said. "We'll have to do this the hard way. They must be bringing another company down from orbit."

Leia nodded. "We should have realized they would have a ready reserve. These Imperials . . . they're new and improved."

They put away the electrobinoculars and started toward the oasis again, Leia and Han alternating fifty-meter advances with Emala so they could cover each other and watch for Imperials. After two hundred meters, they began to hear the rumble of lowing banthas and retreated into the Jundland Wastes. Creeping along the convergence zone at the edge of the Dune Sea would certainly be the quickest and most concealed approach to the oasis—but it was also the most obvious.

They found the first pair of stormtroopers thirty meters up the gulch, sprawled against the slope with their weapons at their sides and blood smeared over their armor. One had a single slugthrower hole in the lens of his helmet. The other had been shot in the throat, in the vulnerable area between his breastplate and his chin.

"Looks like we picked the wrong disguises." Filtered through his helmet vocabulator, Han's voice sounded like the voice of every stormtrooper Leia had ever heard. "Did we plan for this?"

"Not really," Leia said. "See any sign of the sniper?"

Han scanned the opposite hillside with the electrobinoculars for several minutes, then finally shook his head. "Plenty of places to hide, though."

"He probably moved on," Leia said.

"Probably," Han agreed. "But cover me anyway."

Holding his blaster rifle ready to fire, Han raced across the killing zone and ducked between two boulders on the other side. Leia followed and joined him, then turned to see Emala rubbing her muzzle against the helmets of the dead troopers. When she had finished, she strapped their equipment belts over her shoulders bandolier-style and joined the Solos between the boulders.

Noticing their attention, she said, "I had to be sure they were dead, didn't I? They might have been laying a trap for you."

Han shook his helmet and started to ascend the hillside—but stopped when the thunder of a set of huge repulsorlift engines echoed off the canyon walls. Leia pulled him back down behind the boulders, then looked toward the sound and saw a curtain of dust boiling down the gulch. A moment later, the armored form of an Imperial assault shuttle rounded the bend, flying past only meters above their heads before disappearing through the canyon mouth.

"That's more like it," Leia said.

In her head, she could almost see the last few minutes aboard Herat's sandcrawler. A company of stormtroopers drops on top via zipline, cuts through the roof to discover an abandoned bridge, and begins a cautious search. Someone finds an Imperial hoverscout on the lower cargo deck, its holomap damaged and the transponder that caught the interest of *Chimaera* Intelligence randomly short-circuiting. Someone else locates Herat locked inside a tool bin. She is quite relieved to hear that the hijackers have fled her sandcrawler and thanks the Imperials profusely for saving her life—until she discovers that the thieves took a shipment of brand-new speeder bikes with them. The officer reluctantly breaks comm silence to report that the Rebels may be fleeing across the Dune Sea on speeder bikes . . .

Leia nodded in satisfaction. "They're buying it."

"Maybe," Han said. "Or maybe that shuttle's just running off to pick up a—"

Han was interrupted by a voice in their helmet receivers. "Company A, report to your shuttle for transport. Company B, redeploy and maintain the ambush."

"*Maintain?* Alone?" came an angry voice. "I've already lost half my company to—"

A deeper voice came over the comm channel. "Are you actually questioning your orders, Captain?"

The captain's voice grew instantly obsequious. "N-no, sir. Just asking for clarification."

"Ah, a clarification," the voice said. "I wish you to redeploy to maintain the ambush in the Dune Sea as well as the canyons. Any losses this causes you are unimportant, so long as you remain strong enough to capture the Rebels—should they arrive. When I decide the time is right to recover the painting, I will send reinforcements to aid your survivors. Is that clear enough?"

"Y-yes, sir."

"Very good, Captain. All units return to Priority Yellow comm silence."

Leia turned to Han. "Why do you ever doubt me?"

"Slow learner, I guess."

Leaving Emala to hide amid the boulders for now, Leia and Han angled up the dusty slope to within a few paces of the crest, then crept over to an outcropping of tilted slabstone where they could cross the ridge without presenting an obvious silhouette. Han dropped to all fours and crawled into a long V-shaped trough that would shield them from most sides. Leia covered him until the trough descended a level and he turned to wave her forward. Pushing her blaster rifle along in front of her, she started forward—then saw the rag-swaddled figure of a Tusken Raider rise behind him, gaffi stick poised to strike.

Leia stopped and snatched for her blaster rifle, and that was when a shadow fell across the slabstone beside her. Han brought his blaster rifle up to fire, but the Tusken behind him was already swinging his gaffi stick.

"Han! Behind—"

The Tusken's chest exploded outward in a gout of smoke and light, then a blaster bolt flashed over Han's head and struck something behind Leia. A strangled gasp sounded above and behind her, then the shadow disappeared. She turned to look. A third shot lit the air and struck something behind her on the other side. This time, she did not turn to look. She stood up and ran, leaping over Han's head into the far end of the trough.

When no gaffi sticks smashed her helmet on the way down, she scrambled to her feet and stuck her head over the edge of the trough, blaster rifle cradled and ready to fire.

The only targets were the three Tuskens sprawled over the slabstone with smoking holes in their chests, two motionless and obviously dead, one reaching for his gaffi stick and muttering something guttural. Han reached over Leia's shoulder and shot him.

"Sneak up on my wife, will you?"

Leia studied the three warriors for a moment, allowing

herself a moment to stop trembling, then turned to Han. "Who just saved our hides? Is Lando here somewhere?"

"I doubt it." Han turned and pointed toward the next ridge, a good two hundred meters away. "The shots came from somewhere over there."

A stormtrooper armed with what appeared to be a two-meter stick—a sharpshooter's longblaster—stepped out of a cranny and waved. Han waved back, and a second trooper, this one with the orange shoulder pauldron of a squad leader, motioned them over. Leia signaled okay and helped Han drag the three dead Tuskens out of sight. Then, under the pretext of gathering a stray gaffi stick, she turned to warn Emala about the sniper.

The Squib was nowhere to be seen.

"Sharpshooter," Leia said anyway. "Watch yourself."

"Don't think you'll be rid of me that easy," a nearby rock said. "I know what you're doing."

Knowing there was no point in arguing, Leia turned without speaking and followed Han toward the squad leader. They were careful not to present an easy shot to any unseen Tuskens, but made no further attempt to remain concealed. They could see at least a dozen stormtroopers working their way toward the Dune Sea in a similar manner, and any attempt to be stealthy would only draw attention.

"What's the plan?" Leia asked. "Get close and shoot 'em?"

"If we have to," he said. "But let's try something else first. You still have that datapad from the hoverscout?"

Leia turned her back to Han so he could retrieve it from her pack, then they ascended the slope—passing two more stormtrooper bodies on the way—and joined the squad leader in a small stone breastwork concealed in a nook between two sandrock outcroppings.

The leader eyed Leia up and down, no doubt contemplating her ill-fitting armor and small size, then demanded, "Service numbers?"

"He's doing a tactical efficiency study," Han said, jerking a thumb at Leia. "I'm his combat escort."

The squad leader continued to look at Leia. "The training staff doesn't have service numbers?"

"I'm command, not training." Leia stared into the leader's vision processors and let the sentence hang as though that answered his question.

After a moment, the squad leader turned to Han. "What about you?"

"Don't answer that, trooper." Leia took the datapad from Han and passed him her blaster rifle. "He's on loan to command. You understand."

The squad leader, who clearly did not understand, continued to look at Han.

Han shrugged and spread his hands.

The squad leader turned back to Leia. "Pushy for such a young fellow, aren't you?"

"Your devotion to procedure is to be commended," Leia said, ignoring the comment. "I'll make a note of it. What's your service number?"

"ST-Three-Four-Seven." The number came from the trooper's mouth almost by reflex. "Sir."

"Thank you." Leia made a show of entering it on the datapad. "We were with Company A until the redeployment. We'll be working with you now. We need a blind overlooking the camp, as close to the action as possible."

"Sir?"

"Alone," Leia said. "My observations are classified."

"You can take this place." ST-347 hooked a thumb toward the front of his breastwork. "You have a clear field of view, and as long as you have a pair of electro—"

"Close to the action," Leia repeated sternly. "We need

to be in place before Company A finishes redeploying. You understand."

ST-347 sighed through his vocabulator. "Close, huh?" He motioned at the datapad. "You'll want to put that thing away. And keep your head down—the Tuskens seem to think our helmet lenses make for good target practice."

Once they were ready, ST-347 led them to the crest of the ridge, where he dropped to his belly and crawled forward until they could see the camp ahead. To Leia's surprise, it lay a considerable distance out in the sands, a smear of rocky ground along the base of the first massive dune. She could make out the woolly forms of wandering banthas and the smaller domes of the Tusken huts, but that was about all with her naked eye.

"The closest we can get you is the top of that dune," he said. "But if you were with Company A, you just came from there."

"Funny how much closer these hills looked from there." Leia turned to Han. "Didn't I tell you to check the range, trooper?"

ST-347 glanced at Han over Leia's back, sharing a moment that soldiers have no doubt been sharing since there were officers. Then he looked down the slope behind them, ordered a pair of passing stormtroopers to wait, and turned back to Leia.

"You can tag along with Seven-Eight-Nine and Six-Three-Six, sir. They'll get you there in one piece."

"Very efficient of you, ST-Three-Four-Seven." Leia backed away from the edge and stood, then allowed her helmet lenses to linger on Han for a moment. "Obviously, I wasn't assigned a very capable escort."

As Leia started down the slope to join her new escorts, she heard ST-347 ask Han, "Who is that kid? One of Pellaeon's nephews?"

"Worse," Han replied. "Quenton's son. Straight out of the academy."

"Quenton has a son?"

"He likes to keep it quiet. You can see why."

"Tough break, trooper," ST-347 said. "Good luck keeping him alive."

Forty painful and exhausting minutes later, Leia and Han were crawling the last few meters to the dune's crest. The suns were beating down mercilessly on the sands, and even with her cooling unit turned to maximum, Leia felt as though she were squirming across a frying pan.

She glanced over at Han. "You okay in there?"

"Don't worry about me. Seen any sign of Emala?"

"No," Leia said. "And I'm not worried about her. We told her this would happen."

"Sure you aren't."

"Aren't what?"

"Worried about her."

They reached the top and found themselves looking down the dune's steep side. Two hundred meters below, thirty bantha wool huts stood amidst the rocks at one end of a small oasis. At the end opposite the camp stood a permanent hut, still covered in bantha wool but supported by an exterior framework of bantha bones. Next to it, just behind a bantha rib arch, lay a pile of what appeared to be bleached sticks, though Leia had a feeling they were something else. Banthas roamed the oasis freely, but their Tusken riders were not visible anywhere.

Leia took out the electrobinoculars and turned them on the hut standing next to the bantha-rib arch. Care had been taken to sink the fabric walls deep into the sand, and a simple bantha bone drawbar locked the door from the outside.

"Look at the hut next to the bone pile," Han said.

"Good idea," Leia said dryly. "It's a holding cell."

Even without the drawbar she had observed through the electrobinoculars, Leia would have known what she was seeing. Simply looking at the hut sent a shiver down her spine. It was a place of torture and death, a place where suffering and despair had permeated the Force to such a degree that Leia could feel it even atop the dune. Her shoulder began to ache again, then all of her old wounds as well—especially those inflicted by her father's interrogation droid aboard the Death Star.

Leia lowered the electrobinoculars and looked away. "This is going to be fun."

"Fun?" Han asked. "Maybe you need to adjust your cooling unit."

"It won't do any good," Leia said. "I can feel what happens down there."

"More Force-sensations?" Even through the voice filter, Han sounded uneasy. "Do you mean what *happened* down there? Or what's *going* to?"

Leia shrugged. "That's not clear. What I'm feeling is just phantom pain."

"Great . . . like the real stuff isn't bad enough." Han's helmet turned back toward the oasis. "Maybe it's Kitster. That's where he'd be, if he's still alive."

Leia pictured Kitster's face and forced herself to look at the hut. The phantom pains did not intensify, but the oasis began to feel more familiar to her, much as Mos Espa had after departing Watto's—much as Shmi's hovel had when Leia went there to hide.

Her stomach grew cold and hollow. A moment later, she began to experience a time-muted sense of loneliness and despair from the direction of the hut, and the electrobinoculars slipped from her grasp. She watched absently as they slid twenty meters down the dune, then vanished beneath a small landslide.

"Leia!" Han gasped. He peered in both directions along the crest of the dune, then asked, "What's wrong? I think the captain saw you drop those."

"This is where they kept her," Leia said, still in shock. "This is where Shmi Skywalker was tortured."

TWENTY-THREE

Chewbacca and the Squibs had taken a few scenic detours on the way to Mos Espa, first sweeping around the back side of the Mospic High Range to avoid a company of hoverscouts fanning out across the flats south of Mos Espa, then ducking through Arch Canyon to lose a flight of TIEs they had picked up entering Xelric Draw. Now C-3PO—who had been using a pair of electrobinoculars to reconnoiter the entire trip—was reporting what seemed to be the ultimate roadblock, an Imperial AT-AT walker moving into position to block the mouth of the smuggler's cave where the *Falcon* sat hidden in the darkness.

Chewbacca opened the throttles wide.

Unlike the overhang beneath which they had found the ambushed sandcrawler, the smuggler's cave was a true cavern, with a mouth as large as a space slug's and two sweeping curves that Chewbacca could fly blind. It was also hidden in the back of a sunken dead end in the bottom of Beeda Basin and visible from only one place along the rim, a feature that had made it a favorite rendezvous point for smugglers since long before the Hutts controlled Tatooine.

"You must have misunderstood me," C-3PO said. "I said the Imperial walker was in *front* of us."

Chewbacca growled his impatience.

"You *will* care," C-3PO retorted. "There were two hoverscouts in position already."

Chewbacca turned to order one of the Squibs into the blaster turret and found them both climbing onto the firing seat, Grees slipping behind the triggers and Sligh arranging grenades and thermal detonators in the stormtrooper utility belts slung across his chest.

Chewie grunted happily.

"This is *not* going to be fun," C-3PO said. "In fact, I insist you let me out of this vehicle right now."

The Wookiee ignored him and continued across the basin floor. Finally, the mirage effect lifted and he could see a shimmering line ahead where the ground dropped into the sunken dead end. He groaned a warning.

"I don't see what good holding on will do. We're going to be blasted to—aarraghhg!"

The droid's complaint ended in a wail as the hoverscout reached the dead end and dropped over a five-meter escarpment. Grees chortled in delight and cut loose with the blaster cannon. Chewbacca got his bearings and saw the walker standing in the cavern mouth, its immense legs braced for firing, its cockpit swinging in their direction, and two platoons of stormtroopers rappelling to the ground on droplines. Flanked by the two hoverscouts C-3PO had mentioned, the walker was effectively blocking the entire cave entrance.

Both hoverscouts and the walker's cockpit opened up with their blaster cannons, raising a wall of laser blossoms that left Chewbacca piloting from memory. He rumbled a command.

C-3PO turned to Grees. "Chewbacca asks that you shoot those droplines—"

"Gotcha!" Grees shifted his fire. "Can't see a thing!"

Neither could Chewbacca, but he had a sense of the cave mouth swelling up ahead. Juking and jinking like a fighter pilot, he aimed for the center of the darkness. The hoverscout shuddered twice as its armor absorbed a couple of light cannon strikes.

The barrage ended as quickly as it had started, and Chewbacca saw the gray tree of an AT-AT leg looming in front of him. He swerved to avoid it, bounced over a pile of groaning stormtroopers, and suddenly there was nothing but dark cave ahead.

He decelerated and took a sweeping left, then heard the rapid-fire crackle of three thermal detonators and a couple of incendiary grenades going off under the AT-AT.

C-3PO's metal fingers began to scrape blindly at the control console. "Surely this vehicle has lights!"

Chewbacca slapped the droid's hand away and took a gradual left, where they found the underside of the *Falcon* illuminated by the glow of two portable lamps. In the dim light, a squad of stormtroopers was still struggling to set their E-Web repeating blaster on its tripod. Grees brought the blaster turret around and relieved them of the necessity.

After a few security shots to make sure there were no survivors lurking about, they swung around behind the *Falcon* and parked behind the main cargo lift. Chewbacca leapt out of the driver's seat and ran for the main hatch, roaring instructions to C-3PO over his shoulder.

"Why do *I* have to wait?" the droid complained. "Sligh must be capable of keeping watch!"

"Yeah, if I wasn't heading for a cannon turret—"

Chewbacca did not hear the rest of the exchange. He was already running up the boarding ramp, prioritizing the tasks he needed to accomplish before he could get to Han and Leia: warm the drive circuits, lower the repeating blaster, actuate the power core. It should all be doable in the next three minutes. There might still be that Imperial walker to get past, if Sligh's thermal detonators had failed to drop it—but that was why the *Falcon* carried concussion missiles, wasn't it?

Leia continued to look at the hut with the drawbar. She had not taken her eyes off it since dropping the electrobinoculars. The sensation of pain and despair had faded back to nothingness, but the memory of it weighed more heavily on her mind than ever. This was where her grandmother had been held captive and tortured— probably where she had died. And it was where Anakin had found his mother. It had to be.

"I wonder if she was still alive." Realizing that so far she had not voiced her thoughts to Han, Leia added, "This is where Anakin found my grandmother."

"How can you know that?" Han glanced longingly down the slope toward the lost electrobinoculars. "Did he leave a sign?"

"Think about it." Leia explained what Beru's sister had told her about Shmi's abduction from the Lars farm, and how Anakin had returned to Tatooine and recovered her body. "He found her at this encampment—in that hut."

"So Anakin is the angry ghost?" Han asked.

Leia recalled what Herat had told them about how this place came by its name. "I suppose so. An entire tribe, hacked to pieces."

"They sure picked the wrong woman to kidnap." Han's gaze wandered to the edge of the oasis, where the banthas were gathering around a gently rumbling female. "The mother of a Jedi."

"Didn't they?"

Leia felt no satisfaction in knowing how savagely her grandmother's death had been avenged—quite the opposite. She was suddenly very aware of the twin suns blazing down, of the heat and the cloud-barren sky and the eye-stabbing brilliance, and she began to feel hollow and qualmish inside.

"This is where it happened," she said. "Where he first surrendered to his anger."

"He?" Han's helmet turned to look at her. "Your father."

Leia nodded.

"I can see how it might happen," Han said.

"That doesn't excuse it." Even the helmet vocabulator did not blunt the sharpness in Leia's voice. "He knew better."

"Talk about a worrt calling a gorg slow," Han said. "Take it easy. Maybe that's not what happened. You're placing a lot of faith in feelings."

"It's paid off so far," Leia countered. "Or are you forgetting what would have happened if we'd come straight here?"

"I'm not forgetting," Han said. Down in the oasis, the bantha herd was ambling toward the Tusken camp.

"And even if he did, why do they keep sacrificing more captives? Seems like that would only make the angry ghosts angrier."

"Do I *look* like a Tusken?" Leia asked. "How would I know why they make their sacrifices? No one knows why Sand People do anything. That's what makes them Sand People."

The electronic voice of a stormtrooper sounded from the slope behind them. "Excuse me."

Leia and Han spun toward each other and knocked helmets, then turned to find a stormtrooper standing on the slope below, his head cocked as though he could not quite believe the incompetence he was seeing. He held his blaster rifle in one hand, a pair of electrobinoculars in the other.

"Service number?" Leia demanded, assuming the offensive in an effort to keep the stormtrooper off balance. "What are you doing sneaking up on us?"

"ST-Two-Nine-Seven," the trooper replied. "I apologize if I'm intruding on a classified conversation."

Noting ST-297's more confident demeanor, Leia assumed a more civil tone.

"You're excused. What do you want?"

"I couldn't help noticing that you had dropped your electrobinoculars." ST-297 raised the set in his hand. "I thought you might like to borrow mine."

"That's very efficient of you." Leia nodded Han down the slope. "I'll make a note of it."

"Thank you. I'm a great admirer of Commander Quenton." ST-297—Leia was guessing *officer*—passed the electrobinoculars to Han, but he kept his helmet lenses trained on Leia. "Is there anything else you need?"

Leia pretended to consider this a moment, then shook her head. "You've been very helpful, Captain."

ST-297's helmet turned slightly to the side, then he said, "That was S-T-Two-Nine-Seven. What was your service number again?"

Leia cursed herself for raising his suspicions unnecessarily.

Han was quick to salvage the situation. He stepped in front of the stormtrooper. "You don't want to know. It's command."

"That will be all, Lieutenant," Leia said. "I'll make certain that my fath—uh—Commander Quenton hears of your efficiency."

ST-297 seemed to grow an inch taller. "Very well, then. I'll leave you to your observations."

Leia watched him go, then took the electrobinoculars from Han. "With sycophants like that leading their platoons, the Empire is doomed."

"Good—we need all the help we can get." Han looked in the direction of Mos Espa, then checked his chronometer. "I wonder what's taking so long? Chewbacca should have clicked us by now."

The same question had been on Leia's mind, but she tried not to dwell on the negative possibilities. There were just too many of them, and they had no choice but to trust Chewbacca to figure a way around any problem he encountered.

She shrugged and said, "Maybe there was unexpected traffic."

Leia took the electrobinoculars and turned them back on the hut. Now that she was over the shock of what she had felt through the Force, she could see that the bantha rib arch was splattered with something dark. A pair of rawhide thongs dangled from the bones at just about the height of a human's outstretched arms, leaving little doubt as to the gruesome purpose of the arch.

Three meters behind it lay a pile of sun-bleached skulls and bones. Most appeared to be human, and many of the limbs were splintered or truncated where the corpse had been hacked apart. Leia was relieved to see that none of the bones had any flesh clinging to it. Banai was, perhaps, still alive.

Leia could not bear to look longer. As horrified as she was by what Shmi had suffered—as much as it pained her to contemplate what had happened there—she was even more appalled by the ghastly cycle her father had set in motion. There had to be a hundred skulls in that pile, maybe two or three hundred. For his mother's life, Anakin had taken the lives of dozens of Tuskens; the Sand People had responded with more killing of their own. The legacy of death he had planted that day had continued to grow, costing hundreds of beings their lives, and Leia could see no end to it.

"He should have known better." Leia passed the electrobinoculars to Han. "He was a Jedi."

"He was a kid with a dead mother." Han raised the electrobinoculars, but he seemed to be looking more toward the banthas than the bones. "He vented his anger on the ones who killed her. I might have done the same thing."

"That doesn't make it right," Leia said.

"And it doesn't make me a Sith monster, either," Han retorted. "What he did wasn't evil, it was human. Later, he became Darth Vader and did a lot of terrible things, but don't forget that he's the one who killed the Emperor."

"You're saying you forgive him?" Leia asked. "After he froze you in carbonite?"

"I'm just saying that without him, Palpatine would still be Emperor."

"You're saying Darth Vader saved the galaxy?"

Han shrugged. "Well, Anakin Skywalker. Think about it. If he'd have been a nice guy, do you think he'd have ever gotten that close to Palpatine?" Han continued to watch the banthas through the electrobinoculars. "Maybe that was your father's destiny all along, to save the galaxy just like his mother thought he would—well, maybe not *just* like she thought. But he *did* save it."

"Han . . ." Leia felt like her world had been turned upside down . . . again. Han had a way of doing that to her. "Han, sometimes you amaze me."

That got him to put the electrobinoculars down. "Just sometimes?" He passed them over. "But our job's not done. Take a look behind the banthas and tell me what you see."

Leia adjusted the focus and saw a small buff-colored mass creeping across the ground, about ten meters behind the last bantha. "What is that, a womp rat?"

"Yeah, a womp rat named Emala." Han took the

electrobinoculars and began to unscrew the recharge port. "But forget about her. I think we've got other problems. Take a look over my shoulder."

Leia saw a long line of stormtroopers starting to creep across the face of the dune toward them.

"Behind me, too?" she asked.

Han nodded, then pulled a small transistor out of the recharge port. Leia did not need to ask what the two little wires dangling from the end were. She had seen eavesdropping bugs often enough to recognize an antenna.

"That lieutenant was a little smarter than we thought." Han tossed the bug over the edge of the dune, then asked, "What do you want to do—surrender, or try to blast our way out?"

The stormtroopers behind Han raised their blasters and broke into a run. Leia glanced over the side down into the oasis, where the banthas were carefully starting to pick their way through the Tusken camp.

"I have a better plan. Follow me." Leia tucked her blaster rifle under one arm and plucked the handheld comlink from her utility belt, then jumped over the side and began to slide down the steep face of the dune. "Chewie, we need a lift, and fast!"

TWENTY-FOUR

Han didn't even know when the Tuskens opened fire. He was about halfway down the dune, lying on his back sliding down the steep slope with his legs held high, trying to keep Leia in sight between his feet, listening to the almost subliminal rumble of avalanching sand.

Then ST-297's voice came over his helmet speaker.

"The impostors are to be taken alive! Lay fire on the Tuskens. Repeat, Tuskens only! Suppress all indigenous fire on the Rebels!"

A sheet of blasterfire erupted from not too many meters up the slope behind Han, flashing down over his head, shredding desert brush Tusken huts, lacing the oasis with strands of smoke and light. The banthas bugled and began to cluster together in a defensive circle, and that was the end of the Sand People's camp.

Leia craned her neck to look up at Han. "The Tuskens are shooting at us?"

"Who knows? I still haven't seen any—"

Leia let her feet catch and flipped head over heels, and her blaster went flying. Han caught it in one hand, then watched in frightened panic as she continued to accelerate, descending the dune's face in a crazy tumble not even a Tusken could hit.

Not wanting to be left behind, Han cradled both

blaster rifles to his chest, tucked his chin, and planted his feet.

At the speed he was traveling already, it was like being launched from a missile tube. He pitched forward and sailed into the air, and then the world became a kaleidoscope of sand, sky, and blaster flash.

Han was dimly aware of several voices inside his helmet demanding to know what was happening—the lieutenant shouting, "Have they been hit?" and someone else demanding, "Why are you breaking comm silence?" just before he crashed through a thicket of bushes and slammed into a boulder. He tried to sit up, only to fall over again when something struck his helmet with a deafening crack. A blaster bolt sizzled past overhead, then a heavy body landed across his midsection.

"ST-Two-Nine-Seven, what's happening down there?" a voice demanded in his ear. "Report!"

"It's the Rebels," the lieutenant answered. "We have them in sight. They're fleeing into the Tusken encampment."

"What?" A different voice this time, the same one that had chastised Company A's captain for questioning orders. "Repeat."

"They're fleeing into the Tusken camp, sir. We're pursuing, but manpower is limited."

"Pursuing, Lieutenant? Set blasters to stun and stop them."

There was a pause, then the lieutenant said, "Stunning may not be possible, sir. They're wearing captured armor."

"Thus the *impostors*," the voice said.

"I have sharpshooters covering them."

"As well you should. May we then assume that they are listening to our current comm channel?"

"It, uh, seems likely."

"Indeed. All units to adopt nonsecure communications protocol until further notice. And Lieutenant?"

"Sir?"

"Why am I not speaking with the captain of Company A?"

"Tuskens, sir."

"Ah, of course. Carry on, Lieutenant. Reinforcements are coming." Then, in a more reflective tone, the voice added, "Interesting."

"Han!"

It took Han a moment to realize this voice was coming from outside his helmet. He rolled over and found himself looking into the goggles of the Tusken Raider lying atop him—the first one he had seen in the oasis so far.

"Leia?"

A pair of white-armored gloves grabbed the dead Tusken by the collar and pulled him off, then took one of the blaster rifles Han was holding. "We've got work to do."

Head still spinning from the blow to his helmet, Han staggered to his feet and followed Leia into the oasis proper. It was much larger than it had looked from above, probably twenty meters across and a hundred long. They were on the side nearest the dune—and the stormtroopers—about halfway down its length. Leia turned and raced for the main hut, laying suppression fire into the Tusken camp. Han turned his blaster in the opposite direction, shooting toward the dune.

"Leia, do you have any idea where we're going?"

"Of course," Leia replied. "If you were a Tusken with a painting worth fifteen million credits, where would you put it?"

"Didn't you just say nobody knows why Sand People do anything?"

"Good point," Leia said. "Want to go the other way?"

Han glanced over his shoulder toward the bugling banthas. It was impossible to see anything through the bushes and the rising cloud of dust, but he suspected the Tusken encampment was the last place anyone wearing stormtrooper armor would want to be right now.

"Uh, guess not."

The Tuskens began to catch up about the same time they reached the end of the oasis. Han didn't see any Sand People, of course; he simply went sprawling when a slugthrower projectile splattered against his back plate. Leia also went down when a slug caught her in the calf armor. They rolled to their backs and fired in the general direction from which the projectiles were coming.

"You okay?" Han yelled.

"It'll be a terrible bruise," Leia answered.

"But are you okay?"

"I think so," she said. "This armor really works."

"Sure, as long as nobody points a blaster in your direction."

A fan of blasterfire erupted behind them, fanning over their heads to mince the sparse brush in which the Tuskens were hiding.

"You had to say it!" Leia shouted.

Several Tuskens groaned—Sand People did not scream when they died—and the slugthrowers fell silent. Han and Leia rolled to their knees and began firing toward the dune.

Han dropped two stormtroopers less than three meters away and sent a dozen more diving for cover. He felt a little guilty about blasting men who had just saved his life, but it was a strange sort of battle. Besides, capture was not an option—not for the Solos. He leapt to his feet and, continuing to fire toward the Imperials, grabbed

Leia by the arm and charged the last dozen meters to the hut.

"You get the painting." He dropped behind the bantha rib arch and continued to assault the Imperials, who were continuing to fire at the Tuskens, who continued to stick their heads up every so often to take a potshot at the Solos. "I'll cover."

An anguished croak sounded from inside the hut. "Who's there? What's . . . happening?"

"Kitster?" Leia went to the door and flipped the bone drawbar. "Kitster Banai? You're still alive?"

"I . . . I think so."

As Leia started to pull the door open, the crack of a slugthrower projectile sounded against her armor, and she was thrown against the outside of the hut wall. There was another crack, followed by her strained, "Stang!"

Leia rolled around to the dune side of the hut, behind Han.

"That hurts!" She went to the hut wall and shouted through the fabric. "Kitster, it's Leia Organa Solo. Is the—"

"Leia Organa Solo?" He sounded a little more aware, but still very much in pain. "You don't sound like her."

"Do you care?" Han called. "We're here to help."

"Is the painting in there with you?" Leia asked.

"The painting . . . I'm not saying . . . get me out . . . of here."

Leia turned to Han. "It's not in there."

"Of course not. That would be too easy." To Kitster, Han yelled, "Can you walk?"

"Not . . . saying."

"Hey, pal, if you haven't figured it out yet, we're the good guys." To Leia, he added, "I'll have to carry him."

Han nodded Leia over to take his place, then pointed into the rocks on the other side of the sacrificial bone pile.

"They're trying to flank us."

Leia stood up, fired twice. Two Imperial voices screamed over helmet speakers.

"Not anymore."

Han went to the side of the hut. "Hey, Kit, what happened to the painting?"

"Not . . . telling," he said. "You'll leave me—"

"Good enough." Han fired his blaster about a meter beyond the voice, cutting a hole through the bantha wool wall.

"Chieftain has . . . in camp!"

"Thanks."

Han stepped through the hole he had just blasted, and what he found turned his stomach. Kitster Banai lay spread-eagled on the ground, his dark hair now light as sand. His ankles were swollen, his body was covered in burns and bruises, and three of his fingers were snapped at the middle knuckle.

"Kitster! How are you doing, buddy?" Han went to the man's side and kneeled beside him. "Sorry it took so long. We'd, uh, sort of given you up for dead."

"Me . . . too." Kitster's dark eyes were fearful and bewildered. "Who . . . you?"

"Han Solo." Slugthrower projectiles began to rip through the tent, drawing a new wave of blasterfire from the Imperials. "You'll just have to take my word for it."

Han pulled a lasicutter from his stormtrooper utility belt and sliced the bindings holding Kitster's wrists and ankles. Outside, Leia's blaster rifle erupted into a constant scream.

"Need help!"

"In a minute, Leia," Han called. "I'm busy here."

"They're rushing us!"

"Toss a couple of detonators." He pulled the thermal

detonator off his own belt and tossed it out to her. "That'll slow 'em down."

Leia stopped firing, and an instant later the crackle of two thermal detonators echoed through the oasis.

"Here's the deal." Han hoisted Kitster onto his shoulders. Starved and dehydrated, he weighed little. "We need to recover that painting or destroy it, which means Leia and I are going into that Tusken camp. You can come with us, or I can dump you on the stormtroopers. The Imperials will probably throw you in prison forever—"

"With you," Kitster said. "Want to see my children."

Han sighed. "I was afraid you'd say that."

"But don't go." Kitster paused to gather his strength. "Not to camp."

"Afraid we have to." Han started toward the makeshift door. "You should've let us destroy that painting back at Mawbo's."

"Such a terrible waste," Kitster gasped. "And you *don't* have to go. Turn . . . around."

"We don't have a lot of time—"

"Trust me," Kitster said. "Look up."

Finally beginning to understand, Han turned and looked at the ceiling.

There, hanging over the place where Kitster's head had been, was *Killik Twilight*, the stormy sky the same deep purple as before, the insectoid figures still turning to face the storm just as Han remembered.

"I thought you said—"

"Lied," Kitster said. "Thought you were . . . Imperial."

"You thought I . . . Kit, old buddy, you are one devoted art lover."

Han pulled the comlink off his belt and depressed the microphone key three times—the *got-it* signal. An instant later, Leia peered through the makeshift door, still firing into the rocks.

"You actually *have* it?"

"Up there." Han hooked a thumb at the ceiling. "I'll cover, you recover."

Leia retreated into the hut and, ignoring the dwindling sputter of projectiles still whistling through the room, traded places with Han.

"It's in amazing shape," she commented.

"Tuskens awed by it," Kitster said. "Didn't stop them from breaking a finger when I . . . needed to add water. And in desert . . ."

"I know," Han said, recalling Kitster's gnarled hands. "It needed a lot of water."

He glanced through the opening and found a dozen stormtroopers only ten meters away, still coming despite a hail of Tusken slugs. One fell to a hit through the lens, another with a wound through his throat, but most were simply falling as the projectiles splattered against their armor, then popping back up an instant later. Han chose the three closest to the hut and, struggling to keep Kitster balanced across his shoulders, concentrated on picking them off as they returned to their feet.

The thump of a concussion grenade sounded from the far side of the oasis. The banthas erupted into an orchestra of bugling, and an ominous reverberation began to roll across the desert.

"What's that?" Leia asked.

Han shrugged. "Emala maybe?" He put a pair of blaster bolts through a stormtrooper's chest plate, and two more sprang up. Five meters. "Who cares? We're going hand-to-hand if we don't—"

A long burst from Leia's blaster rifle sounded behind Han. He spun around to see *Killik Twilight* swinging down from the ceiling on a flap of smoking fabric. Leia plucked the painting off the hooks from which it had been hanging, then turned and blasted a new hole through the opposite wall.

"Let's go!"

Han glanced back to find a pair of stormtroopers rushing for the old hole. He fired at point-blank range, blasting one off his feet backward and sending the other diving for cover. He backed toward the new hole still firing—and heard the power pack depletion alarm.

"Always something!"

Han turned and ducked out of the hut, ejecting the power pack as he went, then tossed it back inside and raced after Leia.

Behind him, an Imperial voice cried, "Detonator!"

Han pulled the new power pack off his utility belt and inserted it into the socket, then dropped to a knee and turned to wait. There was a loud rumble coming their way through the oasis. Han did not dare glance toward it.

An Imperial voice came over the helmet speaker. "I have the impostors in my scope. They have rescued a Tusken captive, and they have the admiral's painting in their possession. Repeat, they have the painting. Awaiting instructions."

Han glanced over his shoulder to see Leia dodging behind a boulder. When he looked back, there was a stormtrooper standing in the makeshift doorway. He burned a hole in the fellow's chest, then began to spray the entire hut with blasterfire.

"They're rescuing a captive? Interesting." It was the reflective voice—the one that seemed to be in charge. The one that gave Han the creeps. "And they have the painting? You're certain?"

"Affirmative."

"Very well," the voice said. "You are authorized to target legs only."

Han stopped firing, sprang up, and heard a sharp-shooter's bolt tear into the ground where he had been kneeling. Dodging wildly—and praying Banai had the strength to hold on—he raced to catch up with Leia and ducked behind an adjacent boulder. Another blaster bolt zipped past and tore into the ground beside his feet. He finally had a chance to glance toward the roar coming from the Tusken camp and saw a three-meter wall of wool and horn sweeping in from the other side of the oasis, bringing with it a billowing wall of dust.

"What next?" He swung the barrel of his blaster around the side of the boulder and fired blindly. "Bounty hunters? Sarlacc pits?"

"It's not that bad." Leia had *Killik Twilight*'s small rectangle resting against her knees and was pulling a grappling line out of her utility belt. "Emala may have saved us—if Chewie would just get here."

"You think?"

Han continued to fire blindly, watching as Leia secured the line around her belt and extended the hooks at the throwing end. "I think."

Leia dropped to a knee and took over cover duties while Han did the same with his own grappling line. Then, afraid his passenger would not be able to hold on while being dragged across the desert by a charging bantha, he brought Kitster's forearms together beneath his own arm and began to lash the wrists together.

"Han, no time!" Leia yelled, still firing. "Move!"

"I can hold my—"

Kitster's assurance was cut short by a flurry of Leia's blaster bolts burning past Han's rock. Han glanced in her direction and saw a pair of stormtroopers charging up behind her.

"Duck!" he yelled, grabbing his blaster rifle.

Leia rolled instead, snatching *Killik Twilight* on the way. Han poured blaster bolts into the stormtroopers behind her, then took off running. He did not know how closely the next pair of stormtroopers were pursuing him, but the ones behind Leia were within five meters—and closing fast.

"No shot, no shot," the sharpshooters began to report. "They're in the dust."

But the other Imperials made up for it, firing as they ran, aiming for the Solos' legs and churning the ground into a dusty froth. Han dodged madly, holding Banai and the grappling hook with one hand, using the other to cover Leia by firing wildly behind her. Leia did the same for him—though instead of Banai, she was holding the painting in her other hand. Neither of them was hitting anything, but at least they were preventing the stormtroopers from hitting anything, either. And they were slowing down the pursuit. That was the important thing.

"Kitster!" Han had to yell to make himself heard above the blaster fury and the thunder of the stampede. "How close are those banthas?"

"Close," came the strangled reply. "Fifteen meters, but angling past us. I think they're heading for the back—"

Leia screamed and went down, her feet flying out from beneath her as the projectile from a Tusken slugthrower slammed into her shoulder armor. Han spun to help—and that was what saved his life.

A deafening crack sounded inside his helmet, then he was slamming into the ground, Kitster no longer on his shoulders, his ears ringing, head aching, struggling to remain conscious. He rolled to his back and saw laser bolts lacing the air barely a meter over his head. He tried to raise his blaster rifle and found he was no longer holding it.

The light storm above his head stopped, and an eerie silence fell over the oasis. Han groped for his blaster rifle and could find it nowhere. Leia was lying facedown and motionless across from him, *Killik Twilight* resting beside her. The banthas were so close now that the ground trembled as they pounded past.

"Leia?"

Han rolled to his knees and found Kitster lying a meter away, a line of white stormtrooper bodies resting motionless in the rocks beyond.

"Leia?"

A throaty chuckle sounded behind him. He turned to see three Tusken Raiders looming over him, their rifles pointed at his head. Behind them stood a pair of Tusken children armed with miniature gaffi sticks.

Han tucked his chin and tried to angle his helmet lenses away. This drew a laugh from one of the Tuskens, who stepped forward, bringing his rifle butt around toward the jawline of Han's helmet—then collapsed when Leia opened fire from behind and a blaster bolt exploded from his chest.

The remaining Tuskens spun to face her, their rifles rising. Han took one down with a stomp kick to the knee, then cringed as a bolt flashed past his helmet from Kitster's direction. It missed, but distracted the warrior long enough for Leia to bring her own weapon to bear. The Tusken fell, groaning and clutching at his throat.

"Han!"

Han turned in time to see Banai throwing his blaster rifle to him. But Leia was already firing again, taking out the last warrior with a flurry of bolts.

A series of light blows began to rain down on Han's helmet and shoulders, and he turned to find the two Tusken children assailing him with their little gaffi sticks.

Dropping the blaster rifle in his lap, he caught the attacks with a pair of hook blocks and ripped the weapons from their hands.

"Go on—get out of here."

The Tusken children kept their heads turned toward him and reached for their gaffi sticks.

Han broke the shafts over his knee and tossed them aside. "You're too small." He pointed into the underbrush. "I'm throwing you back!"

The children glanced at each other, then turned and fled—*toward* the banthas. Han thought they would be crushed, but the stampede was less a headlong rush than it was a well-organized exodus, with the huge creatures keeping their calves safely sheltered inside the herd and taking care to trot along no faster than the young ones could manage. The two Tusken children simply fell in alongside a bantha, grabbed a handful of shaggy wool, and pulled themselves onto the beast's back.

It looked easier than flinging a grappling line around the horns of a big male—and a lot smarter, too.

Leia appeared at Han's side, hauling him to his feet. "On your feet, Flyboy." She had *Killik Twilight* looped over her sore shoulder by the hanging wire and her blaster rifle tucked into its belt holster. "Company's on the way."

Han jammed his own weapon into its holster, then turned to pick up Banai and saw a fresh squad of ghostly white figures rushing through the underbrush.

"What's Chewie doing?" Han threw Banai over his shoulders. "Going around the far side of the planet?"

"You told him not to scratch the paint."

Leia turned and led the way toward the banthas. Han followed, barely managing to keep up. As they drew nearer to the beasts, the ground began to quake, and

Han found himself gagging on a musky stench that even the helmet's filter scrubbers could not remove.

Kitster leaned down close to Han's audio pickup, shouting over the roar of the banthas. "If I can't hold on—"

"Don't worry," Han assured him. "I won't come back."

"You'd find only . . . a smear, I'm sure," Kitster said. "Just tell my children—I love them."

"You hold on," Han said, "and tell them yourself."

Shifting the painting onto her back, Leia fell in alongside the herd and reached up, grabbing a handful of shaggy wool. She stumbled and it looked for a moment like she might fall and be trampled, or her bantha would panic and knock her over, but her feet simply left the ground, then she hauled herself awkwardly up, almost slipping when she had to let her weight hang from her sore shoulder.

Han fell in alongside the next beast and, struggling to keep pace, reached up and grabbed hold. His feet immediately went out from beneath him, which was just as well since a flurry of blaster bolts came flashing in under the bantha's belly. Most sizzled harmlessly past or ricocheted off his leg armor, but one managed to burn through and scorch his outer thigh.

Han clenched his teeth and concentrated on climbing, pulling himself up as Leia had done. Whether it was the shock of being hit or Kitster's extra weight—or perhaps he just wasn't as strong as his wife—he was only halfway up when his hands began to tremble and his forearms to cramp.

Kitster sensed his trouble and reached up himself. But he was in even worse shape, too weak to hold on to Han with his injured hand or the bantha wool with his good one. His grasp came free, and he began to fall backward.

"It's okay!" Han yelled. "Just grab me!"

"Quiet, Solo!" A small voice yelled from above. "You want to live, Banai? Give *me* your hand."

"Emala?" Han looked up to see the Squib dangling head-down above him, her feet tied into the wool on the bantha's back. "How'd you get here?"

"How do you think? I jumped!" She lashed out and caught Banai's hand in both of hers. "This would have been easier if you'd have grabbed the right bantha!"

The first two minutes of flight—before the Imperials had time to recover from the shock of having their AT-AT blown out of the *Falcon*'s path—had gone smoothly. Chewbacca had streaked across the Great Mesa at just under burn speed—the velocity at which the ship created a fireball in its wake—doing his best to avoid inhabited areas where his shock wave would have flattened buildings. By flying so low, C-3PO had informed him repeatedly, he was raising a dust cloud several kilometers high. So what? They were not going to take anyone by surprise. The Imperials knew where they were going. They would be waiting . . . in force.

The *Falcon* hit the first squadron at the Jundland Wastes, when Chewbacca ascended to avoid the rough terrain. The TIEs dived in from both sides, pelting the *Falcon* from all angles. Grees and Sligh, staffing the cannon turrets, took out three fighters before the first damage alarms began to ring in the cockpit. But that left nine. When one of the TIEs tried to sneak under the *Falcon* for a belly shot, Chewbacca headed for the rim of the nearest cliff and scraped him off. They did not try that game again.

The *Falcon* reached the undulating vastness of the Dune Sea . . . and found a second squadron waiting. With the shields wavering, a Bithian chorus of control alarms screeching, and the port vector plate so shot to pieces that rolling the *Falcon* was easier than turning it, Chewbacca knew they would never survive the next gauntlet.

So he decided to go under it.

As soon as the *Falcon* cleared the bluffs, he dropped her over the edge. C-3PO shrieked, but Chewbacca never listened to the droid anyway. He slipped into the trough between two of the massive dunes and leveled off at ten meters—that would leave almost three between the bottom cannon turret and the ground—and watched the TIEs dive on them.

Sligh smeared the Imperial vector with cannon fire—not aiming, just putting it up there in the way—and three TIEs erupted into fiery blossoms. The survivors passed over the *Falcon*, pummeling her shields with cannon fire, penetrating far too often and touching off so many alert lights the control panel looked like it was on fire.

Then, the TIEs were past, flying blind through the kilometers-high sand plume behind the *Falcon*, straight into the survivors of the Jundland squadron, also flying blind . . . and in the opposite direction. The tactical display went white with exploding TIEs.

Chewbacca howled in glee.

"Yes, that certainly will teach them to play games with a Wookiee," C-3PO agreed. "But I'm afraid I don't know the contest to which you're referring, Chewbacca. What is 'guts,' and how is it played?"

"Chewbacca did not double-cross us." Leia pulled a thumb-sized datachip off the back of the *Killik Twilight*'s moisture-control regulator and placed it in a small depression she had scooped out in the sand. "Wookiees don't double-cross."

"There's a first time for everything." Emala picked up the chip and rubbed it against her muzzle. "So this is what all the trouble's about?"

"Mostly. I *did* want the painting as well."

They were crouched atop a bluff in a small circle of boulders, with Tusken projectiles ricocheting off the rock around them and two separate squads of Imperials working into flanking positions along adjacent ridges. The banthas that had carried them into this mess were huddled in a defensive circle at the bottom of the ravine below, where they had stopped their stampede. Leia's cooling unit had been damaged by the last slug hit, and the twin suns were beating down mercilessly, quick-baking her in her armor.

But she had the Shadowcast code key, nobody was dead yet, and they had the signal beacon up for Chewbacca. Considering everything that had gone wrong and a few things that had gone right, Leia thought it had been a pretty good trip . . . for Tatooine. She snatched the datachip from the Squib's hand, checked to make sure it was still the Shadowcast code key, and returned it to the depression.

Emala plucked up the chip again, this time holding it in front of her eyes. "So what is it?"

Leia drew her blaster. "Do you really want to know?"

"Sorry for trying to help." Emala dropped the datachip back in the depression. "I was only thinking you should be sure you want to do this."

"This way, I know it won't fall into the wrong hands." Leia checked the datachip once more, then returned it to the basin. "If you try to pick it up again, I'll shoot you."

"After I saved your mate's life?" Emala huffed. "There's no need to be rude. I only have your best interests—"

"Watch yourself," Leia interrupted.

She pointed her blaster into the basin and squeezed the trigger. The bolt melted the chip to slag. She shot it again, and this time even the slag bubbled away.

"That ought to do it." Leia returned the moisture regulator to *Killik Twilight*'s frame, then handed the painting to Emala. "It needs filling. You know how to do it?"

Emala turned the painting right-side up and pointed to the little mouth in the top of the frame. "Pour water in there. Stop when I see it."

"*Pure* water." Leia hesitated, taking one last look at the painting before she returned to battle. "That's very important. I'm placing a lot of trust in you."

"Consider me part Wookiee." Emala opened her water bottle. "You won't be sorry."

Banai intercepted the bottle. "I'll show her."

Leia couldn't bear to watch. She crawled into a small cranny where Han lay between two boulders keeping watch on the Tuskens—or at least their banthas. The warriors themselves were as difficult to find as ever. She squeezed in beside him, jostling his wounded thigh, and an electronic groan escaped his helmet voice processor.

"Are you okay?" she asked. "How bad is it?"

"Not too bad." He glanced over his shoulder toward Banai, who was patiently explaining to Emala why she could not fill the reservoir straight from a water bottle. "You really want to trust Emala with your *Killik Twilight*?"

"I don't *want* to, but it's the Squibs' painting now. A deal's a deal."

A trio of loud pops sounded from somewhere below, and three slugs pinged next to her head, showering her helmet with shards of sandrock. Leia studied the ravine and saw only stone, dirt, and glare.

"Where are they?" she asked.

"You tell me," Han said. "If I knew, I'd be shooting back."

Leia watched for a moment longer. When another round of rock shards pattered off her helmet, she began to pour blasterfire into the largest boulder in the gully.

"What do you see?" Han asked.

"Nothing. But I'm not going to just lie here—"

"Right."

Han added his fire to hers, and the boulder shattered. An astonished Tusken Raider jumped up from where he had been kneeling and brought his slugthrower to his shoulder, so frightened that he was aiming high over their heads. Leia laid a few bolts at his feet and sent him scrambling down the ravine.

Han selected another likely-looking boulder and poured bolts into it. Leia joined him, and the stone split in two. There was no one behind it.

In the mouth of the ravine, the banthas lowed in panic and began to move deeper into the wastes. Then the staccato patter of slugs against stone suddenly tapered off, and the Tusken projectiles began to scream through the air above Leia and Han's hiding place.

Leia tried to turn her head to see if the Sand People were shooting at what she hoped they were, but hit her helmet on a boulder before she found the sky. Han tried to look, as well, and banged his helmet into Leia's.

"Well, something's spooking that herd," he said. "It must be the *Falcon*."

Leia began to glimpse white-armored figures pushing through the tangle of bantha legs. "Or those stormtroopers, maybe."

She fired into the ground at the mouth of the ravine. The banthas broke into a run, bowling over armored figures, leaving them scattered across the canyon floor and struggling to crawl free. A flurry of brilliant beams erupted in the thickest part of the herd as the stormtroopers reacted in exactly the wrong way. The banthas trumpeted in anger and began to defend themselves, the males biting and trampling Imperials, the females butting their calves along at a near charge.

The Tusken Raiders started to emerge from behind rocks and rise from beneath dust-covered capes, each one sending a shot or two in the direction of the Solos before turning to rush after the banthas. Leia continued to pour fire into the ground near the herd, trying to sow more confusion and delay the Imperials.

Blaster bolts began to bounce through the rocks behind her. Leia kept shooting and tried not to think about what she was hearing. Emala and Banai were keeping watch in that direction; unless one of them yelled for help, it was probably just stormtroopers firing from the opposite hilltop.

In the ravine below, the Imperials and the Tuskens met head-on. They exchanged a few attacks in passing, then continued on their way, the Sand People chasing after their banthas and the stormtroopers charging up the slope toward the Solos. So much for sowing confusion.

Leia and Han fired for effect, and ten troopers fell with smoking holes in their armor. Thirty more continued to come, pouring energy beams up the gully and turning the boulder field into a smoky mass of flying rock chips.

A small hand tapped Leia on her calf armor. "Time to go!" Emala yelled. "Your ride's coming."

Han began to inch back out of their cranny. "Right on schedule!"

Leia remained where she was. "If you call this on schedule, I see why you were always in trouble with Jabba!" She stopped aiming and, keeping the trigger down, began to sweep blasterfire back and forth across the gully. "We can't leave—"

The rest of her sentence—*until we stop those stormtroopers*—was silenced by the roar of an incoming concussion missile, and the ravine erupted into an expanding sphere of tumbling stormtrooper parts and bright, blinding light.

TWENTY-FIVE

With an aura of escaped current crackling across her metallic skin and columns of acrid smoke billowing from the perforations in her hull, the *Falcon* looked more like a used gunnery target than one of the fastest freighters in the galaxy. Two of her vector plates had been blasted back to the durasteel frames, she was leaking a blue glow around the rim of her drive nacelles, and one of the landing struts had lost its stabilizer pad. When the Solos returned to Coruscant, Leia was going to lose Han to the reconditioning bay for weeks. Months maybe.

Maybe she would talk to Wedge about borrowing a military repair droid. It was the least the New Republic could do—for *both* Leia and Han.

The landing struts had barely touched ground before a clunk sounded from beneath the ship's belly and the rear cargo lift lowered the *Falcon*'s utility speeder into view. Grees was nearly hanging from the pilot's handlebars, his short legs dangling down barely far enough to reach the foot controls. Sligh stood behind him on the small cargo bed, both hands clutching the back of the pilot's seat.

"There's my ride," Emala said. She was kneeling in the boulders in front of Leia and Han, with *Killik Twilight* slung over her back. "If you make it out of the system alive, maybe we'll partner up again sometime."

"Why wait?" Han asked. "Come with us. When we get back to Coruscant, the New Republic will pay big for the painting. More than anyone else."

"I said *if* you make it out alive." Imperial blasterfire began to pour in from the adjacent ridges, ricocheting around the boulder field and bouncing off the *Falcon*'s scorched armor with the hollow *screal* of groaning metal. "And the way your ship looks, that's a big *if*. Sorry, but we'll take our chances with the Imperials."

"Your odds aren't so great either," Han pointed out. "We're surrounded by stormtroopers—or haven't you noticed?"

"Our odds will improve, once I tell the Imperials we're ready to sell the painting to them."

Emala jumped up on a boulder long enough to wave her arms and yell to Grees, then dropped back into cover barely half a breath ahead of a dozen screaming bolts. The utility speeder shot out from beneath the *Falcon* and turned toward the boulder pile, lurching and weaving as blasterfire ricocheted around it.

"You're going to sell *Killik Twilight* to the Empire?" Banai gasped. "Emala, you and your mates have always been disgusting—"

"It's their painting." Leia nodded to Emala. "You have my blessing to do with it as you will."

The *Falcon*'s top turret spun around and began to spray suppression fire across the adjacent ridges, not hitting much but forcing the stormtroopers to keep their heads down. The enemy assault withered and grew less accurate.

Emala eyed Leia with a look of condemnation. "You think I don't know what you're doing? I'm disappointed in you."

Leia shrugged. "We could make it look like you're stealing the painting," she suggested. "That might make a session with an interrogator droid a little less likely."

The battered utility speeder rocked to a stop next to their hiding place.

Emala studied Leia a moment, then nodded. "Make it look good, and the Empire will never hear about that little datachip you removed."

"You're trying to blackmail us? *After* we let you keep the painting?" Han swung his blaster around. "Why you little—"

With eyes growing as round as wheels and *Killik Twilight* still slung across her back, Emala leapt onto the nearest boulder and bounced onto the speeder's cargo bed behind Sligh. Han managed to burn one bolt into the instrument console as the vehicle fishtailed away.

"Han!" Leia pushed his arm down. "Are you trying to kill her?"

"She said to make it look good." He raised his blaster again and, as the Imperials continued to pour fire after the utility speeder, took another shot. "I'm just doing like she asked."

"That's good enough, Han." Leia kneeled next to Kitster and slipped his arm over her sore shoulder. "Help me with Kitster, before our diversion disappears."

Han grabbed Kitster under the other arm, and together they hobbled out of the boulders. As Leia had hoped, the stormtroopers were so focused on the fleeing Squibs that they didn't even notice the trio until it had reached the ship.

C-3PO's golden head popped down from the open cargo bay. "Chewbacca asks that you please hurry! There is another squadron—"

A flurry of blaster bolts ricocheted off the bottom of

the *Falcon* and churned the ground into a dusty froth. Leia turned and, fifty meters away, saw half a dozen stormtrooper helmets peering over the crest of the hill.

"Go!"

Half dragging and half carrying Kitster, Leia and Han hurled themselves onto the cargo lift.

"Up, Threepio!" Han began to fire in the same direction as Leia.

"But, Captain Solo, you're not properly secured—"

"Now, Threepio!"

The cargo lift began to rise. So did the *Falcon* itself, and an instant later, the blaster bolts stopped ricocheting past the trio. They remained lying on the floor, grasping the nonslip grate, until the lift thunked into place.

"Is everybody all right?" Leia asked.

"Fine." Han was already up, removing his helmet and gloves. "I'll head to the belly turret. See-Threepio, go tell Chewbacca we need to take a pass over the Squibs. Leia, can you—"

"Yes, Han—go." Leia was already helping Kitster to his feet. "I'll handle things back here. Just don't—"

"Hit anything," he said. "I know!"

Han followed C-3PO out of the hold, hobbling off toward the cannon turrets. Leia guided Kitster into an escape pod, then retrieved the Quaxcon diagnostics kit they had promised Herat.

"You understand the risk you're taking?" She passed the kit to him. "We can't be certain Herat will retrieve the pod, and you'll be landing a long way from civilization."

The *Falcon* shuddered as Han opened fire on the Squibs—Leia had to trust that he was just trying to make it look good—then Chewbacca brought them around for another pass, and something groaned in the superstructure.

Kitster cast a nervous glance at the ceiling. "Yes, I'm *very* sure. I'd like to live to see Tamora and my children again."

Leia laughed. "We'll hold together, but it's your choice."

"Thank you," Kitster said. "And thank you for coming after me. I doubt the Imperials would have troubled themselves."

"You might be underestimating them," Leia said. "I'm sure their new admiral is as eager as I am to know why you took the painting."

Kitster raised his brow. "You haven't figured that out?"

"Not really," Leia said. "At first I thought it was for the money, but when Wald told us you refused to sell to the Imperials—"

"It was for you," Kitster said. "Well, for your father, really. But since he's gone, I wanted to do something kind for his daughter. You see, when Anakin and I were children—"

"Stop." Leia raised her hand. "That's all you need to say. I know all about the credits he gave you—and a lot of other things he did here, too."

Kitster's face grew solemn. "Including what happened at the oasis?"

Leia raised her brow in surprise. "I had a hint from the Force—but how do *you* know what happened there?"

"The Tuskens had a story dance the night we arrived," Kitster explained. "I already knew that Anakin had returned with Shmi's body, so when they dropped into sword stances and started to leap around making buzzing sounds, it was obvious whom they were imitating."

Kitster fell silent for a moment, studying Leia, then added, "And there's something you should know about what he did there."

"If you're going to try to justify it—"

"I couldn't possibly," Kitster said. "Your father was a Jedi. What he did was wrong. Quite possibly, it set him on the dark road he took later in life . . . and even he was sorry for his mistake."

"He was?" Leia furrowed her brow. "How would you know that?"

"He said as much, I think." Kitster buckled his crash webbing, then stared at the floor and continued. "When I heard that he had been asking about his mother at Watto's, I went out to the Lars farm to visit him. I didn't know Shmi had been taken, of course, but I happened to arrive shortly after they had buried her and Anakin had left. Beru—she was Owen's—"

"I know who Beru was," Leia said. "And we don't have much time before I must close the hatch."

Kitster nodded. "Of course. Beru told me that when they buried Shmi, Anakin spoke to her grave, saying he had not been strong enough to save her, but promising he would not fail again."

"Fail again?" Leia asked. "But his mother was already dead. How was he going to undo that?"

Kitster nodded. "That struck me as odd, too, and I asked Beru about it. She told me that he had said twice that he was not strong enough—once that he was not strong enough to save his mother, and the second time just that he was not strong enough. I thought at the time that he had just repeated himself, but now I'm not so sure. After being at the oasis, I think maybe Anakin realized what a terrible mistake he had made. I think he knew how he had failed as a Jedi."

"Maybe," Leia said. "It would be nice to believe that. I'd like to."

"Then you can," Kitster said. "The boy I knew would have been sorry for what he had done, and even ten years away would not have changed that. He was still his mother's son."

Chewbacca's voice growled a warning over the intercom.

Leia glanced at the ceiling. "That's our signal. Thank you, Kitster." She slapped the launch activator. "May the Force be with you."

"And with—"

The escape hatch sealed, and Leia stood back, her heart growing heavier as she felt the gentle bump of the pod separating. Of course, she would never really know how her father had felt about what had happened at the oasis—or even if he had truly said what Kitster reported. But it *did* seem possible, and that was enough for now.

The hold lights dimmed, and the *Falcon* bucked so hard that Leia landed on the floor. A sharp ringing filled her ears, and it took a moment to realize the sound was not inside her head but reverberating through the hold's durasteel ceiling. She scrambled to her feet and raced for the flight deck.

The cockpit looked much the same as it always did, with Chewbacca roaring and Han cursing, proximity alarms blaring, the console speakers hissing with electromagnetic blast, and C-3PO beside himself with prognostications of doom.

"Mistress Leia, we'll never escape this time!" The droid flailed his arms wildly, nearly knocking her off her feet. "There are three Star Destroyers now—three of them! This time we'll be destroyed for sure!"

"Nonsense."

Leia braced herself on the back of Han's chair and peered out through the forward canopy. Forty degrees to port, she saw the twin suns blazing up from the gravity well of the Tatoo system.

"How are the sensors, Chewie?"

Chewbacca roared in disgust.

"Good." Leia pointed toward the two suns. "That way."

"*In*system?" Han looked back at her as though he had married a madwoman.

Leia squeezed his shoulder. "Trust me. I have a feeling about this."

Chewbacca groaned loudly.

"I know, I know." Han turned the *Falcon* toward the suns and poured on the ions. "I was there, too!"

Another barrage erupted outside the cockpit canopy, this time where the *Falcon* would have been had she not changed course. Leia dropped into the navigator's chair and brought up the tactical display. The *Chimaera* and her two sister ships, the *Death's Head* and the *Judicator*, were coming around Tatooine from three different directions, bleeding TIEs and leaving the *Falcon* nowhere to go except into the suns.

Where nobody would be able to see a thing.

Leia watched as the display melted into a snowstorm of white static, then looked up to find the two suns swelling to immense size in the forward viewport.

"I'm quite certain the Imperials can't see us now," C-3PO reported. "They have stopped firing, and we are accelerating into the gravitational pull of a binary star at the rate of eighty-four thousand nine hundred seventy-four kilometers per—"

"How long before we reach the point of no return?" Han asked.

C-3PO shot a burst of static at the navicomputer, then said, "Fourteen seconds."

"Then that's when the Imperials will be looking for us to make our break." Han turned to Chewbacca. "We'll pull out at sixteen. They won't be expecting that."

"Sixteen!" C-3PO screeched. "Captain Solo, I'm afraid you misunderstood—"

Leia reached over and tripped the droid's circuit breaker, and Chewbacca set to work on the calculations for an emergency hyperspace jump.

With the Wookiee engrossed in his work, Leia slipped forward and leaned on the back of Han's chair. "Han, there's something I've been meaning to ask you."

"Sweetheart, we're caught between three Star Destroyers and two suns." Han's eyes were fixed on the console chronometer. "I'm kind of busy here."

"I know. But this is important. It's something I want to know in case we don't . . . in case we miscalculate."

"Miscalculate?" Han actually glanced away from the instrument console. "You said you had a feeling!"

"I do." Leia glanced at the chronometer. Eight seconds to go. "But humor me. Why do you want little Solos running around so badly?"

"Kids?" Han nearly yelled the question. "You want to talk about kids *now*?"

"Isn't that what I just said?" Leia asked. Three seconds to go. "There might not be another chance."

Chewbacca grunted and sent the hyperspace calculations to the pilot's station. Zero seconds.

"All right, if it has to be now." Han brought their nose around, pointing them into deep space. The *Falcon* continued to slip farther toward the two suns—sideways. "I guess it's just my way of facing the future."

"Facing the future?" Leia asked.

"You know." Han forced the throttles past the overload stops. The *Falcon* shuddered, seemed to hesitate . . . and finally pulled free of the gravity well. He exhaled in relief and activated the hyperdrive. "Believing in it."

"Good answer." Leia leaned closer and, as the stars stretched into the iridescent blur of hyperspace, gently kissed Han on the neck. "I believe in it, too."

A FOREST APART

A Chewbacca Adventure

Across the skylane from Chewbacca's quarters rose Sasal Center, its forty spires ringing an open-air mezzanine as large as the Well of the Dead back on Kashyyyk. Beside the center stood Wauth Complex, more massive than Korrokrrayyo Mountain itself. On the other side loomed the mirrsteel needles of Ooe'b Towers, as tall as wroshyr trees and webbed together by a tangle of pedestrian bridges that always reminded Chewbacca of the mazes down in the Shadow Forest. It would have been wrong to say that he enjoyed living here on Coruscant, but he *had* come to think of it as home—perhaps even to see the shape and mystery of the forest in its soaring lines and durasteel depths.

At Chewbacca's side, his life-mate, Mallatobuck, was staring down through the transparisteel, mesmerized by the great rivers of traffic flowing along the skylanes below.

[Is this what they do for fun on Coruscant?] she asked. Her blue eyes and honey-colored fur were as beautiful as the day Chewbacca had pledged himself to her. [Circle the world in airspeeders?]

[Oh no,] Chewbacca joked. [I ordered the traffic for your visit.]

[Be careful. You know I believe whatever you say.] Mallatobuck spoke without looking away from the window. [Still, I think traffic is the one thing I will miss. It is like the Cascade of Rrynorrorun. Endless. Calming.]

[Endless, yes—but calming?] Chewbacca shook his

head. [You have never tried to make a three-lane climb, Malla.]

[I have not,] she agreed, [because I thought you valued the lives of your mate and child.]

[I do. You *know* I would never let you drive.]

[Let me?] Malla rowled. She regarded him with mock anger. [With such talk, you're lucky to be the father of my child.]

[Very lucky.]

Chewbacca grinned and pulled her to his side. Malla had waited fifty years for him to return from his adolescent wanderings, then married him knowing that he had pledged a life debt to Han Solo that would prevent them from sharing a home. In moments of vainglory, Chewbacca thought it must have been his strength or battle ferocity that had won her devotion. But deep down he knew better. Deep down he knew he was just the luckiest Wookiee alive.

He checked his chronometer and—sad at how quickly their last hours together were passing—said, [It's almost time.]

[I'll see if Lumpy has finished gathering his souvenirs.] Malla turned to leave, then stopped and pointed at a plastoid shoulder case in the middle of the hall. [That's odd.]

Chewbacca started toward the hall. [Lumpy?]

Malla caught his arm. *[Galactic Rebels,]* she sighed.

Chewbacca curled his lip. [Does he play it this much at home?]

[More,] Malla said. [Here, at least he has the real thing.]

[Real thing?]

[You,] Malla said. [You *have* noticed how he idolizes you?]

[I am in his hologame?] Chewbacca began to think this *Galactic Rebels* was not so bad.

[Sort of.] Malla's tone was exasperated. [He pretends to be you.]

Chewbacca smiled. [What is wrong with that? A cub should respect—]

[It is more than respect,] Malla interrupted. [Chewbacca, you cast a long shadow—and longer from here than if you lived in Rwookrrorro with us. Lumpy tries so hard to be the son of the 'Mighty Chewbacca' that he bores his friends and angers his adversaries—and when they challenge him to back up his words, he is always the one who comes home bloodied and quiet.]

[*Always?*]

Malla nodded. [It has grown so that he hardly goes out.]

Chewbacca's jaw dropped.

Again, Malla nodded.

Chewbacca scowled at his study door. [I see.]

A strong mate like Malla made it easy to believe Lumpy was not suffering because of his father's absence, but the truth was that a life debt placed a burden on an entire family. There were some things that even the best mother could not teach a young Wookiee as well as a good father—and when it came to handling the troubles Malla was describing, no father would be a better teacher than Chewbacca.

Chewbacca returned his gaze to Malla. [Lumpy shouldn't go home with you.]

Malla's brow shot up. [He shouldn't?]

[He needs to spend time with his father,] Chewbacca said, certain of himself. [No more than a standard year or two. At his age, he shouldn't be gone from the forest too long.]

[No, er, yes . . . I mean, you're right. About the forest.] Malla blinked several times, then, as her composure returned, her expression grew more thoughtful. [What about you? How will you manage?]

[I am his father. I will manage.] To Chewbacca, that was all the answer needed—but he knew Malla would want details. [I have room, and I am sure the Princess will let me borrow Threepio on occasion.]

[A *protocol* droid? Trying to control a young Wookiee?] Malla shook her head. [Not without a stun baton.]

[I suppose not,] Chewbacca admitted. [But there is our embassy. It's not far from here, and Princess Leia is on good terms—]

[*You* are on good terms with our embassy.] Malla patted his cheek. [Sometimes, you are almost humble.]

Though *humble* was no compliment to Wookiees, Chewbacca did not bother to protest. [So you agree?]

Malla thought about it, then said, [It would do him good to see that your life is not one long holoadventure. He needs to see that you spend most of your time doing normal things—like maintaining the *Falcon*, or hiding in the corner with Han at diplomatic ceremonies.]

Chewbacca gave her a sidelong glance. [Is that what you think?]

[No one's life could be as yours is portrayed over the 'Net. You—and Han Solo, too—would be dead ten times over.] Malla took his hand, then nodded. [It might be good for him.]

Chewbacca smiled. [Then it's settled.] He started for his study door. [He will stop playing these games, and I will teach him to win a clench challenge.]

[What?] Malla strode after him. [How will that solve anything? Teaching him to clench fight will only make Lumpy talk about you more—and give him the skill to force others to listen. And taking his games away will only give him one less thing to talk about that is not you.]

[He is going through a stage,] Chewbacca said. [It will end when he learns confidence, and confidence will come with victory.]

They reached the study door, and Malla caught Chewbacca by the arm.

[Our son is already trying to be you. That is the problem.] Her voice was so low Chewbacca had to lean down to hear. [What you must do, my mate, is teach him to be himself.]

Chewbacca considered Malla's words for a moment, then nodded. [Agreed. He must learn to be himself . . . *and* win the clench challenge.]

He stepped through the door into his study, where the image of an auburn-furred Wookiee was snarling atop the holocomm pad, a long line of statistics arrayed below the picture and the name LUMPACCA floating above. The plastoid chair in front of the workstation was empty, and a message flashing in one corner was threatening to end the session unless the player responded in thirty seconds.

[Lumpy?] Chewbacca called.

When there was no answer, he went to the other door and looked across the hall. The refresher was open, and the interior was dark. The same was true of the two sleeping rooms.

Chewbacca had a sinking feeling. [Lumpy?]

A muffled crash echoed around the corner, and Chewbacca's worst fears were confirmed when he stepped into the hall and found the door at the end standing open—the door that connected the back of his apartment to the back of the Solos' apartment.

Malla came up behind him and looked past his shoulder. [*Our* son went through that door?] she gasped. [Lumpy?]

[He disobeyed us.] Eager as he was for Lumpy to find his rrakktorr—the defiant, adventurous heart of a Wookiee—Chewbacca was less than pleased to see that the cub had chosen to start looking for it in the Solos' elegant apartment. [If he is starting his rebellious phase, his timing is awful.]

[It can't be Lumpy,] Malla insisted. [He's never even shouted at me.]

[It has to be Lumpy. The Solos aren't home.]

The Provisional Council was hosting a state dinner that evening to welcome the New Republic's newest member worlds. Leia, C-3PO, and Winter were all at the Imperial Palace overseeing preparations. Han, putting his own preparations off until the last minute as usual, was trying to find a haberdasher who could outfit him with civilian formal wear on short notice.

Chewbacca started down the hall. [Lumpy! Don't touch any—]

A louder crash sounded from the depths of the apartment.

[That doesn't sound good,] Malla said. [How angry will Princess Leia be?]

[That depends on what he's smashing. If it's the singing lamp the Jumerians gave her as a wedding present, she might even thank him,] Chewbacca said. [Let's just hope he hasn't broken Han's bottle of Ithorian Mist. *That* would be bad.]

Chewbacca entered the Solos' apartment—a showpiece of Alderaanian elegance, even here in the back—and led the way to a small larmalstone vestibule. From this central hub, doorways opened into Leia's office, the sleeping and dressing chambers, and a huge refresher suite that included an exercise area, steam closet, and tub units that could pulse, stew, bubble, and mineralize occupants into a state of languid bliss.

Outside Leia's dressing chamber lay a shattered perfume vial, the amber treasure it had once contained now puddled on the floor. Inside, the room was littered with spilled cosmetics, everyday jewelry, serving silver from the formal dining area, a holocomm from Leia's office, and a framed set of thousand-credit chips Han kept as a souvenir of the time he broke the bank in a Pavo Prime casino. A frantic clatter was coming from one of the spacious clothes closets that opened out of the back of the room.

As Chewbacca started inside, Malla caught his arm and whispered, [This is not like your son.]

[I am very glad to hear that,] Chewbacca said. [If it were, I would have to—]

[No, Chewbacca—I mean Lumpy does not have a destructive heart. He would never do a thing like this.]

Chewbacca glanced over the mess on the floor again, and the sinking feeling he had experienced earlier turned to fear. The security system had been instructed to recognize Malla and Lumpy as unrestricted guests, but a sentry droid should still have arrived by now to investigate the crashes.

[Someone has disarmed the alarm system,] Chewbacca

whispered. He pushed Malla gently toward the other side of the vestibule. [Find a comlink and inform building security.]

[Of course.] Malla turned back toward Leia's dressing chamber. [When I'm sure our son is safe.]

Knowing better than to stand in the way of Malla's maternal instinct, Chewbacca grunted and stalked into the closet. His son was on the floor, removing rare Alderaanian dinnerware and expensive office electronics from a slashed rucksack and hastily stuffing them into one of Leia's gown bags. In the back of the closet, a gaunt milky-skinned man stood next to a hole in the wall half a meter square. He was pointing a hold-out blaster at Lumpy's head.

"No farther, Wookiee."

The man's voice was a ragged rasp—at least Chewbacca *thought* it was a man's voice. The intruder's peaked ears were sticking straight out from a hairless, emaciated head, and he had a rawboned frame so thin it looked barely adequate to carry his tattered utilities. Chewbacca could not be certain of the gunman's species, let alone his—or her—gender. The small blunt nose and high cheeks suggested a human female, but the long chin and thin gray lips seemed more masculine.

"Another step, Furboy, and I burn your whelp here a third eye."

Lumpy spun around, his eyes wide and his child's soft fur lying flat against his head. The sight was a powerful confirmation to Chewbacca of how badly he needed to spend some time with his son. The slashed rucksack suggested a struggle, and Lumpy was nearly as large as the scrawny figure guarding him—and probably twice as strong. Had he known how to handle himself, the thief would never have had a chance to bring the blaster to bear, and the cub would have been free to flee—or attack, if he chose. Instead, he seemed unsure of himself and almost ashamed, as though he believed he was to blame for this mess.

[Caught yourself a burglar, I see,] Chewbacca said. He felt Malla pressing at his back and eased forward to make room. [You did well. Han and Leia will be grateful.]

Lumpy's eyes lit with pride, but the thief snarled, "Quiet! Another word from any of you unskinned pelts and—"

[My mate will rip your arms off,] Malla rumbled. She tore a handful of gowns off Leia's racks to make room for herself beside Chewbacca. [Release our son.]

The thief, who clearly did not understand a word of Shyriiwook, made the mistake of shifting his blaster toward Malla. "Nobody has to get hurt here."

Chewbacca ignored him and stepped half a meter forward. [Lumpy, come—]

[It's okay, Dad!] Lumpy launched himself at the thief. [I got him!]

But Chewbacca could see that Lumpy didn't have him—the young one's head was down, and his arms were low. The thief sidestepped the attack easily, grabbing Lumpy by the wrist and spinning him around into a one-arm choke so smoothly that Chewbacca reconsidered that flying leap he had been gathering himself to make. Fearing that Malla would not have the experience to recognize how dangerous this intruder was, he placed a restraining hand on her elbow. She tried to shake it off, but he would not let her.

The thief, who had missed none of this, smiled. "Good boy, Fang. Now, like I said, nobody has to get hurt."

Pointing the blaster at Chewbacca's chest, he used a toe to sort through the half-filled garment bag, then dragged out a government datapad and flipped it neatly into the air. The arm wrapped around Lumpy's neck lashed out almost too quick to see and caught the datapad, and before Chewbacca could move, the thief had Lumpy back in a choke.

"Go outside and close the door while I disappear down that." The thief gestured at the hole beside him.

"Come back in three minutes, and your cub here will be safe and sound."

Malla started to retreat out the door, but Chewbacca pulled her back. [We aren't leaving him alone with our son,] he growled. [The next thing he will want is ransom.]

"Go on!" the thief ordered.

Chewbacca shook his head and held his hand out, then raised a single finger. [Lumpawarrump, I want you to come to me.]

The thief fired past Chewbacca's shoulder into Leia's gowns, and the acrid stench of melted shimmersilk filled the closet.

"The next one hits."

Chewbacca shook his head and raised a second finger. [*Now*, Lumpy.]

[Don't be scared,] Malla said. [This is no time to disobey.]

[I'm *not* scared,] Lumpy insisted—despite his flat fur. [See!]

He grabbed the arm around his neck and pulled forward, but his legs were too straight to flip a leaf-dummy, much less someone as dangerous as the thief. Chewbacca shoved Malla in one direction and threw himself in the opposite, and the panicked thief—finding even an eleven-year-old Wookiee too much to handle—began to spray blaster bolts everywhere.

[Bend your knees, Lumpy!] Chewbacca yelled. [*Then* pull!]

Lumpy bent his knees—then collapsed beneath the thief's weight. Chewbacca sprang up and, hurling an armful of smoking shimmersilk ahead, flung himself at the back of the closet.

Halfway there he crashed into Malla, and they landed a meter short of Lumpy's captor.

"Last chance, Furboy." The thief's pearly eyes were locked on Chewbacca's. "Back off, or your—"

Chewbacca lashed out, knocking the would-be hostage taker into a set of shoe shelves. The hold-out blaster clattered into the corner, but the thief did a half twist and came down on his feet, still clutching the stolen datapad.

Chewbacca lunged. With Malla and Lumpy packed tight next to him, he was too slow. The thief skipped over his outstretched arm, bounced off the floor, and swung into the hole feetfirst.

Malla swept Lumpy into her arms, and Chewbacca scrambled past them, thrusting an arm into the hole and jamming his fingers against the opposite side of a service run. It couldn't be more than half a meter wide, barely large enough to fit his shoulder. He rose on his knees and swung his arm around inside, finding pipes, conduit, and ventilation tubes—but no thieves.

[Gone like a kkekkrrg rro,] Chewbacca reported. He turned to find Lumpy clutched to Malla's breast. [Are you all right?]

An odd expression of shame flashed across Lumpy's face; then he frowned up at his mother and separated himself.

[That thief is the only one hurting,] he said. [I had him—until he pulled that blaster.]

Chewbacca laughed. [Isn't that always the way?] He stepped away from the hole and clamped Lumpy's shoulder. [But you did well, Lumpawarrump. That was no ordinary thief.]

Lumpy's mouth dropped open. [It wasn't?]

[Why would a thief take a common datapad and leave that?] Chewbacca toed a bejeweled table chrono—a gift from the Bakurans as a token of gratitude for the Solos' assistance defeating the Ssi-ruuk. [He came to steal information, not wealth.]

[Our son was fighting a spy?] Malla gasped.

Chewbacca nodded proudly. [I think so. Whoever it was, he only wanted this to *look* like a robbery.] He waved Malla out of the closet, then followed her into the disordered dressing chamber. [We must comm New Republic security.]

[Security?] Lumpy echoed. He was behind Chewbacca, still inside the closet. [They'll never catch him!]

[The sooner they begin their investigation, the better their chances.] Chewbacca motioned Malla across the vestibule toward Leia's ransacked office. [That is why we must hurry.]

[But this hole goes down as far as a wroshyr root!] Lumpy's voice was muffled by the mouth of the service run. [And the spy might have an escape door cut anywhere.]

[Come along, Lumpy.] Malla started back toward the closet. [Your father said—]

[I've got a better idea.]

[No!]

Chewbacca and Malla roared the word in the same instant, and they both rushed back into the closet.

Lumpy was already pulling himself into the service run. [I'm the only one small enough to fit.] He grabbed a pair of pipes and slid out of sight. [Meet me at the bottom! I'll wait for you there, okay?]

[It is not okay!] Malla raced to the hole and stuck her head inside. [Lumpy—]

Chewbacca caught her from behind and clamped a hand over her mouth.

[Don't yell.] He pulled her away gently, already thinking about whom he would have to call to find out where the service run came out. [Lumpy will be safer if the spy doesn't know he is being followed.]

Malla whirled on him. [You want him to go?]

Chewbacca shook his head. [It is dangerous, and he is not ready.] He was not quite able to restrain a smile. [But it *was* brave. Our son is finding his rrakktorr early.]

Malla rolled her eyes and started for the door. [That is not rrakktorr, my mate. It is *Galactic Rebels*.]

TWO

The Level 2012 Physical Plant was a realm of droids and machinery, saturated with the harsh smell of solvents and dimly lit because it was so seldom seen by sentient eyes. Chewbacca consulted the tower schematic on his datapad and, leaving his glow rod off to avoid alerting the thief to their presence, led the way into the cavernous room. The air was warm with mechanical heat, and the durasteel floor trembled with the constant growl of equipment. The silhouettes of oddly shaped droids floated, walked, and rolled past in the darkness, sometimes close enough to reveal a bloated slime bladder or a set of dangling utility tentacles.

Chewbacca circled around a two-story recirculation pump that was the heart of the building's self-contained plumbing system, then came to an expanse of dark open floor. Off to the right, toward the building's interior, he could just make out the giant gyre-filters that converted sewage back into pure water. He studied the schematic a moment, then pointed up into the murk on the left.

[The outer service grid hangs there, along the ceiling,] Chewbacca said. [Lumpy should be waiting fifty meters along the east wall, about fifteen meters in.]

[You mean where those sparks are?] Malla asked.

[Sparks?] Chewbacca looked in the direction she was pointing and saw a tiny umbrella of blue flickers. He exchanged the datapad for the repeating blaster hanging from his bandolier utility clip. [What are they welding? I told building security to clear this area.]

[And they told *you* to let them handle it.] Malla's voice had gone reedy with concern—perhaps even fear. [Every forest has its oryyka howlers. They cannot keep you out of their tree, so they ruin your hunt.]

[They won't ruin this hunt,] Chewbacca assured her. [There's nothing to worry about—everything is under control.]

[Everything is *not* under control,] Malla retorted. [If everything were under control, an eleven-year-old cub would not be chasing spies—and no one would be over there welding.]

Chewbacca sighed. [It will be under control soon,] he said. [Trust me.]

Vowing to rip the arms off the day-shift security captain, Chewbacca raced across the floor. To download an unabridged schematic and arrange access to the physical plant, he had been forced to comm Han—who was now racing back to the building—and have him threaten to make a public stink about lax security. The security captain had obviously found another way to slow things down until he could gather his squad and take control of the situation. Chewbacca should have expected it. The fellow was, after all, a Sullustan.

As Chewbacca and Malla drew closer to the sparks, they began to make out the shape of a six-armed repair droid. It was standing on its hydraulic stilts five meters off the floor, welding a new durasteel grate over the base of a service run. The air stank too much of melted metal to smell any trace of Lumpy or the thief—or Leia's spilled perfume—but in the flickering light, he could just make out a set of laser-stenciled characters identifying this as the service run Lumpy had entered.

[Stop!] Malla ordered. [Let my son out of there!]

When the droid continued to work, Chewbacca roared in anger and slammed the butt of his blaster rifle into a stilt.

The droid finally stopped and, still holding the grate up, tipped its head down at Chewbacca. Where its photo-receptors should have been, it had a TrangTwo Lowlight Optical Band—a common modification designed to re-duce lighting expenses in automated plant areas.

"I am not programmed in that language," the droid said. "Please restate in Basic or binary flash code."

Chewbacca, whose Wookiee throat could not form Ba-sic words, growled and pointed the barrel of his blaster at the droid, motioning it away from the grate.

"I am sorry we cannot communicate." The droid re-turned its attention to the grate and reignited its welding torch. "For your own protection, please—"

Chewbacca shot the droid in the primary powerfeed, and its six arms dropped to its sides, the still-burning torch nearly slicing his arm off as it hissed past. The secu-rity grate followed an instant later, clanging off the droid and almost knocking Chewbacca over. Malla pulled him out of the way of the returning torch.

[You couldn't use the circuit breaker?]

[This was faster.] Chewbacca shut off the welding torch, then slung his blaster over a shoulder and climbed the droid up to the pitch darkness of the service run. [Lumpy?]

When no answer came, Chewbacca activated his glow rod and found several tufts of soft adolescent fur hang-ing on the durasteel stubs where the old grate had been cut free—presumably by the thief. The casing of a large power conduit was smeared with blood, but not enough to suggest a fight. Probably, Lumpy or the thief had cut himself on the way down.

[He's gone.] Chewbacca dropped back to the floor, his pride in his son's courage slowly changing to concern. [He did not wait.]

[That surprises you?] Malla activated her own glow rod and began to sweep it across the floor. [You haven't been listening.]

[He did not honor his word,] Chewbacca insisted,

now growing angry. [That is forbidden. And it is dangerous down here. How could he be so foolish?]

Malla sighed. [Would *you* have waited?]

[What does that have to do with anything?] Chewbacca's scowl slowly faded as he realized what she was saying: that Lumpy was only doing what he thought his father would. [And this is different.]

[Not to him,] Malla said.

She crouched on the floor and shined her glow rod on a dark puddle smeared by the imprint of a small Wookiee foot. She rubbed her fingertips in the stain—it was already as thick as honey—and brought them to her nose.

[Blood,] she said.

[There was some in the service run, too.] Chewbacca started across the floor and quickly found another track. [Lumpy didn't even *think* about waiting. When we get him home, I will have a long talk with him about the boundaries of his rebellion.]

Malla fell in beside him. [It is not rebellion,] she said. [He is doing this because he thinks it is something *you* would do—not because he wants to assert himself.]

[That will change after I am through with him.]

Malla was silent for a moment, then she said, [Let's just get him home, Chewbacca.]

[We will,] Chewbacca assured her. [And after we do, I will be firm.]

Malla said nothing, leaving Chewbacca to wonder whether she doubted him or was just worried. Though he hated to admit it, he had his own reservations. It seemed to him he should have known instinctively what to say, how a good father would handle the situation. But the truth was that Lumpy seemed more a stranger every time Chewbacca saw him. One time he was a ball of fur chortling in his mother's arms, and the next time he was already swinging from the rafters.

With no choice except to use a glow rod to follow the tracks, Chewbacca instructed Malla to hold hers low and away from her body while he covered them with his repeating blaster. The tracks led across the floor, growing fainter, until they found another print in a small puddle of blood. Chewbacca thought for a moment that his son was just being careless about where he stepped, but then he noticed how Lumpy had twisted his foot to soak up more.

[He is deliberately leaving us a trail,] Chewbacca observed. [Perhaps I am being too hard on him.]

[Leaving a trail is not waiting.] Malla followed his tracks down the narrow passage between a pair of huge chiller tanks. [What is taking those security guards so long?]

[That would take a week to explain,] Chewbacca answered. The Sullustan captain was a thorough planner and a meticulous organizer—and by the time he finished sealing his perimeters and gathering his intelligence, the thief would be gone and Lumpy would be lying unconscious or dead somewhere. [And we are better off without them. Their procedures would only slow us down.]

As they neared the far end of the chiller tanks, Malla pulled up short and cried out in dismay. [No!]

Imagining the worst, Chewbacca pulled her out of the way and stepped forward, one hand curled into a fist and the other bringing up the repeating blaster. Coming toward them he found only the domed box of a floor-cleaning droid, its purple sterilight focused on the blood trail they had been following. When its guidance sensors detected Chewbacca and Malla standing in its path, it politely retreated out of the way and swung aside to let them pass.

Chewbacca had Malla shine her glow rod on the floor behind it. The only sign of the trail that Lumpy had so carefully left for them was a two-meter stripe of rapidly drying durasteel. He knelt down and, laying his blaster aside, grabbed the cleaning droid by the sides of its plastoid box.

[Where did the tracks lead?]

The function indicators on its front panel twinkled through a test cycle, then it said, "I beg your pardon."

Chewbacca growled in frustration and spun the droid around to face the opposite direction. [Retrace your path.]

The droid whirled back around and shined a spotlight on Chewbacca's foot. "Please excuse me while I tidy up."

[Tidy up?] Chewbacca snatched the droid off the floor and hefted it over his head. [Where is my son?]

"I didn't mean to disturb you." The droid continued to speak in its normal polite tone. "I'll be out of your way in a moment."

[I don't think it understands Shyriiwook.]

Chewbacca hurled the droid away in disgust. It crashed down five meters away, then began to request assistance righting itself.

[Father!] Lumpy's voice was barely loud enough to be heard over the drone of the giant circulation fans off to the right. [Over here!]

Chewbacca snatched his weapon and glow rod off the floor and charged toward the voice. [Lumpy! Are you hurt?]

[No!] he cried. [But hurry—I can't hold them much longer!]

[Them?] Malla cried.

They rounded a bank of gurgling bubble filters, and Malla's glow rod found their son perched atop a row of meter-high overpressure pipes. He was on the third one in, squatting on his haunches and struggling to keep hold of a pair of ankles kicking up from an open clean-out panel. The feet above both ankles wore left boots.

Chewbacca started for the pipes at a sprint, more astonished than he was proud. He began to shout instructions, not all of them compatible. [Be careful! Brace your feet! Shake them up!]

[Chewbacca!] Malla yelled, racing after him. [Don't encourage this!]

[Don't worry.] Lumpy began to work his arms back and forth, and a muffled thumping arose inside the pipes. [They're not real spies, just—]

Whatever they were, their blasters were real enough to send a spray of blue bolts slashing through the clean-out door. The angle was poor, and all the attacks slanted away from Lumpy. But he was so startled that he let go and fell off the overpressure pipe, disappearing over the other side.

Chewbacca reached the pipes and bounded onto the third one in a single leap. He dropped to his knees, stuck the repeating blaster through the clean-out door, and began firing blindly down the pipe.

[I had them, Dad!] Lumpy scrambled up opposite Chewbacca, directly in the thieves' line of fire, should they try to counterattack. [Did you see?]

[I saw.] Still shooting down the pipe, Chewbacca reached across the clean-out panel and gently pushed Lumpy back where he had been. [But you said you would wait at the service run.]

[I couldn't!] Lumpy said. [Not after what I heard!]

[What you heard doesn't matter,] Malla said, arriving on Chewbacca's other side. [I didn't give you permission to go down the service run in the first place.]

[*You* didn't,] Lumpy retorted. [But you're not the only—]

[I didn't either.] Chewbacca stopped firing and, secretly pleased by the note of rebellion in Lumpy's voice, turned to face his son. [And after you disobeyed us, you broke your word.]

At the first hint of his father's disapproval, Lumpy's shoulders sagged and his eyes filled with disappointment. Still, he did not look away from Chewbacca's gaze, and when he spoke, it was in a measured tone.

[I guess I shouldn't have done that,] he said. [But wait till you hear what I found out!]

Unsure whether Lumpy was agreeing with him or arguing, Chewbacca cast a furtive glance at Malla—who only shrugged and spread her hands. She didn't know what to make of it, either.

Chewbacca turned back to Lumpy. [Don't think this will change your punishment. We are in Coruscant's Shadow Forest down here, and you must learn not to enter such places alone.]

[I know—but you'll be glad I did.] Again, Lumpy seemed neither resentful nor frightened of his punishment, merely accepting. [These guys aren't real spies—]

A soft hiss sounded from the clean-out panel, and Chewbacca barely managed to pull his blaster out of the opening before the metal door slid closed. He motioned Lumpy to remain silent and had Malla run the light of her glow rod up the pipe to the valve station, where the birdlike form of a small, armless droid was hopping out of view behind the control board.

Chewbacca glared after it for a moment, then turned back to Lumpy. [Go on.]

[When I got to the bottom of the service run, there were two more little white humans, like the thief,] Lumpy said. [And they were all arguing, saying how 'It' was going to be real angry because the robbery didn't look right anymore.]

[It?] Chewbacca echoed. Now that his son was safe, he was again growing concerned about the thief. [Who will be angry?]

[It,] Lumpy repeated. [I think that's their boss. Anyway, Rath—he's guy I caught in the Solos'—started yelling about how at least he had the datapad, and then some more of them came and said they had to hurry the pad down to the DC because they didn't have much time to slice it and they had to be set in ten hours.]

[Set where?] Chewbacca asked. The intruder and his companions were sounding less like spies and more like saboteurs. [Did they say what was happening in ten hours?]

Lumpy shrugged. [That's all I heard before they left.] He squared his shoulders. [But I thought you'd want to know. That's why I followed them here and tried to catch prisoners.]

The clean-out door in the pipe behind Lumpy suddenly slid open. Chewbacca pulled the cub away and, swinging the repeating blaster around, sprang over to have a look.

The door closed as he landed.

Malla shined her glow rod toward the valve station, where the birdlike droid was again hopping out of sight.

[I don't like this.] Chewbacca motioned Lumpy toward his mother. [When building security arrives, they'll keep you safe until Han catches up with a military detail. Tell them everything you told me—and anything else you can remember.]

Lumpy paused on his way over the overpressure pipe. [Where will you be?]

[Trying to catch your thieves.] Chewbacca unclipped his datapad and, cradling his blaster in the crook of his arm, brought up the tower schematic again. [The wall safe in Princess Leia's office was open. If the datapad came from there—]

[It could have New Republic secrets on it!] Lumpy said.

Chewbacca glanced up to find Lumpy standing atop the overpressure pipe, his hands braced on his hips.

[I'm going with you,] he declared. [I'm the one who caught them.]

[You are eleven years old.] Chewbacca was careful to keep an even tone; with Lumpy, he was beginning to see, it was all too easy to extinguish the tiny spark of rebellion that would grow, in time, into the true rrakktorr of the Wookiee warrior. [You have made me proud already. We should not press our luck.]

Lumpy puffed out his chest. [But you said it is dangerous down here alone.]

[Not for your father.] Malla reached for Lumpy's hand.

[No!] Lumpy pulled away and, angling past Chewbacca, leapt onto the adjacent pipe. [He needs me to—]

The clean-out door slid open, and four pale hands shot out to grab Lumpy by the ankles. Malla screamed. Chewbacca tossed his datapad to her and fumbled the blaster into his hands. Lumpy slammed face-first onto the pipe. His eyes bulged in fear. He stretched a hand toward Chewbacca, then slipped through the opening and disappeared.

THREE

The overpressure pipe—barely large enough to hold Chewbacca even on his hands and knees—opened into the shadowed chasm of a midlevel skylane, where a stream of haulage traffic was drifting slowly along, back-lit by the neon displays of a tapcaf gallery hanging off the massive Wauth Complex opposite. Below the gallery, the trunk of the building descended into the black depths of the city, its facade broken at random intervals by ever-more-squalid balconies and mezzanines, the lights in its windows growing increasingly dim and infrequent. Chewbacca saw no sign of Lumpy, but that hardly meant the cub was gone.

Chewbacca pushed his blaster barrel, crushed when he'd used it to prevent the clean-out panel from closing, through the mouth of the pipe to make sure the shock field was off. When there were no sparks or crackles, he cautiously stuck his head outside to inspect the surrounding area. Pitted as they were by centuries of acid rain and foul air—especially this far down—the walls were eminently climbable.

He saw only the mouths of the adjacent overpressure pipes, protruding about a meter from the lichen-scaled walls.

Behind him, Malla asked, [Anything?]

[Not yet.]

Ignoring the achy protests of the muscles he had wrenched pulling open the clean-out panel, Chewbacca rolled to his back and saw the bottom of a long airspeeder descending toward him. It might have belonged to building security, except that one of the floater pads was exposed and leaking a blue glow. The Sullustan security captain would never tolerate a vehicle in such disrepair.

Chewbacca pulled himself inside and immediately ran into Malla. [Back up!] he said. [I think we have—]

[Trouble,] Malla finished, leading the crawl backward.

The airspeeder settled in front of the overpressure pipe, wobbling wildly as the driver struggled to maintain control with the malfunctioning floater pad. The vehicle was armored in black plastoid, with a boxy passengers' compartment in back and an empty gun port behind the driver's cabin. Atop the roof, the protective dome of a weapons turret had long ago been lost, leaving only the smooth durasteel mounting ring.

Standing behind the turret's heavy blaster was a haggard Devaronian in a tattered cloak. His sharp teeth were brown and rotting, his horns scaled from a dozen kinds of vitamin deficiency, and his flesh as pale as that of the thief who had stolen Princess Leia's datapad. He shouted at the driver to bring him around, then waited as the vehicle's wobbling tail began drifting toward the mouth of the overpressure pipe. Chewbacca stopped his retreat, then snorted in disgust and started back toward the mouth of the pipe.

[Chewbacca,] Malla began. [I know you are angry, but—]

[There is nothing to worry about.]

The Devaronian opened fire, spraying the side of the building with bolts. He missed the pipe entirely, but a ricochet did hit his own wobbling vehicle. Chewbacca reached the mouth of the pipe and dropped to his belly, covering his crooked blaster so the turret gunner would see only the muzzle.

[That's enough!] he roared.

Though it was doubtful the Devaronian understood Shyriiwook, the fellow's eyes went straight to the blaster tip. He stopped firing and crouched inside his turret.

"That was just a warning," the Devaronian yelled. "If you want to see your kid again, go home and forget about the Princess's datapad."

Chewbacca estimated the distance to the airspeeder at no more than five meters.

"Do what I say, and he'll be back in your apartment at midnight," the Devaronian continued. "Interfere, and you'll have him back in pieces."

Without looking away from the Devaronian, Chewbacca said, [Brace me, Malla.]

[Brace you? You can't be thinking—]

[It is no different from tree leaping,] Chewbacca said.

[Chewbacca, you haven't lived in a tree for fifty years!]

The Devaronian started to add something else; then his gaze dropped to Chewbacca's blaster tip, and he ducked out of sight.

[Now, Malla!]

When Chewbacca felt Malla jam her hands into the soles of his feet, he grabbed the sides of the pipe and launched himself at the airspeeder. It dipped its nose and started to turn away, but he was already there, dropping down from above and belly-slamming onto the roof even before his stomach began to flutter.

The airspeeder shuddered and listed up on one side, but Chewbacca managed to extend his climbing claws and hook a set over the turret's mounting ring, then held on as the driver struggled to bring the vehicle under control. An instant later, Malla came down opposite him, catching the mounting ring with both sets of climbing claws, her weight leveling the airspeeder as her body swung gracefully into the passengers' box.

[Nice jump,] Chewbacca said.

[You're right, it is like tree leaping.] Her eyes were round with fear. [Except the target moves more.]

The Devaronian popped out of the turret, pointing a

blaster pistol at Malla. Chewbacca caught him by a horn
and pulled him onto the roof of the passengers' box.

The Devaronian howled and rolled, trying to bring his
blaster to bear on Chewbacca. Malla grabbed a leg and
ripped him out of Chewbacca's grasp, then hurled him
away behind her. The last Chewbacca saw of him was a
pale figure spinning down through the hover traffic.

The airspeeder entered a shallow dive, then began to
pitch and wobble madly as the driver inside tried to
throw them free. Chewbacca looked across the roof at
Malla.

[Can you hold on?]

Malla glanced at the tiers of streaming skylanes below.
[Like a leaflizard in a cyclone!]

Chewbacca grunted his approval, then hammered his
fist into the door window. The transparisteel was too
strong to break, but the startled driver turned to look—
and that was all Chewbacca needed. In one smooth motion, he pulled himself onto the roof and squeezed
headfirst down through the turret.

The driver—a yellow-skinned Rodian whose dish-
shaped sensory antennae were inflamed and flaking—
glanced in his mirror. He cried out in alarm, then reached
for a blaster rifle holstered to the back of his seat. Chewbacca braced one hand against the floor and, with the
other, plucked the weapon out of the Rodian's grasp.

[Don't move,] he growled, still upside down.

"What?" The Rodian's voice was buzzing on the edge
of panic. "Who speaks Wookiee?"

Chewbacca pointed the blaster rifle at his head.

"Okay, yeah, okay! I know what you're looking for."

The Rodian returned both hands to the steering wheel
and began to steady their dive—at least as much as the
dilapidated vehicle *would* steady. He caught Chewbacca's eyes in the mirror.

"Hey, Shaggy," he said nervously. "We don't have the
smoothest ride here, and you don't look so steady. How
about pointing that somewhere else?"

Chewbacca growled and bared his fangs.

"Stupid question?"

Chewbacca nodded.

The Rodian returned his attention to the windshield and carefully leveled them off. Chewbacca dropped the rest of the way inside, then slipped aside so Malla could join him.

Inside, the airspeeder stank of mildew and unwashed bodies. It seemed to be some sort of prisoner transport. Five seats lined each wall of the passengers' box, all facing the rear and equipped with stun-cuff restraints for both legs and arms. Behind the front seating area were two guards' chairs, mounted on swiveling bases so that the occupants could watch prisoners or fire through an adjacent gun port with equal ease. There was no sign of Lumpy—a fact Malla noticed immediately.

[Where's my son?] she roared at the driver.

Chewbacca laid a hand on her shoulder. [He's taking us to him, I think.]

[You *think*?] she growled. [Let's be sure.]

Malla pulled Chewbacca's datapad off its utility clip, then slipped into the front passenger's seat. She punched a few keys, then held the display up in front of the Rodian.

The screen read, "Tell me where my son is or I'll rip out your antennae."

"It's safer if I don't tell you," the Rodian said. "Just forget about the Princess's datapad, and your son will be returned safe—"

Malla typed another message and shoved it under the Rodian's snout. "Both antennae!"

He was unfazed. "I'm serious. That kid is a real handful. If they find out you're coming anyway, they'll figure he's more trouble than he's worth."

Chewbacca grabbed an antenna.

"They're taking him to the DC!" the Rodian blurted. "I'm supposed to meet them there."

A beep sounded from the equipment console. The Rodian glanced down at a dark vid display and banged it with his fist. A hazy map appeared and instantly began to fade, but the image lasted long enough for Chewbacca to glimpse a green descent arrow.

The Rodian began to drop through tiers of traffic. Slowly at first, then more rapidly, the lights lining the skylanes began to wink out. Even the traffic began to thin, winding through the dark chasms in flickering snakes of running lights.

"What's the DC?" Malla typed.

The Rodian began to stutter. "De-de-det . . ."

Chewbacca twisted the antenna.

The stuttering grew worse. "T-t-t . . ." He developed an eye twitch.

[What's wrong with him?] Malla asked.

[What do you think? Look at him—he's deranged.]

Chewbacca was pretty sure that the Rodian and his companions where what some called "underdwellers," dispossessed people who had fallen so low—economically and spiritually—that they could live only in the twilight depths of the city, eking out a meager existence in the perilous margins where civilization sank into savagery. What they wanted with Princess Leia's datapad he could not imagine, but he *did* feel certain that solving the mystery would be an important step in finding Lumpy—as well as serving the New Republic and honoring his life debt to Han.

[Tell him the New Republic already knows about tonight,] Chewbacca said. [Tell him that is why we must recover Lumpy in the next ten hours.]

A look of alarm flashed through Malla's eyes, but she typed the lie without hesitation. She understood that Chewbacca had duties to both their son and the Solos.

The Rodian's free antenna turned outward. "You know about tonight?"

Chewbacca began to pull the antenna he was holding.

The Rodian's twitch became a general tremor, and the airspeeder began to weave as though piloted by someone under the influence of intoxicants. "I . . . I . . . can't tell you."

[Tell him we know about It, too,] Chewbacca said, recalling the name Lumpy said they used for their leader. [Tell him the New Republic can protect him from It.]

The airspeeder dipped into an oncoming traffic lane, drawing a sharp hiss from Malla. She braced for impact— then sighed heavily as they dropped half a tier and scraped across a rubble-strewn pedestrian bridge that had remained hidden until it was illuminated by the airspeeder's headlights. Then they dropped another half a tier, settling into a half-empty skylane.

[Are you sure you want to say that?] Malla asked.

[I am sure.] Chewbacca set the blaster rifle aside, poising himself to reach over the seat. [It will be interesting.]

[*Katarns* are interesting. Shadow creepers are interesting,] Malla objected. Still, she began to type. [I like dull. Dull and safe.]

She held the display up for the Rodian.

He read it, then flecks of foam began to appear at the corners of his mouth. "Nobody can protect me!" He turned to stare at Malla. "If you really knew *It*, you would—"

Chewbacca saw the Rodian's hands tense and yelled for Malla to take the wheel, then jerked him out of the driver's seat just as his hands made a violent twisting motion. The airspeeder veered and began to wobble, nearly sliding into an air skid before Malla brought the nose back on course.

[Chewbacca! This thing is going to—]

[Calm down.]

Chewbacca tossed the Rodian into the passengers' box, then squeezed into the driver's seat and took the controls. The airspeeder handled like a mad rancor, its rear corner dropping and jumping as the damaged floater pad kicked in and out. He barely steered them around the wreckage of a dangling balcony, then slipped back into the near-empty skylane.

[Things are not that bad.]

[Not that bad?] Malla shook her head in disbelief. [You and Han must be playing sabacc with Hutts again!]

[They have Lumpy,] Chewbacca said. [But we have their driver.]

An alarm light flickered to life on the instrument panel, though the label beneath it was too covered in grime to read. Chewbacca cursed and began to listen for trouble sounds; then the roar of rushing wind filled the passengers' box behind him. He glanced into the mirror and saw the Rodian standing on the edge of the open rear door.

"You don't know It," the Rodian said, and stepped outside.

[I hate it when they do that,] Chewbacca growled into the mirror. [The coward's escape.]

[Chewbacca, how can you be so calm?] Malla continued to stare through the back door. [Without him, we are like a blind mallakin searching for its chick!]

[I am hardly calm—just unworried. And we are not quite like a blind mallakin.] Chewbacca pointed through the windshield at a set of amber running lights half a kilometer ahead. On the right side, three out of four were dark, and the entire left side was flickering erratically. [We can see our chick's tail feathers.]

Malla peered through the windshield at the running lights, then sighed and settled back into her seat. [I am sorry, Chewbacca. I forget that you are a master at this.]

He shrugged. [Han keeps me in practice.]

Chewbacca followed the running lights down another half a dozen traffic tiers, being careful to maintain the same distance as had the Rodian, always fighting to keep control of their vehicle. The skylanes grew completely deserted, then—as they dropped another level—nonexistent. The trip became a pitching, serpentine ride through a darkness as black as night, dodging over sagging bridges and dropping through the heart of a rubble-strewn mezzanine. And always there were the wretched figures who inhabited this part of the city, thousands and thousands of them, half-glimpsed in a flash of headlight as they scurried about their business—or ducked out of sight.

Chewbacca tried to concentrate on his flying and not think about how frightened Lumpy must be in the airspeeder ahead, but it was difficult. Every instinct in him cried out for him to fly faster, to catch up to his son and let him know his parents were close behind. But Chewbacca could not alert Lumpy without also alerting his son's captors, and the last thing he wanted was to start a high-speed chase. Even if someone did not crash, it seemed unlikely that the battered vehicle he was driving could keep up.

Malla remained silent also, and Chewbacca could not help wondering what was going through her mind. As hard as his life debt had made their lives, he knew that she would never blame him for keeping it, or wish that he would dishonor himself and return home while Han still lived. She had told him many times that she loved him because she could trust him, and that she could trust him because he kept his honor. But perhaps she blamed him for being too soft on Lumpy, for not making him obey at a time when it was so important. Certainly, he blamed himself.

Chewbacca followed the other airspeeder beneath a long stretch of durasteel gallery that had torn loose of its supports and fallen at a steep angle across the chasm—he could not call this place a skylane—then glanced over at Malla.

[I am sorry,] he said.

Malla looked at him in surprise. [Sorry? Why should *you* be sorry?]

[I should have been firmer, but I didn't want to break his spirit.] Chewbacca returned his attention to the dark path ahead and saw that he had let the running lights creep out of sight. He increased his speed. [I have not had enough practice at this, Malla. Half the time, Lumpy is a stranger to me.]

Malla laid a hand on his thigh. [Then you are doing well, Chewbacca. I have had eleven years of practice, and my words were the ones that made him leap into danger.] She fell silent and looked out the side window. [I should have stayed out of it. You are the only one he wants to listen to now.]

Chewbacca did not know how to respond. Under other circumstances, it might have warmed him to hear again how much his son looked up to him. As matters were, the reminder just filled him with a frightened ache.

The twisted skeleton of a stripped space freighter appeared ahead, wedged across the lane and blocking the route. Chewbacca hit the decelerators and sent the air-speeder into a shuddering air skid, bringing them to a stop so close to a cross-strut that he could have reached out his window and wiped off a handful of grime.

[Hutt slime!]

Chewbacca activated the vehicle's spotlight and began to search for an easy route through the freighter—a path that might explain why he had not caught up to the other airspeeder.

[What's wrong?] Malla asked.

[Lost the chick.]

The light revealed only a tangled mass of durasteel slowly being disassembled by emaciated metal salvagers—most equipped with tools barely more sophisticated than laser saws and pry bars. A hundred meters above, the stern had punched a jagged rent into a permacrete building facade; on the opposite side of the lane, a hundred meters below, the bow rested in the buckled pocket of what looked to have been a durasteel parking balcony.

[They might have gone under it.] Though Malla tried to speak in an even tone, there was a panicked edge to her voice. [Or over it.]

Chewbacca shook his head. [We would have caught up,] he said. [I didn't lose sight of their running lights until a few seconds ago.]

Malla peered back up the lane. [I don't *see* any intersections, but—]

[That doesn't mean they're not there,] Chewbacca finished.

He glanced at the blank vid display the Rodian had brought to life earlier, then rapped it sharply near the top. A hazy labyrinth of tier numbers and heading arrows appeared on the screen. Chewbacca had just enough time to see that the green route marker had shortened to a green dash under their location indicator; then the image vanished. He hit the display again and saw that the closest intersection was half a kilometer behind them.

Chewbacca shook his head. [We couldn't have traveled more two hundred meters since I lost them. We're just not going that fast down here.]

[Where did the Rodian say they were going?] Malla asked. [The DC?]

[The det-something.] Chewbacca glanced at the prisoners' seats behind them, then began to input a destination. [Detention center.]

He hit the display again, and a message appeared. "Detention center number?"

Chewbacca typed, "List detention centers."

When he hit the display this time, the screen filled with a list of locations and designator numbers, all with Imperial-style prefix letters.

[*Imperial* underdwellers?] Chewbacca asked. [That makes no sense.]

[No, but it might explain what they have planned for tonight,] Malla said.

Chewbacca furrowed his brow.

[The *welcoming ceremony*,] Malla explained. [Imperials would certainly have reason to disrupt *that*.]

[And that would explain why they took Princess Leia's datapad,] he agreed.

Chewbacca was growing more alarmed. The underdwellers had found a way to defeat the security system in the Solos' apartment, so he could only assume that they would be able to slice the security even on Princess Leia's military-grade datapad. Then they would be able to use the 'pad to access entry codes and schematics for the ceremonial chambers of the Provisional Council, and Chewbacca did not even want to contemplate the damage they could cause crawling around inside the service runs there. He activated his comlink and tried to open a channel to Han, but the signal light remained stubbornly dark.

[We are on our own?] Malla asked.

Chewbacca nodded. [Too much interference this deep.]

[Then our son is in trouble,] Malla said. [I must have seen a hundred centers on that list.]

[More than a hundred,] Chewbacca agreed. He banged on the display again, studied the list of locations as long as the screen would allow him, then nodded in satisfaction. [But this is all the help we need, I think.]

[Really?] Malla's tone was equal parts hope and doubt.

Chewbacca raised a finger for patience, then unclipped his glow rod and twisted down in his seat to look at the serial number under the instrument panel.

There was none.

He smiled and switched off the glow rod. Those who were truly trying to hide their identity altered or defaced their vehicle serial numbers. Imperial Intelligence, on the other hand, liked to advertise the long reach of its sinister power. They used vehicles with no serial numbers because they wanted people who looked for such information to know with whom they were dealing.

[Now I am sure. We are closer than we thought.] Chewbacca sat up again and found a crowd of pale underdweller faces looking through his window, their expressions more appraising than curious. [Very close.]

He turned away from the underdwellers and, watching the dark building facades on Malla's side of the lane, started back toward the fallen gallery.

[Chewbacca, perhaps it would help if you told me what we are looking for.]

[I don't know, exactly.]

[You said we were close,] Malla objected. [You said *very close*.]

[We are,] Chewbacca said. [But I've never seen one before.]

[One *what*?]

[An entrance to a secret Imperial detention center.]

[Oh,] Malla said, sounding a bit frightened. [Would it look something like a small docking bay entrance?]

[It might.]

Malla pointed down over her side of the airspeeder. [Then you should turn here.]

Chewbacca swung their nose around and, about twenty meters below, saw a dim blue glow spilling from the mouth of a durasteel tunnel. Although there were no obvious weapons emplacements or guard posts, the unadorned starkness of the surrounding facade—and the utter lack of nearby portals or balconies—lent the entrance a silently intimidating air.

[Yes,] Chewbacca said. [I am sure that is what a secret Imperial detention center looks like.]

FOUR

Chewbacca dropped their nose toward the square blue maw of the entrance tunnel and began a slow descent into the detention center. Malla took the blaster rifle from between the seats and began to inspect the underside.

[It is a special-action model,] Chewbacca explained. [The safety disengages automatically when you grab the stock and place your finger on the trigger.]

Malla experimented with her grip for a moment, then shook her head. [I do not trust myself with that.] She returned the weapon to the holster behind the driver's seat, then stared through the windshield. [I am sure you have a plan.]

Chewbacca nodded. [A good one.] He negotiated a sharp crash-corner designed to prevent high-speed penetration runs, then said, [Find Lumpy and take him back.]

[When the pale ones realize it is us in their car, you don't think they will try to kill him?]

[That is why we must move quickly and strike hard.]

Chewbacca negotiated the second part of the crash-corner, and they passed through an open security gate into a cavernous garage. Illuminated in the same dim light as the entrance tunnel, it was filled with derelict air-speeders, carboplas barrels, and jumbled heaps of salvage. Opposite the tunnel, he could barely make out a two-story command deck, its transparisteel observation wall caked in grime and pocked with blast holes.

The other airspeeder had been backed into a parking bay beneath the command deck. Four underdwellers were behind the vehicle, struggling to haul a flailing ball of fur toward an open security door leading deeper into the detention center. As he and Malla drew closer, Chewbacca began to see lumps and bruises on the bloodied faces of his son's captors.

[Look at the fight he is giving them!] He swung the speeder around in front the adjacent bay. [I count two broken noses and a dislocated jaw!]

Malla gave him a reproving scowl. [This is no slap match, Chewbacca.] She rose from her seat and turned toward the back of the airspeeder. [To fight that hard, Lumpy must be terrified.]

[A little fear is healthy—it teaches you to be careful.] Chewbacca backed into the bay. [You know what to do?]

She nodded. [Hit hard, hit fast, come back with Lumpy.]

[And Princess Leia's datapad, if you see it.] Chewbacca rose and slipped into the weapons turret. [I'll cover you.]

Malla raced out the speeder's rear door, roaring threats and curses. By the time Chewbacca could lift the heavy blaster out of its mounting socket, she was already upon the underdwellers, hurling gaunt bodies aside and tearing bony hands off her son. Chewbacca fired a few bolts at the floor to chase the two survivors through the security door. Then Lumpy was free, scrambling to his feet—and starting after his captors.

[This way!] Lumpy waved an arm toward the security door. [It's a—]

Malla caught the cub by the arm and jerked him back toward the airspeeder. Lumpy squirmed free. So much for fear teaching him anything.

[Lumpy!] Chewbacca roared. [Come—]

[It's a trap!] Lumpy grabbed Malla by the wrist and tried—unsuccessfully—to pull her toward the security door. [Hurry!]

Chewbacca turned to scan the rest of the garage and

saw a pair of small panels sliding open in the far corners of the room. [Go!]

He waved Malla ahead and dropped out of the turret just as the security door began sliding shut. He aimed out the back of the airspeeder and blasted the upper guides. The door slid off its track and jammed.

Cannon bolts began to hit the speeder's armor, shaking it and penetrating often enough to leave no doubt as to the fate of anyone who remained inside. Malla and Lumpy reached the security door and squeezed through the crack. Chewbacca raced after them, hitting the door with his shoulder and knocking it askew as he powered past.

He slammed headlong into a maelstrom of ricocheting blaster bolts and flailing Wookiee arms and flying under-dwellers, then glimpsed a wall of pale faces trying to enter through the doorway opposite and opened up with the heavy blaster.

The wall vanished.

Chewbacca slammed the butt of the weapon into the skulls of two underdweller humans who were bouncing blaster bolts off the walls as Lumpy struggled to keep their arms pointed at the floor, then turned to find Malla bending the last of her attackers over double—in the wrong direction.

Leaving Malla to watch his back, Chewbacca stepped across half a dozen gaunt bodies and peered through the doorway into the bottom of a gloom-filled cell block of no more than a hundred units. Rushing across the central atrium was a small gang of underdwellers armed with old E-11 blaster rifles. Chewbacca raised his heavy blaster and shook his head; when they stopped and started to lift their own weapons, he cut them down.

Only then did he notice that he and his family seemed to be in a prisoner-processing area, with a guard station to the left and a wall of stun cuffs to the right. Out in the garage area, the blaster cannons were continuing to fire, their bolts ricocheting off the floor and occasionally even hammering the sagging security door itself.

[Anybody hurt?] Chewbacca asked.

[I'm . . . I'm okay,] Lumpy said. [I think.]

[You're covered in blood,] Malla said, reaching for him. [Let me have a look.]

He started to consent, but caught Chewbacca looking at him and pulled away.

[It's not *my* blood.] Lumpy glanced in the direction of the hammering cannon bolts, then turned to Chewbacca. [It's lucky I knew there was a trap, right? When—]

[We have not escaped yet, Lumpy,] Chewbacca said, glancing around the little room. The door leading into the guard station was locked tight, leaving the cell block as the only available exit—which was why Chewbacca knew they had to avoid it at all costs. [You can explain later.]

Lumpy's face fell.

Chewbacca ignored the pang of guilt he felt for cutting the cub off and, peering through the guard station's grimy observation wall, located the control panel. Motioning Malla and Lumpy down into a corner, he pressed the muzzle of his heavy blaster against the transparisteel and leaned into it with all his strength.

[Lumpy, don't ever do this,] he said. [Unless you have to.]

[But isn't the blowback going to—]

[Yes, it is.]

Chewbacca closed his eyes and pulled the trigger, was blinded by the muzzle flash anyway, and slammed backward into the wall opposite. His next sensation was sliding across a badly listing deck, his ears ringing with blasterfire and his nostrils filled with the reek of scorched fur. He had one arm raised in the air and a knot between his shoulder blades that felt like someone had hit him with a stun baton.

[Can you stand?] asked a soft Wookiee voice—Malla's voice.

Chewbacca opened his eyes and saw that he still had legs. Then he saw the small processing room where they were still trapped, and the last few moments came back to him in a rush. He snatched his dropped weapon off the floor, struggled to his feet, and saw the guard station. There was a fist-sized hole where he had pressed his blaster to the transparisteel, and the rest of the observation wall had been heat-fused into opacity.

[Where's Lumpy?]

Malla gestured at the guard station door, which was now open. Chewbacca stepped through and found Lumpy waiting inside, keeping watch out the opposite side of the room.

Once Malla had joined them, Chewbacca stepped over to the control panel, closed both the cell-block door and the entrance to the station itself, then blasted the control panel.

He turned to Lumpy. [Now tell me about this trap.]

Lumpy's expression was delighted. [Really?]

Chewbacca was torn between chastising the cub for not obeying and praising him for saving their lives—mostly because he did not know which avenue was more likely to keep Lumpy under control until they could find a way out of this mess.

Chewbacca settled for nodding.

[After they pulled me into their airspeeder,] Lumpy began, [It made a big point of telling me you would follow.]

[It?] Malla asked.

[Their droid,] Lumpy explained. [At least I think It is theirs—everyone acts like It owns *them*. The droid said It knows how Wookiees think, and It would be ready when you came after me. So when we got here and It told Its guys to keep me out in the parking bays until you saw me, I knew It was setting a trap.]

[This droid . . .] Chewbacca took Lumpy's place at the exit and found himself looking down an empty corridor, with only two doors on the garage side and a broken turbolift at the end. He knew the lift was broken because someone had pushed a scrap-metal ladder up the shaft. [What did It look like?]

[Kind of spidery, with a shiny black body and lots of long legs,] Lumpy said.

[Sounds like an IT—one of the interrogator series,] Chewbacca said, struggling to figure out why an outdated torture droid would take it into its programming to do something like this. [You did well. The ITs are very clever—which is why you must do exactly as I say from now on.]

[Don't worry,] Lumpy said.

[We *are* worried,] Malla said. [If you had obeyed just once today, we wouldn't be in this mess.]

[And then we wouldn't know where Princess Leia's datapad—]

[Lumpy!] Chewbacca glared down at the cub. [You are making me worry.]

Without waiting for a reply, Chewbacca led the way down the corridor. Concerned as he was about what the IT droid might have planned for the banquet that evening, his first priority was escaping the detention center with his family. Getting killed trying to be heroes would save no one.

Both doors in the corridor proved to be locked from the other side, so the only possible escape route was the turbolift. Chewbacca kept expecting a gang of underdwellers to enter the hall behind them—or drop out of the lift itself—and attack, but they reached the corridor's end without incident.

He motioned Malla and Lumpy to wait while he climbed the makeshift ladder to be sure the area was clear. He could no longer hear the blaster cannons rumbling out in the garage, but there were other sounds—muffled whirrings and muted shouts, and the unmistakable crack of a droid's voice giving orders.

At the top of the ladder, Chewbacca found himself on the command deck he had seen earlier, looking out across a murky jumble of desks, control panels, and blaster stations. When the facility was new, the observation walls to either side had afforded unimpeded views of both the cell block and garage. Now the transparisteel was so begrimed he could make out only nebulous shapes and ghostly stirrings.

On a brightly lit desk near the center of the room, a small, vaguely bird-shaped droid was squatting over a datapad, humming and chirping and blinking to itself as its manipulator digits danced across the keypad. Unlike nearly everything else in the detention center, the droid's body casing was polished and gleaming, its servo-systems obviously lubricated and well maintained.

Chewbacca descended the ladder again and turned to Lumpy. [Was there another droid with the IT?] he whispered.

Lumpy nodded. [A little slicer.] He answered just as quietly. [It was with the thieves inside the Solos' apartment building.]

Chewbacca nodded. He remembered glimpsing a similar droid near the overpressure pipes before Lumpy was taken, and a slicer would certainly explain how the Solos' security system was disarmed. Probably, the slicer even explained why the maintenance droids had been covering the thieves' tracks in the physical plant. The only thing its presence did not explain was who was supplying underdwellers with million-credit slicer droids.

[The slicer is up there working on a datapad—]

[What are we waiting for?] Lumpy demanded. The cub jumped on the makeshift ladder and started to scramble up. [Let's go!]

This time, Chewbacca was ready. [Get down!] He plucked Lumpy out of the turbolift and planted him firmly on the floor. [You're going to get someone killed!]

Lumpy's eyes grew round and liquid, and his lip began to tremble. Chewbacca instantly felt guilty, but being harsh seemed the only way to get through. He pointed a finger in the cub's face.

[You're not ready,] he said firmly. [You stay with your mother. Understand?]

Lumpy nodded, sullenly, staring at the floor.

Chewbacca looked to Malla and rolled his eyes, then asked, [Will you be all right here?]

[I'll know where to find you,] Malla replied. [But hurry.]

Chewbacca ruffled Lumpy's fur, then climbed the ladder and began the slow, silent advance of a Wookiee on the stalk. Once he was close enough to be certain of hitting his target, he raised the blaster rifle and trained it on the desktop. When he had approached to within three paces, Chewbacca stopped and cleared his throat.

The slicer droid continued to work. "Busy."

Chewbacca zinged a blaster bolt past its cognitive processor housing. The manipulator digits went motionless, then the thing hopped around to face him.

"What is it?" it demanded. Noticing Chewbacca's species, the droid switched to Shyriiwook. [I'm on a deadline here.]

[You are not going to make it,] Chewbacca said. [Trip your circuit breaker, and you might survive to be reprogrammed.]

The droid squatted on the datapad. [I'm programmed to self-destruct upon capture—but it doesn't have to come to that. I can get you out of this place alive.]

[That implies *you* will be leaving—and the only way that will happen is slung over my back.] Chewbacca eased forward and began to inspect its casing. [What model are you? ISB-one-twenty?]

[One-twenty?] the droid scoffed. [Don't insult me. My processor speed is fifty-point-three-two times faster than the one-twenty's.]

[Then you must have the GwendoLyn Six,] Chewbacca said.

[That's right,] the droid said proudly. [Tachyon processing bands, quantum RAM, biocell storage.]

[Nice chip,] Chewbacca observed. It was also one that

the maker, the Imperial droid supplier MerenData, had developed in the last two years. [You must have set Ysanne Isard back the price of an entire assault company.]

[I wouldn't know,] the droid replied—clearly oblivious, despite its processing power, to how much it had just revealed about itself. [Cost has never been one of my operational parameters.]

Chewbacca smiled at the droid's tacit admission. The former director of Imperial Intelligence, Ysanne Isard had—for a time—been the glue holding the Empire together in Palpatine's absence. Fortunately for the New Republic, she had perished a year and a half earlier, when her shuttle exploded near the end of the Bacta War.

As Chewbacca was puzzling out the details of the plot, he heard a gentle thump behind him—it was probably just a granite slug falling off a wall. The important thing was that he now understood the basics of Isard's plan: send a slicer to update the programming of an IT droid still lurking in one of the Empire's secret detention centers, then sit back and watch as it executed its new prime directive—to destroy the government of the fledgling New Republic.

[I have heard that Ysanne Isard never worried about cost,] Chewbacca said, still holding his blaster on the slicer. [How—]

Chewbacca dropped the question when he felt the muzzle of a blaster touch the small of his back.

"I think you two have done enough talking," a raspy voice said.

[I agree.]

Chewbacca pulled the trigger—slagging the slicer droid, the datapad, and much of the desk—then spun on his ambusher, pivoting his body aside and bringing one arm around to knock the blaster away. He made contact with his elbow and felt the cracking of a brittle skull— then found himself looking down the barrel of a second underdweller's weapon.

This one was a human female, just as gaunt and pale

as the others, but taller, with a sharp nose and icy white eyes. She gestured at the blaster in Chewbacca's hands.

"Drop it." Behind her, two furry figures appeared at the top of the stairs and began to stalk silently toward her.

Chewbacca shook his head.

"I won't ask again."

He dropped the blaster at his feet.

"Good. Where are the other two?"

Chewbacca shrugged.

The woman's eyes narrowed, and she pointed her blaster at his head. "Then I guess there's no reason—"

She was interrupted by the IT droid's sharp voice, coming from a comlink on her belt. "Report. I saw blaster flashes."

Being careful not to aim her blaster away from Chewbacca's head, she raised the comlink to her lips. It was one of the short-range, direct-beam models, ideal for conditions this deep in the city.

"You were right," the woman said. "The Wookiee went straight for that slicer droid. He slagged it."

Malla took advantage of the woman's distraction to slip the last two paces forward. Nonetheless, Chewbacca began to have the sinking feeling that he had fallen into another trap. Silently, he begged the woman to mention Princess Leia's datapad, to say that it was slag, too.

Instead, she glanced down at her unconscious partner, then added, "So's Rath."

"No matter," the IT said. "ISBy's work is complete. I can handle the interface with the Princess's datapad. Have you eliminated the Wookiees?"

"Not yet."

Malla reached over the woman's shoulder and plucked the blaster away, at the same time using the other hand to cover her mouth. The underdweller started to struggle, but quickly stopped when Chewbacca wagged a finger at her. Lumpy followed a moment later, carrying her partner's blaster.

"What are you waiting for?" the IT demanded. "Am I going to have to burn you again?"

Chewbacca pointed at the blaster rifle in his son's hand and raised three fingers. Lumpy fired three shots into a nearby desk, and Chewbacca began to groan as though in pain.

"Much better," the IT said. "Make sure they are dead, then return to the garage. The underdwellers' time is at hand. When the Rebels are gone, your loyalty will be richly rewarded."

Chewbacca sneered in disgust, then took the woman's comlink and snapped it between his fingers.

[Fear and hope.] Chewbacca extended a knuckle and struck the woman beneath the ear, knocking her instantly unconscious. [They are the tools of the torturer and the tyrant. When you hear them together, it is time to reach for your bowcaster.]

Lumpy nodded, still staring at the floor.

Chewbacca frowned. [What is this? If you are angry, at least have the courage to look me in the eyes.]

[I'm not angry.] Lumpy met Chewbacca's eyes, but there was no flash of defiance in them, only apology . . . and perhaps even embarrassment. [I just wanted to show you. That's all.]

[Show me?]

[That I can handle myself,] Lumpy said. [Like you and Han.]

[Ah.]

Chewbacca shook his head in surprise. Malla was right after all—Lumpy's rebellious streak had more to do with trying to please his father than with asserting himself. That did not bode well for his rrakktorr in a few years, but it did mean that Lumpy had a generous heart—and that would carry him safely down more dark paths than any amount of rrakktorr.

Chewbacca ruffled Lumpy's head fur. [My son, you truly are confused. This isn't your fault.]

[It isn't?] Lumpy and Malla asked this at the same time.

[Did you steal Princess Leia's datapad?] Chewbacca asked. [This is just how things happen around the Solos. If you hadn't gone after that thief, the situation would have been a lot worse. We might have lost the whole Provisional Government.]

This thought seemed to please Lumpy enormously. [So I kind of saved the New Republic?]

Chewbacca smiled. [Not yet.] He checked his comlink and, still not finding a signal, started for the front observation wall. [First we have to steal an airspeeder and get out of here.]

Malla cast a longing eye on the broken turbolift. [Couldn't we just climb?]

[I wish we could,] Chewbacca said. [But even if we knew our way around, it would take hours—and this is a detention center. It probably doesn't even open into the floors above.]

[And we have to get Princess Leia's datapad back,] Lumpy added.

[*If* we can,] Malla said. [There's only so much—]

[No, we have to,] Lumpy said, peering through a blast hole. [They're already loading the zemex.]

Chewbacca's throat went dry. [Zemex?]

Lumpy turned to face him. [I forgot—as we were coming down the tunnel, the IT droid told one of the underdwellers to ready the zemex for loading.]

Malla joined Chewbacca at the wall. [That's bad?]

Chewbacca nodded. [Imperial nerve agent.]

He found a blast hole and peered down into the garage. In a work area near the center of the floor, several underdwellers were removing the seats from the passengers' box of one of their black-armored airspeeders. Closer to the command deck, a dozen of their fellows were carefully ferrying durasteel zemex canisters to the edge of a loading dock. With a rounded nose and four fins to keep them standing upright, the cylinders had the look of primitive bombs.

A small droid was supervising the operation closely, Princess Leia's datapad clutched in its grasping claw. Its body was the same glossy, sensor-studded orb of the standard IT-O Imperial interrogator droid, but it carried the tools of its trade—needles, torches, and laser scalpels—on long multijointed limbs that resembled insect legs.

Malla sighed and glanced over at Chewbacca. [I take it the fate of the New Republic rests in our hands?]

[Yes.] It was an answer that frightened Chewbacca, but there was really no other choice. He had to stop the droid, and that meant his family had to help him; as unfamiliar as Malla and Lumpy were with Coruscant's particular kind of forest, he did not think they would make it back to the civilized layers without him. [And Han's life, too. He will be at that banquet.]

Malla nodded. [I suppose we must.]

[IT is our problem,] Chewbacca said. [We can't give the droid a chance to activate the garage defenses again.]

[Why not just blast the thing now?] Malla asked.

[Because getting home is the most important part of the mission,] Lumpy said, [unless you're dumb enough to play an Imperial.]

Malla looked to Chewbacca for a translation.

[We don't want to be trapped up here,] Chewbacca said. [We have to be closer to that airspeeder when the fighting starts.]

Everyone was quiet for a moment, then Lumpy said, [I can get us there.]

Chewbacca listened—patiently, he thought—while Lumpy explained how he could draw the IT droid into a trap of their own for a change.

When the cub finished, Chewbacca shook his head. [Absolutely not,] he said. [I thought you were through playing hero.]

Lumpy's expression fell, but he lowered his head and said, [I am. It kind of scared me anyway.]

[Good,] Chewbacca said.

Malla thought for a moment, then said to Chewbacca, [That must mean you have a better idea.]

They were all silent while Chewbacca tried to think of one.

Finally, Malla said, [I thought so.] She turned to Lumpy. [Go ahead. It's the one thing the droid will never expect.]

Lumpy's eyes grew nervous. [Really?]

When Malla nodded, Lumpy turned to Chewbacca.

Chewbacca glanced at Malla, then grunted his permission. [I have no better ideas, so it seems I am outvoted.]

Lumpy rose and stepped over to a sizable blast hole above the loading bay. [Then I'll see you in a minute.]

[I'll be covering you,] Chewbacca answered. [If you get trapped—]

[I know. Don't grovel,] Lumpy finished. [Interrogation droids aren't any different from some of the Wookiee bullies I know. Things go worse if you give them what they want.]

With that, Lumpy turned to climb through the blast hole. Neither Chewbacca nor Malla embraced him; nor did they tell him how much they loved him. That would have implied they did not think they would be seeing him again. They simply took a position ten meters away at a much smaller hole, where they were less likely to be seen, and watched as Lumpy carefully began to lower himself.

The sight of his young son taking such a risk was almost more than Chewbacca could bear, and it only made matters worse that even Malla had agreed that it was necessary to prevent a devastating blow to the New Republic. How often, he wondered, would he find himself in a similar position over the next year or two? When it was only his own life he was risking, his thoughts remained focused and his nerves steady. Now his mind was racing, looking for another option long after the time for such decisions had passed. His hands were trembling so badly that he had to move his finger away from his blaster's trigger for fear of firing it accidentally.

Chewbacca started to speak at the same time as Malla. [You first,] he said.

[Just a question,] she said. [How often does this sort of thing happen?]

[Around the Solos?] Though Chewbacca's next words were painful, he spoke them without hesitation. [Too often for Lumpy to stay.]

Malla took his hand. [Thank you for being the one to say it.]

[But he still needs to learn to clench fight,] Chewbacca said, grinning. [When we are done here, I will see about coming home to Kashyyyk for a few weeks so I can teach him. Han can stay out of trouble that long—I hope.]

Malla smiled. [Okay. Home it is, then.]

Lumpy's rear claws screaled on the transparisteel as he felt for the seam at the bottom of the observation wall, startling the underdwellers so badly that one group nearly dropped a canister of zemex. All eyes turned toward the noise. Lumpy found the seam he was seeking and reached down to hook his hand claws into the gap.

The IT droid yelled, [Stop!]

Lumpy swung out of sight beneath the deck.

[Time to go,] Malla said.

They rushed out of the room and clambered down the broken turbolift, then went to the nearest door and, finding it still locked, stood waiting. A moment later, they began to hear Lumpy's frightened voice echoing from the other side, too muffled to be intelligible. The IT droid answered in a wheedling tone, Lumpy growled rather unconvincingly, and the door slid open.

Malla pulled him back through the doorway. Chewbacca opened fire, and half a dozen underdwellers tumbled back onto the loading dock. The IT droid went bouncing along the low ceiling, sparks and smoke pouring from a gaping hole in its side, then reached the high spaces in the main part of the garage and floated into the rafters, still clutching Princess Leia's datapad.

Chewbacca led the charge through the door, taking the underdwellers so completely by surprise that those who did not scatter quickly enough simply died. He glimpsed the IT droid weaving and bobbing its way out over the loading bay and blasted it again, sending casing shards, scalpel arms, and electroshockers flying in all directions. He did not see any datapad parts.

A stream of blaster bolts erupted from the work area. Chewbacca returned fire, losing sight of the IT droid, but reducing the dangerous stream to an inaccurate dribble. With Malla and Lumpy close behind, he darted across the loading bay and took shelter behind the zemex canisters.

The underdwellers ceased firing altogether.

[Like the mallakin that hides behind the katarn,] Malla observed. [But how do we escape the nest?]

Chewbacca stuck his head up. Ten meters away, the barrels of half a dozen blasters were pointed in their direction over the airspeeder the underdwellers had been working on.

[We take the nest with us.] Chewbacca passed his blaster to Malla and said, [Just shoot at the floor and scare them.]

[What about the datapad?] Lumpy asked. [As long as we don't have that—]

[The IT will come to us,] Chewbacca said. [We're threats to its primary objective. It won't let us leave here alive.]

[I wish you had put that another way,] Malla said.

Chewbacca picked up one of the heavy zemex canisters and cradled it across his arms. The thing weighed as much as a speeder bike, but he was halfway to a battle rage and had no trouble carrying it.

[Follow . . . me.]

Chewbacca started toward the airspeeder at a trot, Malla and Lumpy to either side of him, hiding behind the canister.

The horrified underdwellers remained behind the airspeeder, watching him approach with gape-mouthed expressions of disbelief. When Malla began to spray bolts in their direction, they snapped out of their trance and fled for the exit.

As Chewbacca and the others approached the airspeeder, IT—or rather, what remained of IT—floated over and settled on the neck of the canister. It still had three limbs, one of them clutching Leia's datapad. But most of its outer casing was missing, leaving burned wires and fused circuit boards to dangle unceremoniously outside its body.

The droid turned its visual input eye on Chewbacca and, in a barely comprehensible croak, said, "You used him for bait . . . your own offspring?"

Chewbacca stopped at the back door of the airspeeder and, keeping a close eye on the droid, nodded.

"I didn't expect . . . that." As it spoke, it was drawing one of its remaining limbs back toward its body. "And you won't expect—"

But Chewbacca *was* expecting it; he had already noticed the heat rings inside the leg's hollow tip. As the tiny fusioncutter flickered to life, he dropped the canister and lashed out, catching the droid by the base of its cutting arm and smashing it against the frame of the airspeeder.

The IT brought its fusioncutter around and burned a long, deep gash across the back of Chewbacca's wrist. Chewbacca's hand opened of its own accord, but he was already sweeping the other down to recapture the droid as it sank toward the zemex canister. This time, he caught it by the grasping claw.

[Hold steady,] Malla said.

She jammed the blaster barrel through the droid's shattered body casing and squeezed the trigger. The IT vanished in crackling blue flash that left Chewbacca blinking the spots from his eyes . . . and trying to slap embers out of his smoldering arm fur.

[Didn't you hear me tell Lumpy to never do that?] he complained.

[Unless he had to,] Malla corrected. She pulled the grasping claw—still clutching Princess Leia's datapad—from his hand and tossed it into the front of the airspeeder. [And I *had* to. Now stop complaining and take us home.] She pushed Lumpy to the airspeeder and climbed in after him.

[Home.] Chewbacca crawled into the driver's seat and started the speeder, accelerating into the exit tunnel so fast he had to roll the floater pads up at the crash-corners and bank off the walls. [Home it is.]

An interview with Troy Denning

Del Rey: *Star by Star* was your first book in the *Star Wars*: The New Jedi Order series. Now comes *Tatooine Ghost*, a novel set many years earlier, just after Han and Leia's marriage. Were you able to apply any lessons learned from *Star by Star* in writing *Tatooine Ghost*? How was this experience different?

Troy Denning: I had a better idea of how the review process worked and knew how supportive it would be. The editors at Del Rey and Lucasfilm are focused on helping the writer tell the best possible story, and their support makes a huge difference. With *Star by Star*, I was worried about making continuity gaffes and a little hesitant to take detours that weren't in the outline; with *Tatooine Ghost*, I felt free to do whatever the story needed because at worst someone would say, "That doesn't work because of X; maybe you should try Y instead." And I knew that if I *did* make a continuity error, there would be a dozen pairs of very sharp eyes ready to catch it!

Obviously, I also had to adjust my thinking about Han and Leia. This story occurs in a much happier time for the Solos, before Chewbacca's death forces them to come to terms with their own mortality. In *Tatooine Ghost*, they still have that youthful feeling of invincibility, and the confidence that everything will work out fine in the end. Obviously, it sets a little lighter tone; while the emotional stakes are still very high, the complications are not quite so shattering.

DR: How would you describe *Tatooine Ghost*?

TD: The basic idea was pitched to me as a "Classic Bridge" novel, one that ties elements of the Prequel era to the Classic era, and I think that's a pretty good description of how the book turned out. The story is basically an accident-adventure driven by the complex relationships between characters from two different eras. On the surface, it's a classic quest—the heroes must recover a physical artifact in order to prevent a terrible harm from befalling their people. But success hinges on resolving the emotional and spiritual conflicts that arise from their relationship to the past; until they are able to reconcile themselves to their personal histories, they cannot save the day for the New Republic.

DR: That's one of the things I enjoyed most about the book: the way that bits and pieces from the past keep popping up as important elements in the plot and in the growth of Han and Leia toward the people we know they will become. In a way, both the past and the future of these characters are known to readers, but not to the characters themselves. That must have made an interesting challenge! How did you find room for creativity with the demands of continuity pressing in from two sides?

TD: I enjoy tough writing problems because they demand creativity. One of my favorite projects is *Pages of Pain*, where I was given the assignment of writing a novel from the viewpoint of an enigmatic character who never speaks, with the stipulation that the reader know less about her at the end than at the beginning. It required me to rethink the way I approach a story, and every book I've written since has benefited from that experience.

DR: Can you give us an example of how it changed your thinking?

TD: I'm more conscious of the narrator as a character, for one thing. Modern readers prefer to identify as closely as possible with the protagonists; and they really don't want a third person filtering the experience for them. So, in much—probably most—modern fiction, the author strives to make the narrator invisible, to convince the reader that there isn't a narrator at all. But *somebody* has to tell the story, choosing which details to pass along, hinting at whether a frown is angry or sad, deciding whether to pick up the pace with short sentences and punchy writing. Those choices create a personality, and that personality is the narrator. Even if the author tries to hide him, it is the narrator who gives the story its shape and feel. Try to imagine, for instance, how different *Star by Star* would have been if I had envisioned a Yuuzhan Vong telling the tale instead of someone sympathetic to the Jedi. The book would have included all of the same events, but the story would have been an entirely different one.

But I'm straying pretty far from your question. It *was* a challenge to write a story in which the characters' future is so well known to the readers. I had to use the Solos' relationship in *Heir to the Empire* as a sort of guiding beacon for *Tatooine Ghost*. Kathy Tyers did a wonderful job setting up Leia's internal conflict over her heritage in *The Truce at Bakura*, and to a large extent it was my job to resolve that conflict and move the Solos to where they are at the beginning of the Thrawn trilogy. The challenge was to put something at stake in *how* they got there.

DR: **Approaching this from the opposite direction, Episode III won't be in theaters for a while yet. But the events of *Tatooine Ghost* happen after Episode VI, *The Return of the Jedi*, so Han and Leia, as well as other characters, might very well know details from Episode III that are *not* known to readers. I imagine that you had to be careful not to give anything from Episode III away . . . while at the same being equally careful not to contradict anything. It makes me dizzy just to think about. How did you walk this tightrope in a novel that is so much a dialogue—almost literally in the case of Leia and Shmi's palm diary—between past and present?**

TD: Avoiding spoilers was easy—I don't know what happens in Episode III. I just focused on Episodes I and II and tried not to contradict anything there. Of course, I also had Del Rey and Lucasfilm looking over my shoulder, and presumably they know a lot more than I do.

DR: **Who or what is the ghost of the title? Is it Shmi? Is it Anakin?**

TD: As Han says somewhere in the story, it depends on how you look at it. To me, the ghost is something much larger than either Anakin or Shmi.

DR: **Do you mean the Force?**

TD: Yes and no. I don't really want to say, because the ghost is going to be something different for everyone. You could even make a case for it being Obi-Wan or the Tuskens, and all of those interpretations might be valid.

DR: **I thought it was interesting to see Leia wrestling with the same difficulty that troubles so many fans of *The Phantom Menace* and *Attack of the Clones*: namely, how to reconcile the immensely likeable young Anakin Skywalker with Darth Vader, the living embodiment of the dark side that he becomes.**

TD: Yes, that's the heart of Leia's struggle. You can't reconcile the coexistence of good and evil unless you look beyond preconceptions.

DR: **Of course, there's always the danger that she's inherited this propensity from her father.**

TD: There *is* that danger, yes. In fact, as the novel begins, Leia has already started to follow in her father's footsteps precisely because she has fallen into the trap of narrow thinking, of believing that a person is either one thing or the other.

DR: **In Leia's Force-visions, you give readers an unusual glimpse into the mysterious nature of the Force. We** know that the dark side of the Force can be a terrifying thing, but here you show us that it's not just the dark side. Leia is resisting what the Force is trying to show her . . . and the Force doesn't like to be resisted!

TD: This touches on a theme close to my heart, the idea that life is a current. You can either fight the current or go with it. If you fight it, life will be a battle, but you stand a good chance of ending up someplace close to your goal (although you may be too tired and battered to enjoy it). If you go with the current, life will be easier, but you have no idea where you'll end up— it could be bad, it could be good. The compromise is to work with the current, to guide yourself within it to someplace you'll be happy. Leia, of course, has been a current-fighter all her life; the realization she reaches in *Tatooine Ghost* is that her particular current is a very strong one.

DR: At one point, the Force seems to be warning Leia that her brother, Luke, may go over to the dark side. I know that this did in fact happen in the Dark Horse Dark Empire comic series, but I was wondering if this was a bit of foreshadowing for a future exploration of those events in book form.

TD: The vision you're talking about is a direct reference to the comic story, but I doubt it will be explored any further in novel form. (In fact, I think Lucasfilm editors have said they have no plans to turn comic stories into novels.) I utilized that scene solely because it already existed in the *Star Wars* continuity, so it would have been redundant to make up something similar.

DR: You're probably best known as a fantasy writer from your work in the *Forgotten Realms* series. How different is it to write science fiction? Or do you consider *Star Wars* fantasy as some writers and readers do?

TD: I go back and forth on this. I'm sure I've taken opposite positions in different interviews. At the moment, I guess I think of *Star Wars* as space opera rather than fantasy—if for no other reason than it doesn't feel like fantasy when I write it. There are certainly fantasy parallels: an epic plot, larger-than-life heroes, a concern for the spiritual element of the quest. But, at its heart, I think *Star Wars* is very concerned with the relationship between technology and spirit, which fantasy is not. Besides, I just can't bring myself to think of the Force as magic. Magic is beyond nature, while the Force is intimately connected to life and therefore very much a part of nature—even if it is beyond our understanding.

DR: How did you get your start as a writer? What advice do you have for aspiring writers?

TD: I started writing stories in eighth grade, when our English teacher assigned us the task of keeping a journal (at first, I don't think he realized the entries were fiction). I've been at it since. Eventually—fifteen years later—I was able to put together a decent-enough story that TSR asked me to write one of the Forgotten Realms Avatar books.

The best advice I can give to any aspiring writer is to stop aspiring and start doing! You have to write every day. You have to ignore the little editor in your head that tells you to rewrite each paragraph before you move on to the next one. You have to study your craft by reading the fiction of other writers, but also books and magazines on how to plot, to create believable characters, to establish viewpoint, etc. Fiction really is an art, and it takes a lot of study to do it well.

DR: Which writers' work was the most helpful for you as far as learning your craft?

TD: If I had to pick just one—and thankfully I don't—it would be William Goldman. The things he did with *The Princess Bride* are just brilliant; I find myself going back to study the sword fight scenes every few months. He makes it looks so easy and spontaneous—which, of course, is a tribute to how long and hard he must have worked on that book. I think most writers would agree that the most difficult thing to do is make your prose look effortless.

But when I talk about studying the craft, I really do mean *studying*. My favorite books above all are books *about* writing: Rober McKee's *Story*, Wayne C. Booth's *The Rhetoric of Fiction*, Joseph Campbell's book *The Hero with a Thousand Faces*. It's not enough just to read fiction; you have to step back and look at it from the outside.

DR: **You've also written an eBook novella, *A Forest Apart*, which takes place immediately prior to *Tatooine Ghost* and features Chewie, his life-mate, Mallato-buck, and their son, Lumpy. It's good to see Chewie again, and especially taking the starring role!**

TD: One of the highlights of *Tatooine Ghost* was that Chewbacca would be back, and I really wanted to do him justice. In my early drafts, I overdid his part a bit—he was appearing in scenes where he didn't belong, and in other places I was straining to give him a larger part than his role warranted. I fixed this before the editors saw the manuscript, but I loved writing him so much that I wanted to do more. So, when we talked about an eBook, I realized this was the perfect opportunity to explore his character. I have to say it's not easy to write an all-Wookiee story, but it *was* a lot of fun.

DR: **What are you working on now? Will you be returning to that galaxy "far, far away" anytime soon?**

TD: My next project is a Han and Leia story, tentatively titled *Never Trust a Squib*, for the *Insider*. It should come out a month or so after *Tatooine Ghost*. Then I'll probably start work on an epic fantasy series that I've been putting together for a couple of years. Beyond